The Leftovers

Also by Tom Perrotta

The Abstinence Teacher

Little Children

Joe College

Election

The Wishbones

Bad Haircut: Stories of the Seventies

The Leftovers

TOM PERROTTA

ST. MARTIN'S PRESS

New York

This is a work of fiction. All of the characters, organizations, and events portrayed in this novel are either products of the author's imagination or are used fictitiously.

THE LEFTOVERS. Copyright © 2011 by Tom Perrotta. All rights reserved. Printed in the United States of America. For information, address St. Martin's Press, 175 Fifth Avenue, New York, N.Y. 10010.

www.stmartins.com

Library of Congress Cataloging-in-Publication Data

Perrotta, Tom.
    The leftovers / Tom Perrotta. — 1st ed.
        p. cm.
        ISBN 978-0-312-35834-1
    1. Life change events—Fiction.   2. Psychological fiction.   I. Title.
    PS3566.E6948L44 2011
    813'.54—dc22   2011019509

First Edition: September 2011

10   9   8   7   6   5   4   3

For Nina and Luke

ACKNOWLEDGMENTS

I count myself lucky to be able to thank the usual suspects—Elizabeth Beier, Maria Massie, Dori Weintraub, and Sylvie Rabineau—for joining me in this Sudden Departure, and for their guidance along the way. Thanks also to Mary, Nina, and Luke, for each and every day.

The Leftovers

PROLOGUE

LAURIE GARVEY HADN'T BEEN RAISED to believe in the Rapture. She hadn't been raised to believe in much of anything, except the foolishness of belief itself.

We're agnostics, she used to tell her kids, back when they were little and needed a way to define themselves to their Catholic and Jewish and Unitarian friends. *We don't know if there's a God, and nobody else does, either. They might say they do, but they really don't.*

The first time she'd heard about the Rapture, she was a freshman in college, taking a class called Intro to World Religions. The phenomenon the professor described seemed like a joke to her, hordes of Christians floating out of their clothes, rising up through the roofs of their houses and cars to meet Jesus in the sky, everyone else standing around with their mouths hanging open, wondering where all the good people had gone. The theology remained murky to her, even after she read the section on "Premillennial Dispensationalism" in her textbook, all that mumbo jumbo about Armageddon and the Antichrist and the Four Horsemen of the Apocalypse. It felt like religious kitsch, as tacky as a black velvet painting, the kind of fantasy that appealed to people who ate too much fried food, spanked their kids, and had no problem with the theory that their loving God invented AIDS to punish the gays. Every once in a while, in the years that followed, she'd spot someone reading one of the Left Behind books in an airport or on a train, and feel a twinge of pity, and even a little bit of tenderness, for the poor sucker who had nothing better to read, and nothing else to do, except sit around dreaming about the end of the world.

And then it happened. The biblical prophecy came true, or at least partly true. People disappeared, millions of them at the same time, all over the world. This wasn't some ancient rumor—a dead man coming back to life during the Roman Empire—or a dusty homegrown legend, Joseph Smith unearthing golden tablets in upstate New York, conversing with an angel. This was real. The Rapture happened in her own hometown, to her best friend's daughter, among others, while Laurie herself was in the house. God's intrusion into her life couldn't have been any clearer if He'd addressed her from a burning azalea.

At least you would have thought so. And yet she managed to deny the obvious for weeks and months afterward, clinging to her doubts like a life preserver, desperately echoing the scientists and pundits and politicians who insisted that the cause of what they called the "Sudden Departure" remained unknown, and cautioned the public to avoid jumping to conclusions until the release of the official report by the nonpartisan government panel that was investigating the matter.

"Something tragic occurred," the experts repeated over and over. "It was a Rapture-like phenomenon, but it doesn't appear to have been the Rapture."

Interestingly, some of the loudest voices making this argument belonged to Christians themselves, who couldn't help noticing that many of the people who'd disappeared on October 14th—Hindus and Buddhists and Muslims and Jews and atheists and animists and homosexuals and Eskimos and Mormons and Zoroastrians, whatever the heck they were—hadn't accepted Jesus Christ as their personal savior. As far as anyone could tell, it was a random harvest, and the one thing the Rapture couldn't be was random. The whole point was to separate the wheat from the chaff, to reward the true believers and put the rest of the world on notice. An indiscriminate Rapture was no Rapture at all.

So it was easy enough to be confused, to throw up your hands and claim that you just didn't know what was going on. But Laurie knew. Deep in her heart, as soon as it happened, she *knew*. She'd been left behind. They all had. It didn't matter that God hadn't factored religion into His decision-making—if anything, that just made it worse, more of a personal rejection. And yet she chose to ignore this knowledge, to banish it to some murky recess of her mind—the basement storage area for things you couldn't bear to think about—the same place you hid the knowledge that you were going to die, so you could live your life without being depressed every minute of every day.

Besides, it was a busy time, those first few months after the Rapture, with school canceled in Mapleton, her daughter home all day, and her son back from college. There was shopping and laundry to do, just like before, meals to cook, and dishes to wash. There were memorial services to attend as well, slide shows to compile, tears to wipe away, so many exhausting conversations. She spent a lot of time with poor Rosalie Sussman, visiting her almost every morning, trying to help her through her unfathomable grief. Sometimes they talked about her departed daughter, Jen—what a sweet girl she was, always smiling, etc.—but mostly they just sat together without speaking. The silence felt deep and right, as if there was nothing either of them could say that could possibly be important enough to break it.

YOU STARTED seeing them around town the following autumn, people in white clothing, traveling in same-sex pairs, always smoking. Laurie recognized a few of them—Barbara Santangelo, whose son was in her daughter's class; Marty Powers, who used to play softball with her husband, and whose wife had been taken in the Rapture, or whatever it was. Mostly they ignored you, but sometimes they followed you around as if they were private detectives hired to keep track of your movements. If you said hello, they just gave you a blank look, but if you asked a more substantive question, they handed over a business card printed on one side with the following message:

> WE ARE MEMBERS OF THE GUILTY REMNANT. WE HAVE
> TAKEN A VOW OF SILENCE. WE STAND BEFORE YOU AS
> LIVING REMINDERS OF GOD'S AWESOME POWER.
> HIS JUDGMENT IS UPON US.

In smaller type, on the other side of the card, was a Web address you could consult for more information: www.guiltyremnant.com.

That was a weird fall. A full year had passed since the catastrophe; the survivors had absorbed the blow and found, to their amazement, that they were still standing, though some were a bit more wobbly than others. In a tentative, fragile way, things were starting to return to normal. The schools had reopened and most people had gone back to work. Kids played soccer in the park on weekends; there were even a handful of trick-or-treaters on Halloween. You could feel the old habits returning, life assuming its former shape.

But Laurie couldn't get with the program. Besides caring for Rosalie, she was worried sick about her own kids. Tom had gone back to college for the spring semester, but he'd fallen under the influence of a sketchy self-appointed "healing prophet" named Holy Wayne, failed all his classes, and refused to come home. He'd phoned a couple of times over the summer to let her know he was okay, but he wouldn't say where he was or what he was doing. Jill was struggling with depression and post-traumatic stress—of course she was, Jen Sussman had been her best friend since preschool—but she refused to talk to Laurie about it or to see a therapist. Meanwhile, her husband seemed bizarrely upbeat, all good news all the time. Business was booming, the weather was fine, he just ran six miles in under an hour, if you could believe that.

"What about you?" Kevin would ask, not the least bit self-conscious in his spandex pants, his face glowing with good health and a thin layer of perspiration. "What'd you do all day?"

"Me? I helped Rosalie with her scrapbook."

He made a face, disapproval mingled with forbearance.

"She's still doing that?"

"She doesn't want to finish. Today we did a little history of Jen's swimming career. You could watch her grow up year by year, her body changing inside that blue bathing suit. Just heartbreaking."

"Huh." Kevin filled his glass with ice water from the built-in dispenser on the fridge. She could tell he wasn't listening, knew that he'd lost interest in the subject of Jen Sussman months ago. "What's for dinner?"

LAURIE COULDN'T say that she was shocked when Rosalie announced that she was joining the Guilty Remnant. Rosalie had been fascinated by the people in white since the first time she saw them, frequently wondering out loud how hard it would be to keep a vow of silence, especially if you happened to bump into an old friend, someone you hadn't seen in a long time.

"They'd have to give you some leeway in a case like that, don't you think?"

"I don't know," Laurie said. "I kind of doubt it. They're fanatics. They don't like to make exceptions."

"Not even if it was your own brother, and you hadn't seen him for twenty years? You wouldn't even be able to say hi?"

"Don't ask me. Ask them."

"How can I ask them? They're not allowed to talk."

"I don't know. Check the website."

Rosalie checked the website a lot that winter. She developed a close I.M. friendship—evidently, the vow of silence didn't extend to electronic communications—with the Director of Public Outreach, a nice woman who answered all her questions and walked her through her doubts and reservations.

"Her name's Connie. She used to be a dermatologist."

"Really?"

"She sold her practice and donated the proceeds to the organization. That's what a lot of people do. It's not cheap to keep an operation like that afloat."

Laurie had read an article about the Guilty Remnant in the local paper, so she knew that there were at least sixty people living in their "compound" on Ginkgo Street, an eight-house subdivision that had been deeded to the organization by the developer, a wealthy man named Troy Vincent, who was now living there as an ordinary member, with no special privileges.

"What about you?" Laurie asked. "You gonna sell the house?"

"Not right away. There's a six-month trial period. I don't have to make any decisions until then."

"That's smart."

Rosalie shook her head, as if amazed by her own boldness. Laurie could see how excited she was now that she'd made the decision to change her life.

"It's gonna be weird, wearing white clothes all the time. I kind of wish it was blue or gray or something. I don't look good in white."

"I just can't believe you're gonna start smoking."

"Ugh." Rosalie grimaced. She was one of those hard-line nonsmokers, the kind of person who waved her hand frantically in front of her face whenever she got within twenty feet of a lit cigarette. "That's gonna take some getting used to. But it's like a sacrament, you know? You have to do it. You don't have a choice."

"Your poor lungs."

"We're not gonna live long enough to get cancer. The Bible says there's just seven years of Tribulation after the Rapture."

"But it wasn't the Rapture," Laurie said, as much to herself as to her friend. "Not really."

"You should come with me." Rosalie's voice was soft and serious. "Maybe we could be roommates or something."

"I can't," Laurie told her. "I can't leave my family."

Family: She felt bad even saying the word out loud. Rosalie had no family to speak of. She'd been divorced for years and Jen was her only child. She had a mother and stepfather in Michigan, and a sister in Minneapolis, but she didn't talk to them much.

"That's what I figured." Rosalie gave a small shrug of resignation. "Just thought I'd give it a try."

A WEEK later, Laurie drove Rosalie to Ginkgo Street. It was a beautiful day, full of sunshine and birdsong. The houses looked imposing—sprawling three-story colonials with half-acre lots that probably would have sold for a million dollars or more when they were built.

"Wow," she said. "Pretty swanky."

"I know." Rosalie smiled nervously. She was dressed in white and carrying a small suitcase containing mostly underwear and toiletries, plus the scrapbooks she'd spent so much time on. "I can't believe I'm doing this."

"If you don't like it, just give me a call. I'll come get you."

"I think I'll be okay."

They walked up the steps of a white house with the word HEAD-QUARTERS painted over the front door. Laurie wasn't allowed to enter the building, so she hugged her friend goodbye on the stoop, and then watched as Rosalie was led inside by a woman with a pale, kindly face who may or may not have been Connie, the former dermatologist.

Almost a year passed before Laurie returned to Ginkgo Street. It was another spring day, a little cooler, not quite as sunny. This time she was the one dressed in white, carrying a small suitcase. It wasn't very heavy, just underwear, a toothbrush, and an album containing carefully chosen photographs of her family, a short visual history of the people she loved and was leaving behind.

Part *One*

THREE-YEAR ANNIVERSARY

HEROES' DAY

IT WAS A GOOD DAY for a parade, sunny and unseasonably warm, the sky a Sunday school cartoon of heaven. Not too long ago, people would have felt the need to make a nervous crack about weather like this—*Hey,* they'd say, *maybe this global warming isn't such a bad thing after all!*—but these days no one bothered much about the hole in the ozone layer or the pathos of a world without polar bears. It seemed almost funny in retrospect, all that energy wasted fretting about something so remote and uncertain, an ecological disaster that might or might not come to pass somewhere way off in the distant future, long after you and your children and your children's children had lived out your allotted time on earth and gone to wherever it was you went when it was all over.

Despite the anxiety that had dogged him all morning, Mayor Kevin Garvey found himself gripped by an unexpected mood of nostalgia as he walked down Washington Boulevard toward the high school parking lot, where the marchers had been told to assemble. It was half an hour before showtime, the floats lined up and ready to roll, the marching band girding itself for battle, peppering the air with a discordant overture of bleats and toots and halfhearted drumrolls. Kevin had been born and raised in Mapleton, and he couldn't help thinking about Fourth of July parades back when everything still made sense, half the town lined up along Main Street while the other half—Little Leaguers, scouts of both genders, gimpy Veterans of Foreign Wars trailed by the Ladies Auxiliary—strode down the middle of the road, waving to the spectators as if surprised to see them there, as if this were some kind of kooky coincidence rather than a national holiday. In Kevin's memory, at least, it all seemed impossibly loud and hectic and innocent—fire trucks, tubas, Irish step dancers, baton twirlers in sequined costumes, one year even a squadron of fez-bedecked Shriners scooting around in those hilarious midget cars. Afterward there were softball games and cookouts, a sequence of comforting rituals culminating in the big fireworks display over Fielding Lake, hundreds of rapt faces turned skyward, oohing and wowing at the sizzling pinwheels and slow-blooming starbursts that lit up the darkness, reminding everyone of who they were and where they belonged and why it was all good.

Today's event—the first annual Departed Heroes' Day of Remembrance and Reflection, to be precise—wasn't going to be anything like that. Kevin could sense the somber mood as soon as he arrived at the high school, the invisible haze of stale grief and chronic bewilderment thickening the air, causing people to talk more softly and move more tentatively than they normally would at a big outdoor gathering.

On the other hand, he was both surprised and gratified by the turn-out, given the cool reception the parade had received when it was first proposed. Some critics thought the timing was wrong ("Too soon!" they'd insisted), while others suggested that a secular commemoration of October 14th was wrongheaded and possibly blasphemous. These objections had faded over time, either because the organizers had done a good job winning over the skeptics, or because people just generally liked a parade, regardless of the occasion. In any case, so many Maple-tonians had volunteered to march that Kevin wondered if there'd be anyone left to cheer them on from the sidelines as they made their way down Main Street to Greenway Park.

He hesitated for a moment just inside the line of police barricades, marshaling his strength for what he knew would be a long and difficult day. Everywhere he looked he saw broken people and fresh reminders of suffering. He waved to Martha Reeder, the once-chatty lady who worked the stamp window at the Post Office; she smiled sadly, turning to give him a better look at the homemade sign she was holding. It fea-tured a poster-sized photograph of her three-year-old granddaughter, a serious child with curly hair and slightly crooked eyeglasses. ASH-LEY, it said, MY LITTLE ANGEL. Standing beside her was Stan Wash-burn—a retired cop and former Pop Warner coach of Kevin's—a squat, no-neck guy whose T-shirt, stretched tight over an impressive beer gut, invited anyone who cared to ASK ME ABOUT MY BROTHER. Kevin felt a sudden powerful urge to flee, to run home and spend the after-noon lifting weights or raking leaves—anything solitary and mindless would do—but it passed quickly, like a hiccup or a shameful sexual fantasy.

Expelling a soft dutiful sigh, he waded into the crowd, shaking hands and calling out names, doing his best impersonation of a small-town politician. An ex–Mapleton High football star and prominent local businessman—he'd inherited and expanded his family's chain of supermarket-sized liquor stores, tripling the revenue during his fifteen-year tenure—Kevin was a popular and highly visible figure around town, but the idea of running for office had never crossed his mind. Then, just last year, out of the blue, he was presented with a petition signed by two hundred fellow citizens, many of whom he knew well: "We, the undersigned, are desperate for leadership in these dark times. Will you help us take back our town?" Touched by this appeal and feeling a bit lost himself—he'd sold the business for a small fortune a few months earlier, and still hadn't figured out what to do next—he accepted the mayoral nomination of a newly formed political entity called the Hopeful Party.

Kevin won the election in a landslide, unseating Rick Malvern, the three-term incumbent who'd lost the confidence of the voters after attempting to burn down his own house in an act of what he called "ritual purification." It didn't work—the fire department insisted on extinguishing the blaze over his bitter objections—and these days Rick was living in a tent in his front yard, the charred remains of his five-bedroom Victorian hulking in the background. Every now and then, when Kevin went running in the early morning, he would happen upon his former rival just as he was emerging from the tent—one time bare-chested and clad only in striped boxers—and the two men would exchange an awkward greeting on the otherwise silent street, a *Yo* or a *Hey* or a *What's up?*, just to show there were no hard feelings.

As much as he disliked the flesh-pressing, backslapping aspect of his new job, Kevin felt an obligation to make himself accessible to his constituents, even the cranks and malcontents who inevitably came out of the woodwork at public events. The first to accost him in the parking lot was Ralph Sorrento, a surly plumber from Sycamore Road, who bulled his way through a cluster of sad-looking women in identical pink T-shirts and planted himself directly in Kevin's path.

"Mr. Mayor," he drawled, smirking as though there were something inherently ridiculous about the title. "I was hoping I'd run into you. You never answer my e-mails."

"Morning, Ralph."

Sorrento folded his arms across his chest and studied Kevin with an unsettling combination of amusement and disdain. He was a big, thick-bodied man with a buzz cut and a bristly goatee, dressed in grease-stained cargo pants and a thermal-lined hoodie. Even at this hour—it was not yet eleven—Kevin could smell beer on his breath and see that he was looking for trouble.

"Just so we're clear," Sorrento announced in an unnaturally loud voice. "I'm not paying that fucking money."

The money in question was a hundred-dollar fine he'd been assessed for shooting at a pack of stray dogs that had wandered into his yard. A beagle had been killed on the spot, but a shepherd-lab mix had hobbled away with a bullet in its hind leg, dripping a three-block trail of blood before collapsing on the sidewalk not far from the Little Sprouts Academy on Oak Street. Normally the police didn't get too exercised about a shot dog—it happened with depressing regularity—but a handful of the Sprouts had witnessed the animal's agony, and the complaints of their parents and guardians had led to Sorrento's prosecution.

"Watch your language," Kevin warned him, uncomfortably aware of the heads turning in their direction.

Sorrento jabbed an index finger into Kevin's rib cage. "I'm sick of those mutts crapping on my lawn."

"Nobody likes the dogs," Kevin conceded. "But next time call Animal Control, okay?"

"Animal Control." Sorrento repeated the words with a contemptuous chuckle. Again he jabbed at Kevin's sternum, fingertip digging into bone. "They don't do shit."

"They're understaffed." Kevin forced a polite smile. "They're doing the best they can in a bad situation. We all are. I'm sure you understand that."

As if to indicate that he did understand, Sorrento eased the pressure on Kevin's breastbone. He leaned in close, his breath sour, his voice low and intimate.

"Do me a favor, okay? You tell the cops if they want my money, they're gonna have to come and get it. Tell 'em I'll be waiting for 'em with my sawed-off shotgun."

He grinned, trying to look like a badass, but Kevin could see the pain in his eyes, the glassy, pleading look behind the bluster. If he remembered correctly, Sorrento had lost a daughter, a chubby girl, maybe nine or ten. Tiffany or Britney, a name like that.

"I'll pass it along." Kevin patted him gently on the shoulder. "Now, why don't you go home and get some rest."

Sorrento slapped at Kevin's hand.

"Don't fucking touch me."

"Sorry."

"Just tell 'em what I told you, okay?"

Kevin promised he would, then hurried off, trying to ignore the lump of dread that had suddenly materialized in his gut. Unlike some of the neighboring towns, Mapleton had never experienced a suicide by cop, but Kevin sensed that Ralph Sorrento was at least fantasizing about the idea. His plan didn't seem especially inspired—the cops had bigger things to worry about than an unpaid fine for animal cruelty—but there were all sorts of ways to provoke a confrontation if you really had your heart set on it. He'd have to tell the chief, make sure the patrol officers knew what they were dealing with.

Distracted by these thoughts, Kevin didn't realize he was heading straight for the Reverend Matt Jamison, formerly of the Zion Bible Church, until it was too late to make an evasive maneuver. All he could do was raise both hands in a futile attempt to fend off the gossip rag the Reverend was thrusting in his face.

"Take it," the Reverend said. "There's stuff in here that'll knock your socks off."

Seeing no graceful way out, Kevin reluctantly took possession of a newsletter that went by the emphatic but unwieldy title *"OCTOBER 14TH WAS NOT THE RAPTURE!!!"* The front page featured a photograph of Dr. Hillary Edgers, a beloved pediatrician who'd disappeared three years earlier, along with eighty-seven other local residents and untold millions of people throughout the world. DOCTOR'S BISEXUAL COLLEGE YEARS EXPOSED! the headline proclaimed. A boxed quote in the article below read, "'We totally thought she was gay,' former roommate reveals."

Kevin had known and admired Dr. Edgers, whose twin sons were the same age as his daughter. She'd volunteered two evenings a week at a free clinic for poor kids in the city, and gave lectures to the PTA on subjects like "The Long-Term Effects of Concussions in Young Athletes" and "How to Recognize an Eating Disorder." People button-holed her all the time at the soccer field and the supermarket, fishing for free medical advice, but she never seemed resentful about it, or even mildly impatient.

"Jesus, Matt. Is this necessary?"

Reverend Jamison seemed mystified by the question. He was a trim, sandy-haired man of about forty, but his face had gone slack and pouchy in the past couple of years, as if he were aging on an acceler-ated schedule.

"These people weren't heroes. We have to stop treating them like they were. I mean, this whole parade—"

"The woman had kids. They don't need to be reading about who she slept with in college."

"But it's the truth. We can't hide from the truth."

Kevin knew it was useless to argue. By all accounts, Matt Jamison used to be a decent guy, but he'd lost his bearings. Like a lot of devout Christians, he'd been deeply traumatized by the Sudden Departure, tormented by the fear that Judgment Day had come and gone, and he'd been found lacking. While some people in his position had re-sponded with redoubled piety, the Reverend had moved in the opposite direction, taking up the cause of Rapture Denial with a vengeance, dedicating his life to proving that the people who'd slipped their earthly chains on October 14th were neither good Christians nor even especially virtuous individuals. In the process, he'd become a dogged investigative journalist and a complete pain in the ass.

"All right," Kevin muttered, folding the newsletter and jamming it into his back pocket. "I'll give it a look."

. . .

THEY STARTED moving at a few minutes after eleven. A police motorcade led the way, followed by a small armada of floats representing a variety of civic and commercial organizations, mostly old standbys like the Greater Mapleton Chamber of Commerce, the local chapter of D.A.R.E., and the Senior Citizens' Club. A couple featured live demonstrations: Students from the Alice Herlihy Institute of Dance performed a cautious jitterbug on a makeshift stage while a chorus line of karate kids from the Devlin Brothers School of Martial Arts threw flurries of punches and kicks at the air, grunting in ferocious unison. To a casual observer it would have all seemed familiar, not much different from any other parade that had crawled through town in the last fifty years. Only the final vehicle in the sequence would have given pause, a flatbed truck draped in black bunting, not a soul on board, its emptiness stark and self-explanatory.

As mayor, Kevin got to ride in one of two honorary convertibles that trailed the memorial float, a little Mazda driven by Pete Thorne, his friend and former neighbor. They were in second position, ten yards behind a Fiat Spider carrying the Grand Marshall, a pretty but fragile-looking woman named Nora Durst who'd lost her entire family on October 14th—husband and two young kids—in what was widely considered to be the worst tragedy in all of Mapleton. Nora had reportedly suffered a minor panic attack earlier in the day, claiming she felt dizzy and nauseous and needed to go home, but she'd gotten through the crisis with the help of her sister and a volunteer grief counselor on hand in the event of just such an emergency. She seemed fine now, sitting almost regally in the backseat of the Spider, turning from side to side and wanly raising her hand to acknowledge sporadic bursts of applause from spectators who'd assembled along the route.

"Not a bad turnout!" Kevin remarked in a loud voice. "I didn't expect this many people!"

"What?" Pete bellowed over his shoulder.

"Forget it!" Kevin shouted back, realizing it was hopeless to try to make himself heard over the band. The horn section was plastered to his bumper, playing an exuberant version of "Hawaii Five-O" that had gone on for so long he was beginning to wonder if it was the only song they knew. Impatient with the funereal pace, the musicians kept surging forward, briefly overtaking his car, and then falling abruptly back, no doubt wreaking havoc on the solemn procession bringing up the rear. Kevin twisted in his seat, trying to see past the musicians to the marchers behind them, but his view was blocked by a thicket of maroon uniforms, serious young faces with inflated cheeks, and brass instruments flashing molten gold in the sunlight.

Back there, he thought, that was the *real* parade, the one no one had ever seen before, hundreds of ordinary people walking in small groups, some holding signs, others wearing T-shirts bearing the image of a friend or family member who'd been taken away. He'd seen these people in the parking lot, shortly after they'd broken into their platoons, and the sight of them—the incomprehensible sum of their sadness—had left him shaken, barely able to read the names on their banners: the Orphans of October 14th, the Grieving Spouses' Coalition, Mothers and Fathers of Departed Children, Bereft Siblings Network, Mapleton Remembers Its Friends and Neighbors, Survivors of Myrtle Avenue, Students of Shirley De Santos, We Miss Bud Phipps, and on and on. A few mainstream religious organizations were participating, too—Our Lady of Sorrows, Temple Beth-El, and St. James Presbyterian had all sent contingents—but they'd been stuck way in the back, almost an afterthought, right in front of the emergency vehicles.

MAPLETON CENTER was packed with well-wishers, the street strewn with flowers, many of which had been crushed by truck tires and would soon be trampled underfoot. A fair number of the spectators were high school kids, but Kevin's daughter, Jill, and her best friend, Aimee, weren't among them. The girls had been sleeping soundly when he left the house—as usual, they'd stayed out way too late—and Kevin didn't have the heart to wake them, or the fortitude to deal with Aimee, who insisted on sleeping in panties and flimsy little tank tops that made it hard for him to know where to look. He'd called home twice in the past half hour, hoping the ringer would roust them, but the girls hadn't picked up.

He and Jill had been arguing about the parade for weeks now, in the exasperated, half-serious way they conducted all the important business in their lives. He'd encouraged her to march in honor of her Departed friend, Jen, but she remained unmoved.

"Guess what, Dad? Jen doesn't care if I march or not."

"How do you know that?"

"She's gone. She doesn't give a shit about anything."

"Maybe so," he said. "But what if she's still here and we just can't see her?"

Jill seemed amused by this possibility. "That would suck. She's probably waving her arms around all day, trying to get our attention." Jill scanned the kitchen, as if searching for her friend. She spoke in a loud voice, suitable for addressing a half-deaf grandparent. "Jen, if you're in here, I'm sorry I'm ignoring you. It would help if you could clear your throat or something."

Kevin withheld his protest. Jill knew he didn't like it when she joked about the missing, but telling her for the hundredth time wasn't going to accomplish anything.

"Honey," he said quietly, "the parade is for us, not for them."

She stared at him with a look she'd recently perfected—total incomprehension softened by the slightest hint of womanly forbearance. It would have been even cuter if she still had some hair and wasn't wearing all that eyeliner.

"Tell me something," she said. "Why does this matter so much to you?"

If Kevin could have supplied a good answer for this question, he would've happily done so. But the truth was, he really didn't know why it mattered so much, why he didn't just give up on the parade the way he'd given up on everything else they'd fought about in the past year: the curfew, the head-shaving, the wisdom of spending so much time with Aimee, partying on school nights. Jill was seventeen; he understood that, in some irrevocable way, she'd drifted out of his orbit and would do what she wanted when she wanted, regardless of his wishes.

All the same, though, Kevin really wanted her to be part of the parade, to demonstrate in some small way that she still recognized the claims of family and community, still loved and respected her father and would do what she could to make him happy. She understood the situation with perfect clarity—he knew she did—but for some reason couldn't bring herself to cooperate. It hurt him, of course, but any anger he felt toward his daughter was always accompanied by an automatic apology, a private acknowledgment of everything she'd been through, and how little he'd been able to help her.

Jill was an Eyewitness, and he didn't need a psychologist to tell him that it was something she'd struggle with for the rest of her life. She and Jen had been hanging out together on October 14th, two giggly young girls sitting side by side on a couch, eating pretzels and watching YouTube videos on a laptop. Then, in the time it takes to click a mouse, one of them is gone, and the other is screaming. And people keep disappearing on her in the months and years that follow, if not quite so dramatically. Her older brother leaves for college and never comes home. Her mother moves out of the house, takes a vow of silence. Only her father remains, a bewildered man who tries to help but never manages to say the right thing. How can he when he's just as lost and clueless as she is?

It didn't surprise Kevin that Jill was angry or rebellious or depressed. She had every right to be all those things and more. The only thing that surprised him was that she was still around, still sharing a house with him when she could just as easily have run off with the

Barefoot People or hopped on a Greyhound Bus to parts unknown. Lots of kids had. She looked different, of course, bald and haunted, like she wanted total strangers to understand exactly how bad she felt. But sometimes when she smiled, Kevin got the feeling that her essential self was still alive in there, still mysteriously intact in spite of everything. It was this other Jill—the one she never really got a chance to become— that he'd been hoping to find at the breakfast table this morning, not the real one he knew too well, the girl curled up on the bed after coming home too drunk or high to bother scrubbing off last night's makeup.

He thought about phoning again as they approached Lovell Terrace, the exclusive cul-de-sac where he and his family had moved five years earlier, in an era that now seemed as distant and unreal as the Jazz Age. As much as he wanted to hear Jill's voice, though, his own sense of decorum held him back. He just didn't think it would look right, the mayor chatting on his cell phone in the middle of a parade. Besides, what would he say?

Hi, honey, I'm driving past our street, but I don't see you . . .

EVEN BEFORE he lost his wife to them, Kevin had developed a grudging sense of respect for the Guilty Remnant. Two years ago, when they'd first appeared on his radar screen, he'd mistaken them for a harmless Rapture cult, a group of separatist fanatics who wanted nothing more than to be left alone to grieve and meditate in peace until the Second Coming, or whatever it was they were waiting for (he still wasn't clear about their theology and wasn't sure they were, either). It even made a certain kind of sense to him that heartbroken people like Rosalie Sussman would find it comforting to join their ranks, to withdraw from the world and take a vow of silence.

At the time, the G.R. seemed to have sprung up out of nowhere, a spontaneous local reaction to an unprecedented tragedy. It took him a while to realize that similar groups were forming all over the country, linking themselves into a loose national network, each affiliate following the same basic guidelines—white clothes and cigarettes and two-person surveillance teams—but governing itself without much in the way of organized oversight or outside interference.

Despite its monastic appearance, the Mapleton Chapter quickly revealed itself to be an ambitious and disciplined organization with a taste for civil disobedience and political theater. Not only did they refuse to pay taxes or utilities, but also they flouted a host of local ordinances at their Ginkgo Street compound, packing dozens of people into homes built for a single family, defying court orders and foreclosure notices, building barricades to keep out the authorities. A series of confrontations ensued, one of which resulted in the shooting death of a G.R. member who threw rocks at police officers trying to execute a search warrant. Sympathy for the Guilty Remnant had spiked in the wake of the botched raid, leading to the resignation of the Chief of Police and a severe loss of support for then Mayor Malvern, both of whom had authorized the operation.

Since taking office, Kevin had done his best to dial down the tension between the cult and the town, negotiating a series of agreements that allowed the G.R. to live more or less as it pleased, in exchange for nominal tax payments and guarantees of access for police and emergency vehicles in certain clearly defined situations. The truce seemed to be holding, but the G.R. remained an annoying wild card, popping up at odd intervals to sow confusion and anxiety among law-abiding citizens. This year, on the first day of school, several white-clad adults had staged a sit-in at Kingman Elementary School, occupying a second-grade classroom for an entire morning. A few weeks later, another group of them had wandered onto the high school football field in the middle of a game, lying down on the turf until they were forcibly removed by angry players and spectators.

FOR MONTHS now, local officials had been wondering what the G.R. would do to disrupt Heroes' Day. Kevin had sat through two planning meetings at which the subject was discussed in detail, and had reviewed a number of likely scenarios. All day he'd been waiting for them to make their move, feeling an odd combination of dread and curiosity, as if the party wouldn't really be complete until they'd crashed it.

But the parade had come and gone without them, and the memorial service was nearing its close. Kevin had laid a wreath at the foot of the Monument to the Departed at Greenway Park, a creepy bronze sculpture produced by one of the high school art teachers. It was supposed to show a baby floating out of the arms of its astonished mother, ascending toward heaven, but something had misfired. Kevin was no art critic, but it always looked to him like the baby was falling instead of rising, and the mother might not be able to catch it.

After the benediction by Father Gonzalez, there was a moment of silence to commemorate the third anniversary of the Sudden Departure, followed by the pealing of church bells. Nora Durst's keynote address was the last item on the program. Kevin was seated on the makeshift stage with a few other dignitaries, and he felt a little anxious as she stepped up to the podium. He knew from experience how daunting it could be to deliver a speech, how much skill and confidence it took to command the attention of a crowd even half the size of this one.

But he quickly realized that his worries were misplaced. A hush came over the spectators as Nora cleared her throat and shuffled through her note cards. She had suffered—she was the Woman Who Had Lost Everything—and her suffering gave her authority. She didn't have to earn anyone's attention or respect.

On top of that, Nora turned out to be a natural. She spoke slowly and clearly—it was Oratory 101, but a surprising number of speakers missed that day—with just enough in the way of stumbles and hesitations to keep everything from seeming a bit too polished. It helped that she was an attractive woman, tall and well-proportioned, with a soft but emphatic voice. Like most of her audience, she was casually dressed, and Kevin found himself staring a little too avidly at the elaborate stitching on the back pocket of her jeans, which fit with a snugness one rarely encountered at official government functions. She had, he noticed, a surprisingly youthful body for a thirty-five-year-old woman who'd given birth to two kids. *Lost two kids,* he reminded himself, forcing himself to keep his chin up and focus on something more appropriate. The last thing he wanted to see on the cover of *The Mapleton Messenger* was a full-color photograph of the mayor ogling a grieving mother's butt.

Nora began by saying that she'd originally conceived of her speech as a celebration of the single best day of her life. The day in question had occurred just a couple of months before October 14th, during a vacation her family had taken at the Jersey Shore. Nothing special had happened, nor had she fully grasped the extent of her happiness at the time. That realization didn't strike until later, after her husband and children were gone and she'd had more than enough sleepless nights in which to take the measure of all that she'd lost.

It was, she said, a lovely late-summer day, warm and breezy, but not so bright that you had to think constantly about sunscreen. Sometime in the morning, her kids—Jeremy was six, Erin four; it was as old as they'd ever get—started making a sand castle, and they went about their labor with the solemn enthusiasm that children sometimes bring to the most inconsequential tasks. Nora and her husband, Doug, sat on a blanket nearby, holding hands, watching these serious little workers run to the water's edge, fill their plastic buckets with wet sand, and then come trudging back, their toothpick arms straining against the heavy loads. The kids weren't smiling, but their faces glowed with joyful purpose. The fortress they built was surprisingly large and elaborate; it kept them occupied for hours.

"We had our video camera," she said. "But for some reason we didn't think to turn it on. I'm glad in a way. Because if we had a video of that day, I'd just watch it all the time. I'd waste away in front of the television, rewinding it over and over."

Somehow, though, thinking about that day made her remember another day, a terrible Saturday the previous March when the entire family was laid low by a stomach bug. It seemed like every time you turned around, someone else was throwing up, and not always in a toilet. The house stunk, the kids were wailing, and the dog kept whimpering to be let outside. Nora couldn't get out of bed—she was feverish, drifting in and out of delirium—and Doug was no better. There was a brief period in the afternoon when she thought she might be dying. When she shared this fear with her husband, he simply nodded and said, "Okay." They were so sick they didn't even have the sense to pick up the phone and call for help. At one point in the evening, when Erin was lying between them, her hair crusty with dried vomit, Jeremy wandered in and pointed tearfully at his foot. *Woody pooped in the kitchen,* he said. *Woody pooped and I stepped in it.*

"It was hell," Nora said. "That was what we kept telling each other. *This is truly hell.*"

They got through it, of course. A few days later, everyone was healthy again, and the house was more or less in order. But from then on, they referred to the Family Puke-A-Thon as the low point in their lives, the debacle that put everything else in perspective. If the basement flooded, or Nora got a parking ticket, or Doug lost a client, they were always able to remind themselves that things could have been worse.

"*Well,* we'd say, *at least it's not as bad as that time we all got so sick.*"

It was around this point in Nora's speech that the Guilty Remnant finally made their appearance, emerging en masse from the small patch of woods flanking the west side of the park. There were maybe twenty of them, dressed in white, moving slowly in the direction of the gathering. At first they seemed like a disorganized mob, but as they walked they began to form a horizontal line, a configuration that reminded Kevin of a search party. Each person was carrying a piece of posterboard emblazoned with a single black letter, and when they got to within shouting distance of the stage, they stopped and raised their squares overhead. Together, the jagged row of letters spelled the words STOP WASTING YOUR BREATH.

An angry murmur arose from the crowd, which didn't appreciate the interruption or the sentiment. Nearly the entire police force was present at the ceremony, and after a moment of uncertainty, several officers began moving toward the interlopers. Chief Rogers was on-stage, and just as Kevin rose to consult him about the wisdom of provoking a confrontation, Nora addressed the officers.

"Please," she said. "Leave them alone. They're not hurting anyone."

The cops hesitated, then checked their advance after receiving a signal from the Chief. From where he sat, Kevin had a clear view of the protesters, so he knew by then that his wife was among them. Kevin hadn't seen Laurie for a couple of months, and he was struck by how much weight she'd lost, as if she'd disappeared into a fitness center instead of a Rapture cult. Her hair was grayer than he'd ever seen it—the G.R. wasn't big on personal grooming—but on the whole, she looked strangely youthful. Maybe it was the cigarette in her mouth—Laurie had been a smoker in the early days of their relationship—but the woman who stood before him, the letter N raised high above her head, reminded him more of the fun-loving girl he'd known in college than the heavyhearted, thick-waisted woman who'd walked out on him six months ago. Despite the circumstances, he felt an undeniable pang of desire for her, an actual and highly ironic stirring in his groin.

"I'm not greedy," Nora went on, picking up the thread of her speech. "I'm not asking for that perfect day at the beach. Just give me that horrible Saturday, all four of us sick and miserable, but alive, and together. Right now that sounds like heaven to me." For the first time since she'd begun speaking, her voice cracked with emotion. "God bless us, the ones who are here and the ones who aren't. We've all been through so much."

Kevin attempted to make eye contact with Laurie throughout the sustained, somewhat defiant applause that followed, but she refused even to glance in his direction. He tried to convince himself that she was doing this against her will—she was, after all, flanked by two large bearded men, one of whom looked a little like Neil Felton, the guy who used to own the gourmet pizza place in the town center. It would have been comforting to think that she'd been instructed by her superiors not to fall into temptation by communicating, even silently, with her husband, but he knew in his heart that this wasn't the case. She could've looked at him if she'd wanted to, could've at least acknowledged the existence of the man she'd promised to spend her life with. She just didn't want to.

Thinking about it afterward, he wondered why he hadn't climbed down from the stage, walked over there, and said, *Hey, it's been a while. You look good. I miss you.* There was nothing stopping him. And yet he just sat there, doing absolutely nothing, until the people in white lowered their letters, turned around, and drifted back into the woods.

A WHOLE CLASS OF JILLS

JILL GARVEY KNEW HOW EASY it was to romanticize the missing, to pretend that they were better than they really were, somehow superior to the losers who'd been left behind. She'd seen this up close in the weeks after October 14th, when all sorts of people—adults, mostly, but some kids, too—said all kinds of crazy stuff to her about Jen Sussman, who was really nobody special, just a regular person, maybe a little prettier than most girls their age, but definitely not an angel who was too good for this world.

God wanted her company, they'd say. *He missed her blue eyes and beautiful smile.*

They meant well, Jill understood that. Because she was a so-called Eyewitness, the only other person in the room when Jen departed, people often treated her with creepy tenderness—it was as if she were a grieving relative, as if she and Jen had become sisters after the fact—and an odd sort of respect. No one listened when she tried to explain that she hadn't actually *witnessed* anything and was really just as clueless as they were. She'd been watching YouTube at the crucial moment, this sad but hilarious video of a little kid punching himself in the head and pretending like it didn't hurt. She must have watched it three or four times in a row, and when she finally looked up, Jen was gone. A long time passed before Jill realized she wasn't in the bathroom.

You poor thing, they'd insist. *This must be so hard on you, losing your best friend like that.*

That was the other thing nobody wanted to hear, which was that she and Jen weren't best friends anymore, if they ever had been, which she doubted, even though they'd used the phrase for years without giving it a second thought: *my best friend, Jen; my best friend, Jill.* It was their mothers who were best friends, not them. The girls just tagged along because they had no choice (in that sense they really were like sisters). They carpooled to school, slept at each other's houses, went on combined family vacations, and spent countless hours in front of the TV and computer screens, killing time while their mothers drank tea or wine at the kitchen table.

Their makeshift alliance was surprisingly durable, lasting all the way from pre-K to the middle of the eighth grade, when Jen underwent a sudden and mysterious transfiguration. One day she had a new body—at least that's the way it seemed to Jill—the next day new clothes, and the day after that new friends, a clique of pretty and popular girls led by Hillary Beardon, whom Jen had previously claimed to despise. When Jill asked her why she'd want to hang out with people she herself had accused of being shallow and obnoxious, Jen just smiled and said they were actually pretty nice when you got to know them.

She wasn't mean about it. She never lied to Jill, never mocked her behind her back. It was like she just drifted slowly away, into a different, more exclusive orbit. She made a token effort to include Jill in her new life, inviting her (most likely on instructions from her mother) on a day trip to Julia Horowitz's beach house, but all that really did was make the gulf between them more obvious than it had been before. Jill felt like a foreigner the whole afternoon, a pale and mousy interloper in her hopeless one-piece bathing suit, watching in silent bewilderment as the pretty girls admired one another's bikinis, compared spray-on tans, and texted boys on candy-colored phones. The thing that amazed her most was how comfortable Jen looked in that strange context, how seamlessly she'd merged with the others.

"I know it's hard," her mother told her. "But she's branching out and maybe you should, too."

That summer—the last one before the disaster—felt like it would never end. Jill was too old for camp, too young to work, and too shy to pick up the phone and call anyone. She spent way too much time on Facebook, studying pictures of Jen and her new friends, wondering if they were all as happy as they looked. They'd taken to calling themselves the Classy Bitches, and almost every photo had that nickname in the heading: *Classy Bitches Chillin'; Classy Bitches Slumber Party; Hey CB what ru drinking?* She kept a close eye on Jen's status, tracking the ups and downs of her budding romance with Sam Pardo, one of the cutest guys in their class.

Jen is holding hands with Sam and watching a movie.

Jen is THE BEST KISS EVER!!!

Jen is the longest two weeks of my life.

Jen is . . . WHATEVER.

Jen is Guys Suck!

Jen is All Is Forgiven (and then some).

Jill tried to hate her, but she couldn't quite pull it off. What was the point? Jen was where she wanted to be, with people she liked, doing things that made her happy. How could you hate someone for that? You just had to figure out a way to get all that for yourself.

By the time September finally rolled around, she felt like the worst was over. High school was a clean slate, the past wiped away, the future yet to be written. Whenever she and Jen passed in the hall, they just said hi and left it at that. Every now and then, Jill would look at her and think, *We're different people now.*

The fact that they were together on October 14th was pure coincidence. Jill's mother had bought some yarn for Mrs. Sussman—the two moms were big on knitting that fall—and Jill happened to be in the car when she decided to drop it off. Out of old habit, Jill ended up in the basement with Jen, the two of them chatting awkwardly about their new teachers, then turning on the computer when they ran out of things to say. Jen had a phone number scribbled on the back of her hand—Jill noticed it when she pressed the power switch, and wondered whose it was—and chipped pink polish on her nails. The screen saver on her laptop was a picture of the two of them, Jill and Jen, taken a couple of years earlier during a snowstorm. They were all bundled up, red-cheeked and grinning, both of them with braces on their teeth, pointing proudly at a snowman, a lovingly constructed fellow with a carrot nose and borrowed scarf. Even then, with Jen sitting right beside her, not yet an angel, it felt like ancient history, a relic from a lost civilization.

IT WASN'T until her mother joined the G.R. that Jill began to understand for herself how absence could warp the mind, make you exaggerate the virtues and minimize the defects of the missing individual. It wasn't the same, of course: Her mother wasn't *gone* gone, not like Jen, but it didn't seem to matter.

They'd had a complicated, slightly oppressive relationship—a little closer than was good for either of them—and Jill had often wished for a little distance between them, some room to maneuver on her own.

Wait'll I get to college, she used to think. *It'll be such a relief not to have her breathing down my neck all the time.*

But that was the natural order of things—you grew up, you moved out. What wasn't natural was your mother walking out on you, moving across town to live in a group house with a bunch of religious nuts, cutting off all communication with her family.

For a long time after she left, Jill found herself overwhelmed by a childlike hunger for her mother's presence. She missed everything about the woman, even the stuff that used to drive her crazy—her off-key singing, her insistence that whole-wheat pasta tasted just as good as the regular kind, her inability to follow the storyline of even the simplest TV show (*Wait a second, is that the same guy as before, or someone else?*). Spasms of wild longing would strike her out of nowhere, leaving her dazed and weepy, prone to sullen fits of anger that inevitably got turned against her father, which was totally unfair, since he wasn't the one who'd abandoned her. In an effort to fend off these attacks, Jill made a list of her mother's faults and pulled it out whenever she felt herself getting sentimental:

Weird, high-pitched totally fake laugh
Crappy taste in music
Judgmental
Wouldn't say hi if she met me on the street
Ugly sunglasses
Obsessed with Jen
Uses words like *hoopla* and *rigamarole* in conversation
Nags Dad about cholesterol
Flabby arm Jello
Loves God more than her own family

It actually worked a little, or maybe she just got used to the situation. In any case, she eventually stopped crying herself to sleep, stopped writing long, desperate letters asking her mother to please come home, stopped blaming herself for things she couldn't control.

It was her decision, she learned to remind herself. *No one made her go.*

...

THESE DAYS, the only time Jill consistently missed her mother was first thing in the morning, when she was still half-asleep, unreconciled to the new day. It just didn't feel right, coming down for breakfast and not finding her at the table in her fuzzy gray robe, no one to hug her and whisper, *Hey, sleepyhead,* in a voice full of amusement and commiseration. Jill had a hard time waking up, and her mother had given her the space to make a slow and grumpy transition into consciousness, without a whole lot of chitchat or unnecessary drama. If she wanted to eat, that was fine; if not, that was no problem, either.

Her father tried to pick up the slack—she had to give him that—but they just weren't on the same wavelength. He was more the up-and-at-'em type; no matter what time she got out of bed, he was always perky and freshly showered, looking up from the morning paper—amazingly, he still read the morning paper—with a slightly reproachful expression, as if she were late for an appointment.

"Well, well," he said. "Look who's here. I was wondering when you were gonna put in an appearance."

"Hey," she muttered, uncomfortably aware of herself as the object of parental scrutiny. He eyeballed her like this every morning, trying to figure out what she'd been up to the night before.

"Bit of a hangover?" he inquired, sounding more curious than disapproving.

"Not really." She'd only had a couple of beers at Dmitri's house, maybe a toke or two off a joint that made the rounds at the end of the night, but there was no point in going into detail. "Just didn't get enough sleep."

"Huh," he grunted, not bothering to hide his skepticism. "Why don't you stay home tonight? We can watch a movie or something."

Pretending not to hear him, Jill shuffled over to the coffeemaker and poured herself a mug of the dark roast they'd recently started buying. It was a double-edged act of revenge against her mother, who hadn't allowed Jill to drink coffee in the house, not even the lame breakfast blend she thought was so delicious.

"I can make you an omelette," he offered. "Or you can just have some cereal."

She sat down, shuddering at the thought of her father's big sweaty omelettes, orange cheese oozing from the fold.

"Not hungry."

"You have to eat something."

She let that pass, taking a big gulp of black coffee. It was better that way, muddy and harsh, more of a shock to the system. Her father's eyes strayed to the clock above the sink.

"Aimee up?"

"Not yet."

"It's seven-fifteen."

"There's no rush. We're both free first period."

He nodded and turned back to his paper, the way he did every morning after she told him the same lie. She was never quite sure if he believed her or just didn't care. She got the same distracted vibe from a lot of the adults in her life—cops, teachers, her friends' parents, Derek at the frozen yogurt store, even her driving instructor. It was frustrating, in a way, because you never really knew if you were being humored or actually getting away with something.

"Any news on Holy Wayne?" Jill had been following the story of the cult leader's arrest with great interest, grimly amused by the sordid details included in the articles, but also embarrassed on behalf of her brother, who'd cast his lot with a man who turned out to be a charlatan and a pig.

"Not today," he said. "I guess they used up all the good stuff."

"I wonder what Tom will do."

They'd been speculating about this for the past few days but hadn't gotten too far. It was hard to imagine what Tom might be thinking when they didn't know where he was, what he was doing, or even if he was still involved with the Healing Hug Movement.

"I don't know. He's probably pretty—"

They stopped talking when Aimee walked into the kitchen. Jill was relieved to see that her friend was wearing pajama bottoms—it wasn't always the case—though the relative modesty of this morning's outfit was undercut by a cleavage-baring camisole. Aimee opened the refrigerator and peered into it for a long time, tilting her head as if something fascinating was going on in there. Then she pulled out a carton of eggs and turned toward the table, her face soft and sleepy, her hair a glorious mess.

"Mr. Garvey," she said, "any chance you could whip up one of those yummy omelettes?"

AS USUAL, they took the long way to school, ducking behind the Safeway to smoke a quick joint—Aimee did her best not to set foot inside Mapleton High without some sort of buzz going—then heading across Reservoir Road to see if anyone interesting happened to be hanging out at Dunkin' Donuts. The answer, not surprisingly, turned out to be no—unless you thought old men gnawing on crullers qualified as interesting—but the moment they poked their heads in, Jill was overcome by a wicked sugar craving.

"You mind?" she asked, glancing sheepishly toward the counter. "I didn't have any breakfast."

"I don't mind. It's not my fat ass."

"Hey." Jill swatted her in the arm. "My ass isn't fat."

"Not yet," Aimee told her. "Have a few more donuts."

Unable to decide between the glazed and the jelly, Jill split the difference and ordered both. She would've been perfectly happy to eat on the run, but Aimee insisted on getting a table.

"What's the hurry?" she asked.

Jill checked the time on her cell phone. "I don't wanna be late for second period."

"I have gym," Aimee said. "I don't care if I miss that."

"I have a Chem test. Which I'm probably gonna fail."

"You always say that, and you always get As."

"Not this time," Jill said. She'd skipped too many classes in the past few weeks, and had been stoned for too many of the ones she'd managed to attend. Some subjects mixed okay with weed, but Chemistry wasn't one of them. You get high and start thinking about electrons, and you can end up a long way from where you're supposed to be. "This time I'm screwed."

"Who cares? It's just a stupid test."

I do, Jill wanted to say, but she wasn't sure if she meant it. She used to care—used to care a lot—and hadn't quite gotten used to the feeling of not caring, though she was doing her best.

"You know what my mom told me?" Aimee said. "She said that when she was in high school, girls could get out of gym just for having their period. She said there was this one teacher, this Neanderthal football coach, and she told him every class that she had cramps, and he always said, *Okay, go sit in the bleachers.* The guy never even noticed."

Jill laughed, even though she'd heard the story before. It was one of the few things she knew about Aimee's mother, besides the fact that she was an alcoholic who'd disappeared on October 14th, leaving her teenage daughter alone with a stepfather she didn't like or trust.

"You want a bite?" Jill held out her jelly donut. "It's really good."

"That's okay. I'm stuffed. I can't believe I ate that whole omelette."

"Don't blame me." Jill licked a tiny jewel of jelly off the tip of her thumb. "I tried to warn you."

Aimee's expression turned serious, even a bit stern.

"You shouldn't make fun of your father. He's a really nice guy."

"I know."

"And he's not even a bad cook."

Jill didn't argue. Compared to her mother, her father was a terrible cook, but Aimee had no way of knowing that.

"He tries," she said.

She scarfed down her glazed donut in three quick bites—it was so airy inside, almost like there was nothing beneath the sugary coating—then gathered up her trash.

"Ugh," she said, dreading the prospect of the test she was about to take. "I guess we better go."

Aimee studied her for a moment. She glanced at the display case behind the counter—tiers of donuts arrayed in their metal baskets, iced and sprinkled and powdered and plain and full of sweet surprises—and then back at Jill. A mischievous smile broke slowly across her face.

"You know what?" she said. "I think I will have something to eat. Maybe some coffee, too. You want coffee?"

"We don't have time."

"Sure we do."

"What about my test?"

"What about it?"

Before Jill could reply, Aimee was out of her seat, moving toward the counter, her jeans so tight and her stride so liquid that everyone in the place turned to stare.

I have to go, Jill thought.

A feeling of unreality came over her just then, a sudden awareness of being trapped in a bad dream, that panicky sense of helplessness, as if she possessed no will of her own.

But this was no dream. All she had to do was stand up and start walking. And yet she remained frozen in her pink plastic seat, smiling foolishly as Aimee turned and mouthed the word *Sorry,* though it was clear from the look on her face that she wasn't sorry at all.

Bitch, Jill thought. *She wants me to fail.*

AT MOMENTS like this—and there were more of them than she would have liked to admit—Jill wondered what she was doing, how she'd allowed herself to get so tangled up with someone as selfish and irresponsible as Aimee. It wasn't healthy.

And it had happened so quickly. They'd only gotten to know each other a few months ago, at the beginning of summer, two girls working side by side in a failing frozen yogurt store, chatting during the slow times, some of which lasted for hours.

They were wary of each other at first, conscious of their membership in different tribes—Aimee sexy and reckless, her life a cluttered saga of bad decisions and emotional melodrama; Jill straitlaced and reliable, an A student and model teenage citizen. *I wish I had a whole class of Jills,* more than one teacher had written in the comments box on her report card. No one had ever written that about Aimee.

As the summer wore on, they began to relax into what felt like a genuine friendship, a connection that made their differences seem increasingly trivial. For all her social and sexual confidence, Aimee turned out to be surprisingly fragile, quick to tears and violent bouts of self-loathing; she required a lot of cheering up. Jill was better at hiding her sadness, but Aimee had a way of coaxing it out of her, getting her to open up about things she hadn't discussed with anyone else—her bitterness toward her mother, her trouble communicating with her father, the feeling that she'd been cheated, that the world she'd been raised to live in no longer existed.

Aimee took Jill under her wing, bringing her to parties after work, introducing her to what she'd been missing. Jill was intimidated at first—everybody she met seemed a little older and a little cooler than she was, even though most of them were her own age—but she quickly overcame her shyness. She got drunk for the first time, smoked weed, stayed up till dawn talking to people she used to ignore in the hallway, people she'd written off as losers and burnouts. One night, on a dare, she took off her clothes and jumped into Mark Sollers's pool. When she climbed out a few minutes later, naked and dripping in front of her new friends, she felt like a different person, like her former self had been washed away.

If her mother had been home, none of it would have happened, not because her mother would've stopped her, but because Jill would've stopped herself. Her father tried to intervene, but he seemed to have lost faith in his authority. He grounded her once in late July, after finding her passed out on the front lawn, but she ignored the punishment and he never mentioned it again.

Nor did he complain when Aimee started sleeping over, even though Jill hadn't consulted him before inviting her. By the time he finally got around to asking what was up, Aimee was already a fixture in the house, sleeping in Tom's old bedroom, adding her own peculiar requests to the family shopping lists, the kind of stuff that would have given her mother a heart attack—Pop-Tarts, Hot Pockets, ramen noodles. Jill told the truth, which was that Aimee needed a break from her stepfather, who sometimes "bothered" her when he came home drunk. He hadn't touched her yet, but he watched her all the time and said creepy things that made it hard for her to fall asleep.

"She shouldn't live there," Jill told him. "It's not a good situation."

"Okay," her father said. "Fair enough."

The last two weeks of August were especially giddy, as if both girls sensed an expiration date on the fun and wanted to drink every drop while they still could. One morning, Jill came down from the shower, complaining about how much she hated her hair. It was always so dry and lifeless, nothing like Aimee's, which was soft and radiant and never looked bad, not even when she'd just rolled out of bed in the morning.

"Cut it off," Aimee told her.

"What?"

Aimee nodded, her face full of certainty.

"Just get rid of it. You'll look better without it."

Jill didn't hesitate. She went upstairs, hacked away at her dull tresses with a pair of sewing scissors, then finished the job with the electric clippers her father kept under the bathroom sink. It was exhilarating to feel the past falling away in clumps, to watch a new face emerge, her eyes big and fierce, her mouth softer and prettier than it used to be.

"Holy shit," Aimee said. "That is fucking awesome."

Three days later Jill had sex for the first time, with a college guy she barely knew, after a drunken spin-the-bottle marathon at Jessica Marinetti's house.

"I never did it with a bald girl," he confided while they were still in the middle of the act.

"Really?" she said, not bothering to inform him that she'd never done it at all. "Is it okay?"

"It's nice," he told her, nuzzling her scalp with the tip of his nose. "Feels like sandpaper."

She didn't start to feel self-conscious until school started and she saw the way her old friends and teachers looked at her when she walked down the hall with Aimee, the mix of pity and loathing in their eyes. She knew what they were thinking—that she'd been led astray, that the bad girl had corrupted the good one—and wanted to tell them that they were wrong. She was no victim. All Aimee had done was show her a new way of being herself, a way that made as much sense right now as the old way had before.

Don't blame her, Jill thought. *I made the choice.*

She was grateful to Aimee, she really was, and glad she'd been able to help her out with a place to stay when she needed it. Even so, all this togetherness was starting to get to her, the two of them living like sisters, sharing clothes and meals and secrets, partying together every night and then starting up again in the morning. This month they even got their periods at the same time, which was kind of freaky. What she needed was a breather, a little time to catch up on schoolwork, hang out with her dad, maybe go through some of the college material that kept arriving in the mail every day. Just a day or two to get her bearings, because sometimes she had a little trouble locating the boundary between the two of them, the place where Aimee left off and Jill began.

THEY WERE only a few blocks from school when the Prius pulled up silently beside them. It was one of those things that never used to happen to Jill but happened all the time now that she was hanging out with Aimee. The passenger window slid down, releasing a cloud of pot-scented reggae into the chilly November morning.

"Hey, ladies," Scott Frost called out. "What's up?"

"Not much," Aimee replied. Her voice changed color when she talked to guys—it sounded deeper to Jill, infused with a teasing lilt that made even the most banal statements seem vaguely intriguing. "What's up with you?"

Adam Frost leaned in from the driver's seat, his head staggered a few inches behind his brother's, creating a kind of mini–Mount Rushmore effect. The Frost twins were famously handsome—identical dreadlocked slackers with square jaws, sleepy eyes, and the lithe bodies of the athletes they might have been if they hadn't been wasted all the time. Jill was pretty sure they'd graduated the year before, but she still saw them a lot in school, mostly in the art room, though they never seemed to do any art. They just sat around like retired guys, observing the young strivers with an air of benevolent amusement. The drawing teacher, Ms. Coomey, seemed to enjoy their company, chatting and laughing with them while her students worked independently. She was around fifty, married, and overweight, but a rumor had nonetheless spread through the school that she and the Frost brothers sometimes got it on in the supply closet during her free periods.

"Hop in," Adam called out. He had a row of piercings in his right eyebrow, which was the main way people distinguished him from Scott. "Let's go for a ride."

"We have to go to school," Jill muttered, speaking more to Aimee than the twins.

"Fuck that," said Scott. "Come hang out at our house, it'll be fun."

"What kind of fun?" Aimee inquired.

"We have a Ping-Pong table."

"And some Vicodin," Adam added.

"Now you're talking." Aimee turned to Jill with a hopeful smile. "Whaddaya think?"

"I don't know." Jill felt the heat of embarrassment spreading across her face. "I've been missing a lot of school lately."

"Me too," Aimee said. "One more day's not gonna matter."

It was a reasonable point. Jill glanced at the twins, who were nodding in unison to "Buffalo Soldier," sending out a subliminal message of encouragement.

"I don't know," she said again.

Aimee released a pointed sigh, but Jill remained motionless. She couldn't understand what was holding her back. The Chemistry test was already under way. The rest of the day would just be a footnote to her failure.

"Whatever." Aimee opened the door and climbed into the backseat, staring at Jill the whole time. "You coming?"

"That's okay," Jill told her. "You guys go ahead."

"You sure?" Scott asked as Aimee shut the door. He seemed genuinely disappointed.

Jill nodded and Scott's window hummed shut, slowly obscuring his beautiful face. The sealed-up Prius didn't move for a second or two, and neither did Jill. A sharp feeling of regret took hold of her as she stared at the tinted glass.

"Wait!" she called out.

Her voice sounded loud in her own ears, almost desperate, but they must not have heard her, because the car lurched into motion just as she was reaching for the door, and moved noiselessly down the street without her.

SHE WAS still high when she got to school, but not in the giggly way that made most mornings with Aimee feel like a goofy adventure, the two of them pretending to be spies or cracking up at things that weren't even funny, which somehow made them laugh even harder. Today's buzz felt heavy and sad, just a weird bad mood.

Technically, she was supposed to sign herself in at the main office, but that was one of those regulations nobody paid much attention to anymore, a holdover from a more orderly and obedient time. Jill had only been in high school for five weeks before the Sudden Departure, but she still had a vivid memory of what it was like back then, the teachers serious and demanding, the kids focused and motivated, full of energy. Almost everybody played an instrument or went out for a sport. Nobody smoked in the bathroom; you could get suspended for making out in the hall. People walked faster in those days—at least that's how she remembered it—and they always seemed to know exactly where they were going.

Jill opened her locker and grabbed her copy of *Our Town,* which she hadn't even started, despite the fact that they'd been discussing it in English for the past three weeks. There were still ten minutes to go before the end of second period, and she would have been happy to plop down on the floor and at least skim the first few pages, but she knew she wouldn't be able to concentrate, not with Jett Oristaglio, Mapleton High's wandering troubadour, sitting directly across from her, strumming his acoustic guitar and singing "Fire and Rain" for the thousandth time. That song just gave her the creeps.

She thought about ducking into the library, but there wasn't enough time to get anything done, so she figured she'd just head upstairs to English. On the way, she took a quick detour past Mr. Skandarian's room, where her classmates were finishing up the Chem test.

She wasn't sure what possessed her to look inside. The last thing she wanted was for Mr. S. to see her and realize that she wasn't sick. That would totally blow any chance she had of getting him to let her take a makeup test. Luckily, he was filling in a Sudoku when she peeked through the window, completely absorbed in the little boxes.

It must have been a hard test. Albert Chin was finished, of course—he was messing with his iPhone to kill time—and Greg Wilcox had gone to sleep, but everybody else was still working, doing the kind of stuff you do when you're trying to think and the clock is running out—lips were being bitten; hair was being wound around fingers; legs were bouncing up and down. Katie Brennan was scratching at her arm like she had a skin disease, and Pete Rodriguez kept tapping himself in the forehead with the eraser end of his pencil.

She only stood there for a minute or two, but even so, you might have expected someone to look up and see her, maybe smile or throw a quick wave. That's what usually happened when somebody peered into a classroom during a test. But everybody just kept working or sleeping or spacing out. It was as if Jill no longer existed, as if all that remained of her was an empty desk in the second row, a memorial to the girl who used to sit there.

SPECIAL SOMEONE

TOM GARVEY DIDN'T HAVE TO ask why the girl was standing on his doorstep, suitcase in hand. For weeks now, he'd felt the hope leaving his body in a slow leak—it was a little like going broke—and now it was gone. He was emotionally bankrupt. The girl smiled wryly, as if she could read his thoughts.

"You Tom?"

He nodded. She handed him an envelope with his name written across the front.

"Congratulations," she said. "You're my new babysitter."

He'd seen her before, but never up close, and she was even more beautiful than he'd realized—a tiny Asian girl, sixteen at most, with impossibly black hair and a perfect teardrop of a face. *Christine,* he remembered, the fourth bride. She let him stare for a while, then got tired of it.

"Here," she said, pulling out her iPhone. "Why don't you just take a picture?"

Two days later, the FBI and Oregon State Police arrested Mr. Gilchrest in what the TV news insisted on calling a "surprise early-morning raid," even though it was no surprise to anyone, least of all Mr. Gilchrest himself. Ever since Anna Ford's betrayal, he'd been warning his followers of dark times ahead, trying to convince them it was all for the best.

"Whatsoever happens to me," he'd written in his last e-mail, "do not despair. It happens for a reason."

Though he'd expected the arrest, Tom was taken aback by the severity of the charges—multiple counts of second- and third-degree rape and sodomy, as well as tax evasion and illegal transportation of a minor across state lines—and offended by the obvious pleasure the newscasters took in what they called "the spectacular downfall of the self-styled messiah," the "shocking allegations" that left his "saintly reputation in tatters" and "fast-growing youth movement in disarray." They kept showing the same unflattering video clip of a handcuffed Mr. Gilchrest being escorted into the courthouse in rumpled silk pajamas, his hair flattened on one side of his head, as if he'd just been hauled out of bed. The scroll bar at the bottom of the screen read: HOLY WAYNE? HOLY S**T! DISGRACED CULT LEADER BUSTED ON SEX RAP. FACES UP TO 75 YEARS IN PRISON.

There were four of them watching—Tom and Christine, and Tom's housemates, Max and Luis. Tom didn't know either of the guys very well—they'd just been rotated in from Chicago to assist him at the San Francisco Healing Hug Center—but from what he could tell, their reactions to the news were completely in character: sensitive Luis weeping softly, hotheaded Max shouting obscenities at the screen, insisting Mr. Gilchrest had been framed. For her part, Christine seemed oddly unruffled by the coverage, as if everything were unfolding according to plan. The only thing that bothered her was her husband's pajamas.

"I told him not to wear those," she said. "They make him look like Hugh Hefner."

She got a little more animated when Anna Ford's milkmaid face appeared on the screen. Anna was spiritual bride number six, and the only non-Asian girl in the bunch. She'd disappeared from the Ranch in late August, only to turn up a couple of weeks later on *60 Minutes,* where she told the world about the harem of underaged girls who catered to Holy Wayne's every need. She claimed to have been fourteen years old at the time of her marriage, a desperate runaway who'd been befriended by two nice guys at the Minneapolis bus station, given food and shelter, and then transported to the Gilchrest Ranch in southern Oregon. She must have made a good impression on the middle-aged Prophet; three days after her arrival, he slipped a ring on her finger and took her to bed.

"He's not a messiah," she said, in what became the defining sound bite of the scandal. "He's just a dirty old man."

"And you're Judas," Christine told the television. "Judas with a big fat ass."

IT WAS all in ruins, everything Tom had worked for and hoped for over the past two and a half years, but for some reason he didn't feel as heartbroken as he'd expected to. There was a definite sense of relief beneath the pain, the knowledge that the thing you'd been dreading had finally come to pass, that you no longer had to live in fear of it. Of course, there was a whole slew of new problems to worry about, but there would be time to deal with them later on.

He'd given his bed to Christine, so he stayed in the living room after everyone called it a night. Before turning off the lamp, he took out the picture of his Special Someone—Verbecki with the sparkler—and pondered it for a few seconds. For the first time since he could remember, he didn't whisper his old friend's name, nor did he make his nightly plea for the missing to return. What was the point? He felt like he'd just woken up from a sleep that had lasted way too long, and could no longer remember the dream that had detained him.

They're gone, he thought. *I've got to let them go.*

THREE YEARS ago, when he first arrived at college, Tom had been just like everybody else—a normal American kid, a B+ student who wanted to major in business, pledge a cool frat, drink a ton of beer, and hook up with as many reasonably hot girls as possible. He'd felt homesick for the first couple of days, nostalgic for the familiar streets and buildings of Mapleton, his parents and sister, and all his old buddies, scattered to institutions of higher learning across the country, but he knew the sadness was temporary, and even kind of healthy. It bothered him when he met other freshmen who spoke about their hometowns, and sometimes even their families, with casual disdain, as if they'd spent the first eighteen years of their lives in prison and had finally busted out.

The Saturday after classes began, he got drunk and went to a football game with a big gang from his floor, his face painted half orange and half blue. All the students were concentrated in one section of the domed stadium, roaring and chanting like a single organism. It was exhilarating to melt into the crowd like that, to feel his identity dissolving into something bigger and more powerful. The Orange won, and that night, at a frat kegger, he met a girl whose face was painted the same as his, went home with her, and discovered that college life exceeded his highest expectations. He could still vividly remember the feeling of walking home from her dorm as the sun came up, his shoes untied, his socks and boxers missing in action, the spontaneous high five he exchanged with a guy who staggered past him on the quad like a mirror image, the smack of their palms echoing triumphantly in the early-morning silence.

A month later, it was all over. School was canceled on October 15th; they were given seven days to pack up their stuff and vacate the campus. That final week existed in his memory as a blur of baffled farewells—the dorms slowly emptying, the muffled sound of someone crying behind a closed door, the soft curses people uttered as they pocketed their phones. There were a few desperate parties, one of which ended in a sickening brawl, and a hastily arranged memorial service in the Dome, at which the Chancellor solemnly recited the names of the university's victims of what people had just begun to call the Sudden Departure. The roll call included Tom's Psych instructor and a girl from his English class who'd overdosed on sleeping pills after learning of the disappearance of her identical twin.

He hadn't done anything wrong, but he remembered feeling a weird sense of shame—of personal failure—returning home so soon after he'd left, almost as if he'd flunked out or gotten expelled for disciplinary reasons. But there was comfort as well, the reassurance of returning to his family, finding them all present and accounted for, though his sister had apparently had a pretty close call. Tom asked her about Jen Sussman a couple of times, but she refused to talk, either because it was too upsetting—that was his mother's theory—or because she was just sick of the whole subject.

"What do you want me to say?" she'd snapped at him. "She just fucking vaporized, okay?"

They hunkered down for a couple of weeks, just the four of them, watching DVDs and playing board games, anything to distract themselves from the hysterical monotony of the TV news—the obsessive repetition of the same few basic facts, the ever-rising tally of the missing, interview upon interview with traumatized eyewitnesses, who said things like *He was standing right next to me* . . . , or *I just turned around for a second* . . . , before their voices trailed off into embarrassed little chuckles. The coverage felt different from that of September 11th, when the networks had shown the burning towers over and over. October 14th was more amorphous, harder to pin down: There were massive highway pileups, some train wrecks, numerous small-plane and helicopter crashes—luckily, no big passenger jets went down in the United States, though several had to be landed by terrified co-pilots, and one by a flight attendant who'd become a folk hero for a little while, one bright spot in a sea of darkness—but the media was never able to settle upon a single visual image to evoke the catastrophe. There also weren't any bad guys to hate, which made everything that much harder to get into focus.

Depending upon your viewing habits, you could listen to experts debating the validity of conflicting religious and scientific explanations for what was either a miracle or a tragedy, or watch an endless series of gauzy montages celebrating the lives of departed celebrities—John Mellencamp and Jennifer Lopez, Shaq and Adam Sandler, Miss Texas and Greta Van Susteren, Vladimir Putin and the Pope. There were so many different levels of fame, and they all kept getting mixed together—the nerdy guy in the Verizon ads and the retired Supreme Court Justice, the Latin American tyrant and the quarterback who'd never fulfilled his potential, the witty political consultant and that chick who'd been dissed on *The Bachelor*. According to the Food Network, the small world of superstar chefs had been disproportionately hard hit.

Tom didn't mind being home at first. It made sense, at a time like that, for people to stick close to their loved ones. There was an almost unbearable tension in the air, a mood of anxious waiting, though no one seemed to know whether they were waiting for a logical explanation or a second wave of disappearances. It was as if the whole world had paused to take a deep breath and steel itself for whatever was going to happen next.

. . .

NOTHING HAPPENED.

As the weeks limped by, the sense of immediate crisis began to dissipate. People got restless hiding out in their houses, marinating in ominous speculation. Tom started heading out after dinner, joining a bunch of his high school friends at the Canteen, a dive bar in Stonewood Heights that wasn't particularly diligent about ferreting out fake IDs. Every night was like a combination Homecoming Weekend and Irish wake, all sorts of unlikely people milling around, buying rounds and trading stories about absent friends and acquaintances. Three members of their graduating class were among the missing, not to mention Mr. Ed Hackney, their universally despised vice principal, and a janitor everybody called Marbles.

Nearly every time Tom set foot in the Canteen, a new piece got added to the mosaic of loss, usually in the form of some obscure person he hadn't thought about for years: Dave Keegan's Jamaican housekeeper, Yvonne; Mr. Boundy, a junior high substitute teacher whose bad breath was the stuff of legend; Giuseppe, the crazy Italian guy who used to own Mario's Pizza Plus before the surly Albanian dude took over. One night in early December, Matt Testa sidled up while Tom was playing darts with Paul Erdmann.

"Hey," he said, in that grim voice people used when discussing October 14th. "Remember Jon Verbecki?"

Tom tossed his dart a little harder than he'd meant to. It sailed high and wide, almost missing the board altogether.

"What about him?"

Testa shrugged in a way that made his reply unnecessary.

"Gone."

Paul stepped up to the tape mark on the floor. Squinting like a jeweler, he zipped his dart right into the middle of the board, just an inch or so above the bullseye and a little to the left.

"Who's gone?"

"This was before your time," Testa explained. "Verbecki moved away the summer after sixth grade. To New Hampshire."

"I knew him all the way back in preschool," Tom said. "We used to have playdates. I think we went to Six Flags once. He was a nice kid."

Matt nodded respectfully. "His cousin knows my cousin. That's how I found out."

"Where was he?" Tom asked. This was the obligatory question. It seemed important, though it was hard to say why. No matter where the person was when it happened, the location always struck him as eerie and poignant.

"At the gym. On one of the ellipticals."

"Shit." Tom shook his head, imagining a suddenly empty exercise machine, the handles and pedals still moving as if of their own accord, Verbecki's final statement. "It's hard to picture him at the gym."

"I know." Testa frowned, as if something didn't add up. "He was kind of a pussy, right?"

"Not really," Tom said. "I think he was just a little sensitive or something. His mother used to have to cut the labels out of his clothes so they wouldn't drive him crazy. I remember in preschool he used to take his shirt off all the time because he said it itched him too much. The teachers kept telling him it was inappropriate, but he didn't care."

"That's right." Testa grinned. It was all coming back to him. "I slept over his house once. He went to bed with all the lights on, and this one Beatles song playing over and over. 'Paperback Writer' or some shit."

" 'Julia,' " Tom said. "That was his magic song."

"His what?" Paul fired off his last dart. It landed with an emphatic *thunk,* just below the bullseye.

"That's what he called it," Tom explained. "If 'Julia' wasn't playing, he couldn't go to sleep."

"Whatever." Testa didn't appreciate the interruption. "He tried sleeping at my house a bunch of times, but it never worked. He'd roll out his sleeping bag, change into pj's, brush his teeth, the whole nine yards. But then, just when we were about to go to bed, he'd lose it. His bottom lip would get all quivery and he'd be like, *Dude, don't be mad, but I gotta call my mom.*"

Paul glanced over his shoulder as he extracted his darts from the board.

"Why'd they move?"

"Fuck if I know," Testa said. "His dad probably got a new job or something. It was a long time ago. You know how it is—you swear you're gonna keep in touch, and you do for a little while, and then you never see the guy again." He turned to Tom. "You even remember what he looked like?"

"Kinda." Tom closed his eyes, trying to picture Verbecki. "Sorta pudgy, blond hair with bangs. Really big teeth."

Paul laughed. "Big teeth?"

"Beavery," Tom explained. "He probably got braces right after he moved."

Testa raised his beer bottle.

"Verbecki," he said.

Tom and Paul clinked their bottles against his.

"Verbecki," they repeated.

That was how they did it. You talked about the person, you drank a toast, and then you moved on. Enough people had disappeared that you couldn't afford to get hung up on a single individual.

For some reason, though, Tom couldn't get Jon Verbecki out of his mind. When he got home that night, he went up to the attic and looked through several boxes of old photographs, faded prints from the days before his parents owned a digital camera, back when they used to have to ship the film off to a mail-order lab for processing. His mother had been bugging him for years to get the pictures scanned, but he hadn't gotten around to it.

Verbecki appeared in a number of photos. There he was at a school Activities Day, balancing an egg on a teaspoon. One Halloween, he was a lobster among superheroes and didn't look too happy about it. He and Tom had been T-ball teammates; they sat beneath a tree, grinning with almost competitive intensity, wearing identical red hats and shirts that said SHARKS. He looked more or less as Tom remembered—blond and toothy, in any case, if not quite as pudgy.

One picture made a special impression. It was a close-up, taken at night, when they were six or seven years old. It must have been around the Fourth of July, because Verbecki had a lit sparkler in his hand, an overexposed cloud of fire that looked almost like cotton candy. It would have seemed festive, except that he was staring fearfully into the camera, like he didn't think it was a very good idea, holding a sizzling metal wand so close to his face.

Tom wasn't sure why he found the picture so intriguing, but he decided not to put it back in the box with the others. He brought it downstairs and spent a long time studying it before he fell asleep. It almost seemed like Verbecki was sending a secret message from the past, asking a question only Tom could answer.

IT WAS right around this time that Tom received a letter from the university informing him that classes would resume on February 1st. Attendance, the letter stressed, would not be mandatory. Any student who wished to opt out of this "Special Spring Session" could do so without suffering any financial or academic penalty.

"Our goal," the Chancellor explained, "is to continue operating on a scaled-down basis during this time of widespread uncertainty, to perform our vital missions of teaching and research without exerting undue pressure on those members of our community who are unprepared to return at the present moment."

Tom wasn't surprised by this announcement. Many of his friends had received similar notifications from their own schools in recent days. It was part of a nationwide effort to "Jump-Start America" that had been announced by the President a couple of weeks earlier. The economy had gone into a tailspin after October 14th, with the stock market plunging and consumer spending falling off a cliff. Worried experts were predicting "a chain reaction economic meltdown" if something wasn't done to halt the downward spiral.

"It's been nearly two months since we suffered a terrible and unexpected blow," the President said in his prime-time address to the nation. "Our shock and grief, while enormous, can no longer be an excuse for pessimism or paralysis. We need to reopen our schools, return to our offices and factories and farms, and begin the process of reclaiming our lives. It won't be easy and it won't be quick, but we need to start now. Each and every one of us has a duty to stand up and do our part to get this country moving again."

Tom wanted to do his part, but he honestly didn't know if he was ready to go back to school. He asked his parents, but their opinions only mirrored the split in his own thinking. His mother thought he should stay home, maybe take some classes at community college, and then return to Syracuse in September, by which time everything would presumably be a lot clearer.

"We still don't know what's going on," she told him. "I'd be a lot more comfortable if you were here with us."

"I think you should go back," his father said. "What's the point of hanging around here doing nothing?"

"It's not safe," his mother insisted. "What if something happens?"

"Don't be ridiculous. It's just as safe there as it is here."

"Is that supposed to make me feel better?" she asked.

"Look," his father said. "All I know is that if he stays here, he's just gonna keep going out and getting drunk with his buddies every night." He turned to Tom. "Am I wrong?"

Tom gave a shrug of nondenial. He knew he'd been drinking way too much and was beginning to wonder if he needed some kind of professional help. But there was no way to talk about his drinking without talking about Verbecki, and that was a subject he really didn't feel like discussing with anyone.

"You think he's gonna drink any less in college?" his mother asked. Tom found it both troubling and interesting to listen to his parents discuss him in the third person, as if he weren't actually there.

"He'll have to," his father said. "He won't be able to get drunk every night and keep up with his work."

His mother started to say something, then decided it wasn't worth the trouble. She looked at Tom, holding his gaze for a few seconds, making a silent plea for his support.

"What do you want to do?"

"I don't know," he said. "I'm pretty confused."

In the end, his decision was influenced less by his parents than his friends. One by one over the next few days, they told him that they would be heading back to their respective schools for second semester—Paul to FIU, Matt to Gettysburg, Jason to U. of Delaware. Without his buddies around, the idea of staying home lost a lot of its appeal.

His mother reacted stoically when he informed her of his decision. His father gave him a congratulatory slap on the shoulder.

"You'll be fine," he said.

The drive to Syracuse felt a lot longer in January than it had in September, and not just because of the intermittent snow squalls that blew across the highway in swirling gusts, turning the other vehicles into ghostly shadows. The mood in the car was oppressive. Tom couldn't think of much to say, and his parents were barely speaking to each other. That was how it had been since he'd come home—his mother gloomy and withdrawn, brooding about Jen Sussman and the meaning of what had happened; his father impatient, grimly cheerful, a little too insistent that the worst was over and they needed to just get on with their lives. If nothing else, he thought, it would be a relief to get away from them.

His parents didn't stay long after dropping him off. There was a big storm coming, and they wanted to get on the road before it hit. His mother handed him an envelope before leaving the dorm.

"It's a bus ticket." She hugged him with a tenacity that was almost alarming. "Just in case you change your mind."

"I love you," he whispered.

His father's hug was quick, almost perfunctory, as if they'd be seeing each other again in a day or two.

"Have fun," he said. "You only get one shot at college."

• • •

DURING THE Special Spring Session, Tom pledged Alpha Tau Omega. Joining a frat was something he'd wanted to do for so long—in his mind, it was synonymous with college itself—that the process was well under way before he was able to admit that it no longer mattered to him in the least. When he tried to project himself into the future, to envision the life that awaited him at ATO—the big house on Walnut Place, the wild parties and nutty pranks, the late-night bull sessions with brothers who would go on to be his lifelong friends and allies—it all seemed hazy and unreal to him, images from a movie he'd seen a long time ago and whose plot he could no longer remember.

He could've withdrawn, of course, maybe rushed again in the fall when he felt better, but he decided to tough it out. He told himself that he didn't want to bail out on Tyler Rucci, his floormate and pledge brother, but in his heart he knew that the stakes were higher than that. He'd pretty much stopped going to classes by the end of February—he was finding it impossible to concentrate on academics—so the pledge process was all he had left, his only real link to normal college life. Without it, he would've become one of those lost souls you saw all over campus that winter, pale, vampiry kids who slept all day and drifted from the dorm to the student center to Marshall Street at night, habitually checking their phones for a message that never seemed to come.

Another benefit of pledging was that it gave him something to talk about with his parents, who called almost every day to check up on him. He wasn't a particularly good liar, so it helped to be able to say, *We went on a scavenger hunt,* or *We had to cook breakfast in bed for the older brothers, and then serve it to them in flowery aprons,* and to have details at the ready to back up these claims. It was a lot harder when his mother grilled him about his schoolwork, and he was forced to improvise about essays and exams and the brutal problem sets in Statistics.

"What'd you get on that paper?" she'd ask.

"Which paper?"

"Poli Sci. The one we talked about."

"Oh, that one. Another B+."

"So he liked the thesis?"

"He didn't really say."

"Why don't you e-mail me the essay? I'd like to read it."

"You don't need to read it, Mom."

"I'd like to." She paused. "You sure you're okay?"

"Yeah, everything's fine."

Tom always insisted everything was fine—he was busy, making friends, keeping up a solid B average. Even when discussing the frat, he made sure to emphasize the positive, focusing on things like the weekday study groups and the all-night intra-frat karaoke blowout, while avoiding any mention of Chip Gleason, the only active ATO brother who'd gone missing on October 14th.

Chip loomed large around the frat house. There was a framed portrait of him in the main party room, and a scholarship fund dedicated to his memory. The pledges had been required to memorize all sorts of personal information about him: his birthday, the names of his family members, his top-ten movies and bands, and the complete list of all the girls he'd hooked up with in his sadly abbreviated life. That was the hard part—there were thirty-seven girlfriends in all, starting with Tina Wong in junior high and ending with Stacy Greenglass, the buxom Alpha Chi who'd been in bed with him on October 14th—riding him reverse cowgirl-style, if legend were to be believed—and who had to be hospitalized for several days as a result of the severe emotional trauma brought on by his sudden midcoitus departure. Some of the brothers told this story as if it were a funny anecdote, a tribute to the studliness of their beloved friend, but all Tom could think of was how awful it must have been for Stacy, the kind of thing you'd never recover from.

One night at a Tri Delt mixer, though, Tyler Rucci pointed out a hot sorority girl on the dance floor, grinding with a varsity lacrosse player. She was tanned and wearing an incredibly tight dress, leaning forward as she moved her ass in slow circles against her partner's crotch.

"You know who that is?"

"Who?"

"Stacy Greenglass."

Tom watched her dance for a long time—she looked happy, running her hands over her breasts and then down over her hips and thighs, making porn star faces for the benefit of her friends—trying to figure out what she knew that he didn't. He was willing to accept the possibility that Chip hadn't meant much to her. Maybe he was just a one-time hookup, or a casual friend with benefits. But still, he was a real person, someone who played an active and reasonably important part in her life. And yet here she was, just a few months after he'd disappeared, dancing at a party as though he'd never even existed.

It wasn't that Tom disapproved. Far from it. He just couldn't figure out how it was possible that Stacy could get over Chip while he remained haunted by Verbecki, a kid he hadn't seen for years and probably wouldn't have even recognized if they'd bumped into each other on October 13th.

But that was how it was. He thought about Verbecki all the time. If anything, his obsession had deepened since he'd returned to school. He carried that stupid picture—Little Kid with Sparkler—everywhere he went and looked at it dozens of times a day, chanting his old friend's name in his head as though it were some kind of mantra: *Verbecki, Verbecki, Verbecki.* It was the reason he was flunking out, the reason he was lying to his parents, the reason he no longer painted his face blue and orange and screamed his head off at the Dome, the reason he could no longer imagine his own future.

Where the hell did you go, Verbecki?

A BIG part of the pledge process was getting to know the Older Brothers, convincing them that you were a good fit with ATO. There were poker nights and pizza lunches and marathon drinking games, a series of interviews masquerading as social events. Tom thought he was doing a decent job of hiding his obsession, impersonating a normal, well-adjusted freshman—the guy he should have been—until he was approached one night in the TV room by Trevor Hubbard, a.k.a. Hubbs, a junior who was the frat's resident bohemian/intellectual. Tom was leaning against a wall, pretending to be interested in a Wii bowling match between two of his pledge brothers, when Hubbs suddenly appeared at his side.

"This is fucked," he said in a low voice, nodding at the wide-screen Sony, the virtual ball knocking down the virtual pins, Josh Freidecker flipping a celebratory double bird at Mike Ishima. "All this fraternity bullshit. I don't know how anybody stands it."

Tom grunted ambiguously, not sure if this was a ploy designed to catch him in an act of disloyalty. Hubbs hardly seemed the type to play that sort of game, though.

"Come here," he said. "I need to talk to you."

Tom followed him into the empty hallway. It was a weeknight, still pretty early, not much going on in the house.

"You feeling okay?" Hubbs asked him.

"Me?" Tom said. "I'm fine."

Hubbs regarded him with a certain skeptical amusement. He was a small, wiry guy—an accomplished rock climber—with scraggly facial hair and a sour expression that was more a default mode than a reflection of his actual mood.

"You're not depressed?"

"I don't know." Tom gave an evasive shrug. "A little, maybe."

"And you really want to join this frat, live here with all these douchebags?"

"I guess. I mean, I thought I did. Everything's just kinda fucked up right now. It's hard to know what I want."

"I hear you." Hubbs nodded appreciatively. "I used to be pretty happy here myself. Most of the brothers are pretty cool." He glanced left and right, then lowered his voice to a near whisper. "The only one I didn't like was Chip. He was the biggest asshole in the whole house."

Tom nodded cautiously, trying not to look too surprised. He'd only ever heard people say nice things about Chip Gleason—great guy, good athlete, six-pack abs, ladies' man, natural leader.

"He kept a hidden camera in his bedroom," Hubbs said. "Used to tape the girls he fucked, then show the videos down in the TV room. One girl was so humiliated she had to leave school. Good old Chip didn't care. Far as he was concerned, she was just a stupid whore who got what she deserved."

"That sucks." Tom was tempted to ask the girl's name—it must have been among those he'd memorized—but decided to let it pass.

Hubbs stared at the ceiling for a few seconds. There was a smoke detector up there, red light glowing.

"Like I said, Chip was a dick. I should be happy he's gone, you know?" Hubbs's eyes locked on Tom's. They were wide and frightened, full of a desperation Tom had no trouble recognizing, since he saw it all the time in the bathroom mirror. "But I dream about that fucker every night. I'm always trying to find him. I'll be running through a maze, screaming his name, or tiptoeing through a forest, looking behind every tree. It's got to the point I don't even want to go to sleep anymore. Sometimes I write him letters, you know, just telling him what's going on around here. Last weekend, I got so hammered, I tried to get his name tattooed on my forehead. The tattoo guy wouldn't do it—that's the only reason I'm not walking around with Chip Fucking Gleason written on my face." Hubbs looked at Tom. It almost felt like he was pleading. "You know what I'm talking about, right?"

Tom nodded. "Yeah, I do."

Hubbs's face relaxed a little. "There's this guy I've been reading about on the Web. He's speaking at a church in Rochester on Saturday afternoon. I think he might be able to help us."

"He's a preacher?"

"Just a guy. He lost his son in October."

Tom gave a sympathetic groan, but it didn't mean anything. He was just being polite.

"We should go," Hubbs said.

Tom was flattered by the invitation, but also a little scared. He had the feeling that Hubbs was a little unhinged.

"I don't know," he said. "Saturday's the hot dog–eating contest. The pledges are supposed to cook."

Hubbs looked at Tom in amazement.

"A hot dog–eating contest? Are you fucking kidding me?"

TOM STILL marveled at the humble circumstances of his first encounter with Mr. Gilchrest. Later he would see the man speak in front of adoring crowds, but on that frigid March Saturday, no more than twenty people had gathered in an overheated church basement, small puddles of melted snow spreading out from each pair of shoes on the linoleum floor. Over time, the Holy Wayne movement would come to be associated primarily with young people, but that afternoon, the audience was mostly middle-aged or older. Tom felt out of place among them, as if he and Hubbs had wandered by mistake into a retirement planning seminar.

Of course, the man they'd come to see wasn't famous yet. He was still, as Hubbs had said, "just a guy," a grieving father who spoke to anyone who would listen, wherever they would have him—not just in houses of worship, but in senior centers, VFW halls, and private homes. Even the host of the event—a tall, slightly stooped, youngish man who introduced himself as Reverend Kaminsky—seemed a bit fuzzy about who Mr. Gilchrest was and what he was doing there.

"Good afternoon, and welcome to the fourth installment of our Saturday lecture series, 'The Sudden Departure from a Christian Perspective.' Our guest speaker today, Wayne Gilchrest, hails from just down the road in Brookdale and comes highly recommended by my esteemed colleague, Dr. Finch." The Reverend paused, in case anyone wanted to applaud for his esteemed colleague. "When I asked Mr. Gilchrest to provide a title for his lecture so I could list it on our website, he told me it was a work in progress. So I'm just as curious as all of you to hear what he has to say."

People who only knew Mr. Gilchrest in his later, more charismatic incarnation wouldn't have recognized the man who rose from a chair in the front row and turned to face the meager crowd. Holy Wayne's future uniform consisted of jeans and T-shirts and studded leather wristbands—one reporter dubbed him the "Bruce Springsteen of cult leaders"—but back then he favored more formal attire, on that day an ill-fitting funeral suit that seemed to have been borrowed from a smaller, less powerful man. It looked uncomfortably tight across the chest and shoulders.

"Thank you, Reverend. And thanks, everybody, for coming out." Mr. Gilchrest spoke in a gruff voice that radiated masculine authority. Later, Tom would learn that he drove a delivery van for UPS, but if he'd had to guess that afternoon, he would've pegged him for a police officer or high school football coach. He glanced at his host, frowning an insincere apology. "I guess I didn't realize that I was supposed to be speaking from a Christian perspective. I'm really not sure what my perspective is."

He began by passing out a flyer, one of those missing person notices you saw all over the place after October 14th, on telephone poles and supermarket corkboards. This one featured a color photograph of a skinny kid standing on a diving board, hugging himself against the cold. Beneath his crossed arms, his ribs were clearly visible; his legs jutted like sticks from billowy trunks that looked like they would have fit a grown man. He was smiling but his eyes seemed troubled; you got the feeling he didn't relish the prospect of plunging into the dark water. HAVE YOU SEEN THIS BOY? The caption identified him as Henry Gilchrest, age eight. It included an address and phone number, along with an urgent plea for anyone who may have seen a child resembling Henry to contact his parents immediately. PLEASE!!! WE ARE DESPERATE FOR INFORMATION REGARDING HIS WHEREABOUTS.

"This is my son." Mr. Gilchrest stared fondly at the flyer, almost as if he'd forgotten where he was. "I could spend the whole afternoon telling you about him, but it's not gonna do much good, is it? You never smelled his hair after he just got out of the bath, or carried him from the car after he'd fallen asleep on the way home, or heard the way he laughed when someone tickled him. So you'll just have to take my word for it: He was a great kid and he made you glad to be alive."

Tom glanced at Hubbs, curious to know if this was what they'd come for, a blue-collar guy reminiscing about his departed son. Hubbs just shrugged and turned back to Mr. Gilchrest.

"You can't really tell from the picture, but Henry was a little small for his age. He was a good athlete, though. Lotta quickness. Good reflexes and hand-eye coordination. Soccer and baseball were his games. I tried to get him interested in basketball, but he didn't go for it, maybe because of the height thing. We took him skiing a couple of times, but he wasn't crazy about that, either. We didn't push too hard. We figured he'd let us know when he was ready to try again. You know what I'm saying, right? Seemed like there was time enough for everything."

In school, Tom couldn't sit still for lectures. After the first few minutes, the professor's words blurred into a meaningless drone, a sluggish river of pretentious phrases. He got jittery and lost his focus, becoming intensely and unhelpfully conscious of his physical self— twitchy legs, dry mouth, grumbly digestive organs. No matter how he arranged himself on his chair, the posture always struck him as awkward and uncomfortable. For some reason, though, Mr. Gilchrest had the opposite effect on him. Tom felt calm and lucid as he listened, almost bodiless. Settling back into his chair, he had a sudden bewildering vision of the hot dog–eating contest he'd blown off at the frat house, big guys cramming their faces full of meat and bread, cheeks bulging, their eyes full of fear and disgust.

"Henry was smart, too," Mr. Gilchrest continued, "and I'm not just saying that. I'm a pretty good chess player and I'm telling you, he could give me a run for my money by the time he was seven. You should have seen the look on his face when he played. He got real serious, like you could see the wheels turning in his head. Sometimes I made bone-headed moves to keep him in the game, but that just ticked him off. He'd be like, *Come on, Dad. You did that on purpose.* He didn't want to be patronized, but he didn't want to lose, either."

Tom smiled, remembering a similar father-son dynamic from his own childhood, a weird mixture of competition and encouragement, worship and resentment. He felt a brief stab of tenderness, but the sensation was muffled somehow, as if his father were an old friend with whom he'd fallen out of touch.

Mr. Gilchrest pondered the flyer again. When he looked up, his face seemed naked, utterly defenseless. He took a deep breath, as if he were preparing to go underwater.

"I'm not gonna say much about what it was like after he left. To tell the truth, I barely remember those days. It's a blessing, I think, like the traumatic amnesia people get after a car accident or major surgery. I can tell you one thing, though. I was awful to my wife in those first few weeks. Not that there was anything I could've done to make her feel better—there was no such thing as *feeling better* back then. But what I did, I made things worse. She needed me, and I couldn't say a kind word, couldn't even look at her sometimes. I started sleeping on the couch, sneaking out in the middle of the night and driving around for hours without telling her where I was going or when I'd be back. If she called, I wouldn't answer my phone.

"I guess in some way I blamed her. Not for what happened to Henry—I knew that was nobody's fault. I just . . . I didn't mention this before, but Henry was an only child. We wanted to have more, but my wife had a cancer scare when he was two, and the doctors recommended a hysterectomy. Seemed like a no-brainer at the time.

"After we lost Henry, I kind of got obsessed with the idea that we needed to have another kid. Not to replace him—I'm not crazy like that—but just to start over, you know? I had it in my head that that was the only way we could live again, but it was impossible, because of her, because she was physically incapable of bearing me another child.

"I decided that I would leave her. Not right away, but in a few months, when she was stronger and people wouldn't judge me so harshly. It was a secret I had, and it made me feel guilty, and somehow I blamed her for that, too. It was a feedback loop, and it just kept getting worse. But then, one night, my son came to me in a dream. You know how sometimes you see people in dreams, and it's not really them, but somehow it is them? Well, this wasn't like that. This was my son, clear as day, and he said, *Why are you hurting my mother?* I denied it, but he just shook his head, like he was disappointed in me. *You need to help her.*

"I'm embarrassed to admit this, but it had been weeks since I'd touched my wife. Not just sexually—I mean I literally hadn't *touched* her. Hadn't stroked her hair or squeezed her hand or patted her on the back. And she was crying all the time." Mr. Gilchrest's voice cracked with emotion. He wiped the back of his hand almost angrily across his mouth and nose. "So the next morning I got up and gave her a hug. I put my arms around her and told her I loved her and didn't blame her for anything, and it was almost like saying it made it true. And then something else came into my mind. I don't know where it came from. I said, *Give me your pain. I can take it.*" He paused, looking at his audience with an almost apologetic expression. "This is the part that's hard to explain. Those words were barely out of my mouth when I felt a weird jolt in my stomach. My wife let out a gasp and went limp in my arms. And I knew right then, as clearly as I'd ever known anything, that an enormous amount of pain had been transferred from her body into mine.

"I know what you're thinking, and I don't blame you. I'm just telling you what happened. I'm not saying I fixed her or cured her, or anything like that. To this day, she's still sad. Because there's not some finite amount of pain inside us. Our bodies and minds just keep manufacturing more of it. I'm just saying that I took the pain that was inside of her *at that moment* and made it my own. And it didn't hurt me at all."

A change seemed to come over Mr. Gilchrest. He stood up straighter and placed his hand over his heart.

"That was the day I learned who I am," he declared. "I'm a sponge for pain. I just soak it up and it makes me stronger."

The smile that spread across his face was so joyful and self-assured he seemed almost like a different person.

"I don't care if you believe me. All I ask is that you give me a chance. I know you're all hurting. You wouldn't be here on a Saturday afternoon if you weren't. I want you to let me hug you and take away your pain." He turned to Reverend Kaminsky. "You first."

The minister was clearly reluctant, but he was the host and couldn't see any polite way out. He rose from his chair and approached Mr. Gilchrest, casting a skeptical sidelong glance at the audience on the way, letting them know he was just being a good sport.

"Tell me," Mr. Gilchrest said. "Is there a special someone you've been missing? A person whose absence seems especially troubling to you? Anyone at all. Doesn't have to be a close friend or member of your family."

Reverend Kaminsky seemed surprised by the question. After a brief hesitation he said, "Eva Washington. She was a classmate of mine in divinity school. I didn't know her that well, but . . ."

"Eva Washington." Mr. Gilchrest stepped forward, the sleeves of his suit jacket creeping toward his elbows as he spread his arms. "You miss Eva."

At first it seemed like an unremarkable social hug, the kind people exchange all the time. But then, with startling abruptness, Reverend Kaminsky's knees buckled and Mr. Gilchrest grunted, almost as if he'd been punched in the gut. His face tightened into a grimace, then relaxed.

"Wow," he said. "That was a lot."

The two men held each other for a long time. When they separated, the Reverend was sobbing, one hand clamped over his mouth. Mr. Gilchrest turned to the audience.

"Single file," he said. "I have time for everybody."

Nothing happened for a moment or two. But then a heavyset

woman in the third row stood up and made her way to the front. Before long, all but a few members of the audience had left their seats.

"No pressure," Mr. Gilchrest assured the holdouts. "I'm here when you're ready."

Tom and Hubbs were near the end of the line, so they were familiar with the process by the time their turns arrived. Hubbs went first. He told Mr. Gilchrest about Chip Gleason, and Mr. Gilchrest repeated Chip's name before pulling Hubbs against his chest in a strong, almost paternal embrace.

"It's okay," Mr. Gilchrest told him. "I'm right here."

Several seconds passed before Hubbs let out a yelp and Mr. Gilchrest staggered backward, his eyes widening with alarm. Tom thought they were about to crash onto the floor like wrestlers, but somehow they managed to remain upright, performing a precarious dance until they regained their balance. Mr. Gilchrest laughed and said, "Easy, partner," patting Hubbs gently on the back before letting him go. Hubbs looked wobbly and dazed as he returned to his seat.

Mr. Gilchrest smiled as Tom stepped forward. Up close his eyes seemed brighter than Tom had expected, as if he were glowing from within.

"What's your name?" he asked.

"Tom Garvey."

"Who's your special someone, Tom?"

"Jon Verbecki. This kid I used to know."

"Jon Verbecki. You miss Jon."

Mr. Gilchrest opened his arms. Tom stepped forward, into his strong embrace. Mr. Gilchrest's torso felt broad and sturdy, but also soft, unexpectedly yielding. Tom felt something loosen inside of him.

"Give it here," Mr. Gilchrest whispered in his ear. "It doesn't hurt me."

Later, in the car, neither Tom nor Hubbs had much to say about what they'd felt in the church basement. They both seemed to understand that describing it was beyond their powers, the gratitude that spreads through your body when a burden gets lifted, and the sense of homecoming that follows, when you suddenly remember what it feels like to be yourself.

SHORTLY AFTER midterms, Tom received a flurry of increasingly agitated voice, text, and e-mail messages from his parents, imploring him to contact them *immediately*. From what he could gather, the university had sent them some sort of formal warning that he was in danger of failing all his classes.

He didn't respond for a few days, hoping the delay would give them time to cool off, but their attempts to reach him only grew more frantic and aggressive. Finally, unnerved by their threats to alert the campus police, cancel his credit card, and cut off his cell phone service, he gave in and called them back.

"What the hell's going on up there?" his father demanded.

"We're worried about you," his mother cut in, speaking on a separate handset. "Your English teacher hasn't seen you in weeks. And you didn't even *take* your Poli Sci exam, the one you said you got a B on."

Tom winced. It was embarrassing to be caught in a lie, especially one so big and stupid. Unfortunately, all he could think to do was lie again.

"That was my bad. I overslept. I was too embarrassed to tell you."

"That's not gonna cut it," his father said. "You know how much it costs for one semester of college?"

Tom was surprised by the question, and a bit relieved. His parents had money. It was a lot easier to apologize for wasting some of it than to explain what he'd been doing for the past two months.

"I know it's expensive, Dad. I really don't take it for granted."

"That's not the issue," his mother said. "We're happy to pay for your college. But something's wrong with you. I can hear it in your voice. We should never have let you go back there."

"I'm fine," Tom insisted. "It's just that the frat stuff's been taking up way more of my time than I thought it would. Hell Week's the end of this month, and then everything'll get back to normal. If I work hard, I'm pretty sure I can pass all my classes."

He heard an odd silence at the other end of the connection, as if each of his parents was waiting for the other one to speak.

"Honey," his mother said softly. "It's too late for that."

AT THE frat house that night, Tom told Hubbs that he was withdrawing from school. His parents were coming on Saturday to take him home. They had his whole life figured out—a full-time job at his father's warehouse, and two sessions a week with a therapist who specialized in young adults with grief disorders.

"Apparently I have a grief disorder."

"Welcome to the club," Hubbs told him.

Tom hadn't mentioned it to his parents, but he'd already seen a psychologist at the University Health Service, a mustachioed Middle Eastern guy with watery eyes who'd informed him that his obsession with Verbecki was just a defense mechanism, and a common one at that, a smoke screen to distract him from more serious questions and troubling emotions. This theory made no sense to Tom—what good was a defense mechanism if it fucked up your whole life? What the hell was it defending you from?

"Damn," said Hubbs. "What are you gonna do?"

"I don't know. But I can't go back home. Not right now."

Hubbs looked worried. The two of them had grown closer in the past couple of weeks, bonding over their shared fascination with Mr. Gilchrest. They'd attended two more of his lectures, each with an audience double the size of the previous one. The most recent had been at Keuka College, and it had been thrilling to see the way he connected with a young audience. The hugging session lasted almost two hours; when it was over, he was dripping wet, barely able to stand, a fighter who'd gone the distance.

"I have some friends who live off campus," Hubbs told him. "If you want, you can probably crash there for a few days."

Tom packed his things, drained his bank account, and slipped out of the dorm on Friday night. When his parents showed up the next day, all they found were some books, a disconnected printer, and an unmade bed, along with a letter in which Tom told them a little about Mr. Gilchrest and apologized for letting them down. He told them that he would be traveling for a while, and promised to keep in touch via e-mail.

"I'm sorry," he wrote. "This is a really confusing time for me. But there are some things I need to figure out on my own, and I hope you'll respect my decision."

HE STAYED with Hubbs's buddies through the end of the semester, then sublet their apartment when they headed home for summer vacation. Hubbs moved in with him; they got hired as detailers at a car dealership and did volunteer work for Mr. Gilchrest in their spare time, passing out leaflets, setting up folding chairs, collecting addresses for an e-mail list, whatever he needed.

That summer things really started to take off. Someone posted a clip of Mr. Gilchrest on YouTube—it was tagged I AM A SPONGE FOR YOUR PAIN—and it went viral. The crowds at his lectures grew bigger, the invitations to speak more frequent. By September, he was renting a mothballed Episcopal church in Rochester, holding marathon Hugfests every Saturday and Sunday morning. Tom and Hubbs sometimes manned the merch table in the lobby, selling lecture DVDs, T-shirts—the most popular one said GIVE IT TO ME on the front, and I CAN TAKE IT on the back—and a self-published paperback memoir entitled *A Father's Love.*

Mr. Gilchrest traveled a lot that fall—it was the first anniversary of the Sudden Departure—giving lectures all over the country. Tom and Hubbs were among the volunteers who drove him to and from the airport, getting to know him as a person, gradually earning his trust. When the organization began expanding that spring, Mr. Gilchrest asked the two of them to run the Boston chapter, organizing and promoting a multi-campus speaking tour and doing whatever else they saw fit to increase awareness among the local college population of what he'd begun calling the Healing Hug Movement. It was exhilarating to be given so much responsibility, to have gotten in on the ground floor of a phenomenon that had taken off so unexpectedly—like working at an Internet start-up back in the day, Tom thought—but also a little dizzying, everything growing so quickly, shooting off in so many different directions at once.

During that first summer in Boston, Tom and Hubbs began hearing disturbing rumors from people they knew back at the Rochester headquarters. Mr. Gilchrest was changing, they said, letting the fame go to his head. He'd bought a fancy car, started wearing different clothes, and was paying a little too much attention to the adoring young women and teenage girls who lined up to hug him. He'd apparently begun calling himself "Holy Wayne" and hinting about some sort of special relationship with God. On a couple of occasions, he had referred to Jesus as his brother.

When he arrived in September to give his first lecture to a packed house at Northeastern, Tom could see that it was true. Mr. Gilchrest was a new man. The heartbroken father in the shabby suit was gone, replaced by a rock star in sunglasses and a tight black T-shirt. When he greeted Tom and Hubbs there was an imperious coolness in his voice, as if they were simply hired help, rather than devoted followers. He instructed them to give backstage passes to any cute girls who seemed promising, "especially if they're Chinese or Indian or like that." Onstage, he didn't just offer hugs and sympathy; he spoke of accepting a God-given mission to fix the world, to somehow undo the damage caused by the Sudden Departure. The details remained vague, he explained, not because he was holding out, but because he himself didn't know them all yet. They were coming to him piecemeal, in a series of visionary dreams.

"Stay tuned," he told the audience. "You'll be the first to know. The world is depending on us."

Hubbs was troubled by what he saw that night. He thought Mr. Gilchrest had gotten drunk on his own Kool-Aid, that he'd morphed from an inspirational figure to the CEO of a messianic Cult of Personality (it wasn't the last time Tom would hear this accusation). After a few days of soul-searching, Hubbs told Tom that he was done, that while he loved Mr. Gilchrest, he couldn't in good conscience continue to serve Holy Wayne. He said he would be leaving Boston, heading back to his family on Long Island. Tom tried to talk to him out of it, but Hubbs was beyond persuasion.

"Something bad's gonna happen," he said. "I can feel it."

IT TOOK a whole year for Hubbs to be proven right, and during that time, Tom remained a loyal follower and valued employee of the Healing Hug Movement, helping to launch new field offices in Chapel Hill and Columbus before landing a plum job at the San Francisco Center, training new teachers to run Special Someone Meditation Workshops. Tom loved the city and enjoyed meeting a batch of new students every month. He had a few affairs—the novice teachers were mostly women—but not nearly as many as he could have. He was a different person now, more self-contained and contemplative, a far cry from the frat boy with the painted face, out to get laid by any means necessary.

On paper, the movement was thriving—membership was growing steadily, money was pouring in, the media was paying attention—but Mr. Gilchrest's behavior was becoming increasingly erratic. He was arrested in Philadelphia after being found in a hotel room with a fifteen-year-old girl. The case was eventually dismissed for lack of evidence—the girl insisted that they were "just talking"—but Mr. Gilchrest's reputation suffered a serious blow. Several of his college lectures were canceled, and for a while, Holy Wayne became a punch line on late-night TV, the most recent incarnation of that age-old scoundrel, the Horny Man of God.

Stung by the ridicule, Mr. Gilchrest abandoned his headquarters in Upstate New York and moved to a ranch in a remote part of southern Oregon, far from prying eyes. Tom had visited only once, in mid-June, to take part in a gala three-day celebration of what would have been Henry Gilchrest's eleventh birthday. The accommodations weren't much—the hundred or so guests had to sleep in tents and share a few nasty Porta-Johns—but it was an honor just to be invited, a sign of membership in the inner circle of the organization.

For the most part, Tom liked what he saw—big weathered house, swimming pool, working farm, stables. Only two things bothered him: the contingent of gun-toting security guards patrolling the grounds—there had supposedly been some death threats against Holy Wayne—and the inexplicable presence of six hot teenage girls, five of them Asian, who were living in the main house with Mr. Gilchrest and his wife, Tori. The girls—they were jokingly referred to as the "Cheerleading Squad"—spent their days sunning themselves beside the pool while Tori Gilchrest power-walked by herself around the outskirts of the property, breathing forcefully through her nose while performing an elaborate series of arm exercises with light dumbbells.

Tom didn't think she looked too happy, but on the final night of the party, Tori was the one who stepped up to the microphone on the outdoor stage and introduced the girls as Mr. Gilchrest's "spiritual brides." She admitted that it was an unconventional arrangement, but she wanted the community to know that her husband had asked for—and received—her blessing for each and every one of these new marriages. The girls—they were standing behind her, smiling nervously in their pretty dresses—were all sweet and modest and surprisingly mature for their ages, not to mention completely adorable. As everyone knew, she herself could no longer bear children, and this was a problem, because God had recently revealed to Holy Wayne that it was his destiny to father a child who would repair the broken world. One of these girls—Iris or Cindy or Mei or Christine or Lam or Anna—would be the mother of this miracle child, but only time would tell which one. Mrs. Gilchrest concluded by saying that the love between her and Holy Wayne remained as strong and vibrant as it had been on their wedding day. She assured everyone that they continued to live together very happily as husband and wife, partners and best friends forever.

"Whatever my husband does," she said, "I support him a hundred and ten percent and I hope you will, too!"

There was a roar from the crowd as Mr. Gilchrest bounded up the steps and made his way across the stage to present his wife with a bouquet of roses.

"Isn't she the greatest?" he asked. "Am I the luckiest guy in the world or what?"

The spiritual brides began to applaud as Mr. Gilchrest kissed his legal wife, and the crowd followed suit. Tom did his best to clap along with everyone else, but his hands felt huge and leaden, so heavy he could barely pry them apart.

CHRISTINE SAID she was bored, trapped in the house all day like a prisoner, so Tom took her for a whirlwind tour of the city. He was glad for an excuse to get away from the office. It was like a funeral in there—no seminars in session, nothing to do except sit around with Max and Luis, answering e-mails and the occasional phone call, parroting the talking points they'd been given by headquarters: The charges are bogus; Holy Wayne is innocent until proven guilty; an organization is bigger than one man; our faith remains unshakable.

It was a classic San Francisco day, cool and bright, milky morning fog surrendering reluctantly to a clear blue sky. They did the usual stuff—cable car and Fisherman's Wharf, Coit Tower and North Beach, Haight-Ashbury and Golden Gate Park—Tom playing the role of jovial guide, Christine chuckling at his lame jokes, grunting politely at his half-remembered facts and recycled anecdotes, just as happy as he was to think about something besides Mr. Gilchrest for a while.

He was surprised at how well they were getting along. Back at the house, she'd been a bit of a problem, a little too interested in pulling rank, reminding everyone of her exalted status within the organization. Nothing was good enough—the futon was lumpy, the bathroom was gross, the food tasted weird. But the fresh air brought out a previously concealed sweetness in her, a bouncy teenage energy that had been hidden beneath the regal attitude. She dragged him into vintage clothing stores, apologized to homeless guys for her lack of spare change, and stopped every couple of blocks to gaze down at the bay and pronounce it awesome.

Christine kept moving in and out of focus on him. Yes, she was a visiting dignitary—Mr. Gilchrest's wife or whatever—but she was also just a kid, younger than his own sister and a lot less worldly, a small-town Ohio girl, who, until she ran away from home, had never been to a city bigger than Cleveland. But not really like his sister, either, because people didn't stop and stare at Jill when she walked down the street, tripped up by her unearthly beauty, trying to figure out if she was famous, if they'd seen her on TV or something. He wasn't sure how to treat Christine, if he should think of himself as a personal assistant or a surrogate big brother, or maybe just a helpful friend, a caring, slightly older guy showing her around an unfamiliar metropolis.

"I had a nice day," she told him over a late-afternoon snack at Elmore's, a café on Cole Street that was full of Barefoot People, hippies with bullseyes painted on their foreheads. The Bay Area was their spiritual homeland. "It's good to be out of the house."

"Anytime," he said. "I'm happy to do it."

"Sooo." Her voice was low, slightly flirtatious, as if she suspected him of withholding good news. "Have you heard anything?"

"About what?"

"You know. When he's getting out. When I can go back."

"Back where?"

"To the Ranch. I really miss it."

Tom wasn't sure what to tell her. She'd seen the same TV reports he had. She knew that Mr. Gilchrest had been denied bail, and that the authorities were playing hardball, seizing the organization's assets, arresting several top and midlevel people, squeezing them for damaging information. The FBI and State Police made no secret of the fact that they were actively searching for the underage girls Mr. Gilchrest claimed to have married—not because they'd done anything wrong, but because they were victims of a serious crime, endangered minors in need of medical care and psychological counseling.

"Christine," he said, "you can't go back there."

"I have to," she told him. "It's where I live."

"They'll make you testify."

"No, they won't." She sounded defiant, but he could see the doubt in her eyes. "Wayne said everything would be okay. He's got really good lawyers."

"He's in big trouble, Christine."

"They can't put him in jail," she insisted. "He didn't do anything wrong."

Tom didn't argue; there was no point. When Christine spoke again, her voice was small and frightened.

"What am I supposed to do?" she asked. "Who's gonna take care of me?"

"You can stay with us for as long as you want."

"I don't have any money."

"Don't worry about it."

This didn't seem like the right time to tell her that he didn't have any money, either. He and Max and Luis were technically volunteers, donating their time to the Healing Hug Movement in exchange for room and board and a paltry stipend. The only cash in his pocket had come from the envelope Christine had handed him when she'd arrived, two hundred dollars in twenties, the most money he'd seen in a long time.

"What about your family?" he asked. "Is that a possibility?"

"My family?" The idea seemed funny to her. "I can't go back to my family. Not like this."

"Like what?"

She tucked her chin, examining the front of her yellow T-shirt, as if searching for a stain. She had narrow shoulders and very small breasts, hardly there at all.

"Didn't they tell you?" She ran her palm over her flat belly, smoothing the wrinkles from her shirt.

"Tell me what?"

When she looked up, her eyes were shining.

"I'm pregnant," she said. He could hear the pride in her voice, a dreamy sense of wonder. "I'm the One."

Part *Two*

MAPLETON MEANS FUN

THE CARPE DIEM

JILL AND AIMEE HEADED OUT right after dinner, cheerfully informing Kevin that they didn't know where they were going, what they were doing, who they would be with, or when they might be home.

"Late," was all Jill could tell him.

"Yeah," agreed Aimee. "Don't wait up."

"It's a school night," Kevin reminded them, not bothering to add, as he sometimes did, that it was odd how going nowhere and doing nothing could take up so much time. The joke just didn't seem that funny anymore. "Why don't you try to stay sober for once? See what it's like to wake up in the morning with a clear head."

The girls nodded earnestly, assuring him that they had every intention of heeding this excellent advice.

"And be careful," he continued. "There are a lot of freaks out there."

Aimee grunted knowingly, as if to say that no one needed to tell her about freaks. She was wearing kneesocks and a short cheerleader skirt—light blue, not the maroon and gold of Mapleton High—and had deployed her usual unsubtle arsenal of cosmetics.

"We'll be careful," she promised.

Jill rolled her eyes, unimpressed by her friend's good-girl act.

"You're the biggest freak of all," she told Aimee. Then, to Kevin, she added, "She's the one people need to watch out for."

Aimee protested, but it was hard to take her seriously, given that she looked less like an innocent schoolgirl than a stripper halfheartedly pretending to be one. Jill gave the opposite impression—a scrawny child playing dress-up—in her cuffed jeans and the oversized suede coat she'd borrowed from her mother's closet. Kevin experienced the usual mixed feelings seeing them together: a vague sadness for his daughter, who was so clearly the sidekick in this duo, but also a kind of relief rooted in the thought—or at least the hope—that her unprepossessing appearance might function as a form of protective camouflage out in the world.

"Just watch out for yourselves," Kevin told them.

He hugged the girls good night, then stood in the doorway as they headed down the stairs and across the lawn. He'd tried for a while to restrict his hugs to his own child, but Aimee didn't like being left out. It was awkward at first—he was far too conscious of the contours of her body and the length of their embraces—but it had gradually become part of the routine. Kevin didn't exactly approve of Aimee, nor was he thrilled to have her living under his roof—she'd been staying there for three months and showed no signs of leaving anytime soon—but he couldn't deny the benefits of having a third person in the mix. Jill seemed happier with a friend around, and there was a lot more laughter at the dinner table, fewer of those deadly moments when it was just the two of them, father and daughter, and neither had a word to say.

KEVIN LEFT the house a little before nine. As usual, Lovell Terrace was lit up like a stadium, the big houses preening like monuments in the glow of their security floodlights. There were ten dwellings in all, "Luxury Homes" built in the last days of SUVs and easy credit, nine of them still occupied. Only the Westerfelds' house was empty—Pam had died last month, and the estate remained unsettled—but the Homeowners' Association made sure the lawn was cared for and the lights stayed on. Everyone knew what happened when deserted houses fell into disrepair, drawing the attention of bored teenagers, vandals, and the Guilty Remnant.

He headed out to Main Street and turned right, setting off on his nightly pilgrimage. It was like an itch—a physical compulsion—this need to be among friends, away from the gloomy, frightened voice that often held court in his head but always seemed so much louder and surer of itself in a quiet house after dark. One of the most frequently noted side effects of the Sudden Departure had been an outbreak of manic socializing—impromptu block parties that lasted for entire weekends, potluck dinners that stretched into sleepovers, quick hellos that turned into marathon gabfests. Bars were packed for months after October 14th; phone bills were exorbitant. Most of the survivors had settled down since then, but Kevin's urge for nocturnal human contact remained as powerful as ever, as if a magnetic force were propelling him toward the center of town, in search of like-minded souls.

THE CARPE Diem was an unassuming place, one of the few blue-collar taverns that had weathered Mapleton's late-twentieth-century transformation from factory town to bedroom community. Kevin had been going there since he was a young man, back when it was called the Midway Lounge, and the only drafts you could get were Bud and Mich.

He entered through the restaurant door—the bar was in an adjoining room—nodding at the familiar faces as he made his way to the booth in the back, where Pete Thorne and Steve Wiscziewski were already deep in conversation over a pitcher of beer, passing a legal pad back and forth across the table. Unlike Kevin, both men had wives at home, but they usually arrived at the Carpe Diem long before he did.

"Gentlemen," he said, sliding in beside Steve, a bulky, excitable guy who Laurie always said was a heart attack waiting to happen.

"Don't worry," Steve said, filling a clean glass with the dregs from the pitcher and handing it to Kevin. "There's another on the way."

"We're going over the roster." Pete held up the legal pad. The top page featured a rough sketch of a baseball diamond with names scrawled in the filled positions and question marks by the empty ones. "All we really need is a center fielder and a first baseman. And a couple of subs for insurance."

"Four or five new players," said Steve. "That should be doable, right?"

Kevin studied the sketch. "What happened with that Dominican guy you were telling me about? Your housecleaner's husband?"

Steve shook his head. "Hector's a cook. He works nights."

"He might be able to play on the weekends," Pete added. "That's at least something."

Kevin was gratified by the amount of thought and effort the guys were giving to a softball season that was still five or six months away. It was exactly what he'd been hoping for when he convinced the town council to restore funding for the adult recreation programs that had been suspended after the Sudden Departure. People needed a reason to get out of their houses and have a little fun, to look up and realize that the sky hadn't fallen.

"I'll tell you what would help," said Steve. "If we could find a couple left-handed hitters. Right now every guy on the squad is a righty."

"So what?" Kevin polished off his flat beer in a single gulp. "It's slow-pitch. None of that strategy stuff really matters."

"No, you gotta mix it up," Pete insisted. "Keep the other guys off balance. That's why Mike was so great. He really gave us that extra dimension."

The Carpe Diem team had lost only one player on October 14th—Carl Stenhauer, a mediocre pitcher and second-string outfielder—but Mike Whalen, their cleanup hitter and star first baseman, was an indirect casualty as well. Mike's wife was among the missing, and he still hadn't recovered from his loss. He and his sons had painted a crude, almost unrecognizable portrait of Nancy on the back wall of their house, and Mike spent most of his nights alone with the mural, communing with her memory.

"I talked to him a few weeks ago," Kevin said. "But I don't think he's gonna play this year. He says his heart's just not in the game."

"Keep working on him," Steve said. "The middle of our lineup's pretty weak."

The waitress came by with a new pitcher and refilled everyone's glasses. They toasted to fresh blood and a winning season.

"It'll be good to get back on the field," Kevin said.

"No kidding," agreed Steve. "Spring's not spring without softball."

Pete put down his glass and looked at Kevin.

"So there's one other thing we wanted to run by you. You remember Judy Dolan? I think she was in your son's class."

"Sure. She was a catcher, right? All-county or something?"

"All-state," Pete corrected him. "She played varsity in college. She's graduating in June, moving back home for the summer."

"She'd be quite an asset," Steve pointed out. "She could take over for me behind the plate, and I could move to first. It would solve a lot of our problems."

"Wait a second," Kevin said. "You want the league to go coed?"

"No," Pete said, exchanging a wary glance with Steve. "That's exactly what we don't want."

"But it's the Men's Softball League. If you have women playing, then it's coed."

"We don't want *women*," Steve explained. "We just want Judy."

"You can't discriminate," Kevin reminded them. "If you admit one woman, you gotta admit them all."

"It's not discrimination," Pete insisted. "It's an exception. Besides, Judy's bigger than I am. If you didn't look too close, you wouldn't even know she was a girl."

"You ever play coed softball?" Steve asked. "It's about as much fun as all-male Twister."

"They do it with soccer," Kevin said. "Everybody seems fine with that."

"That's soccer," Steve said. "They're all pussies to begin with."

"Sorry," Kevin told them. "You can have Judy Dolan or you can have a men's league. But you can't have both."

THE MEN'S room was a tight squeeze—a dank, windowless space outfitted with a sink, a hand dryer, a trash can, two side-by-side urinals, and a toilet stall—in which it was theoretically possible to have five individuals rubbing shoulders at the same time. Usually this only happened late at night, when guys had drunk so much beer that waiting politely was no longer an option, and by then, everybody was cheerful enough that the obstacle-course aspect of it just seemed like part of the fun.

Right now, though, Kevin had the whole place to himself, or at least he would have if he hadn't been so aware of Ernie Costello's friendly face gazing down at him from a framed photograph hanging above and between the two urinals. Ernie was the Midway's former bartender, a big-bellied guy with a walrus mustache. The wall around his portrait was full of heartfelt graffiti scrawled by his friends and former customers.

We miss you buddy.
You were the best!!!
It's not the same without you
You're in our hearts. . . .
Better make it a double!

Kevin kept his head down, doing his best to ignore the bartender's beseeching gaze. He'd never been a fan of the memorials that had sprung up all over town in the wake of the Sudden Departure. It didn't matter if they were discreet—a roadside flower arrangement, a name soaped on the rear window of a car—or big and flashy, like the mountain of teddy bears in a little girl's front yard, or the question WHERE'S DONNIE? burned into the grass along the entire length of the high school football field. He just didn't think it was healthy, being reminded all the time of the terrible and incomprehensible thing that had happened. That was why he'd pushed so hard for the Heroes' Day Parade—it was better to channel the grief into an annual observance, relieve some of the day-to-day pressure on the survivors.

He washed his hands and rubbed them under the useless dryer, wondering if Pete and Steve had inadvertently stumbled onto something with their idea of inviting Judy Dolan onto the team. Like those guys, Kevin preferred to play in a competitive all-male league, where you didn't have to watch your language or think twice about barreling into the catcher to break up a close play at the plate. But it was starting to look like finding enough players for a serious league was going to be a heavy lift, and he thought a fun coed league might be an alternative worth considering, the greatest good for the greatest many.

KEVIN LITERALLY bumped into Melissa Hulbert on his way out of the restroom. She was leaning against the wall in the dim alcove, waiting her turn for the ladies' room, which could accommodate only one person at a time. Later on, he realized that their meeting probably wasn't a coincidence, but it felt like one. Melissa acted surprised and seemed happier to see him than he might have expected.

"Kevin." She kissed him on the cheek. "Wow. Where've you been hiding?"

"Melissa." He made an effort to match the warmth of her greeting. "It's been a while, huh?"

"Three months," she informed him. "At least."

"That long?" He pretended to do the math in his head, then expelled a grunt of fake wonderment. "So how've you been?"

"Good." She shrugged to let him know that *good* was a bit of an overstatement, then studied him for an anxious moment or two. "Is this okay?"

"What?"

"Me being here."

"Sure. Why not?"

"I don't know." Her smile didn't quite cancel out the edge in her voice. "I just assumed—"

"No, no," he assured her. "It's not like that."

An older woman Kevin didn't know emerged from the ladies' room, mumbling an apology as she slipped by, trailing a vapor cloud of sweet perfume.

"I'm at the bar," Melissa said, touching him lightly on the arm. "If you feel like buying me a drink."

Kevin groaned an apology. "I'm here with some friends."

"Just one drink," she told him. "I think you owe me that much."

He owed her a lot more than that, and they both knew it.

"Okay," he said. "Fair enough."

MELISSA WAS one of three women Kevin had attempted to sleep with since his wife had left, and the only one close to his own age. They'd known each other since they were kids—Kevin was a year ahead of her in school—and they'd even had a little teenage fling the summer before his senior year, a heavy makeout session at the end of a keg party. It was one of those free-pass things—he had a girlfriend, she had a boyfriend, but the girlfriend and the boy-friend both happened to be on vacation—that hadn't gone nearly as far as he would've liked. She was a hottie back then, a wholesome, freckle-faced redhead, with what were widely considered to be the nicest tits in all of Mapleton High. Kevin managed to put his hand on the left one, but only for a tantalizing second or two before she removed it.

Some other time, she told him, with a sadness in her voice that sounded sincere. *I promised Bob I'd be good.*

But there was no other time, not that summer, and not for the next quarter century. Bob and Melissa went steady all the way through high school and college and ended up getting married. They bounced around a bit before coming home to Mapleton, right around the time Kevin moved back with his own family. Tom was just two at the time, the same age as Melissa's younger daughter.

They saw each other a lot when the kids were small, at playgrounds and school events and spaghetti dinners. They were never close—never socialized or exchanged more than the usual parental small talk—but there was always that little secret between them, the memory of a sum-mer night, the awareness of a road not taken.

HE ENDED up buying her three drinks, the first to discharge his debt, the second because he'd forgotten how easy it was to talk to her, and the third because it felt good to have her leg pressing against his while he sipped his bourbon, which was exactly how he'd gotten into trouble the last time.

"Any word from Tom?" she asked.

"Just an e-mail a few months ago. He didn't say much."

"Where is he?"

"I'm not exactly sure. Somewhere on the West Coast, I think."

"But he's okay?"

"Seemed like it."

"I heard about Holy Wayne," she said. "What a creep."

Kevin shook his head. "I don't know what the hell my son was thinking."

Melissa's face clouded over with maternal concern.

"It's hard being young now. It was different for us, you know? It was like a Golden Age. We just didn't realize it."

Kevin wanted to object on principle—he was pretty sure most people thought of their own youth as some kind of Golden Age—but in this case she had a point.

"What about Brianna?" he asked. "How's she doing?"

"Okay." Melissa sounded like she was trying to convince herself. "Better than last year anyway. She's got a boyfriend now."

"That's good."

Melissa shrugged. "They met over the summer. Some kind of survivors' network. They sit around and tell each other how sad they are."

IN THEIR previous meeting at the Carpe Diem—the night they ended up going home together—Melissa had talked a lot about her divorce, which had been a minor local scandal. After almost twenty years of marriage, Bob had left her for a younger woman he'd met at work. Melissa was only in her early forties at the time, but it had felt to her as if her life were over, as if she'd been abandoned like some crappy old car on the side of the highway.

Aside from alcohol, the main thing that kept her going was her hatred of the woman who'd stolen her husband. Ginny was twenty-eight, a slim, athletic woman who'd worked as Bob's assistant. They married as soon as the divorce was final, and tried to start a family. They were apparently having trouble getting pregnant, but Melissa didn't take much comfort in that. The very thought of Bob even wanting children with another woman was infuriating. What made it even more galling was the fact that her own kids actually *liked* Ginny. They were more than happy to call their father a cheating bastard, but all they would ever say about his new wife was that she was *really nice*. As if to prove their point, Ginny made multiple attempts to smooth things over with Melissa, writing several letters in which she apologized for the pain she'd caused, and asking for forgiveness.

I just wanted to hate her in peace, Melissa said. *And she wouldn't even let me do that.*

Melissa's rage was so pure that her main thought on October 14th—once she'd ascertained that her kids were safe—was a wild, unspoken hope that Ginny would be among the victims, that her problematic existence would simply be erased from the world. Bob would suffer as she had suffered; the score would be settled. It might even be possible, under those circumstances, for her to take him back, for the two of them to start over and find a way to reclaim some of what they'd lost.

Can you imagine? she said. *That's how bitter I was.*

Everybody had thoughts like that, Kevin reminded her. *It's just that most of us won't admit it.*

Of course it wasn't Ginny who vanished; it was Bob, while riding the elevator in a parking garage next to his office. There were disruptions in phone and Internet service that day, and Melissa didn't find out he was missing until around nine o'clock that night, when Ginny herself showed up to break the news. She seemed dazed and groggy, like someone had just awoken her from a long afternoon nap.

Bobby's gone, she kept muttering. *Bobby's gone.*

You know what I said to her?

Melissa had closed her eyes, as if she were trying to wish away the memory.

I said, Good, now you know how it feels.

• • •

THE YEARS had changed some things but not others. Melissa's freckles had faded, and her hair was no longer red. Her face was fuller, her figure less defined. But her voice and eyes were exactly the same. It was like the girl he'd known had been absorbed into the body of a middle-aged woman. It was Melissa, and it wasn't.

"You should've called me," she said, pouting sweetly as she laid her hand on his thigh. "We wasted the whole summer."

"I was embarrassed," he explained. "I felt like I let you down."

"You didn't let me down," she assured him, her long fingernails tracing cryptic designs on the fabric of his jeans. She was wearing a gray silk blouse, unbuttoned to reveal the scalloped edge of a maroon bra. "It's no big deal. It happens to everyone."

"Not to me," he insisted.

This wasn't exactly true. He'd had similar malfunctions with Liz Yamamoto, a twenty-five-year-old grad student he'd met on the Internet, and then again with Wendy Halsey, a thirty-two-year-old marathon-running paralegal, but he'd chalked those up to performance anxiety caused by the relative youth of his partners. It was sadder with Melissa, and harder to account for.

They'd gone back to her house, had a glass of wine, and then headed into the bedroom. It felt good, relaxed and natural and totally right—like they were finishing what they'd started back in high school—until the very last moment, when all the life drained out of him. That was a defeat of a different magnitude, a blow from which he still hadn't recovered.

"It's scary the first time with a new partner," she told him. "It hardly ever works right."

"The voice of experience, huh?"

"Trust me, Kevin. The second time's a charm."

He nodded, fully prepared to accept this as a general rule, but just as willing to bet he'd be the exception that proved it wrong. Because even now, with the back of her thumb resting ever so lightly against his crotch, he still wasn't feeling much of anything beyond a dull throb of anxiety, the vestigial guilt of a married man out in public with another woman. It didn't seem to matter that his wife had moved out, or that people his age hooked up all the time at the Carpe Diem. Some were married, some weren't; things were a lot looser on that front than they used to be. It was as if his conscience were stuck in the past, tethered to a set of conditions that no longer existed.

"I don't know." He smiled sadly, trying to let her know it was nothing personal. "I just don't think it's gonna work."

"I've got some pills," she whispered. "They'll fix you right up."

"Really?" Kevin was intrigued. He'd been thinking about asking his doctor to prescribe something, but hadn't worked up the nerve. "Where'd you get them?"

"They're around. You're not the only guy with this issue."

"Huh." His eyes drifted south. Unlike her face, her breasts were still freckled. He remembered them fondly from their previous encounter. "That might work."

Melissa leaned closer, until her nose was almost touching his. Her hair smelled good, a subtle aura of almonds and honeysuckle.

"If you have an erection that lasts for more than four hours," she told him, "I'm probably gonna need a break."

IT WAS funny—once Kevin knew that pharmaceutical assistance would be available in case of emergency, he realized that he probably wouldn't need it. He sensed this even before they left the bar, and his optimism only grew on the way to Melissa's house. It felt good to be walking down a dark, tree-lined street, holding hands with an attractive woman who'd made it quite clear that he was welcome in her bed. It felt even better when she stopped him in front of Bailey Elementary, pushed him against a tree, and kissed him long and hard. He couldn't remember the last time he'd experienced that distinctive, double-sided sensation, warm body softening against his front, cold bark jabbing roughly into his back. *Sophomore year?* he wondered. *Debbie DeRosa?*

Melissa's hips were rocking gently, creating some sweet, intermittent friction. He reached around and cupped her ass; it was soft and womanly, heavy in his hand. She made a purring sound as her tongue swirled around the inside of his mouth.

Nothing to worry about, he thought, picturing the two of them on the living room floor, Melissa on top, his cock as hard as a frat boy's. *I got this covered.*

It was the smell of smoke that made them pull apart, a sudden awareness of company. They turned and saw the two Watchers hurrying toward them from the direction of the school—they must have been hiding in the bushes by the main entrance—moving with that strange sense of urgency they all had, as if you were an old friend they'd just spotted at the airport. He was relieved to see that neither one of them was Laurie.

"Oh, Jesus," Melissa muttered.

Kevin didn't recognize the older woman, but the younger one—a thin girl with a bad complexion—was familiar to him from the Safeway, where she'd worked as a cashier. She had a strange name he couldn't quite remember, something that always seemed misspelled on her name tag.

"Hi, Shana," he said, trying to be polite, treating her the way he'd treat anyone else. "It's Shana, right?"

The girl didn't answer, not that he expected her to. She hadn't been all that chatty even when she'd been free to talk. She just locked eyes with him, as if she were trying to read his mind. Her partner did the same to Melissa. There was something harsher in the older woman's gaze, Kevin thought, a smug note of judgment.

"You bitch," Melissa told her. She sounded angry and a little drunk. "I warned you about this."

The older Watcher brought her cigarette to her lips, the wrinkles around her mouth deepening as she inhaled. She blew the smoke right in Melissa's face, a thin, contemptuous jet.

"I told you to leave me alone," Melissa continued. "Didn't I tell you that?"

"Melissa." Kevin put his hand on her shoulder. "Don't do this."

She jerked away from his touch. "This bitch is stalking me. It's the third time this week. I'm sick of it."

"It's okay," Kevin told her. "Let's just walk away."

"It's not okay." Melissa stepped closer to the Watchers, shooing them like pigeons. "Go on! Get the fuck outta here! Leave us alone!"

The Watchers didn't retreat, nor did they flinch at the foul language. They just stood there, calm and expressionless, sucking on their cigarettes. It was supposed to remind you that God was watching, keeping track of your smallest actions—at least that was what Kevin had heard—but the effect was mostly just annoying, something a little kid would do to get on your nerves.

"Please," Kevin said, not quite sure if he was addressing Melissa or the Watchers.

Melissa gave up first. She shook her head in disgust, turned away from the Watchers, and took a tentative step in Kevin's direction. But she stopped, made a hawking sound in her throat, then whirled and spit in the face of her tormentor. Not a fake spit, either—the kind that's more noise than saliva—but a juicy schoolboy gob that struck the woman directly on the cheek, landing with an audible splat.

"Melissa!" Kevin cried out. "Jesus Christ!"

The Watcher didn't flinch, didn't even wipe at the foamy spittle as it dripped off her chin.

"Bitch," Melissa said again, but the conviction had gone out of her voice. "You made me do that."

THEY WALKED the rest of the way in silence, no longer holding hands, doing their best to ignore their white-clad chaperones, who were following so close behind it felt like they were a single group, four friends out for the evening.

The Watchers stopped at the edge of Melissa's lawn—they rarely trespassed on private property—but Kevin could feel their eyes on his back as he made his way up the front steps. Melissa stopped by the door, reaching into her purse, groping for the keys.

"We can still do this," she told him, without a whole lot of enthusiasm. "If you want to."

"I don't know." There was a melancholy weight in his chest, as if they'd skipped right past the sex to the disappointment afterward. "You mind if I take a rain check?"

She nodded, as if she'd suspected as much, squinting past him to the women on the sidewalk.

"I hate them," she said. "I hope they all get cancer."

Kevin didn't bother to remind her that his wife was one of them, but then she remembered it herself.

"I'm sorry."

"It's okay."

"I just don't understand why they have to ruin it for the rest of us."

"They think they're doing us a favor."

Melissa laughed softly, as if at a private joke, then kissed Kevin chastely on the cheek.

"Give me a call," she told him. "Don't be a stranger."

The Watchers were waiting on the sidewalk, their faces blank and patient, freshly lit cigarettes in their hands. He thought about making a break for it—they usually wouldn't chase you—but it was late and he was tired, so they set off together. He sensed a certain lightness in their steps as they moved beside him, the satisfaction that comes from a job well done.

BLUE RIBBON

NORA DURST HATED TO ADMIT it, but *SpongeBob* wasn't working anymore. It was probably inevitable—she'd seen some episodes so many times she basically had them memorized—but that didn't make it any easier. The show was a ritual she'd come to depend on, and these days rituals were pretty much all she had.

For about a year—the last year they had together—Nora and her family had watched *SpongeBob* in the evening, right before bed. Erin was too young to get most of the jokes, but her brother, Jeremy—he was three years older, a kindergarten man of the world—stared at the TV with an awestruck expression, as if a miracle were unfolding before his eyes. He chuckled at almost every line, but when he really cut loose, the laughter exploded from his mouth in loud whoops that mixed approval and amazement in equal measure. Every so often— usually in response to physical violence, bodies being stretched, flat- tened, spun, distorted, dismembered, or propelled at high speed across improbable distances—hilarity got the better of him, and he had to launch himself off the couch and onto the floor, where he could pound on the rug until he managed to calm down.

Nora was surprised by how much she enjoyed the show herself. She'd gotten used to the bland crap her kids insisted on watching— *Dora* and *Curious George* and the Big Red Dog—but *SpongeBob* was refreshingly clever, and even a bit edgy, a harbinger of better days down the road, when they'd all be liberated from the ghetto of chil- dren's programming. Because she was such a fan, she was puzzled by her husband's indifference. Doug sat with them in the living room, but rarely bothered to lift his eyes from his BlackBerry. That was the way he was those last few years, so absorbed in his work that he was rarely more than half there, a hologram of himself.

"You should watch," she told him. "It's really pretty funny."

"No offense," he said. "But SpongeBob's a little retarded."

"He's just sweet. He gives everyone the benefit of the doubt, even if they don't deserve it."

"Maybe," Doug conceded. "But retarded people do that, too."

She didn't have much more luck with her friends, the mothers she went to yoga class with on Tuesday and Thursday mornings, and oc- casionally out for drinks with at night, if their husbands were around to hold down the fort. These women didn't share Doug's Olympian disdain for childish things, but even they grew skeptical when she rhapsodized about her favorite cartoon invertebrate.

"I can't stand that show," Ellen Demos said. "But the song at the beginning's a real hoot."

"The squid is awful," added Linda Wasserman. "He's got that creepy phallic nose. I hate the way it just *dangles* there."

After October 14th, of course, Nora forgot about *SpongeBob* for a long, long time. She moved out of her house and spent several heavily medicated months at her sister's, trying to come to grips with the nightmare that had replaced her life. In March, against the advice of her friends, family, and therapist, she returned home, telling herself that she needed some quiet time alone with her memories, a period of reflection in which she might be able to answer the question of whether it would be desirable, or even possible, to go on living.

The first few weeks passed in a fog of misery and confusion. She slept at odd hours, drank too much wine to substitute for the Ambien and Xanax she'd sworn off, and spent entire days wandering through the cruelly empty house, opening closets and peering under beds, as if she half expected to find her husband and children hiding out, grinning like they'd just pulled off the best practical joke ever.

"I hope you're happy!" she imagined scolding them, pretending to be upset. "I was going out of my mind."

One evening, aimlessly flipping through the channels, she happened upon a familiar episode of *SpongeBob,* the one where it snows in Bikini Bottom. The effect on her was instantaneous and exhilarating: Her head was clear for the first time in ages. She felt okay, better than okay. It wasn't just that she could sense her little boy in the room, sitting right beside her on the couch; at times it was almost as if she *were* Jeremy, as if she were watching the show through his eyes, experiencing a six-year-old's wild pleasure, laughing so hard she almost lost her breath. When it was over, Nora cried for a long time, but it was a good cry, the kind that makes you stronger. Then she grabbed a notepad and wrote the following:

I just saw the episode of the snowball fight. Do you remember that one? You liked playing in the snow, but only if it wasn't too cold or windy out. I remember the first time we went sledding on that old wooden toboggan, and you cried because you got snow on your face. It was a whole year before you let us take you again, but then you liked it better because instead of the toboggan we had snow tubes, which took a really long time to blow up. You would have enjoyed watching *SpongeBob* tonight, especially the part where he jams a funnel in his head and turns his face into a snowball machine gun. I'm sure you would have tried to imitate the sound he made while he was shooting them, and I bet you would have done it really well, because I know how much you like to make funny noises.

The next morning, she drove to Best Buy, picked up a complete set of *SpongeBob* DVDs, and spent the better part of the day watching several episodes from Season One, a marathon that left her feeling cranky, hollowed out, and in desperate need of fresh air. For this very reason, she'd been careful about rationing her kids' TV time, and understood that she needed to do the same for herself.

Before long, she'd developed what turned out to be a surprisingly durable strategy: She allowed herself to watch *SpongeBob* twice a day, once in the morning and then again at night, never failing to write a brief entry about each episode in her notebook. This practice—it came to feel vaguely religious—gave structure and focus to her life, and helped her not to feel so lost all the time.

There were a couple of hundred episodes in all, which meant that she saw each one three or four times in the course of a year. It was okay, though, at least until recently. Nora still had something to write after each rerun, some fresh memory or observation triggered by what she'd just seen, even the handful of shows that she'd grown to actively dislike.

In the past few months, however, something fundamental had changed. She almost never laughed at SpongeBob's antics anymore; shows that she'd found amusing in the past now struck her as desperately sad. This morning's episode, for example, felt like some sort of allegory, a bitter commentary on her own suffering:

Today was the dance contest, the one where Squidward takes over SpongeBob's body. To do this, he climbs inside SpongeBob's conveniently empty head, then pulls off SpongeBob's arms and legs so he can replace them with his own. Yes, I realize that SpongeBob's limbs can regenerate themselves, but come on, it's still horrible. During the competition, Squidward gets a cramp and SpongeBob's body ends up writhing on the floor in agony. The audience thinks this is pretty cool and gives him First Prize. Quite a metaphor. The person in the most pain wins. Does that mean I get a Blue Ribbon?

In her heart, she understood that the real problem wasn't the show so much as the feeling that she was losing her son again, that he was no longer there in the room with her. It made sense, of course: Jeremy would be nine now, probably past the age where he would be watching *SpongeBob* with any real enthusiasm. Wherever he was, he was onto something else, growing up without her, leaving her more alone than she already was.

What she needed to do was retire the DVDs—donate them to the library, put them out for garbage, whatever—before SpongeBob and everything associated with him got permanently poisoned in her mind. It would have been easier if she had something to replace him with, some new show to fill the empty space, but every time she tried to ask her old friends what their boys were watching, the women just hugged her and said, *Oh, honey,* in their smallest, most sorrowful voices, as if they hadn't understood the question.

BEFORE LUNCH, Nora took a long ride on the Mapleton-to-Rosedale Bike Trail, a seventeen-mile stretch of land that used to be a railroad line. She liked riding there on weekday mornings when it was relatively uncrowded and the people using it were mostly adults, a lot of them retired, out for some joyless, life-prolonging exercise. Nora made it a point to stay far away on sunny weekend afternoons, when the path was crowded with families on bikes and Rollerblades, and the sight of a little girl with a too-big helmet, or a scowling boy pedaling furiously on a bike equipped with rickety training wheels, could leave her bent over and gasping on the grassy margin of the path, as if she'd been punched in the stomach.

She felt strong and blissfully empty gliding through the crisp November air, enjoying the intermittent warmth of the sun as it filtered down through the overhanging trees, which were mostly stripped of their foliage. It was that trashy, post-Halloween part of the fall, yellow and orange leaves littering the ground like so many discarded candy wrappers. She'd keep riding into the cold weather for as long as she could, at least until the first big snowfall. That was the lowest time of the year, dim and claustrophobic, a funk of holidays and grim inventories. She was hoping that she could escape to the Caribbean or New Mexico for a while, anyplace bright and unreal, if she could only find someone to go with who wouldn't drive her crazy. She'd visited Miami on her own last year, and it had been a mistake. As much as she liked solitude and strange places, the two of them together did a number on her, releasing a flood of memories and questions that she managed to keep a fairly tight lid on at home.

THE PATH was more or less a straight shot, a car's width of aging blacktop that took you from Point A to Point B without a whole lot of fanfare. In theory, you were free to double back at any point, but Nora either went halfway—turning around at the edge of Mapleton for an easy sixteen-mile round-trip—or all the way to the terminus in Rosedale, for a grand total of thirty-four, a distance that was no longer the least bit daunting to her. If the path had continued for another ten miles, she would have followed it to the end without complaint.

Not too long ago she would have laughed if someone had suggested that a three-hour bike ride would become an unremarkable part of her daily routine. Back then her life was so crowded with tasks and errands, the everyday emergencies and constantly expanding to-do list of a full-time wife and mother, that she could barely squeeze in a couple of yoga classes a week. But these days she literally had nothing better to do than ride her bike. Sometimes she dreamed about it right before falling asleep, the hypnotic sight of the ground disappearing beneath her front wheel, the jittery sensation of the world humming up through her handlebars.

One day she'd have to get a job, she understood that, not that there was any particular hurry on that front. With the generous survivor's benefits she'd received—three lump-sum six-figure payments from the federal government, which had stepped in after the insurance companies had ruled the Sudden Departure an "Act of God" for which they could not be held accountable—she figured she'd be okay for at least five years, even more if she ever decided to sell the house and move into someplace smaller.

Still, the day would eventually come when she'd have to start supporting herself, and she did her best to think about it sometimes, not that she ever got too far. She could see herself getting up in the morning full of purpose, putting on clothes and makeup, and then heading out the door, but her fantasy always petered out right there. Where was she going? To an office? A school? A store? She had no idea. She had a degree in Sociology and had spent several years with a research firm that rated corporations based on their records of social and environmental responsibility, but the only thing she could really imagine herself doing at this point was working with children. Unfortunately, she'd tried that last year, helping out a couple of afternoons a week at Erin's old day care, and it hadn't gone very well. She'd cried too much in front of the kids, and hugged a few of them a little too hard, and had been gently and respectfully asked to take a leave of absence.

Oh well, she told herself. *Maybe it won't matter. Or maybe none of us will even be around in five years.*

Or maybe she'd meet a nice man, get married, and start a new family—maybe even a family just like the one she'd lost. It was a seductive idea, until she got around to thinking about the replacement children. They would be a disappointment, she was sure of it, because her real children had been perfect, and how could you compete with that?

She turned off her iPod and checked her jacket pocket to make sure her pepper spray was handy before crossing Route 23 and entering the long, slightly freaky stretch of the trail that ran between an industrial wasteland to the south and a scrubby forest that was under the nominal control of the County Parks Commission to the north. Nothing bad had ever happened to her there, but she'd seen some weird stuff in the past few months—a pack of dogs shadowing her at the edge of the woods, a muscular man whistling cheerfully as he pushed an empty wheelchair down the path, and a stern-looking Catholic priest with a salt-and-pepper beard who reached out and squeezed her arm as she rode by. Then, just last week, she happened upon a man in a business suit sacrificing a sheep in a small clearing near an algae-covered pond. The man—a chubby middle-aged guy with curly hair and round glasses—had a large knife pressed to the animal's throat, but hadn't yet begun his incision. Both the man and the sheep gazed at Nora with startled, unhappy expressions, as if she'd caught them in an act they would have preferred to remain private.

MOST EVENINGS she ate dinner at her sister's house. It got a little tedious sometimes, being a perpetual appendage to someone else's family, having to play the role of Aunt Nora, pretending to be interested in her nephews' inane banter, but she was grateful nonetheless for a few hours of low-stress human contact, a respite from what would otherwise start to feel like a long and very lonely day.

Afternoons remained her biggest problem, a dull, amorphous chunk of solitude. That's why she'd been so upset about losing the day care job—it filled the empty hours so perfectly. She ran errands when she was lucky enough to have some—they weren't nearly as plentiful or pressing as they used to be—and occasionally cracked open a book she'd borrowed from her sister: one of the Shopaholics, *Mr. Right,*

Good in Bed, the kind of fun, frothy stuff she used to enjoy. But these days reading just made her sleepy, especially after a long ride, and the one thing she couldn't afford to do was nap, not if she didn't want to find herself wide-awake in the dark at three in the morning, with nothing but the inside of her own head to keep her company.

Today, though, Nora had an unexpected visitor, the first in a long time. Reverend Jamison pulled up in his Volvo just as she was wheeling her bike into the garage, and she was surprised by how pleased she was to see him. People used to drop by all the time, just to check up on her, but some sort of statute of limitations seemed to have kicked in about six months ago. Apparently even the most awful tragedies, and the people they'd ruined, got a little stale after a while.

"Hey, there," she called out, pressing the button that lowered the automatic door, and then heading down the driveway to meet him, moving with the stiff-legged waddle of a newly dismounted cyclist, the cleats of her bike shoes clicking against the pavement. "How are you?"

"Okay." The Reverend smiled unconvincingly. He was a lanky, troubled-looking man in jeans and a partially untucked white Oxford shirt, tapping a manila envelope against the side of his leg. "Yourself?"

"Not bad." She brushed some hair out of her eyes, then immediately regretted the gesture, which revealed the decorative pattern of pink dents her helmet left in the tender skin of her forehead. "All things considered."

Reverend Jamison nodded somberly, as if to acknowledge all the things that needed to be considered.

"You have a few minutes?" he asked.

"Now?" she said, feeling suddenly self-conscious about her spandex tights and sweaty face, the yeasty odor of exertion that was undoubtedly trapped beneath her Gore-Tex windbreaker. "I'm kind of a mess."

Even as she said this, she took a moment to marvel at the persistence of her own vanity. She'd thought she was through with all that—what use could she possibly have for it anymore?—but apparently it was too deep a reflex to ever really go away.

"Take your time," he said. "I can wait out here while you get cleaned up."

Nora couldn't help smiling at the absurdity of the offer. Reverend Jamison had sat up with her on nights when she was out of her mind with grief, and had cooked her breakfast when she woke up wild-haired and drooling on the living room couch, still in yesterday's clothes. It was a little late in the day to get all girly and modest on him.

"Come on in," she said. "I'll just be a minute."

UNDER OTHER circumstances, Nora might have found it vaguely exciting, stepping into a steamy shower while a reasonably handsome man who wasn't her husband waited patiently downstairs. But Reverend Jamison was too grim and preoccupied, too wrapped up in his own bitter obsessions to be conscripted into even the flimsiest romantic scenario.

Actually, Nora wasn't even sure if Matt Jamison on was a Reverend anymore. He no longer preached at the Zion Bible Church, no longer seemed to do much of anything except research and distribute that horrible newsletter, the one that had turned him into a pariah. From what she'd heard, his wife and kids had abandoned him, his friends no longer spoke to him, and total strangers sometimes found it necessary to punch him in the face.

She was pretty sure he deserved whatever he got, but she still harbored a soft spot for the man he'd been, the one who'd helped her through the blackest hours of her life. Of all the would-be spiritual advisors who'd inflicted themselves on her after October 14th, Matt Jamison was the only one she'd been able to tolerate for more than five minutes at a time.

She'd resented him at first, the way she'd resented all the others. Nora wasn't religious and couldn't understand why every priest, minister, and New Age quack within a fifty-mile radius of Mapleton thought they had a right to intrude upon her misery, and assumed she would find it comforting to hear that what had happened to her—the annihilation of her family, to be precise—was somehow part of God's plan, or the prelude to a glorious reunion in heaven at some unspecified later date. The Monsignor of Our Lady of Sorrows even tried to convince her that her suffering wasn't all that unique, that she was really no different than a parishioner of his, a woman who'd lost her husband and three children in a car accident and still somehow managed to live a reasonably happy and productive life.

"Sooner or later we all lose our loved ones," he said. "We all have to suffer, every last one of us. I stood beside her while she watched all four of those coffins go into the ground."

Then she's lucky! Nora wanted to scream. *Because at least she knows where they are!* But she held her tongue, understanding how inhuman it would sound, calling a woman like that lucky.

"I want you to leave," she told the priest in a calm voice. "Go home and say a million Hail Marys."

Reverend Jamison had been foisted upon her by her sister, who'd been a member of the Zion Bible Church for many years, along with Chuck and the boys. The whole family claimed to have been born again at the exact same moment, a phenomenon that Nora found highly improbable, though she kept this opinion to herself. At Karen's urging, Nora and her kids had once attended a worship service at Z.B.C.— Doug had refused to "waste a Sunday morning"—and she'd been a little put off by the Reverend's evangelical fervor. It was a style of preaching she'd never encountered close up, having spent her childhood as a halfhearted Catholic and her adulthood as an equally passionless nonbeliever.

Nora had been living at her sister's for a few months when the Reverend started dropping by—at Karen's invitation—for informal, once-a-week "spiritual counseling" sessions. She wasn't happy about it, but by that point she was too weak and beaten down to resist. It wasn't quite as bad as she'd feared, though. In person, Reverend Jamison turned out to be far less dogmatic than he'd been in the pulpit. He had no platitudes or canned sermons to offer, no obnoxious certainty about God's wisdom and good intentions. Unlike the other clergymen she'd dealt with, he asked a lot of questions about Doug and Erin and Jeremy and listened carefully to her answers. When he left, she was often surprised to realize that she felt a little better than she had when he'd arrived.

She terminated the sessions when she moved back home, but soon found herself calling him late at night, whenever her insomniac reveries turned suicidal, which was fairly often. He always came right over, no matter what time it was, and stayed for as long as she needed him. Without his help, she never would have made it through that dismal spring.

As she grew stronger, though, she began to realize that it was the Reverend who was falling apart. There were nights when he seemed just as despondent as she was. He wept frequently and kept up a running monologue about the Rapture and how unfair it was that he'd missed the cut.

"I gave everything to Him," he complained, his voice infused with the bitterness of a spurned lover. "My entire life. And this is the thanks I get?"

Nora didn't have a lot of patience for this kind of talk. The Reverend's family had emerged unscathed from the disaster. They were still right where he'd left them, a lovely wife and three sweet kids. If anything, he should get down on his knees and thank God every minute of the day.

"Those people were no better than I was," he continued. "A lot of them were worse. So how come they're with God and I'm still here?"

"How do you know they're with God?"

"It's in the Scriptures."

Nora shook her head. She'd considered the possibility of the Rapture as an explanation for the events of October 14th. Everyone had. It couldn't be avoided, not when so many people were proclaiming it from the rooftops. But it never made any sense to her, not even for a second.

"There was no Rapture," she told him.

The Reverend laughed as if he pitied her. "It's right there in the Bible, Nora. 'Two men will be in the field; one will be taken and the other left.' The truth is right in front of us."

"Doug was an atheist," Nora reminded him. "There's no Rapture for atheists."

"It's possible he was a secret believer. Maybe God knew his heart better than he did."

"I don't think so. He used to brag about how there wasn't a religious bone in his body."

"But Erin and Jeremy—they weren't atheists."

"They weren't anything. They were just little kids. All they believed in was their mommy and daddy and Santa Claus."

Reverend Jamison closed his eyes. She couldn't tell if he was thinking or praying. When he opened them, he seemed just as bewildered as before.

"It doesn't make any sense," he said. "I should've been first in line."

Nora remembered that conversation later in the summer when Karen informed her that Reverend Jamison had suffered a nervous breakdown and taken a leave of absence from the church. She considered stopping by his house to see how he was doing, but she couldn't find the strength. She just mailed him a get-well-soon card and left it at that. Not long afterward, right around the first anniversary of the Sudden Departure, his newsletter made its first appearance, a self-published five-page compendium of scurrilous accusations against the missing of October 14th, none of whom were in any kind of position to defend themselves. This one embezzled from his employer. That one drove drunk. Another one had disgusting sexual appetites. Reverend Jamison stood on street corners and passed them out for free, and even though most people claimed to be appalled by what he was doing, he never had any shortage of takers.

• • •

AFTER HE left, Nora wondered how she could have been so stupid, so utterly unprepared for something that should have been obvious the moment he'd stepped out of his car. And yet she'd invited him into her kitchen and even made him a cup of tea. He was an old friend, she told herself, and they had some catching up to do.

But it was more than that, she'd realized, studying his sallow, haunted face from across the breakfast island. Reverend Jamison was a wreck, but some part of her respected him for that, the same part that sometimes felt ashamed of her own shaky sanity, the way she'd managed to keep going after everything that had happened, clinging to some pathetic idea of a normal life—eight hours of sleep, three meals a day, lots of fresh air and exercise. Sometimes that felt crazy, too.

"How *are* you?" she asked in a probing tone, letting him know that she wasn't just making small talk.

"Exhausted," he said, and he looked it. "Like my body's full of wet cement."

Nora nodded sympathetically. Her own body felt great just then, warm and loose from the shower, her muscles pleasantly sore, her wet hair gathered snugly in a terry-cloth turban on top of her head.

"You should take a rest," she told him. "Go on vacation or something."

"Vacation." He chuckled scornfully. "What would I do on vacation?"

"Sit by the pool. Forget about things for a while."

"We're past that, Nora." He spoke sternly, as if addressing a child. "There's no sitting by the pool anymore."

"Maybe not," she conceded, remembering her own misguided attempts at fun in the sun. "It was just a thought."

He stared at her in a way that didn't feel particularly friendly. As the silence grew strained, she wondered if it would be a good idea to ask him about his kids, find out if they'd had some sort of reconciliation, but she decided against it. If people had good news, you didn't have to drag it out of them.

"I saw your speech last month," he said. "I was impressed. It must have taken a lot of courage for you to do that. You had a really natural delivery."

"Thank you," she said, pleased by the compliment. It meant something coming from a veteran public speaker like the Reverend. "I didn't think I could, but . . . I don't know. It just felt like something I needed to do. To keep their memory alive." She lowered her voice, trusting him with a confession. "It's just three years, but sometimes it feels like ages ago."

"A lifetime." He lifted his mug, sniffed at the steam curling up from the liquid, then set it back down without taking a sip. "We were all living in a dreamworld."

"I look at pictures of my kids," she said, "and sometimes I don't even cry. I can't tell if that's a blessing or a curse."

Reverend Jamison nodded, but she could tell that he wasn't really listening. After a moment, he reached down for something on the floor—it turned out to be the manila envelope he'd been holding in the driveway—and set it down on the countertop. Nora had forgotten all about it.

"I brought you the new issue of my paper," he said.

"That's okay." She raised her hand in a gesture of polite refusal. "I really don't—"

"No." There was a sharp note of warning in his voice. "You really do."

Nora stared dumbly at the envelope, which the Reverend was nudging toward her with the tip of his index finger. A strange sound came out of her mouth, something between a cough and a laugh.

"Are you kidding me?"

"It's about your husband." To his credit, he looked genuinely embarrassed. "I could've run it in the October issue, but I held it until after your speech."

Nora shoved the envelope back across the counter. She had no idea what secret it contained, and no desire to find out.

"Please get out of my house," she said.

Reverend Jamison stood up slowly from his stool, as if his body really were full of wet cement. He stared regretfully at the envelope for a moment, then shook his head.

"I'm sorry," he told her. "I'm just the messenger."

VOW OF SILENCE

IN THE EVENING, AFTER DAILY Sustenance and the Hour of Self-Accusation, they reviewed the folders of the people they were hoping to shadow. In theory, of course, they were open to shadowing everyone, but certain individuals had been singled out for special attention, either because one of the Supervisors thought they were ripe for recruitment, or because a resident had made a Formal Request for increased surveillance. Laurie glanced at the folder in her lap: *ARTHUR DONOVAN, age 56, 438 Winslow Road, Apt. 3.* The photo stapled to the inside cover showed a completely ordinary middle-aged

man—balding, big-bellied, scared to death—pushing an empty shopping cart through a parking lot, his comb-over dislodged by a stiff
breeze. A divorced father of two grown children, Mr. Donovan worked
as a technician for Merck and lived alone. According to the most recent entry on the log, Donovan had spent the previous Thursday night
at home, watching television by himself. He must have done that a lot,
because Laurie had never once laid eyes on him in all her nocturnal
wanderings.

Without bothering to recite the required silent prayer for Arthur
Donovan's salvation, she closed the folder and handed it to Meg Lo-
max, the new convert she was helping to train. Every night in Self-
Accusation, Laurie took herself to task for this exact failing, but
despite her repeated vows to do better, she kept bumping against the
limits of her own compassion: Arthur Donovan was a stranger, and
she couldn't work up a whole lot of concern about what happened to
him on Judgment Day. That was the sad truth, and there wasn't much
sense in pretending otherwise.

I'm only human, she told herself. *There's not enough room in my*
heart for everyone.

Meg, on the other hand, studied Donovan's photo with a melancholy expression, shaking her head and clucking her tongue at a volume that would have been unacceptable for anyone but a Trainee.
After a moment, she took out her notepad, scribbled a few words, and
showed the message to Laurie.

Poor man. He looks so lost.

Laurie nodded briskly, then reached for the next file on the coffee
table, resisting the urge to take out her notepad and remind Meg that
she didn't need to write down every single thought that passed through
her head. It was something she'd figure out soon enough on her own.
Everybody did, eventually, once the initial shock of not speaking wore
off. It just took some people a little longer than others to realize how
few words they needed to get by, how much of life they could negotiate
in silence.

There were twelve of them in the smoke-filled room, tonight's contingent of Watchers, passing the folders in a clockwise direction. It was meant to be a solemn activity, but there were times when Laurie forgot her purpose and began to enjoy herself, culling juicy tidbits of local gossip from the logs, or simply renewing her connection to the sinful but colorful world she was supposed to have renounced. She felt herself falling into this temptation as she read the file of Alice Souderman, her old friend from the Bailey Elementary School PTA. The two of them had cochaired the auction committee for three years in a row and had remained close, even during the turbulent period that preceded Laurie's conversion. She couldn't help but be intrigued by the news that, just last week, Alice had been observed having dinner at Trattoria Giovanni with Miranda Abbott, another of Laurie's good friends, a harried mother of four with a great sense of humor and a wicked talent for mimickry. Laurie hadn't known that Alice and Miranda were friends, and felt pretty sure that they must have spent a good part of the meal talking about *her* and how much they missed her company. Probably they were mystified by her decision to withdraw from their world and scornful of the community in which she now lived, but Laurie chose not to think about that. She focused instead on the vegetarian lasagna at Giovanni's—it was the specialty of the house, the cream sauce luscious but not too rich, the carrots and zucchini sliced to an almost translucent thinness—and on an image of herself as the third person at the table, drinking wine and laughing with her old friends. She felt an urge to smile, and had to consciously tighten her mouth against it.

Please help Alice and Miranda, she prayed as she closed the folder. *They're good people. Have mercy on them.*

What mostly struck her, reading the files, was how deceptively *normal* things seemed in Mapleton. Most people just put on blinders and went about their trivial business, as if the Rapture had never even happened, as if they expected the world to last forever. Tina Green, age nine, attended her weekly piano lesson. Martha Cohen, twenty-three, spent two hours at the gym, then stopped at CVS on the way home for a box of tampons and a copy of *US Weekly*. Henry Foster, fifty-nine, walked his West Highland terrier around the path at Fielding Lake, stopping frequently so the dog could interact with its peers. Lance Mikulski, thirty-seven, was seen entering the Victoria's Secret store at Two Rivers Mall, where he purchased several unspecified items of lingerie. This was an awkward revelation, given that Lance's wife, Patty, happened to be sitting across the room from Laurie at that very moment and would soon have a chance to review the file for herself. Patty seemed like a nice enough woman—of course, most people seemed nice enough when they weren't allowed to talk—and Laurie's heart went out to her. She knew exactly how it felt, reading embarrassing revelations about your husband while a roomful of people who'd read the same information pretended not to notice. But you knew they were looking, wondering if you'd be able to maintain your composure, to detach yourself from petty emotions like jealousy and anger and keep your mind where it belonged, firmly fixed on the world to come.

Unlike Patty Mikulski, Laurie hadn't made a Formal Request for surveillance of her husband; the only request she'd made was for her daughter. As far as she was concerned, Kevin was on his own: He was a grown man and could make his own decisions. It just so happened that those decisions included going home with two different women whose files she'd had the bad luck to review, and whose souls she was supposed to pray for, like that was ever gonna happen.

It had hurt more than she expected to imagine her husband kissing a strange woman, undressing her in an unfamiliar bedroom, lying peacefully beside her after they'd finished making love. But she hadn't cried, hadn't betrayed an iota of the pain she was feeling. That had only happened once since she'd come to live here, the day she opened her daughter's file and discovered that the familiar photo on the inside cover—a soulful school portrait of a long-haired, sweetly smiling sophomore—had been replaced by what looked to her like a mug shot of a teenage criminal with big dead eyes and a shaved head, a girl in desperate need of a mother's love.

THEY CROUCHED behind some bushes on Russell Road, peering through the foliage at the front door of a white colonial with a brick sunporch that belonged to a man named Steven Grice. There were lights on both downstairs and up, and it seemed likely that the Grice family was in for the night. Even so, Laurie decided to sit tight for a while—it would be a lesson in persistence, the most important quality a Watcher could cultivate. Meg shifted beside her, hugging herself to ward off a chill.

"Damn," she whispered. "I'm freezing."

Laurie pressed a finger to her lips and shook her head.

Meg grimaced, mouthing the word *Sorry.*

Laurie shrugged, trying not to make too big a deal of the faux pas. This was Meg's first shift on the Night Watch; it would take some time for her to get used to it. Not just the physical hardship and the boredom, but the social awkwardness—the *rudeness,* even—of not being able to fill the silence with conversation, of more or less ignoring the person who was breathing right next to you. It went against every social impulse that had been drummed into you as a child, especially if you were a woman.

And yet Meg would get used to it, just as Laurie had. She might even come to appreciate the freedom that came with silence, the peace that followed surrender. That was one thing Laurie had learned the winter after the Rapture, when she'd spent all that time with Rosalie Sussman. When your words are futile, you're better off keeping them to yourself, or never even thinking them in the first place.

A car turned off Monroe onto Russell, catching them in a silvery wash of light as it rumbled by. The hush seemed deeper in its wake, the stillness more complete. Laurie watched a leaf from a nearly bare curbside maple topple through the glow of a streetlamp and drop soundlessly onto the pavement, but the perfection of the moment was overtaken by the bustle of Meg rooting around in her coat pocket. After what sounded like a prolonged struggle, she managed to extract her notebook and scrawl a brief question, barely legible in the moonlight:

What time is it?

Laurie raised her right arm, tugging at her sleeve and tapping several times on her watchless wrist, a gesture meant to convey the idea that time was irrelevant to a Watcher, that you had to empty yourself of expectations and sit quietly for however long it took. If you were lucky you might even come to enjoy it, to experience the waiting as a form of meditation, a way of connecting with God's presence in the world. Sometimes it happened: There had been nights over the summer when the air seemed infused with divine reassurance; you could just close your eyes and breathe it in. But Meg looked frustrated, so Laurie took out her own pad—something she'd been hoping not to do—and wrote a single word in big block letters:

PATIENCE.

Meg squinted at it for a few seconds, as if the concept were unfamiliar to her, before venturing a small nod of comprehension. She smiled bravely as she did so, and Laurie could see how grateful she was for this little scrap of communication, the simple kindness of a reply.

Laurie smiled back, remembering her own training period, the feeling she'd had of being completely isolated, cut off from everyone she'd ever loved—Rosalie Sussman had transferred out of Mapleton by then, helping to launch a start-up chapter on Long Island—a loneliness made even harder by the fact that she'd chosen it of her own free will. It hadn't been an easy decision, but in retrospect it seemed not only right, but inevitable.

After Rosalie moved to Ginkgo Street, Laurie had done her best to reclaim her life as wife and mother and involved citizen. For a little while it felt like a blessing to escape the force field of her best friend's grief—once again doing yoga and volunteer work, taking long walks around the lake, monitoring Jill's homework, worrying about Tom, and trying to repair her relationship with Kevin, who made no secret of the fact that he'd been feeling neglected—but that sense of liberation didn't last for long.

She told her therapist that it reminded her of coming home the summer after her freshman year at Rutgers, stepping back into the warm bath of family and friends, loving it for a week or two, and then feeling trapped, dying to return to school, missing her roommates and her cute new boyfriend, the classes and the parties and the giggly talks before bed, understanding for the first time that *that* was her real life now, that *this,* despite everything she'd ever loved about it, was finished for good.

Of course what she was missing this time around wasn't the excitement and romance of college; it was the sadness she'd shared with Rosalie, the oppressive gloom of their long, silent days, sorting through photographs of Jen, taking the measure of a world that no longer contained this sweet and beautiful girl. It had been horrible, living inside that knowledge, accepting its brutal finality, but it felt real in a way that paying the bills didn't, or planning the spring library benefit, or reminding yourself to pick up a box of linguine at the supermarket, or congratulating your own daughter on the 92 she got on a math quiz, or waiting patiently for your husband to finish grunting and extract himself from your body. That was what she'd needed to escape now, the unreality of pretending things were more or less okay, that they'd hit a bump on the road and should just keep on going, attending to their duties, uttering their empty phrases, enjoying the simple pleasures that the world still insisted on offering. And she'd found what she was looking for in the G.R., a regimen of hardship and humiliation that at least offered you the dignity of feeling like your existence bore some sort of relationship to reality, that you were no longer engaged in a game of make-believe that would consume the rest of your life.

But she was a middle-aged woman, a forty-six-year-old wife and mother whose best years were behind her. Meg was a sexy, wide-eyed girl in her midtwenties with waxed eyebrows, blond highlights, and the vestiges of a professional manicure. There was an engagement ring taped into her Memory Book, a pebble-sized rock that must have made her friends scream with envy. These were terrible days to be young, Laurie thought, to have all your hopes and dreams stripped away, to know that the future you'd been counting on was never going to arrive. It must have felt like going blind or losing a limb, even if you believed that God had something better for you just around the corner, something wonderful that you couldn't quite imagine.

Flipping to a fresh page of the notepad, Meg started to write a new message, but Laurie never saw what it was. A door scraped open and they turned in unison to see Steven Grice stepping onto his front stoop, an average-looking guy with glasses and a little paunch, wearing a warm-looking fleece pullover, which Laurie couldn't help coveting. He hesitated for a moment or two, as if acclimating himself to the night, then headed down the steps and across the lawn to his car, which flashed a chirpy welcome as he approached.

They set off in pursuit, but lost sight of the vehicle when it turned right at the end of the block. Laurie's hypothesis, based on nothing more than a hunch, was that Grice was probably headed to the Safeway for some kind of nighttime treat, blueberry pound cake or butter pecan ice cream or maybe a slab of dark chocolate studded with almonds, any one of the many, many foods she found herself fantasizing about at odd moments throughout the day, usually in the vast famished interlude that separated the morning bowl of oatmeal from the evening bowl of soup.

The supermarket was a brisk ten-minute walk from Russell Road, which meant that if she was right and if they hurried, they might be able to catch up with Grice before he left the store. Of course, he'd probably just get back in his car and drive right back home after that, but there was no point in getting too far ahead of herself. Besides, she wanted Meg to understand that Watching was a fluid, improvisational activity. It was entirely possible that Grice wasn't going to the Safeway and that they'd lose track of him altogether. But it was just as likely that, while searching for him, they'd bump into someone else on the list and could shift their attention to that subject. Or they could stumble upon some wholly unforeseen situation involving individuals whose names they didn't even know. The goal was to keep your eyes open and go wherever you'd be able to do the most good.

At any rate, it was a relief to be on the move, no longer hiding in the shrubbery. As far as Laurie was concerned, the exercise and fresh air were the best parts of the job, at least on a night like this, when the sky was clear and the temperature was still above forty. She tried not to think about what it was going to be like in January.

At the corner, she stopped to light a cigarette and offered one to Meg, who recoiled slightly before raising her hand in a futile gesture of refusal. Laurie jabbed the pack more insistently. She hated being a hardass, but the rule was absolutely clear: *A Watcher in Public View Must Carry a Lit Cigarette at All Times.*

When Meg continued to resist, Laurie jammed a cigarette—the G.R. provided a generic brand with a harsh taste and suspiciously chemical odor, purchased in bulk by the regional office—between the younger woman's lips and held a match to it. Meg choked violently on the first drag, as she always did, then released a small whimper of revulsion after the fit had passed.

Laurie patted her on the arm, letting her know she was doing just fine. If she could've spoken, she would've recited the motto both of them had learned in Orientation: *We don't smoke for enjoyment. We smoke to proclaim our faith.* Meg smiled queasily, sniffling and wiping at her eyes as they resumed their walk.

In a way, Laurie envied Meg her suffering. That was how it was supposed to be—a sacrifice for God, a mortification of the flesh, as if every puff were a profound personal violation. It was different for Laurie, who'd been a smoker throughout college and into her twenties, only quitting with difficulty at the beginning of her first pregnancy. For her, starting again after all those years was like a homecoming, an illicit pleasure smuggled into the grueling regimen of privations that made up life in the G.R. The sacrifice in her case would have been quitting a second time, not being able to savor that first cigarette in the morning, the one that tasted so good she sometimes found herself lying in her sleeping bag and blowing smoke rings at the ceiling just for the fun of it.

THERE WEREN'T many cars in the Safeway lot, but Laurie couldn't rule out the possibility that one of them belonged to Grice—he drove a nondescript, dark-colored sedan, and she'd neglected to note the make, model, or license plate—so they headed inside to search the store, splitting up to cover more ground.

She started in the Produce section, circling the fruit to avoid temptation—it was painful to look at the strawberries, to even think their name—and hustling past the vegetables, which looked so impossibly fresh and inviting, each one an advertisement for the doomed planet that had produced it: dark green broccoli, red peppers, dense orbs of cabbage, damp heads of romaine lettuce, their broad leaves held in place by shiny wire bands.

The Bakery aisle was torture, even this late in the day—just a few stray baguettes here, a sesame bagel and banana nut muffin there, leftovers bound for tomorrow's day-old bin. A lingering odor of fresh-baked bread permeated the area, mingling with the bright lights and piped-in music—"Rhinestone Cowboy," oddly enough, a song she hadn't heard in years—to induce a kind of sensory overload. She felt almost giddy with desire, amazed to remember that the supermarket had once seemed painfully dull to her, just another obligatory stop on the mundane circuit of her life, no more exciting than the gas station or post office. In a matter of months, it had become exotic and deeply affecting, a garden from which she and everyone she knew had been expelled, whether they knew it or not.

She didn't breathe any easier until she turned her back on the deli counter and took refuge among the packaged foods—cans of beans and boxes of dried pasta and bottles of salad dressing—all sorts of good stuff, but nothing you had to stop yourself from grabbing and shoving into your mouth. The sheer variety of products was overwhelming, somehow ridiculous and impressive at the same time: four shelves devoted to barbecue sauce alone, as if each brand possessed its own unique and powerful properties.

The Safeway felt half asleep, only one or two customers per aisle, most of them moving slowly, scanning the shelves with dazed expressions. To her relief, all of them drifted by without saying a word or even nodding hello. According to G.R. protocol, you were supposed to return a greeting not with a smile or a wave, but by looking directly into the eyes of the person who'd greeted you and counting slowly to ten. It was awkward enough with strangers and casual acquaintances, but completely unnerving if you found yourself face-to-face with a close friend or family member, both of you blushing and uncertain— hugs were expressly prohibited—a flood of unspeakable sentiments rising into your throat.

She'd expected to reconnect with Meg somewhere around the frozen food aisle—the geographical center of the store—but didn't get alarmed until she made her way through Beverages, Coffee and Tea, and Chips and Snacks without catching a glimpse of her. Was it possible that they'd crossed without realizing it, each one rounding the corner of the aisle the other one had just vacated at exactly the same time?

Laurie was tempted to backtrack, but she kept going all the way to the dairy case, where Meg had begun her search. It was empty, except for a single shopper standing in front of the sliced cheese, a bald man with a wiry runner's build she recognized too late as Dave Tolman, the father of one of her son's former schoolmates. He turned and smiled, but she pretended not to notice.

She knew she'd been irresponsible, letting Meg out of her sight like that. The first few weeks at the compound could be hard and disorienting; newcomers had a tendency to flee back to their old lives if given half a chance. That was okay, of course: The G.R. wasn't a cult, as lots of ignorant people liked to claim. Every resident was free to come and go as they pleased. But it was a Trainer's job to provide guidance and companionship during this vulnerable time, helping the Trainee through the inevitable crises and moments of weakness, so she didn't lose heart and do something she'd regret for all of eternity.

She thought about making a quick loop around the perimeter of the store to double-check, then decided to head straight out into the parking lot in case Meg was making a run for it. She cut between two unmanned checkout counters, trying not to think about what it would be like, arriving back at the compound without her Trainee, having to explain that she'd left her alone in the supermarket, of all places.

The automatic doors parted sluggishly, releasing her into the night, which seemed to have gotten noticeably colder. She was just about to break into a run when she saw, to her immense relief, that it wouldn't be necessary. Meg was standing right in front of her, a contrite young woman in shapeless white clothes, holding a piece of paper in front of her chest.

Sorry, it read. **I couldn't breathe in there.**

IT WAS way past midnight when they got back to Ginkgo Street, slipping between two concrete barriers and signing in at the sentry house. These security measures had been put in place a couple of years earlier, after the police raid that resulted in the martyrdom of Phil Crowther—a forty-two-year-old husband and father of three—and the wounding of two other residents. The cops had entered the compound in the middle of the night, armed with search warrants and battering rams, hoping to rescue two little girls who, their father claimed, had been abducted and were being held against their will by the Guilty Remnant. Angered by what they saw as Gestapo tactics, some residents threw rocks and bottles at the invaders; the outnumbered cops panicked and responded with gunfire. A subsequent investigation exonerated the officers, but criticized the raid itself as "legally flawed and badly executed, based on the uncorroborated allegations of an embittered, noncustodial parent." Since then—and

Laurie had to give Kevin most of the credit for the change—the Mapleton Police had adopted a less confrontational attitude toward the G.R., doing their best to employ diplomacy rather than force when inevitable disputes and crises arose. Even so, the memory of the shootings remained fresh and painful on Ginkgo Street. She'd never heard anyone even speculate about the possibility of removing the traffic barriers, which in any case doubled as memorials, spray-painted with the words WE LOVE YOU, PHIL—SEE YOU IN HEAVEN.

They'd been assigned a bedroom on the third floor of Blue House, which was reserved for female Trainees. Laurie normally lived in Gray House, the women's dorm next door, where an average-sized room accommodated as many as six or seven people, all of them in sleeping bags on a bare floor. Every night was a somber, adults-only slumber party—no giggles or whispers, just lots of coughing and farting and snoring and groaning, the sounds and smells of too many stressed-out people packed into too small a space.

Blue House was highly civilized by comparison, almost luxurious, just the two of them in a child-sized room with twin beds and pale green walls, a soft beige carpet that felt good against your bare feet, and, best of all, a bathroom right across the hall. *A little vacation,* Laurie thought. She got undressed while Meg was showering, exchanging her dirty clothes for a loose-fitting G.R. nightgown—an ugly but comfortable garment sewn from an old sheet—then knelt to say her prayers. She took her time, focusing on her children and then moving down the list to Kevin, her mother, her siblings, her friends and former neighbors, trying to visualize every one of them dressed in white garments and bathed in the golden light of forgiveness, as she'd been taught to do. It was a luxury to pray like this, in an empty room with no distractions. She knew that God didn't care if she was kneeling or standing on her head, but it just felt better to do it right, her mind clear and her attention undivided.

Thank you for bringing Meg to us, she prayed. *Give her strength and grant me the wisdom to guide her in the right direction.*

The Night Watch had gone pretty well, she thought. They'd lost track of Grice and hadn't run into anyone else whose files they'd reviewed, but they saw a fair amount of action in the town center, accompanying people from bars and restaurants to their cars, and walking home with a trio of teenage girls who chatted cheerfully among themselves about boys and school as if Laurie and Meg weren't even there. They'd had only one unpleasant encounter, with a couple of twentysomething jerks outside the Extra Inning. It wasn't horrible, just the usual insults and a crude sexual invitation from the drunker of the two, a good-looking guy with an arrogant grin, who put his arm around Meg as if she were his girlfriend. ("I'll fuck the pretty one," he told his buddy. "You can have Grandma.") But even that was a useful lesson for Meg, a little taste of what it meant to be a Watcher. Sooner or later, someone would hit her, or spit on her, or worse, and she'd have to be able to endure the abuse without protesting or trying to defend herself.

Meg emerged from the bathroom, smiling bashfully, her face pink, her body lost inside her tentlike nightgown. It was almost cruel, Laurie thought, draping a lovely young woman in such a dull and baggy sack, as if her beauty had no place in the world.

It's different for me, she told herself. *I'm just as happy being hidden.*

The water in the bathroom was still warm, a luxury she no longer took for granted. In Gray House there was a chronic lack of hot water—it was inevitable, with so many people living there—but regulations required two showers a day regardless. She stayed in for a long time, until the air was thick with steam, which wasn't much of a problem since the G.R. prohibited mirrors. It still felt weird to her, brushing her teeth in front of a blank wall, using chalky no-name paste and a crappy manual brush. She'd accepted most of the hygiene restrictions without complaint—it was easy to see why perfumes and conditioners and antiaging creams might be considered extravagances—but she remained unreconciled to the loss of her electric toothbrush. She'd pined for it for weeks before realizing that it was more than the sensation of a clean mouth that she missed—it was her marriage, all those years of mindless domestic happiness, long, crowded days that culminated with her and Kevin standing side by side in front of the dual sinks, battery-operated wands buzzing in their hands, their mouths full of minty froth. But that was all over. Now it was just herself in a quiet room, her fist moving doggedly in front of her face, no one smiling into the mirror, no one smiling back.

DURING THE Training Period, the Vow of Silence wasn't absolute. There was a brief interlude after lights-out—usually no more than fifteen minutes—when you were allowed to speak freely, to verbalize your fears and ask any questions that had gone unanswered during the day. The Unburdening was a recent innovation, meant to function as a kind of safety valve, a way to make the transition to not talking a little less abrupt and intimidating. According to a PowerPoint Laurie had seen—she was a member of the Committee on Recruitment and Retention—the dropout rate among Trainees had declined by almost a third since the new policy had been adopted, which was one of the main reasons why the compound had become so crowded.

"So how you doing?" Laurie asked, just to get the ball rolling. Her own voice sounded strange to her, a rusty croak in the darkness.

"Okay, I guess," Meg replied.

"Just okay?"

"I don't know. It's hard to just walk away from everything. I still can't believe I did it."

"You seemed a little nervous at the Safeway."

"I was afraid I was gonna see somebody I knew."

"Your fiancé?"

"Yeah, but not just Gary. Any of my friends." Her voice was a bit wobbly, like she was trying hard to be brave. "I was supposed to get married this weekend."

"I know." Laurie had read Meg's file and understood that she was going to require some special attention. "That must've been hard."

Meg made a funny sound, something between a chuckle and a groan.

"I feel like I'm dreaming," she said. "I keep waiting to wake up."

"I know what that's like," Laurie assured her. "I still feel like that sometimes. Tell me a little about Gary. What's he like?"

"Great," Meg said. "Really cute. Broad shoulders. Sandy hair. This sweet little cleft in his chin. I used to kiss him there all the time."

"What's he do?"

"He's a securities analyst. Just got his MBA last spring."

"Wow. He sounds impressive."

"He is." She said it matter-of-factly, as if there weren't any room for debate. "He's a great guy. Smart, good-looking, lots of fun. Loves to travel, goes to the gym every day. My friends call him Mr. Perfect."

"Where'd you meet?"

"In high school. He was a basketball player. My brother was on the team, so I went to a lot of games. Gary was a senior and I was a sophomore. I didn't think he even knew I was alive. And then, one day, he just walked up to me and said, *Hey, Chris's sister. You want to go to a movie?* Can you believe that? He didn't even know my name and he asked me on a date."

"And you said yes."

"Are you kidding? I felt like I won the lottery."

"You hit it off right away?"

"God, yeah. The first time he kissed me, I thought, *This is the boy I'm gonna marry.*"

"It took you long enough. That must've been what, eight or nine years ago?"

"We were in school," Meg explained. "We got engaged right after I graduated, but then we had to postpone the wedding. Because of what happened."

"You lost your mother."

"It wasn't just her. One of Gary's cousins, he also . . . two girls I knew in college, my father's boss, a guy Gary used to work out with. A whole bunch of people. You remember what it was like."

"I do."

"It just didn't feel right, getting married without my mother. We were really close, and she was so excited when I showed her the ring. I was gonna wear her wedding dress and everything."

"And Gary was okay with the postponement?"

"Totally. Like I said, he's a really nice guy."

"So you rescheduled the wedding?"

"Not right away. We didn't even talk about it for two years. And then we just decided to go for it."

"And you felt ready this time?"

"I don't know. I guess I just finally accepted the fact that my mother wasn't coming back. Nobody was. And Gary was starting to get impatient. He kept telling me that he was tired of being sad all the time. He said my mom would have wanted us to get married, to start a family. He said she would've wanted us to be happy."

"What did you think?"

"That he was right. And I was tired of being sad all the time, too."

"So what happened?"

Meg didn't speak for a few seconds. It was almost like Laurie could hear her thinking in the dark, trying to formulate her answer as clearly as she could, as if a lot depended on it.

"We made all the arrangements, you know? We rented a hall, picked out a DJ, interviewed caterers. I should've been happy, right?" She laughed softly. "It felt like I wasn't even there, like it was all happening to someone else, someone I didn't even know. Look at her, designing the invitations. Look at her, trying on the dress."

"I remember that feeling," Laurie said. "It's like you're dead and you don't even know it."

"Gary got mad. He couldn't understand why I wasn't more excited."

"So when did you decide to bail out?"

"It was on my mind for a while. But I kept waiting, you know, hoping it would get better. I went to a therapist, got medication, did a lot of yoga. But nothing worked. Last week I told Gary that I needed another postponement, but he didn't want to hear it. He said we could get married or we could break up. It was my choice."

"And here you are."

"Here I am," she agreed.

"We're glad to have you."

"I really hate the cigarettes."

"You'll get used to them."

"I hope so."

Neither one of them spoke after that. Laurie rolled onto her side, savoring the softness of the sheets, trying to remember the last time she'd slept in such a comfortable bed. Meg only cried for a little while, and then she was quiet.

GET A ROOM

NORA HAD BEEN LOOKING FORWARD to the dance, less for the event itself than for the chance to make a public statement, to let her little world know that she was okay, that she'd recovered from the humiliation of Matt Jamison's article and didn't need anyone's pity. She'd felt defiantly upbeat all day long, trying on the sexiest clothes in her closet—they still fit, some even better than before—and practicing her moves in front of the mirror, the first time she'd danced in three years. *Not bad,* she thought. *Not bad at all.* It was like traveling back in time, meeting the person you used to be, and recognizing her as a friend.

The dress she'd finally settled on was a slinky red-and-gray wrap-around with a plunging neckline that she'd last worn to Doug's boss's daughter's wedding, where it had received a slew of compliments, including one from Doug himself, the master of withholding. She knew she'd made the right choice when she modeled it for her sister and saw the sour look on Karen's face.

"You're not wearing *that,* are you?"

"Why? Don't you like it?"

"It's just a little . . . *flashy,* isn't it? People might think—"

"I don't care," Nora said. "Let them think whatever they want."

A jittery, mostly pleasant sense of anticipation—Saturday-night butterflies—took hold of her in Karen's car, a feeling she remembered from college, back when every party seemed like it had the potential to change her life. It stuck with her through the entire drive and the short walk through the middle school parking lot, only to abandon her at the front entrance of the building when she saw the flyer advertising the dance:

MAPLETON MEANS FUN PRESENTS:
NOVEMBER ADULT MIXER
DJ, DANCING, REFRESHMENTS, PRIZES
8 P.M.–MIDNIGHT
HAWTHORNE SCHOOL CAFETERIA

Mapleton means fun? she thought, catching a sudden mortifying glimpse of herself in the glass door. *Is that a joke?* If it was, then the joke was on her, a no-longer young woman in a party dress about to enter a school her children would never get a chance to attend. *I'm sorry,* she told them, as if they were hiding in her mind, judging everything she did. *I didn't think this through.*

"What's the matter?" Karen asked, peering over her shoulder. "Is it locked?"

"Of course it's not *locked.*" Nora pushed open the door to show her sister what a stupid question it was.

"I didn't think it was," Karen said testily.

"Then why'd you ask?"

"Because you were just standing there, that's why."

Shut up, Nora thought as they stepped into the main hallway, a bright tunnel with a waxed brown floor and a multitude of institutional green lockers stretching into the distance on either side. *Just please shut up.* A collection of student self-portraits hung on the wall across from the main office, above a banner that read: WE ARE THE MUSTANGS! It hurt her to look at all those fresh, hopeful, clumsily rendered faces, to think of all the lucky mothers sending them off in the morning with their backpacks and lunch boxes, and then picking them up at the curb in the afternoon.

Hey, sweetie, how was your day?

"They have an excellent art program," Karen said, as if she were giving a tour to a prospective parent. "They're strong on music, too."

"Great," Nora muttered. "Maybe I should enroll."

"I'm just making conversation. You don't have to get all huffy about it."

"Sorry."

Nora knew she was being a bitch. It was especially unfair given that Karen was the only date she could scrounge up on such short notice. That was the thing about her sister—Nora didn't always like her and hardly ever agreed with her, but she could always count on her. Everyone else she'd called—her allegedly close friends from the mommy group in which she could no longer claim membership—had begged off, citing family obligations or whatever, but only after trying to talk her out of coming here at all.

Are you sure it's a good idea, honey? Nora hated the condescending way they called her "honey," as if she were a child, incapable of making her own decisions. *Don't you want to wait a little longer?*

What they meant was wait a little longer for the dust to settle from the article, the one that everyone in town was probably still whispering about: PLAYS WELL WITH OTHERS: "HERO" DAD'S STEAMY TRYST WITH PRESCHOOL HOTTIE. Nora had only read it once, in her kitchen after Matt Jamison's surprise visit, but once was enough for all the grisly details of Doug's torrid affair with Kylie Mannheim to permanently engrave themselves on her memory.

Even now, two weeks later, it was still hard for her to accept the idea of Kylie as the Other Woman. In Nora's mind, she was still her kids' beloved teacher from the Little Sprouts Academy, a lovely, energetic girl, fresh out of college, who somehow managed to seem innocent and wholesome despite having a pierced tongue and a tattoo sleeve on her left arm that fascinated the toddlers. She was the author of a beautiful evaluation letter that Nora had once believed she would treasure forever, a carefully observed three-page analysis of Erin's first year at Little Sprouts that praised her "uncommon social skills," her "inexhaustibly curious mind," and her "fearless sense of adventure." For a couple of months after October 14th, Nora had carried the letter everywhere, so she could read it whenever she wanted to remember her daughter.

Unfortunately, there was no doubt about the veracity of the Reverend's accusations. He'd rescued an old, apparently broken laptop of Kylie's from the trash—the guy at the computer store had told her the hard drive was shot—and used his recently acquired data recovery skills to unearth a treasure trove of incriminating e-mails, compromising photos, and "shockingly explicit" chat sessions between "the handsome father of two" and "the fetching young educator." The newsletter included several damning excerpts from this correspondence, in which Doug revealed a hitherto hidden flair for erotic writing.

Nora had been devastated, not only by the tawdry revelations—she hadn't suspected a thing, of course—but also by the Reverend's obvious delight in making them public. She hid out for several days after the scandal broke, mentally reviewing her entire marriage, wondering if every minute of it had been a lie.

Once the initial shock wore off, she noticed that she also felt a kind of relief, a lightening of her burden. For three years she'd been grieving for a husband who didn't really exist, at least not in the way she'd imagined. Now that she knew the truth, she could see that she'd lost a little less than she thought she had, which was almost like getting something back. She wasn't a tragic widow, after all, just another woman betrayed by a selfish man. It was a smaller, more familiar role, and a lot easier to play.

"You ready?" Karen asked.

They were standing in the doorway of the cafeteria, watching the activity on the dimly lit dance floor. It was surprisingly crowded, a bunch of middle-aged people, mostly women, moving enthusiastically, if a bit awkwardly, to Prince's "Little Red Corvette," trying to find a way back to their younger, more limber selves.

"I think so," Nora replied.

She could sense the heads turning as they entered the cavernous party space, the attention of the room swiveling in their direction. This was what her friends had been hoping to protect her from, but she really didn't care one way or the other. If people wanted to look at her, they were welcome to look.

Yup, it's me, she thought. *The Saddest Woman in the World.*

She waded straight into the fray, raising her arms overhead and letting her hips take the lead. Karen was right there with her, elbows and knees chugging away. Nora hadn't seen her sister dance in years and had forgotten how much fun it was to watch her, a short, heavy woman with lots of moving parts, sexy in a way you couldn't have predicted from encountering her in any other context. They leaned in close, smiling at each other as they sang along: *Little red Corvette, baby you're much too fast!* Nora spun to the left, then snapped her upper body back to the right, her long hair whipping across her face. For the first time in ages, she felt almost human again.

~~~~~

THE GAME they played was called Get a Room. It was a lot like Spin the Bottle, except the group as a whole got to vote on whether a couple could leave the circle and retire to a private space. The voting added an element of strategy into what was otherwise a simple game of chance. You had to keep track of a whole range of possibilities, recalculating with every spin who you wanted to keep around and who you wanted to eliminate as a rival. The goal—aside from the obvious one of hooking up with someone you were attracted to—was to avoid being one of the last two players in the circle, because they had to get a room, too, though Jill knew from experience that they mostly just sat around feeling like losers. In a way it was better with an uneven number of players, despite the embarrassment of finding yourself alone at the end, the odd one out.

Aimee rubbed her hands together for luck, smiled at Nick Lazarro—he was every girl's first choice—and flicked the spinner, which came from a game of Twister. The arrow blurred, then slowed, regaining its shape as it ticked around the circle, inching past Nick to land squarely on Zoe Grantham.

"Jesus," Zoe groaned. She was a pretty, voluptuously chunky girl with Cleopatra bangs and juicy red lips that left their marks all over people's necks and faces. "Not again."

"Oh, come on," Aimee pouted. "It's not that bad."

They scuttled toward each other on their hands and knees and kissed in the center of the circle. It was nothing special—no tongue, no groping, just a polite liplock—but Jason Waldron started clapping and hooting as if they were going at it like porn stars.

"Hell, yeah!" he bellowed, the way he always did when there was lesbian action under way, no matter how listless. "These bitches need to get a room!"

No one seconded the motion. Nick spun next, but the arrow landed on Dmitri, so he got to go again. Those were the sexist rules they played by: Girls had to make out with each other, but the guys didn't, for reasons that were supposed to be self-explanatory. Jill was annoyed by this double standard, not because she had anything against kissing girls—she liked it just fine, with the single exception of Aimee, who was a little too much like a sister—but because it was bound up with a second injustice: Girls could kiss, but they could never get a room, on the grounds that that would mean stranding two guys without female partners, disturbing the heterosexual symmetry of the game. Jill had tried a couple of times to get the others to reconsider this policy, but no one backed her up on it, not even Jeannie Chun, who would have been the most obvious beneficiary of the change.

On his second spin, Nick got Zoe, and they went at it enthusiastically enough that Max Connolly suggested they get a room. Jeannie seconded the motion, but everyone else voted no—Jill and Aimee because they wanted to keep Nick in the game, Dmitri because he had a crush on Zoe, and Jason because he was Nick's lackey and never voted for Nick to get a room with anyone but Aimee.

That was the problem these days—there weren't enough players, and all the suspense was gone. Back in the summer, it had been crazy; on some nights they had close to thirty people in the circle—this was out in Mark Sollers's backyard—many of whom were strangers to one another. The voting was raucous and unpredictable; you were just as likely to get a room for a lame kiss as a steamy one. The first time she played, Jill ended up with a college guy who turned out to be a good friend of her brother's. They fooled around a bit, but then gave up and spent a long time talking about Tom, a conversation that taught her more about her brother than she knew from living in the same house with him for all those years. The second time she got a room with Nick, whom she knew from school but had never spoken to. He was beautiful, a quiet, dark-eyed boy with lank hair and a watchful expression, and she felt beautiful with him, absolutely certain that she belonged in his arms.

The game got smaller and duller in September, when the college kids headed back to school, and it continued to shrink throughout the fall, their number dwindling down to a hard core of eight players, and every session was more or less the same: Aimee went off with Nick, Jill and Zoe duked it out for Max and Dmitri, and Jeannie and

Jason ended up together by default. Jill didn't even know why they bothered anymore—the game mostly felt like a bad habit to her, a ritual that had outlived its usefulness, but it was always accompanied by a slender hope that the group dynamic might shift in such a way that she'd find herself alone with Nick again and could remind him of how perfectly their bodies and minds fit together.

Unfortunately, it wasn't going to happen tonight. She got him on her fourth spin, felt the familiar jolt of excitement as his face moved toward hers, and the equally familiar letdown when they kissed. He wasn't even pretending to be interested, his lips dry and only slightly parted, his tongue stubbornly passive in response to the eager, questioning flicks of her own. It was such a lethargic performance—way less hot than the kiss he'd given Zoe; Jill wasn't even in second place anymore!—that nobody even bothered to suggest that they get a room. When it was over, he wiped his mouth, gave a languid nod of approval, and said, "Thanks, that was great," but it was just good manners. They might as well have just shaken hands, or waved at each other from across the street. It made her wonder if their summer hookup had even happened, if the glorious hour and a half they'd spent on Mark's parents' bed wasn't just a figment of her imagination, a bad case of wishful thinking.

But it wasn't—the sheets had been cool and white, with little blue flowers on them, really delicate and innocent-looking, and Nick had been really into it. The only thing that had changed since then was that he'd fallen in love with Aimee, the way every guy eventually did. You could see it in the way his face lit up when the arrow finally pointed in her direction, and in the slow, serious way he kissed her, as if there were no one else in the room, as if what they were sharing wasn't part of a game at all. Aimee couldn't match his sincerity—there was something inescapably theatrical about the way she melted onto the floor, pulling him on top of her and arching her back so she could grind her pelvis against his—but the combination of the two styles had a potent effect on the judges. When Jason suggested that they get a room, Zoe seconded the motion, and the vote in favor was unanimous, not a single abstention.

~~~~~

THE BARRIER that separated Nora from the people around her thinned and softened as she danced; the others didn't seem as far away or strange as they often did when she passed them in the supermarket or on the bike path. When they bumped into her on the dance floor, the contact wasn't intrusive or unpleasant. If someone smiled at her, she smiled back, and most of the time it felt okay, like something her face was meant to do.

She took a break after a half hour and headed for the refreshment table, where she poured herself a plastic cup of chardonnay and downed it in two big gulps. The wine was lukewarm, a bit too sweet, but she thought it might be okay with ice and a little seltzer.

"Excuse me, Mrs. Durst?"

Nora turned toward the voice, which was soft and eerily familiar. For a long, blank moment, it felt like she'd lost the powers of thought and speech.

"I'm sorry to bother you," Kylie said. She'd cut her hair boyishly short, and it looked cute on her, a nice contrast to all that hipster ink on her arm, which Doug had apparently found so arousing. *I luv ur tats,* he'd told her in one of the text messages Reverend Jamison had published in his newsletter. *I asked my wife to get one but she said no :(.* "Can we talk for a minute?"

Nora remained mute. The crazy thing was, she'd imagined a version of this moment so clearly that she knew it by heart. For the first couple of days after learning about Doug's affair, she'd fantasized repeatedly, and in great detail, about barging into Little Sprouts in the middle of naptime and slapping Kylie across the face, really hard, with all the other teachers and kids looking on.

Slut, she would say matter-of-factly, as if this were Kylie's real name. (She'd experimented with an alternate scenario in which she screamed the word like a curse, but it was too melodramatic, not nearly as satisfying.) *You are a disgusting person.*

And then she would slap her on the other side of her cheating face, the sound of the blow reverberating like a gunshot in the darkened playroom. There were a bunch of other things she planned to say after that, but the words weren't really the point. The slaps were.

"I totally understand if you don't want to," Kylie went on. "I know this is awkward."

Nora stared at her, remembering how good—how cathartic and even righteous—it had felt to confront her in those daydreams, as if she were an instrument of divine justice. But she understood now that it was an imaginary Kylie that she'd wanted to punish, a prettier and more confident woman than the one standing in front of her. The real Kylie looked too flustered and contrite to slap. She also seemed a lot shorter than Nora remembered, maybe because she wasn't surrounded by a sea of toddlers.

"Mrs. Durst?" Kylie squinted worriedly at Nora. "Are you okay, Mrs. Durst?"

"Why do you keep calling me that?"

"I don't know." Kylie studied her retro suede sneakers. In her skinny jeans and tight little T-shirt—it was also black, with a white exclamation point between what Doug had called her "little cheerleader boobs"—she looked like she belonged in a basement rock club, not a middle school cafeteria. "I just don't feel like I have the right to use your first name anymore."

"How considerate."

"I'm sorry." Kylie's face turned a more intense shade of pink. "I just didn't expect to see you here. You never came to the mixers before."

"I don't get out much," Nora explained.

Kylie ventured a tentative smile. Her face was a little fuller than it used to be, a little more ordinary. *Not so young anymore, are we?* Nora thought.

"You're a really good dancer," Kylie told her. "It looked like you were having fun out there."

"I'm all about the fun," Nora said. She could sense people watching them from a distance, homing in on the drama. "How about you? Enjoying yourself?"

"I just got here."

"Lots of older guys," Nora pointed out. "Maybe even some married ones."

Kylie nodded, as if she appreciated the dig.

"I deserve that," she said. "And I just want you to know how sorry I am for what happened. Believe me, you can't even imagine how terrible I've felt . . ."

She kept talking, but all Nora could think about was the silver piercing in the middle of her tongue, the dull metallic pearl she could occasionally glimpse when Kylie opened her mouth a little wider than usual. This was another of Doug's favorite things, the subject of an e-mail rhapsody that Nora been unable to expunge from her memory:

Your BJs are amazing!!! Four fucking stars! Best I ever had. I love the way u go down on me so slow and sexy and lick me with your magic tongue and I love how much u love it too. What was it u said—better than an ice cream cone? I gotta stop now—I'm gonna cum just thinking about your hot little mouth. Love, kisses, and ice cream,
D.

Best I ever had. That was the line that had killed her, the one that had seemed like more of a betrayal than the actual sex. During the twelve years she and Doug had been together, she'd given him a lot of blowjobs, and he'd seemed happy enough about them at the time. Maybe even a little too happy, she'd come to think, and a little too entitled. She'd complained on a couple of occasions about the way he used to just shove her head down toward his crotch—no words, no tenderness, just a silent command—and he'd made a show of listening carefully, promising to be more considerate in the future. And he always was, for a little while, until he wasn't anymore. It reached the point, near the end, where the whole act got poisoned for her, and she could no longer tell if she was doing it because she wanted to or because he expected it. Apparently Kylie was a much better sport.

"I wanted to call you," she was saying, "but then I just, I don't know, after everything that happened—"

She stopped in midstream, her eyes widening as she spotted Karen moving toward them with belligerent urgency, big sister to the rescue. She stepped protectively in front of Nora, getting right in Kylie's face.

"What is wrong with you?" she demanded, her voice stoked with indignation. "Are you crazy?"

"It's okay," Nora muttered, laying a restraining hand on her sister's arm.

"No, it's not okay," Karen said, never taking her eyes off Kylie. "I'm just amazed that you have the nerve to show your face around here. After what you did . . ."

Kylie leaned to one side, trying to reestablish eye contact with Nora.

"I'm sorry," she said. "I think I better go."

"Good idea," Karen told her. "You never should have come here in the first place."

Nora stood beside her sister and watched, along with just about everybody else at the dance, as Kylie turned and made the long walk of shame across the cafeteria to the exit doors. She kept her shoulders back and her chin up the whole way there, compensating with good posture for the fact that she was no longer welcome.

~~~~~~

THE RULES didn't require a couple to have sex once they got behind closed doors, but they did require both players to strip to their underwear. Jill and Max knew the drill and began undressing as soon as they entered Dmitri's little sister's pink-walled bedroom.

"You again," he said, flopping onto the bed in a pair of tartan-plaid boxers that Jill had seen a couple of times before.

"Yup." Jill was pretty sure he was equally familiar with her black panties and beige bra. "It's Groundhog Day."

"Oh, well." He plucked a bit of fluff from his navel and dropped it on the floor. "Could be worse, right?"

"Definitely." She climbed in beside him, using her hip to shove him close to the wall. "It could totally be worse."

She wasn't just being nice. Max was a sweet, smart guy, and she was always relieved to find herself alone with him. He was easy to talk to, and they'd figured out a long time ago that they didn't click as sexual partners, so there was no pressure on that front. It was more complicated with Dmitri, who was better-looking than Max and more interested in sex, but who also made it clear in all sorts of ways that he would have preferred to be with Aimee or Zoe. Sometimes they hooked up, but she was always a little sad afterward. The real disaster was getting stuck with Jason, but that almost never happened. She didn't know how Jeannie could stand it. Maybe they just surfed girl-on-girl porn together.

Max poked her arm. "You cold?"

"A little."

He unfurled the duvet at the foot of the bed and spread it over them.

"Better, huh?"

"Yeah, thanks."

She patted him on the thigh, then rolled onto her side to turn off the lamp, because they both liked lying in the dark. Sometimes it felt like they were an old married couple, the way her parents used to be. She remembered going into their room to say good night, the two of them looking so cozy and contented in their pajamas, reading with their glasses on. These days, her father seemed a little lost up there, the bed off balance, like it was about to tip over. She figured that was why he slept on the couch so much.

"You have Mr. Coleman for Biology?" Max asked.

"No, I had Ms. Gupta."

"Coleman was really good. I don't think they should've fired him."

"He said some pretty mean things."

"I know. I'm not defending what he said."

A few weeks earlier, Mr. Coleman had told one of his classes that the Sudden Departure was a natural phenomenon, a kind of global autoimmune reaction, a way for the earth to fight off the raging infection of humanity. *It's us,* he'd said. *We're the problem. We're making the planet sick.* A couple of kids had been upset by this—one of them had lost his mother on October 14th—and some parents lodged an official complaint. Just last week the school board announced that Mr. Coleman had agreed to take an early retirement.

"I don't know," Max said. "I really don't think what he said was so crazy."

"It was harsh," Jill reminded him. "He said the people who got taken were Rejects. The families didn't like it."

"A lot of people say it the other way," Max pointed out. "They say the rest of us are the Rejects."

"That sucks, too."

They were quiet for a while. Jill felt pleasantly drowsy—not sleepy, just relaxed. It felt good to be lying there in the dark, under the covers, a warm body beside her.

"Jill?" Max whispered.

"Mmm?"

"You mind if I jerk off?"

"No," she told him. "Go right ahead."

~~~~~

KYLIE WAS all the way down by the main office by the time Nora caught up with her. The hallway was empty, the fluorescent lights oppressively bright; Kylie's face was wet with tears. Embarrassed, Nora diverted her gaze to the bewildering stain on her arm, a multicolored explosion of vines, leaves, bubbles, and flowers that must have hurt like hell going on.

"Don't you have a coat?"

Kylie sniffled and wiped her eyes. "It's in the car."

"Can I ask you something?" Nora's voice was oddly calm, despite her inner agitation. "Was he gonna leave me?"

Kylie shook her head. "At the beginning I thought he might, but it was just wishful thinking."

"What do you mean?"

"I don't know. After the first few times, we stopped talking about it. It just kinda dropped off the agenda."

"You were okay with that?"

"Not really." Kylie tried to smile, but she didn't look any happier. "I just wasn't thinking straight. I mean, I know better than to get involved with a married guy. But I did it anyway. What's that about?"

Nora assumed the question was rhetorical. In any case, Kylie would have to work it out on her own.

"I'm curious," she said. "How did it start?"

"It just kinda happened." Kylie shrugged, as if the affair remained a mystery to her. "I mean, we flirted a little in the mornings, you know, when he dropped Erin off. I'd compliment his tie, and he'd tease me about looking tired, ask me what I'd been up to the night before. But lots of the dads—"

"When did it turn . . . ?"

Kylie hesitated. "You sure you want to hear this?"

Nora could hear music wafting out of the cafeteria—"Burning Down the House," a song she'd always liked—but it sounded watery and remote, like it was emanating from the past, rather than from a room down the hall. She nodded for Kylie to go ahead.

"Okay." Kylie looked unhappy, like she knew she was making a mistake. "It was the holiday party. You took the kids home, but Doug stuck around to help with the cleanup. We ended up going out for a drink afterward. We just kinda hit it off."

Nora could remember the party—Erin hadn't napped that day and spent most of the evening in tears—but she couldn't remember Doug even being there, let alone what time he'd come home, or how he'd acted when he did. All that was gone, irretrievable.

"You kept it up for a long time. Almost a year."

Kylie frowned, as if something was wrong with Nora's math. "It didn't feel like that. We hardly ever saw each other. He'd drop by once a week for an hour or two, if I was lucky, and then he'd leave. And I couldn't complain, right? That was what I'd signed up for."

"But you must've talked about the future. What was gonna happen. I mean, you couldn't just go on indefinitely."

"I tried, believe me. But he had no patience for relationship talk. He was always like, *Not tonight, Kylie. I can't deal with this right now.*"

Nora couldn't help laughing. "Sounds like Doug."

"He was such a *guy*." Kylie shook her head, smiling fondly at the memory. But then her expression clouded over. "I think I just made him feel like he was cool again, you know? Mr. Dull Corporate Family Man, with a girlfriend like me. Like he was a secret agent."

Nora grunted, struck by the plausibility of this theory. Doug had been a bit of a hipster when she'd met him in college—he wrote music reviews for the school paper, cultivated scruffy facial hair, and played ultimate Frisbee—but he'd discarded that version of himself the day he started business school. It happened so suddenly and irrevocably that Nora had spent the whole first semester trying to figure out where the guy she'd been sleeping with had gone. *Hey,* he told her, *if you're gonna sell out, at least have the guts to admit it.* But maybe he missed his old self more than he'd let on.

"He loved my crappy apartment," Kylie went on. "I have this studio over on Rankin, behind the hospital? Kind of a dump, but I just got tired of psycho roommates, you know? Anyway, it's basically one big room, with a foldout futon and a little table with two chairs that I found in the garbage. Totally cluttered. Doug thought it was hilarious. He thought my car was funny, too. It's like twelve years old."

"He could be a little snobby about stuff like that."

"He wasn't mean about it. More just amazed that I could live that way. Like I had a choice, right? I mean, your house is so beautiful, he must have thought that everybody . . ." Her voice trailed off as she belatedly recognized her mistake.

"You were in my house?"

"Just once," Kylie assured her. "During the spring vacation? You took your kids to your parents' and Doug stayed home to work?"

"Oh, God." That trip had been a minor disaster. She and the kids had gotten stuck in a brutal traffic jam on the Garden State Parkway, and she'd had to pull over so Jeremy could take an emergency dump on the shoulder of the highway. She'd just stood there holding his hand, staring up at the sky while he did his business, that sluggish river of cars crawling past, moving more slowly than a person could walk. When Doug caught up with them on the weekend, he'd seemed strangely cheerful, much nicer to her parents than usual. "Did you sleep there? In our bed?"

Kylie looked mortified. "I'm sorry. I shouldn't have done that."

"It's all right." Nora gave a little shrug, as if nothing could hurt her anymore. Some days she actually felt like that. "I don't even know why I'm asking you all these questions. It's not like it matters anymore."

"Of course it matters."

"Not really. I mean, he left me anyway. He left both of us."

"Not on purpose," Kylie said. She seemed pleased to be included.

They both turned at the same time, startled by the rapid clop of footsteps in the otherwise quiet hallway. Nora knew it was Karen even before she burst into view, rounding the corner like she was late for class.

"I'm fine," Nora said, holding up her hand like a traffic cop.

Karen stopped. Her gaze shifted warily from Nora to Kylie and back to Nora.

"You sure?"

"We're just talking."

"Forget about her," Karen said. "Come back to the dance."

"Just give me a minute, okay?"

Karen raised both hands in a gesture of saintly surrender. Then she gave a little suit-yourself shrug and headed back toward the cafeteria, her heels tapping out a reproachful rhythm. Kylie waited for the sound to die out.

"Is there anything else you want to know? It's kind of a relief to tell you about it."

Nora knew what she meant. As distressing as it was to learn the details of Doug's affair, it also felt therapeutic, as if a missing chunk of the past were being returned to her.

"Just one more thing. Did he ever talk about me?"

Kylie rolled her eyes. "Only all the time."

"Really?"

"Yeah. He always said he loved you."

"You're kidding." Nora couldn't hide her skepticism. "He hardly ever said that to me. Not even when I said it first."

"It was like a ritual. Right after we had sex, he'd get all serious and say, *This isn't about me not loving Nora.*" She uttered these words in a deep, manly voice, not at all like Doug's. "Sometimes I said it along with him. *This isn't about me not loving Nora.*"

"Wow. You must've hated me."

"I didn't hate you," Kylie said. "I was just jealous."

"Jealous?" Nora tried to laugh, but the sound died in her throat. It had been a long time since she'd thought of herself as someone other people could be jealous of. "Why?"

"You had everything, you know? The husband, the house, those beautiful kids. All your friends and your nice clothes, the yoga and the vacations. And I couldn't even make him forget you when he was in my bed."

Nora closed her eyes. Doug had been foggy in her mind for a long time, but all at once he was clear again. She could see him lying beside Kylie, naked and smug after fucking her, earnestly reminding her of his family commitments, his enduring love for his wife, letting her know that she could only have so much, and nothing more.

"He didn't care about me," Nora explained. "He just couldn't stand to see you happy."

〜〜〜〜〜

JUDGING FROM the careless way she was slumped against the locker, Kevin thought at first that Nora Durst might be asleep, or possibly drunk. As he got closer, though, he saw that her eyes were open and reasonably alert. She even managed a wan smile when he asked if she was okay.

"Fine," she told him. "I'm just taking a little break."

"Me, too," he said, because that seemed more diplomatic than the truth, which was that he'd come to check on her after a couple of different people had reported seeing her alone in the hall, looking pretty distraught. "It's kinda loud in there. You can barely hear yourself think."

She nodded the way you do when you're not actually listening to the other person and are just waiting for them to go away. Kevin didn't want to impose on her, but he also had a feeling that she could use a little company.

"It's great that you came," he said. "It looked like you were having a good time. You know, earlier."

"I was." Nora had to tilt her head at what looked like an uncomfortable angle to meet his eyes. "Earlier."

It was awkward looming over her like that, especially since it afforded him what felt like an unfair glimpse of her cleavage. Without asking, he lowered himself onto the floor beside her and stuck out his hand.

"I'm Kevin."

"The Mayor," she said.

"That's right. We met at the parade."

He was about to withdraw his hand when she reached up and shook it, sparing him the embarrassment. She had bony fingers and a surprisingly firm grip.

"I remember."

"You gave a nice speech."

Nora turned her head to get a better look at him, as if to judge his sincerity. She was wearing makeup, so the bruised-looking skin below her eyes was less noticeable than usual.

"Don't remind me," she said. "I'm trying to forget about that."

Kevin nodded. He wanted to say something sympathetic about the article in Matt Jamison's newsletter—it was an incredibly low blow, even for the bottom-feeder Matt had become—but he figured she was trying to forget about that, too.

"I wish I'd kept my mouth shut," she muttered. "I feel like such an idiot."

"It's not your fault."

"Nothing's my fault. But I still feel like shit."

Kevin wasn't sure what to say to that. Without thinking, he stretched out his legs so they were parallel to hers on the floor, his dark jeans next to her bare skin. The symmetry reminded him of an article he'd read about body language, how we unconsciously mirror the postures of people we're attracted to.

"So, how do you like the DJ?" he asked.

"Good." She sounded like she meant it. "A little old-school, but pretty good."

"He's new. The last guy talked too much. He had a microphone and he used to yell at people to get on the dance floor, and not in a nice way. He'd be like, *What's the matter, Mapleton? It's a party, not a funeral!* Sometimes it got kinda personal. *Yo, Tweed Jacket? Are you even breathing?* We got a lot of complaints."

"Let me guess," she said. "You were Tweed Jacket?"

"No, no." Kevin smiled. "That was just an example."

"You sure?" she said. "'Cause I didn't see you out on the dance floor."

"I wanted to. I just got sidetracked."

"By what?"

"It's like a council meeting in there. Every time I turn around, somebody's yelling at me about potholes or the planning commission or nobody collected their yard waste. I can't really loosen up, not the way I used to."

She leaned forward and gathered her knees to her chest. There was something girlish in the posture, a touching counterpoint to her face, which seemed older than the rest of her. It startled him when she smiled, like someone had turned on a light beneath her skin.

"Yo, Tweed Jacket," she said.

"Just for the record, I don't even own a tweed jacket."

"You should get one," she told him. "With patches on the sleeves. I bet it'd look good on you."

JILL LAY awake in the darkness for a long time before getting up and putting her clothes on. She planted a soft kiss on Max's forehead, but he didn't stir. He'd fallen asleep right after jerking off and looked like he was out for the count. Next time she'd have to ask him to keep the light on while he did it, so she could watch his face. That was the best part of the whole thing as far as she was concerned, the way a guy's face contorted so violently and then relaxed, as if some terrible mystery had just been solved.

She headed downstairs, surprised to find the living room empty, eerie and unfamiliar-looking in the light of the muted TV. That stupid "Miracle Spotters" infomercial was on again, the one that showed a family of four—Mom, Dad, their son and daughter—walking through the woods with military-style night-vision goggles strapped over their eyes. On cue, they all stopped and looked up, pointing in amazement at something in the sky. She knew the narration by heart: *Buy two Miracle Spotters at our everyday low price, and get two more ABSO-LUTELY FREE! That's right, buy two and get another pair free! As an added bonus, we'll throw in a set of four Home Safe Family Communication Devices for NO CHARGE WHATSOEVER! That's a sixty-dollar value!* On-screen, the little boy cowered in the forest, speaking worriedly into his Family Communication Device, which looked to Jill like a garden-variety walkie-talkie. His face broke into a wide grin as his parents and sister emerged from the trees, clutching their own devices, and rushed to embrace him. *Order now! You'll thank God you did!* Jill would've died before she admitted it, but the cheesy commercial always got her choked up, the joy of the reunited family, all that sentimental crap.

Not that it was her job, but she took a few minutes to tidy up while she waited for Aimee. She knew how depressing it could be to wake up in a messy house, how it could make you feel like the new day was already old. Of course, Dmitri's house was party central—his parents and two little sisters had been "away" for as long as Jill had known him, and no one expected them back anytime soon—so maybe he didn't mind so much. Maybe chaos was the normal state for him, order the puzzling exception.

She carried a bunch of empty beer bottles into the kitchen and rinsed them under the faucet. Then she wrapped up the cold pizza, put it in the fridge, and crammed the box into the trash can. She'd just finished loading the dishwasher when Aimee came in, smiling sheepishly, holding one arm straight out in front of her. A pair of panties was dangling from her hand, pinched between her thumb and forefinger like a piece of suspicious roadside trash.

"I am such a slut," she said.

Jill stared at the panties. They were light blue, with a pattern of yellow daisies.

"Are those mine?"

Aimee opened the cabinet under the sink and shoved the underwear deep into the trash can.

"Believe me," she said. "You don't want them back."

~~~~~

AS MUCH as he enjoyed it, Kevin had never been much of a dancer. It was the football, he thought—he was too tense in the hips and shoulders, a little too rooted to the ground, as if he expected dancers from an opposing team to come crashing into him. As a result, he tended to get locked into simple repetitive motions that made him feel like he was impersonating a cheap battery-operated toy.

Nora made him even more conscious of his shortcomings in this department than usual. She moved with a relaxed grace, apparently unaware of any distinction between her body and the music. Luckily, she didn't seem the least bit put off by Kevin's incompetence. Most of the time, she didn't even seem to know he was there. She kept her head down, her face partially concealed by a swaying curtain of dark, sleek hair, so fine it looked almost liquid. On those rare occasions when their eyes met, she gave him a sweet, startled smile, as if she'd forgotten all about him.

The DJ played "Love Shack" and "Brick House" and "Sex Machine," and Nora knew most of the words. She shimmied and spun and kicked off her shoes, dancing barefoot on the hardwood floor. The exuberance she displayed was especially impressive because she must have known how closely she was being watched. Kevin could feel it himself, as if he'd accidentally wandered into the beam of a harsh spotlight. The scrutiny wasn't exactly rude, he thought— there was something furtive and helpless about it—but it was relentless, and he grew increasingly self-conscious in its glare. He glanced around, smiling sheepishly, apologizing to the room for his clumsiness.

They danced for seven songs straight, but when Kevin asked if Nora wanted a break—he certainly could have used one himself—she shook her head. Her face was gleaming with sweat, her eyes bright.

"Let's keep going."

He was exhausted after the one-two punch of "I Will Survive" and "Turn the Beat Around." Luckily, the song after that was "Surfer Girl," the first slow number since they'd started. There was a moment of awkwardness during the opening arpeggio, but she answered his questioning glance by stepping forward and draping her arms around his neck. He completed the embrace, placing one hand on her shoulder and the other on the small of her back. She dropped her head on his shoulder, as if he were her prom date.

He took a little shuffle step forward and one to the side, breathing in the mingled scents of her sweat and shampoo. She followed his lead, her body pressing into his as they moved. He could feel the humid heat of her skin rising through the thin fabric of her dress. Nora murmured something, but her words got lost in his collar.

"Sorry," he said. "I didn't hear you."

She lifted her head. Her voice was soft and dreamy.

"There's a pothole on my street," she told him. "When are you gonna fix it?"

Part *Three*

HAPPY HOLIDAYS

DIRTBAGS

TOM WAS JITTERY IN THE terminal. He would have preferred to keep hitchhiking, sticking to the back roads, camping in the woods, saving their money for emergencies. They'd made it all the way from San Francisco to Denver like that, but Christine had gotten tired of it. She never told him so straight out, but he could see that she thought it was beneath her, having to stick out her thumb and pretend to be grateful to people who had no idea what an honor it was to play even a bit part in her story, people who acted like they were the ones doing the favor, picking up a couple of scruffy, barefoot kids in the middle of nowhere and taking them a little farther down the road.

It was two days before Thanksgiving—Tom had forgotten all about the holiday, which used to be one of his favorites—and the waiting area was choked with travelers and luggage, not to mention a problematic number of cops and soldiers. Christine spotted an empty seat—it was a single in the middle of a row—and rushed to grab it. Trying to control his irritation, Tom lumbered after her, weighed down by his overstuffed backpack, reminding himself that her needs came first.

Shrugging off the ungainly pack—it contained her stuff as well as his own, plus the tent and sleeping bag—he sat down at her feet like a loyal dog positioning himself at an angle to avoid eye contact with the pack of soldiers sitting directly across the way, all of them dressed in desert fatigues and combat boots. Two were napping and one was texting, but the fourth—a skinny, redheaded dude with rabbity, pink-rimmed eyes—was studying Christine with an intensity that made him nervous.

This was exactly what he'd been worried about. She was so cute that you couldn't *not* check her out, not even when she was dressed in these filthy hippie rags and a hand-knitted stocking cap, with a big blue-and-orange bullseye painted in the middle of her forehead. More than a month had passed since Mr. Gilchrest's arrest, and the story had pretty much faded away, but he figured it was just a matter of time before some busybody noticed Christine and connected her with the fugitive brides.

The soldier's gaze shifted to Tom. He tried to ignore it, but the guy apparently had all the time in the world and nothing to do but stare. Eventually, Tom had no choice but to turn and meet his eyes.

"Yo, Pigpen," the soldier said. The stitching on his shirt pocket identified him as HENNING. "That your girlfriend?"

"Just a friend," Tom replied, a bit grudgingly.

"What's her name?"

"Jennifer."

"Where you heading?"

"Omaha."

"Hey, me too." Henning seemed pleased by the coincidence. "Got a two-week leave. Gonna spend Thanksgiving with the family."

Tom gave a minimal nod, trying to let the guy know he wasn't in the mood for a big get-to-know-you chat, but Henning didn't take the hint.

"So what brings you to Nebraska?"

"Just passing through."

"Where you coming from?"

"Phoenix," he lied.

"Hot as a bitch down there, huh?"

Tom looked away, trying to signal that the conversation was over. Henning pretended not to notice.

"So what is it with you guys and showers? You allergic to water or something?"

Oh, God, Tom thought. *Not this again.* When they'd decided to disguise themselves as Barefoot People, he figured they'd get teased a lot about drugs and free love, but he had no idea how much time he was going to have to devote to the subject of personal hygiene.

"We value cleanliness," Tom told him. "We're just not obsessed with it."

"I can see that." Henning glanced at Tom's grimy feet as if they were Exhibit A. "I'm curious. What's the longest you've ever gone without a shower?"

If Tom had any interest in being honest, he would have said seven days, which was the extent of his current streak. In the interest of verisimilitude, he and Christine had stopped showering three days before leaving San Francisco, and during their time on the road they'd only had access to public restrooms.

"None of your business."

"All right, fine." Henning seemed to be enjoying himself. "Just answer me this. When was the last time you changed your underwear?"

The soldier next to Henning, a bald black guy who'd been texting like his life depended on it, looked up from his phone and chortled.

Tom remained silent. There was no dignified way to answer a question about your underwear.

"Come on, Pigpen. Just give me a ballpark figure. Extra points if it's less than a week."

"Maybe he's a commando," the black guy speculated.

"Purity comes from within," Tom explained, echoing one of the Barefoot People's favorite slogans. "What's on the outside is irrelevant."

"Not to me," Henning shot back. "I'm the one that has to sit on the bus with you for twelve hours."

Tom didn't say so, but he knew the guy had a point. For the past couple of days, he'd been uncomfortably aware of the funk he and Christine were giving off in close quarters. Every driver who picked them up immediately cracked the windows, no matter how cold or rainy it was. Verisimilitude was no longer an issue.

"I'm sorry if we offend you," he said, a bit stiffly.

"Don't get mad, Pigpen. I'm just fucking with you."

Before Tom could reply, Christine kicked him softly in the back. He ignored the summons, wanting to keep her out of the conversation. But then she kicked him again, hard enough that he had no choice but to turn around.

"I'm starving," she said, jutting her chin in the direction of the Food Court. "Could you get me a slice of pizza?"

HENNING WASN'T the only one who resented their presence on the overnight bus. The driver didn't look too happy as he took their tickets; several passengers muttered disparaging comments as they made their way down the aisle toward the empty seats in back.

It was almost enough to make Tom feel sorry for the Barefoot People. Until he'd started impersonating one, he had no idea how unpopular they were with the general public, at least once you got out of San Francisco. But whenever he found himself wishing that he and Christine had chosen a more respectable cover—something that would have allowed them to blend in a little better and not attract so much free-floating hostility—he reminded himself that the weaknesses of this particular disguise were also its strengths. The more conspicuous you were, the easier it was for people to take you at face value—they just wrote you off as a couple of harmless dirtbags and left it at that.

Christine slid into the window seat in the very last row, unpleasantly close to the restroom. She seemed puzzled when Tom sat down across the aisle.

"What's the matter?" She patted the empty seat beside her. "Aren't you gonna keep me company?"

"I figured we could spread out. Be easier to get some rest."

"Oh." She looked disappointed. "I guess you don't love me anymore."

"I forgot to tell you," he said. "I met someone else. On the Internet."

"Is she pretty?"

"All I know is, she's clean Russian girl, looking for rich American stud."

"Good thing it's not the other way around."

"Very funny."

They'd been teasing each other like this for the past couple of weeks, pretending to be boyfriend and girlfriend, hoping to joke away some of the sexual tension that always seemed to be hanging in the air, but only making it thicker in the process. It had been distracting enough back at the house, but it had become excruciating now that they were on the road, twenty-four-hour-a-day companions, eating together, sleeping side by side in the little pup tent. He'd heard Christine snoring and seen her squatting in the woods, and had held her hair away from her face when she threw up in the morning, but all that familiarity hadn't managed to breed even the smallest sliver of contempt. He still got flustered every time she brushed up against him, and knew it would be pure insomniac torture, sitting right next to her for twelve hours, his eyes wide open, her knee just inches from his own.

Despite a multitude of opportunities, Tom still hadn't made any moves on her—hadn't tried to kiss her in the tent, or even hold her hand—and he didn't intend to. She was sixteen years old and four months pregnant—her belly had just begun to bulge—and the last thing she needed to deal with were sexual advances from her traveling companion, the guy who was supposed to be watching out for her. His mission was simple: All he had to do was deliver her safely to Boston, where some sympathetic friends of Mr. Gilchrest had offered to take her in and provide her with food and shelter and medical care until the baby arrived, the one who was supposed to save the world.

Tom didn't believe all this nonsense about the Miracle Child, of course. He didn't even understand what it would mean to *save the world*. Would the people who'd disappeared come back? Or would things just get better for the ones left behind, less sadness and worry all around, a brighter future ahead? The prophecy was maddeningly vague, which led to all sorts of groundless rumors and wild speculation, none of which he took seriously, for the simple reason that his faith in Mr. Gilchrest was pretty much shot to hell. He was only helping Christine because he liked her, and because this seemed like a good time to get out of San Francisco and on to the next chapter in his life, whatever that was going to be.

Even so, just for fun, he sometimes allowed himself to entertain the remote possibility that it could all be true. Maybe Mr. Gilchrest really was a holy man, despite all his flaws, and the baby really was some kind of savior. Maybe everything really did depend on Christine, and therefore, on him. Maybe Tom Garvey would be remembered thousands of years from now as the guy who'd helped her when she needed it most, and had always acted like a gentleman, even when he didn't have to.

That's me, he thought with grim satisfaction. *The guy who kept his hands to himself.*

IT WAS early evening by the time they got moving, too late to enjoy the Rocky Mountain scenery. The bus was new and clean, with plush reclining seats, onboard movies, and free wireless, though neither Tom nor Christine had any use for that. The bathroom didn't even smell that bad, at least not yet.

He tried watching the movie—*Bolt,* a cartoon about a dog who mistakenly believes he has superpowers—but it was hopeless. He'd lost his taste for pop culture after the Sudden Departure and hadn't been able to get it back. It all seemed so hectic and phony now, so desperate to keep you looking over there so you didn't notice the bad news right in front of your face. He didn't even follow sports anymore, had no idea who'd won the World Series. All the teams were patched together anyway, the holes in their rosters plugged by minor leaguers and old guys who'd come out of retirement. All he really missed was music. It would have been nice to have his metallic green iPod along for the ride, but that was long gone, lost or stolen in Columbus, or possibly Ann Arbor.

At least Christine seemed to be enjoying herself. She was giggling at the tiny screen in front of her, sitting with her dirty feet on the seat cushion and her knees hugged tightly to her breasts, which she claimed were a lot bigger than they used to be, though Tom couldn't really see much of a difference. From this angle, with her little bump hidden beneath a baggy sweater and a ratty fleece jacket, she just looked like a kid, someone who should have been worrying about homework and soccer practice, not sore nipples and whether she was getting enough folic acid. He must've stared a little too long, because she turned suddenly, as if he'd spoken her name.

"What?" she asked, a little defensively. The bullseye on her forehead was a bit faded; she'd have to touch it up when they got to Omaha.

"Nothing," he said. "I was just spacing out."

"You sure?"

"Yeah, go back to your movie."

"It's pretty funny," she told him, her eyes crinkling with pleasure. "That little dog's a trip."

• • •

THERE WAS a run on the bathroom when the movie ended. The line moved efficiently at first, but it came to a standstill after an older guy with a cane and a grimly determined expression ducked inside and stayed put. The people behind him grew visibly annoyed as the minutes ticked by, sighing with increasing frequency, instructing their colleagues up front to knock and see if he was alive in there, or at least find out if *War and Peace* was all it was cracked up to be.

As luck would have it, Henning happened to be second in line during the traffic jam. Tom kept his head down, pretending to be engrossed in the freebie paper he'd picked up at the terminal, but he could feel the soldier's insistent gaze boring into the center of his bullseye.

"Pigpen!" he cried when Tom finally looked up. He sounded pretty drunk. "My long-lost buddy."

"Hey."

"Yo, Grampa!" Henning barked, addressing the closed door of the restroom. "Time's up!" He turned back to Tom with an aggrieved expression. "What the fuck's he doing in there?"

"Can't rush Mother Nature," Tom reminded him. This seemed like something a Barefoot Person would say.

"Fuck that," Henning replied, drawing an agitated nod of agreement from the middle-aged woman in front of him. "I'm gonna count to ten. If he's not outta there, I'm gonna kick the door down."

Just then the toilet flushed, sending a visible wave of relief down the aisle. This was followed by an extended, oddly suspenseful interlude of silence, at the end of which the toilet flushed a second time. When the door finally opened, the now-famous occupant stepped out and surveyed his public. He mopped his sweaty brow with a paper towel and made a humble appeal for forgiveness.

"Had a little problem." He rubbed his stomach, a bit tentatively, as if things still weren't quite right. "Nothin' I could do."

Tom caught a whiff of misery as the old guy limped off and his replacement stepped into the restroom, uttering a soft cry of protest as she shut the door.

"So what's going on back here?" Henning asked, a lot more cheerful now that the logjam had been broken. "You guys partying?"

"Just hanging out," Tom told him. "Trying to get some rest."

"Yeah, right." Henning nodded, like he was in on the joke, and patted one of his back pockets. "I got some Jim Beam. I'm happy to share."

"We're not really into alcohol."

"I get it." Henning pinched his thumb and forefinger together and brought them to his lips. "You like the herb, huh?"

Tom gave a judicious nod. The Barefoot People definitely liked the herb.

"I got some of that, too," Henning reported. "There's a rest stop in a few hours if you want to join me."

Before Tom could answer, the toilet flushed.

"Thank you, Jesus," Henning muttered.

Stepping out of the bathroom, the middle-aged woman smiled queasily at Henning.

"It's all yours," she told him.

On his way in, Henning took another toke on his imaginary joint. "Catch you later, Pigpen."

LULLED BY the hum of the big tires, Tom drifted off to sleep somewhere outside of Ogallala. He was awakened a while later—he had no idea how long he'd been napping—by the sound of voices and a muddled sense of alarm. The bus was dark except for the glow of a few scattered reading lights and laptop screens, and it took him a few seconds to get his bearings. He turned instinctively to check on Christine, but the soldier was in the way. He was sitting right next to her, a pint of whiskey in his hand, talking in a low, confidential tone.

"Hey!" Tom's voice came out louder than he meant it to, earning him several annoyed glances and a couple of shushes from his fellow passengers. "What are you—?"

"Pigpen." Henning spoke softly. There was a sweet expression on his face. "Did we wake you?"

"Jennifer?" Tom leaned forward, trying to get a glimpse of Christine. "Are you okay?"

"I'm fine," she said, but Tom thought he detected a note of reproach in her voice, which he knew he deserved. He was supposed to be her bodyguard, and here he was, sleeping on the job. God only knew how long she'd been trapped like this, fending off the advances of a drunken soldier.

"Go back to sleep." Henning reached across the aisle and patted him on the shoulder with what felt like parental reassurance. "There's nothing to worry about."

Tom rubbed his eyes and tried to think. He didn't want to antagonize Henning or cause any sort of disturbance. The one thing they didn't need was to draw any unnecessary attention to themselves.

"Listen," he said, in the friendliest, most reasonable tone he could muster. "I don't mean to be a jerk, but it's really late, and we haven't had a lot of sleep in the past few days. It would be really cool if you just went back to your seat and let us get some rest."

"No, no," Henning protested. "It's not like that. We're just having a conversation."

"It's nothing personal," Tom explained. "I'm asking you nicely."

"Please," Henning said. "I just need somebody to talk to. I'm going through some bad shit right now."

He sounded sincere, and Tom started to wonder if maybe he'd overreacted. But he just didn't like the whole situation, the stranger pressed up against Christine, occupying the seat that Tom had so stupidly surrendered.

"It's okay," Christine told him. "I don't mind if Mark stays."

"Mark, huh?"

Henning nodded. "That's my name."

"All right. Whatever." Tom sighed, acknowledging his defeat. "If it's okay with her, I guess it's okay with me."

Henning extended the bottle like a peace offering. *What the hell,* Tom thought. He took a small sip, wincing as the liquor ignited in his throat.

"There you go," Henning said. "It's a long way to Omaha. Might as well enjoy ourselves."

"Mark was telling me about the war," Christine explained.

"The war?" Tom shuddered as a bourbon aftershock traveled through his body. All at once he felt clearheaded, wide awake. "Which one?"

"Yemen," he said. "Fucking hellhole."

CHRISTINE DOZED off, but Tom and Henning kept talking softly, trading the bottle back and forth across the aisle.

"I ship out in ten days." Henning sounded like he didn't quite believe it. "Twelve-month deployment."

He said he came from a military family. His father served; so had two uncles and an aunt. Henning and his older brother, Adam, had made a pact to enlist right after October 14th. He came from a small rural town full of Bible-believing Christians, and back then just about everyone he knew believed that the End Times were upon them. They were expecting a major war to break out in the Middle East, the battle foretold in the Book of Revelation. The opponent would be nothing less than the army of the Antichrist, the honey-tongued leader who would unite the forces of evil under a single banner and invade the Holy Land.

So far, though, none of that had happened. The world was full of corrupt and despicable tyrants, but in the past three years, none of them had emerged as a plausible Antichrist, and no one had invaded Israel. Instead of one big new war, there was just the usual bunch of crappy little ones. Afghanistan was mostly over, but Somalia was still a mess, and Yemen was getting worse. A few months ago, the President had announced a big troop escalation.

"I talked to a guy who just got back," Henning told him. "He said it's like the Stone Age over there, just sand and rubble and I.E.D.'s."

"Damn." Tom took another hit of bourbon. He was starting to feel pretty loose. "You scared?"

"Fuck, yeah." Henning tugged on his earlobe like he was trying to yank it off. "I'm nineteen years old. I don't wanna wake up in Germany with one of my legs cut off."

"That's not gonna happen."

"Did to my brother." Henning spoke matter-of-factly, his voice flat and distant. "Fucking car bomb."

"Oh, man. That sucks."

"I'm gonna see him tomorrow. First time since it happened."

"How's he doing?"

"Okay, I guess. They got him in a wheelchair, but he's gonna get a new leg pretty soon. One of those high-tech ones."

"Those are pretty cool."

"Maybe he'll be one of those bionic sprinters. I saw an article about this one guy, he's actually faster now than he used to be." Henning swallowed the last few drops of bourbon, then shoved the empty bottle into the seat pocket in front of him. "It's gonna be weird seeing him like that. My big brother."

Henning leaned back and closed his eyes. Tom thought he was drifting off to sleep, but then he gave a soft grunt, as if something interesting had just occurred to him.

"You got it right, Pigpen. Just go wherever you want, do whatever you want. Nobody ordering you around or trying to blow your head off." He looked at Tom. "That's the deal, right? You just wander around, looking for the party?"

"It's our duty to enjoy ourselves," Tom explained. He was pretty familiar with the theology; a lot of the teachers he'd been training in San Francisco had gone through a Barefoot phase before becoming Holy Wayners. "We believe that pleasure is the creator's gift, and that we glorify the creator whenever we have a good time. The only sin is misery. For us, that's Rule Number One."

Henning grinned. "That's my kinda religion."

"It sounds simple, but it's not as easy as you think. It's like the human race has been programmed for misery."

"I hear that," Henning said, with surprising conviction. "How long you been doing it?"

"About a year." Tom and Christine had been honing their cover stories in preparation for exactly this sort of interrogation, and he was glad they had—he was a little too drunk to be improvising. "I was in college, but it all felt so pointless. Like, the world's coming to an end, and I'm getting a degree in Accounting. What good's that gonna do me?"

Henning tapped his forehead. "What's with the circle thing?"

"It's a bullseye. A target. So the Creator will recognize us."

Henning glanced at Christine. She was breathing softly, her head resting against the window, her features delicate in repose, as if they'd been sketched on her face rather than sculpted.

"How come hers is a different color? Does it mean something?"

"It's a personal choice, like a signature. I do maroon and gold 'cause those were my high school colors."

"I could do green and beige," Henning said. "Kind of a camo thing."

"Nice." Tom nodded his approval. "I haven't seen that before."

Henning leaned across the aisle, like he wanted to share a secret.

"So is it true?"

"What?"

"You guys are into orgies and shit?"

From what Tom had heard, the Barefoot People held these big solstice gatherings out in the desert, where everybody ate mushrooms and dropped acid and danced and fucked. It didn't sound all that great to him, just a big, sloppy frat party.

"We don't call them orgies," he explained. "It's more like a spiritual retreat. You know, like a bonding ritual."

"I'm down with that. I wouldn't mind bonding with a few cute hippie girls."

"Really?" Tom couldn't resist. "Even if they hadn't changed their underwear for a week?"

"What the hell?" Henning said with a grin. "Purity comes from within, right?"

CHRISTINE NUDGED him awake as they pulled into the terminal in Omaha. Tom's head felt big and unsupportable, way too heavy for his neck.

"Oh, God." He shut his eyes against the onslaught of daylight through the tinted windows. "Don't tell me it's morning."

"Poor baby." She patted him gently on the forearm. They were sitting next to each other, Tom in the seat where Henning had been.

"Ugh." He swirled his tongue around the inside of his mouth. There was a vile taste in there—stale bourbon, pot smoke, bus exhaust, sadness. "Just shoot me and get it over with."

"No way. It's more fun to watch you suffer."

Henning was gone. They'd hugged him goodbye around four in the morning, at a travel plaza in the dead center of the middle of nowhere.

"I hope he's okay," she said, as if reading his mind.

"Me, too."

He was on his way to San Francisco, hitchhiking westward with a piece of paper in his wallet, on which Tom had written the address of Elmore's Café and instructions to "Ask for Gerald." There was no Gerald, as far as Tom knew, but it didn't matter. The Barefoot People would take him in, with or without an introduction. Everybody was welcome, even—especially—a soldier who'd decided that he wanted no part of the killing and dying.

"It's kind of amazing," Christine remarked, as they stood with the other passengers on the concrete apron, waiting to retrieve their luggage. "You converted him to a religion you don't even believe in yourself."

"I didn't convert him. He converted himself."

The driver was in a bad mood, tossing suitcases and canvas bags onto the ground behind him, paying no attention to where they landed. The crowd retreated a few steps, giving him room.

"You can't really blame him," Christine said. "He'll have more fun in San Francisco."

Their backpack landed with a thud. Tom bent down to get it, but must have straightened up a little too quickly. His legs went rubbery and he wobbled in place for a second or two, waiting for the dizziness to pass. He could feel the sweat breaking out on his forehead, one clammy drop at a time.

"Oh man," he said. "Today is gonna suck."

"Welcome to my life," she told him. "Maybe we can throw up together."

A redheaded family was standing inside the terminal, anxiously scanning the arriving passengers. There were four of them: a skinny father and a plump mother—they were around the same age as Tom's own parents—a sullen teenage girl, and a haggard, one-legged guy in a wheelchair. *Adam,* Tom thought. He was smiling wryly, holding up a piece of paper, like an airport chauffeur.

MARK HENNING, it said.

The Hennings barely noticed Tom and Christine. They were too busy checking every new face that came through the door, waiting patiently for the right one to appear, the only face that mattered.

SNOWFLAKES AND CANDY CANES

KEVIN GOT TO TOWN HALL around eight that morning, an hour earlier than usual, hoping to squeeze in a little work before heading to the high school for a meeting with Jill's guidance counselor. Fulfilling a campaign pledge, he'd opted for a hands-on style of governing, making himself available to meet with constituents on a first-come, first-served basis for an hour every day. This was partly a matter of good politics, and partly a coping strategy. Kevin was a social animal: He liked having somewhere to go in the morning, a reason to shave and shower and put on decent clothes. He liked feeling busy and impor-

tant, certain that his sphere of influence extended beyond the boundaries of his own backyard.

He'd learned this the hard way after selling Patriot Liquor Mega-
stores, a sweet deal that left him financially independent at the age
of forty-five. Early retirement had been the dream at the center of his
marriage, a goal he and Laurie had been moving toward for as long as
he could remember. They never said it out loud, but they aspired to
be one of those couples you saw on the cover of *Money Magazine*—
vigorous middle-aged people riding a tandem bike or standing on the
deck of their sailboat, cheerful refugees from the daily grind who'd
managed, through a combination of luck and hard work and careful
planning, to get a chunk of the good life while they were still young
enough to enjoy it.

But it hadn't worked out that way. The world had changed too
much and so had Laurie. While he was busy managing the sale of the
business—it was a stressful, protracted transaction—she was drifting
away from the life they'd known, mentally preparing herself for an entirely different future, one that didn't include a tandem bike or a
sailboat, or even a husband, for that matter. Their shared dream had
become Kevin's exclusive property, and useless to him as a result.

It took him a while to figure this out. All he really knew at the time
was that retirement didn't agree with him, and that it was possible to
feel like an unwelcome guest in your own home. Instead of doing all
the exciting things he'd dreamed about—training for an over-forty tri-
athlon, learning to fly-fish, reigniting the passion in his marriage—he
mostly just moped around, an aimless man in baggy sweatpants who
couldn't understand why his wife was ignoring him. He put on weight,
micromanaged the grocery shopping, and developed an unhealthy
interest in his son's old video games, especially John Madden Football, which could consume whole afternoons if you weren't careful.
He grew a beard, but there was too much gray in it, so he shaved it off.
That was what passed for a big event in the life of a retired man.

Running for office turned out to be the perfect antidote for what ailed him. It got him out of the house and into contact with lots of other people without being anywhere near as demanding as a real job. As Mayor of a smallish town, he rarely worked more than three or four hours a day—a good part of which was spent wandering around the municipal complex, chatting with various clerks and department heads—but that little bit of structure made all the difference in his daily routine. Everything else fell into place around it—afternoons were for errands and exercise, evenings for relaxing; later on, there was always the Carpe Diem.

ON THE way up to his office, he popped into police headquarters for his daily briefing and caught Chief Rogers eating a massive blueberry muffin, a clear violation of his heart-healthy diet.

"Oh." The Chief cupped his hand over the broken dome of his muffin, as if to protect its modesty. "Little early, isn't it?"

"Sorry." Kevin retreated a step. "I can come back later."

"That's all right." The Chief waved him in. "It's no big deal. You want some coffee?"

Kevin filled a foam cup from a silver push-button thermos, stirred in a packet of creamer, then took a seat.

"Alice would kill me." The Chief nodded with guilty pride in the direction of his muffin. He was a sad-eyed, flabby man who'd had two heart attacks and a triple bypass before the age of sixty. "But I already gave up booze and sex. I'll be damned if I'm gonna give up breakfast."

"It's your call. We just don't wanna see you back in the hospital."

The Chief sighed. "Let me tell you something. If I die tomorrow, I'm gonna regret a lot of things, but this muffin won't be one of them."

"I wouldn't worry about that. You'll probably outlast all of us."

The Chief didn't seem to think this was a very likely scenario.

"Do me a favor, okay? If you come in here some morning and find me keeled over on my desk, just wipe the crumbs off my face before the ambulance comes."

"Sure," Kevin said. "You want me to comb your hair, too?"

"It's a matter of dignity," the Chief explained. "At a certain point, that's all you have left."

Kevin nodded, letting his silence mark the transition to official business. If you weren't careful, small talk with Ed Rogers could last all morning.

"Any trouble last night?"

"Not much. One DUI, one domestic, a pack of stray dogs on Willow Road. The usual crap."

"What was the domestic?"

"Roy Grandy threatened his wife again. He spent the night in the holding cell."

"Figures." Kevin shook his head. Grandy's wife had gotten an order of protection over the summer, but she'd allowed it to lapse. "What are you gonna do?"

"Not much. By the time we got there, the wife was claiming it was all a big misunderstanding. We're gonna have to turn him loose."

"Anything new on the Falzone thing?"

"Nah." The Chief looked exasperated. "Same old story. Nobody knows anything."

"Well, let's keep digging."

"It's blood from a stone, Kevin. You can't get information from people who won't talk. They're gonna have to realize this is a two-way street. If they want us to protect them, they're gonna have to play ball."

"I know. I'm just worried about my wife. In case there's some kinda nut out there."

"I hear you." The Chief's somber expression turned sly. "Though I gotta tell you, if my wife took a vow of silence, I'd support her a hundred and ten percent."

• • •

THREE WEEKS had passed since the body of a murdered Watcher had been found near the Monument to the Departed in Greenway Park. Since then, aside from conducting routine ballistics tests and identifying the victim—he was Jason Falzone, twenty-three, a former barista from Stonewood Heights—the police had made very little progress with the investigation. A door-to-door canvas of the neighborhood bordering the park had failed to locate a single witness who'd seen or heard anything suspicious. It wasn't all that surprising: Falzone had been killed after midnight, in a deserted area several hundred yards from the nearest house. Only one shot had been fired from close range, a single bullet in the back of the head.

The investigators had also been stymied in their efforts to locate the victim's partner, or interview anyone within the G.R. itself, which refused, on principle, to cooperate with the police or any other government agency. After a contentious negotiation, Patti Levin, the Mapleton Chapter's Director and spokesperson, had agreed "as a courtesy" to respond in writing to a series of questions, but the information she provided led absolutely nowhere. The detectives were especially skeptical about her insistence that Falzone was alone on the night of the murder, since it was common knowledge that the Watchers traveled in pairs.

We don't always have an even number of personnel on duty, she wrote. *Simple math dictates that some of our people will have to work independently.*

Offended by what they saw as stonewalling, not to mention Levin's condescending tone, some members of the investigation team had raised the possibility of using more aggressive measures—subpoenas, search warrants, etc.—but Kevin had convinced them to hold off. One of his priorities as Mayor was to dial down the tension between the town and the Guilty Remnant; you didn't do that by sending a group of heavily armed officers into the compound on a vague mission to round up potential witnesses, not after what had happened the last time.

As the days went by without an arrest, Kevin expected the police to come under fire from frightened residents—murders were exceedingly rare in Mapleton, and unsolved, apparently random ones were unheard-of—but the outcry never materialized. Not only that—if the letters to the local paper were any indication, a fair number of citizens believed that Jason Falzone had gotten more or less what he deserved. *I'm not trying to justify what happened,* one writer declared, *but troublemakers who deliberately and repeatedly make nuisances of themselves shouldn't be surprised if they provoke a reaction.* Other commentators were more blunt: *It's long past time to expel the G.R. from Mapleton. If the police won't do it, someone else will.* Even the victim's parents took a measured view of his death: *We mourn the loss of our beloved son. But the truth is, Jason had become a fanatic. Before he vanished from our lives, he spoke frequently of his wish to die as a martyr. It appears that wish has been granted.*

So that was where they were: a brutal, execution-style murder, no witnesses, no one clamoring for justice—not the victim's family, not the G.R., and not the good people of Mapleton. Just a dead kid in the park, one more sign that the world had lost its mind.

DAISY'S DINER was one of those retro places with lots of stainless steel and maroon Naugahyde. It had been lovingly renovated about twenty years ago and was now getting old all over again—the banquettes patched with duct tape, the coffee mugs chipped, the once-dazzling checkerboard floor dull and scuffed.

Bing Crosby's version of "The Little Drummer Boy" was playing on the sound system. Rubbing a clear spot into the fogged-up window, Kevin gazed with satisfaction on the holiday scene outside—oversized snowflakes and candy canes suspended from wire stretched across Main Street, real evergreen wreaths on the lampposts, the business district bustling with cars and pedestrians.

"It's looking good this year," he said. "All we need's a little snow."

Jill grunted noncommittally as she bit into her veggie burger. He felt a little guilty about letting her skip class to eat lunch with him, but they needed to talk, and it was hard to do that at home, with Aimee always hovering around. Besides, at this point in the semester, the damage was already done.

The conference with the guidance counselor had not gone well, to put it mildly. In some vague way, Kevin had known that Jill's grades were slipping, but he'd misjudged the gravity of the situation. A former straight-A student with stellar SAT scores, his daughter was failing Math and Chemistry and might eke out Cs at best in A.P. English and World History—two of her best subjects—if she aced her finals and handed in a number of overdue assignments before Christmas break, eventualities that were seeming more remote by the day.

"I'm at a loss," the counselor told him. She was an earnest young woman with long, straight hair and rimless octagonal glasses. "It's a complete academic meltdown."

Jill had just sat there, poker-faced, her expression wavering between polite boredom and mild amusement, as if they were talking about someone else, a girl she barely knew. Kevin came in for some pretty harsh criticism himself. Ms. Margolis couldn't understand his blasé attitude, the fact that he hadn't spoken to any of Jill's teachers or responded to the many e-mails informing him of his daughter's unsatisfactory progress.

"What e-mails?" he said. "I didn't get any e-mails."

It turned out that the messages were still going to Laurie's account, so he'd never actually seen them, but the mix-up just proved the counselor's larger point, which was that Jill wasn't getting enough supervision and support at home. Kevin didn't argue with that; he knew he'd dropped the ball. Ever since Tom had started kindergarten, Laurie had been the parent in charge of education. She supervised the homework, signed the report cards and permission slips, and met the new teachers on back-to-school night. All Kevin had to do for all those years was try to look interested when she told him what was going on; he obviously hadn't come to terms with the fact that all this responsibility now belonged to him.

"I realize there's been some . . . upheaval at home," Ms. Margolis said. "Clearly, Jill's having some adjustment issues."

She concluded the meeting by scrawling a big *X* through the college wish list that she and Jill had drawn up at the beginning of the school year. Williams, Wesleyan, Bryn Mawr—they were all out of the question now. It was late in the process, but what they needed to do in the upcoming weeks was shift their focus to less selective institutions, schools that might be a little more forgiving of a semester's worth of terrible grades from an otherwise excellent student. It was unfortunate, she said, but that was where they found themselves, so they might as well face reality.

I'll play my drum for him, pa rum pum pum pum . . .

"So what do you think?" Kevin asked, eyeing his daughter across the narrow Formica table.

"About what?" She stared right back, her face patient and unreadable.

"You know. College, next year, the rest of your life . . ."

Her mouth puckered with distaste. "Oh, that."

"Yeah, that."

She dipped a french fry into a little pot of ketchup, then popped it into her mouth.

"I'm not sure. I don't even know if I want to go to college."

"Really?"

She shrugged. "Tommy went to college. Look what happened to him."

"You're not Tommy."

She dabbed at her mouth with a napkin. A faint flush had crept into her cheeks.

"It's not just that," she told him. "It's just . . . we're the only ones left. If I go you'll be all alone."

"Don't worry about me. You just do what you need to do. I'll be fine." He tried to smile, but only got halfway there. "Besides, last time I checked there were three of us living in the house."

"Aimee's not part of the family. She's just a guest."

Kevin reached for his glass—it was empty except for the ice—and brought his mouth to the straw, vacuuming up a few stray droplets of moisture. She was right, of course. They were the only ones left.

"What do you think?" she asked. "Do you want me to go away to school?"

"I want you to do whatever you want. Whatever makes you happy."

"Gee, thanks, Dad. You're a big help."

"That's why they pay me the big bucks."

She brought her hand to the top of her head, pinching absent-mindedly at her stubble. It had grown noticeably thicker and darker in the past few weeks, much less severe without the pale scalp shining through.

"I've been thinking," she said. "I'd rather just stay home next year, if that's okay with you."

"Of course it's okay."

"Maybe I could commute to Bridgeton State. Take a few classes. Maybe get a part-time job."

"Sure," he said. "That would work."

They finished their food in silence, barely able to look at each other. Kevin knew that a less selfish parent would have been disappointed—Jill deserved way better than Bridgeton State, everybody's college of last resort—but all he felt was a relief so intense it was almost embarrassing. It wasn't until the waitress took their plates that he trusted himself enough to speak.

"So, uh, I've been meaning to ask what you want for Christmas."

"Christmas?"

"Yeah," he said. "Big holiday? Right around the corner?"

"I haven't really thought about it."

"Come on," he said. "Help me out."

"I don't know. A sweater?"

"Color? Size? I could use a little guidance."

"Small," she told him, grimacing as if the information were painful to disclose. "Black, I guess."

"Great. What about Aimee?"

"Aimee?" Jill sounded surprised, even a bit annoyed. "You don't have to get anything for Aimee."

"What's she gonna do, sit there and watch us open presents?"

The waitress returned with the check. Kevin glanced at it, then reached for his wallet.

"Maybe some gloves," Jill suggested. "She's always borrowing mine."

"Okay." Kevin took out his credit card and set it on the table. "I'll get her some gloves. Let me know if you think of anything else."

"What about Mom?" Jill said after a few seconds. "Should we get something for her?"

Kevin almost laughed, but stopped himself when he saw the serious expression on his daughter's face.

"I don't know," he said. "We're probably not gonna see her."

"She used to like earrings," Jill murmured. "But I guess she can't wear them anymore."

THEY WERE standing at a pedestrian crosswalk right outside the diner when a woman rode by on an orange bike. She called out to Kevin as she zipped past, a terse greeting he couldn't quite decipher.

"Hey." He raised his hand in a delayed salute, addressing the space she no longer occupied. "How's it going?"

"Who's that?" Jill's eyes followed the cyclist as she headed down the street, rounding the bend toward Pleasant Street, flowing at the same speed as the car that hemmed her in.

"No one you know," Kevin said, wondering why he didn't want to say her name.

"That's hard-core," Jill observed. "Riding a bike in December."

"She's dressed for it," he said, hoping it was true. "They have all that Gore-Tex and whatnot."

He spoke casually, waiting for the emotional disturbance to pass. He hadn't seen or spoken to Nora Durst since the mixer, the night they'd danced together until the lights came on. He'd walked her to her car and said good night like a gentleman, shaking her hand, telling her how much he had enjoyed her company. Her sister was standing right there, a squat, impatient-looking woman, so it didn't go any further than that.

"Call me sometime," she told him. "I'm in the book."

"Absolutely," he said. "I'll do that."

He'd meant it, too. Why wouldn't he? She was smart and pretty and easy to talk to, and it wasn't like he had a whole lot going on at the moment. But three weeks had passed and he still hadn't made the call. He'd thought about it a lot, enough that he no longer had to look up her number in the Mapleton white pages. But dancing with her was one thing, and going on a date, actually getting to know her, getting close to whatever it was she had to live with—that was something else entirely.

She's out of my league, he told himself, without really knowing what he meant by that, what league either one of them belonged to.

He drove Jill back to school, then went home and lifted weights in his basement, an ambitious dumbbell workout that got a nice pump going in his arms and chest. He cooked roast chicken and potatoes for the girls, read a chapter of *American Lion* after dinner, and then wandered over to the Carpe Diem, where the night passed without any surprises, just the familiar faces and pleasant banter of people who knew each other a little too well and would be doing the exact same thing tomorrow.

It wasn't until he got into bed that his thoughts returned to Nora, the jolt he'd felt when she passed him on her bike. In the daylight, the moment had come and gone in a jumbled rush, but in the dark, in the hush of his bedroom, it slowed and sharpened. In this simplified version, Jill wasn't with him; Main Street was empty. Not only that, Nora wasn't wearing spandex or a helmet, just the same pretty dress she'd worn at the dance. Her hair was loose and flowing, her voice clear and firm as she floated by.

"Coward," she said, and all he could do was nod.

THE BEST CHAIR IN
THE WORLD

IN THE CAR, NORA DID her best to act like it was no big deal, like going to the mall at the height of the holiday season was just something you did—because you were an American, because Christmas was right around the corner, because you were part of an extended family whether you liked it or not, and needed to buy gifts for a certain number of your relatives. Karen followed her lead, keeping the conversation light and casual, not saying anything to call attention to the significance of the journey, to suggest that Nora was "being brave" or "taking a step forward" or "getting on with her life," any of the patronizing phrases she'd come to despise.

"It's hard to shop for teenage boys," Karen said. "They won't even tell me which video games they want, like I'm supposed to know the difference between Brainwave Assassin 2 and Brainwave Assassin Special Edition. Plus, I told them I wouldn't get anything rated M—I don't even like the T games, to be honest—so that really limits my options. And the boxes they come in are so small, it just looks . . . *empty* under the tree, not like when they were little and you had all these presents spilling out, taking up the whole living room. *That* really felt like Christmas."

"Maybe books?" Nora said. "They like to read, right?"

"I guess." Karen kept her eyes straight ahead, fixed on the glowing taillights of the Explorer in front of them. Traffic was heavy for seven-thirty in the evening, almost like rush hour; apparently, the herd had made a collective decision to do some shopping. "They like that fantasy crap, and all the titles sound the same. Last Christmas I got Jonathan one of those boxed set trilogies—*The Werewolves of Necropolis,* or something—and it turned out he already owned them. They were right there on his bookshelf. It was like that with everything. I don't think the boys got anything that really made them happy."

"Maybe you should surprise them. Don't focus so much on the things you know they want. Introduce them to something new."

"Like what?"

"I don't know. Like surfboards or something. Gift certificates for rock climbing or scuba lessons, that kind of thing."

"Hmmm." Karen seemed intrigued. "That's not such a bad idea."

Nora couldn't tell if her sister was being sincere, but it didn't really matter. It was a half hour to the mall, and they needed to talk about *something.* If nothing else, it was a chance for her to practice her small talk, to remember what it felt like to be a normal person having a harmless little chat, nothing too heavy or disturbing. It was a skill she'd need to develop if she was ever going to reenter the social world in a serious way—get through a job interview, say, or a dinner date with an interesting man.

"It's—it's pretty warm for this time of year," she ventured.

"I know!" Karen's reply was oddly emphatic, as if she'd been waiting all day for a chance to discuss the weather. "Yesterday afternoon I went out in just a sweater."

"Wow. In December. That's crazy."

"It's not gonna last."

"No?"

"Cold front's moving in tomorrow. I heard it on the radio."

"That's too bad."

"What can you do?" Karen's high spirits returned as abruptly as they'd vanished. "Be nice if it snowed for Christmas. We haven't had a white one in a while."

There was nothing to it, Nora thought. You just kept babbling, piling one inane remark on top of another. The trick was to sound like you were interested, even if you weren't. You had to be careful about that.

"I talked to Mom this afternoon," Karen said. "She might not make a turkey this year. She says maybe a big roast beef or possibly a leg of lamb. I reminded her that Chuck doesn't like lamb, but you know how she is. Things go in one ear and out the other."

"Tell me about it."

"Though I have to say, I do kind of sympathize with her on the turkey question. I mean, we just had turkey for Thanksgiving and the leftovers lasted forever. It's like, enough with the turkey already."

Nora nodded, though she didn't really care one way or the other—she wasn't eating any meat these days, not even poultry or fish. It wasn't so much an ethical objection as a conceptual shift, as though food and animals had ceased to be overlapping categories. Even so, she was relieved to hear that there might not be a turkey at Christmas dinner. Karen had made a big one for Thanksgiving, and the whole family had gathered around it for what felt like an excruciating length of time, rhapsodizing about its golden brown skin and moist interior. *What a beautiful bird*, they kept telling one another, which was a weird thing to say about a dead thing without a head. And then her cousin Jerry had made everyone pose for a group photograph, with the beautiful bird occupying the place of honor. At least nobody would do that with a roast beef.

"This is so great!" Karen said, as they waited at a red light on the mall access road. She squeezed Nora's leg, just above the knee. "I can't believe we're doing this."

The truth was, Nora could hardly believe it herself. It was all part of an experiment, the impulsive decision she'd made to stay home this year and face the holidays head-on, instead of running away to Florida or Mexico for a week, baking in the sun, pretending that there was no such thing as Christmas. All the same, she'd surprised herself by taking Karen up on her invitation to go to the mall, the epicenter of all the madness.

It was mostly Kevin Garvey's fault, she was pretty sure of that. A month had passed since they'd danced at the mixer, and she still hadn't figured out what to do about him. All she knew was that anything—even a trip to the mall with her sister—beat the prospect of another night of sitting at home like a teenager, waiting for him to call. It should've been obvious by now that it wasn't going to happen, but some part of her brain wasn't getting the message—she kept checking her e-mail every five minutes, carrying the phone everywhere she went, just in case he decided to get in touch while she was in the shower or the laundry room.

Sure, she could've picked up the phone or shot him a casual e-mail. He was the Mayor, after all; if she wanted, she could've just dropped in on him during his office hours, started complaining about parking meters or something. Back when she was young and single, she'd never had a problem taking the initiative, asking a guy out or at least smoothing the way for him to do the asking. But that wasn't the point anymore. Kevin had said he would call her, and he seemed like a guy who could be trusted to keep his word. If he wasn't that kind of guy, then the hell with him—he wouldn't be any good to her anyway.

On some level, she understood that he'd danced with her out of pity. She was totally willing to admit that that was how it had started—a philanthropist and a charity case—but it had ended somewhere else entirely, her head on his shoulder, his arms wrapped tight around her, some kind of current running between their bodies, making her feel like a dead woman who'd been shocked back to life. And it wasn't just her: She'd seen the look on his face when the lights came on, the tenderness and curiosity in his eyes, the way he kept holding her and shuffling his feet well after the music had stopped.

It was hard at first when he didn't call—really hard—but a month is a long time, and she'd pretty much reconciled herself to the fact that it had all been a false alarm, at least until last week, when she'd passed him on her bike and everything got stirred up again. He was just standing there on Main Street with his punky-looking daughter at his side; all Nora had to do was squeeze the brakes, glide right up to them, and say, *Hey, how's it going?* Then, at least, she would've been able to study his face, maybe get a clearer sense of what was going on. But she'd been a coward—she froze, forgot to hit the brakes, sped right past as if she were late for an appointment, as if she had someplace better to go than a house where the phone never rang and no one ever visited.

"Oh, look!" Karen said. They were cruising through the parking lot, trying to locate a space that wasn't half a mile away from the entrance. She was pointing at a mother and daughter, the mom close to Nora's age, the child maybe eight or nine, both of them wearing fuzzy reindeer antlers on their heads, the girl's complete with blinking red lights. "Isn't that adorable?"

TWO WHITE-CLAD Watchers were standing in front of the Macy's entrance, along with a grizzled-looking guy ringing a bell for the Salvation Army. Out of politeness, Nora accepted a leaflet from one of the G.R. guys—*Have you forgotten already?* the cover inquired—then dropped it in a trash can conveniently situated just inside the door.

She felt a mini panic attack coming on as they passed the fragrance counter, a small animal's sense of imminent danger. It was partly a re-action to the stench of a dozen different perfumes spritzed into the air by heavily made-up young women who seemed to think they were per-forming a public service, and partly a more general feeling of sensory overload brought on by the sudden onslaught of bright lights, bouncy music, and eager consumers. The blank-faced mannequins didn't help, their paralyzed bodies decked out in the latest fashions.

It was easier to breathe once they entered the main concourse, with its high glass ceiling—the mall was built on three levels, with balconies on the upper two—and vast white floor, which reminded her of an old-fashioned train station. Beyond the central fountain, an enormous Christmas tree towered over a line of children waiting to meet Santa Claus, its angel-tipped peak rising past the first mezza-nine. The tree reminded her of a ship in a bottle, so big you had to wonder how it got there.

Karen was a brutally efficient shopper, one of those people who always knows exactly what she's looking for and where it can be found. She strode through the mall with an air of fierce concentra-tion, eyes straight ahead, no aimless browsing or impulse buying. She was the same way in the supermarket, crossing off each item on her list with a red Sharpie, never passing the same spot twice.

"What do you think?" she asked, holding up an orange-and-blue-striped tie in the Big Guys Wearhouse. "Too bold?"

"For Chuck?"

"Who else?" She tossed the tie back onto the clearance table. "The boys never dress up."

"Pretty soon they will. They'll have proms and stuff, right?"

"I guess." Karen plunged her hand back into the serpentine tangle of neckties. "They'll have to start showering first."

"They don't shower?"

"They *say* they do. But their towels are always dry. Hmm." She selected a more likely candidate, yellow diamonds on a field of green silk. "What do you think?"

"It's nice."

"I don't know." Karen frowned. "He's got too many green ties as it is. He has too many ties, period. Whenever anybody asks what he wants for Christmas, he always says, *Just a tie. A tie will be fine.* So that's what he gets. For birthdays and Father's Day, too. And he always seems perfectly happy with them." She released the tie, then glanced up at Nora. There was a sweet look on her face, affection and resignation and amusement all mixed together. "God, he's so boring."

"He's not boring," Nora said. "He's just . . ."

She faltered, for lack of a better adjective.

"Boring," Karen said again.

It was hard to argue with that. Chuck was a good provider, a solid, colorless guy who worked as a Quality Assurance Supervisor for Myriad Laboratories. He liked steak, Springsteen, and baseball, and had never once expressed an opinion that Nora had found remotely surprising. *Always a dull moment with Chuck,* Doug used to say. Of course, Doug was Mr. Unpredictable, charming and quirky, a new passion every month—Tito Puente and Bill Frisell, squash, libertarianism, Ethiopian food, sexy young women with lots of tattoos and a flair for fellatio.

"It's the same with everything," Karen said, examining a wide red tie with a mix of black pinstripes and wider silver stripes. "I try to get him to think outside the box, to wear a blue shirt with his gray suit, or God forbid a pink one, and he just looks at me like I'm crazy. *You know what, let's just stick with the white.*"

"He likes what he likes," Nora said. "He's a creature of habit."

Karen stepped away from the clearance table. Apparently the red one was a keeper.

"I guess I shouldn't complain," she said.

"No," Nora agreed. "You really shouldn't."

ON HER way to the Food Court, Nora passed the Feel Better Store and decided to check it out. She still had twenty minutes to kill before she was supposed to rendezvous with Karen, who had slipped off for a little "private shopping time," family code for *I'm going to buy you a present and need you to get lost for a while.*

Her heart was still racing when she stepped inside, her face hot with pride and embarrassment. She'd just forced herself to make a solo circuit of the big Christmas tree on the main level, where all the parents and kids were waiting to meet Santa Claus. It was another holiday challenge, an attempt to face her fear head-on, to break her shameful habit of avoiding the sight of small children whenever possible. That wasn't the kind of person she wanted to be—shut down, defensive, giving a wide berth to anything that might remind her of what she'd lost. A similar logic had inspired her to apply for the day-care job last year, but that had been too much, too soon. This was more controlled, a one-time-only, bite-the-bullet sort of thing.

It actually went okay. The way it was set up, the kids lined up on the right, met Santa in the middle, then exited on the left. Nora approached from the exit side, walking briskly, like an ordinary shopper on her way to Nordstrom. Only one child passed, a stocky boy talking excitedly to his goateed father. Neither one of them paid the slightest attention to her. Behind them, up on the makeshift stage, an Asian boy in a dark suit was shaking hands with Santa.

The hard part came after she looped around the tree—there was a giant model train set running in a frantic circle around the trunk—and headed in the opposite direction, walking slowly along the entire length of the line, like a general reviewing her troops. The first thing she noticed was that morale was low. It was late; most of the kids looked dazed, ready to collapse. A few of the toddlers were crying or squirming in their parents' arms, and some of the older kids seemed on the verge of making a break for the parking lot. The parents mostly looked grim, the invisible cartoon balloons above their heads filled with thoughts like, *Stop your whining. . . . We're almost there. . . . This is supposed to be fun. . . . You're going to do this whether you like it or not!* Nora remembered the feeling, had the pictures to prove it, both of her kids sitting teary-eyed and forlorn in the lap of a defeated Santa.

There must have been thirty children in line, and only two of the boys reminded her of Jeremy, far fewer than she'd expected. There had been times in the past when almost any little boy could tear her heart out, but now she was pretty much okay as long as he wasn't blond and very skinny with toy soldier spots on his cheeks. Just one girl made her think of Erin, and the resemblance wasn't really physical—it was more something in her expression, a premature wisdom that seemed heartbreaking in such an innocent face. The girl— she was a thumb-sucking beauty with a wild tangle of dark hair—stared at Nora with such solemn curiosity that Nora stopped and stared right back, probably for a little too long.

"Can I help you?" her father asked, glancing up from his Black- Berry. He was around forty, gray-haired but fit-looking in a rumpled business suit.

"You have a lovely daughter," Nora told him. "You should treasure her."

The man placed his hand protectively on his daughter's head.

"I do," he replied a bit grudgingly.

"I'm happy for you," Nora said. And then she walked away, before she had a chance to add anything that would upset him or ruin her own day, the way she had too many times in the past.

THE FEEL Better Store had an interesting motto—Everything You Need for the Rest of Your Life—but it turned out to be one of those yuppie emporia specializing in self-indulgent products for people who had way too much to begin with, things like heated slippers and bath- room scales that offered hearty personalized congratulations when you met your weight-loss goals and constructive personalized criticism when you didn't. Even so, Nora made a long, slow journey through the inte- rior, examining the hand-cranked emergency radios, programmable pillows, and noiseless nose-hair trimmers, appreciating the pleasantly austere environment—New Age soundscapes instead of Christmas carols—and the advanced age of the clientele. No beautiful little kids staring at you in the Feel Better Store, just middle-aged men and women nodding politely to one another as they loaded up on towel warmers and high-tech wine accessories.

She didn't notice the chair until she was on her way out. It occupied its own dim corner of the showroom, an ordinary-looking brown leather recliner resting like a throne on a low, carpeted pedestal, bathed in the soft glow of an overhead light. She wandered over for a closer look and was startled to discover that it cost nearly ten thousand dollars.

"It's worth it," the salesman told her. He had sidled up and spoken before she even realized he was there. "That's the best chair in the world."

"It better be," Nora said with a laugh.

The salesman nodded thoughtfully. He was a shaggy-haired, youngish guy in an expensive suit, the kind of suit you didn't expect to see on someone who worked at the mall. He leaned forward, as if to tell her a secret.

"It's a massage chair," he said. "You like massages?"

Nora frowned—this was a complicated question. She used to *love* massages. She'd had a standing twice-a-month Integrative Bodywork appointment with Arno, a squat Austrian genius who worked out of the spa in her health club. An hour with him, and it didn't matter what ailed her—PMS, bad knee, mediocre marriage—she felt reborn, able to meet the world with positive energy and an open heart. She'd tried going back to him about a year ago, but found that she could no longer stand to be touched so intimately.

"They're okay," she replied.

The salesman smiled and gestured toward the chair.

"Try it," he said. "You can thank me later."

NORA WAS alarmed at first, the way the headrest lurched so violently into motion, the hard rubber balls—or whatever they were—swirling up against the soft leather upholstery, digging into the knotty muscles surrounding her spine, grabby fingerlike devices pinching at her neck and shoulders. The vibrating seat cushion was undulating indecently, shooting warm, intermittent pulses of electricity into her butt and thighs. It was all too much until the salesman showed her how to work the control pad. She experimented with the settings—speed, temperature, intensity—until she hit upon the optimal combination, then cranked up the leg rest, closed her eyes, and surrendered.

"Pretty nice, huh?" the salesman observed.

"Mmmm," Nora agreed.

"Bet you didn't realize how tense you were. This is a stressful time of year." When she didn't reply, he added, "Take your time. Ten minutes of this and you'll be as good as new."

Whatever, Nora thought, too pleased by the chair to be irritated by the man's presumption. It really was a remarkable piece of equipment, unlike anything she'd ever tried before. In a normal massage, what you experienced was a slightly alarming sense of being pressed down, your body flattening against the table, your face mashed into the hole, a powerful, if mostly benevolent, force manhandling you from above. This was just the opposite, all the energy surging from below, your body rising and softening, nothing holding you down but air.

There was a time, not so long ago, when the idea of a ten-thousand-dollar massage chair would have seemed obscene to her, a shameful form of self-indulgence. But really, when you thought about it, it wasn't that high a price to pay for something so therapeutic, especially if you spread out the cost over ten or twenty years. In the end, a massage chair wasn't all that different from a hot tub or a Rolex or a sports car, any of the other luxury items people bought to cheer themselves up, many of them more cheerful than Nora to begin with.

Besides, who would even know? Karen, maybe, but Karen wouldn't care. She was always encouraging Nora to pamper herself, buy some new shoes or a piece of jewelry, take a cruise, spend a week at Canyon Ranch. Not to mention that Nora would let her sister use the chair anytime she wanted. They could make it a regular thing, a Wednesday-night massage date. And even if the neighbors did find out, what did Nora care? What were they gonna do, say mean things and hurt her feelings?

Good luck with that, she thought.

No, the only thing holding her back was the thought of what would happen if she actually owned the chair, if she could feel this good anytime she wanted. What would happen if there were no other customers milling around, no salesman hovering nearby, no Karen to meet in five or ten minutes? What if it were just Nora in an empty house, the whole night ahead of her, and no reason to hit the off switch?

THE BALZER METHOD

ON CHRISTMAS MORNING THEY WATCHED a PowerPoint presentation, the eighteen female residents of Blue House gathered in the chilly basement meeting room. That was how they did it for now, simultaneous showings in each house within the compound, as well as the various outposts scattered throughout town. There had been some talk within the Mapleton Chapter about the necessity of building or acquiring a structure large enough to accommodate the entire membership, but Laurie preferred it this way—more intimate and communal, less like a church. Organized religion had failed; the G.R. had nothing to gain by turning into a new one.

The lights went out and the first slide appeared on the wall, a photo of a wreath hanging on the door of a generic suburban house.

TODAY IS "CHRISTMAS."

Laurie shot a quick sidelong glance at Meg, who still looked a bit shaky. They'd stayed up late the night before, working through Meg's conflicted feelings about the holiday season, the way it made her miss her family and friends and question her commitment to her new life. She'd even found herself wishing that she'd waited to join the G.R., so she could have had one last Christmas with her loved ones, just for old times' sake. Laurie told her it was natural to feel nostalgia at this time of year, that it was similar to the pain amputees felt in a phantom limb. The thing was gone, but it was still somehow a part of you, at least for a little while.

The second slide showed a shabby Christmas tree festooned with a few meager scraps of tinsel, lying by the curb on a bed of dirty snow, waiting for a garbage truck to cart it away.

"CHRISTMAS" IS MEANINGLESS.

Meg sniffled softly, like a child trying to be brave. During last night's Unburdening, she'd told Laurie about a vision she'd had when she was four or five years old. Unable to sleep on Christmas Eve, she'd tiptoed downstairs and seen a fat bearded man standing in front of her family's tree, checking items off a list. He wasn't wearing a red suit—it was more like a blue bus driver's uniform—but she still recognized him as Santa Claus. She watched him for a while, then snuck back upstairs, her body filled with an ecstatic sense of wonder and confirmation. As a teenager, she convinced herself that the whole thing had been a dream, but it had seemed real at the time, so real that she reported it to her family the next morning as a simple fact. They still jokingly referred to it that way, as though it were a documented historical event—the Night Meg Saw Santa.

In the slide that followed, a group of young carolers stood in a semicircle, their mouths open, their eyes shining with joy.

WE WON'T JOIN THE CELEBRATION.

Laurie barely remembered her own childhood Christmases. Being a parent had obscured all that; what stuck in her memory was the excitement on the faces of her own kids, their contagious holiday pleasure. That was something Meg would never get to experience. Laurie assured her that it was okay to feel anger about that, and healthy to acknowledge and express her anger, much better than feeding it with denial.

The vow of silence forbade laughter as well as speech, but a few people forgot themselves and chuckled at the next slide, a house lit up like a Vegas bordello, the front yard crowded with random yuletide statuary—a nativity scene, a herd of reindeer, an inflatable Grinch, some elves and toy soldiers and angels and a plastic snowman, plus a sour, top-hatted fellow who must have been Ebenezer Scrooge.

"CHRISTMAS" IS A DISTRACTION. WE CAN NO LONGER AFFORD TO BE DISTRACTED.

Laurie had watched a lot of PowerPoints over the past six months, and had even helped to put a few of them together. They were an essential mode of communication within the G.R., a kind of portable, preacherless sermon. She understood the structure by now, knew that they always took a turn somewhere in the middle, away from the topic at hand to the only subject that really mattered.

"CHRISTMAS" BELONGS TO THE OLD WORLD.

The caption remained constant while a series of images flashed by, each one representing the world of the past: a Walmart superstore, a man on a riding lawn mower, the White House, the Dallas Cowboys cheerleaders, a rapper whose name Laurie didn't know, a pizza she couldn't bear to look at, a handsome man and an elegant woman sharing a candlelit dinner, a European cathedral, a jet fighter, a crowded beach, a mother nursing an infant.

THE OLD WORLD IS GONE. IT DISAPPEARED THREE YEARS AGO.

In G.R. PowerPoints, the Rapture was illustrated by photos from which particular individuals had been clumsily deleted. Some of the Photoshopped people were famous; others were of more local interest. One picture in this series had been taken by Laurie, a candid snapshot of Jill and Jen Sussman on an apple-picking expedition when they were ten years old. Jill was grinning and holding up a shiny red apple. The Jen-shaped space beside her was empty, a pale gray blob ringed by brilliant autumnal colors.

WE BELONG TO THE NEW WORLD.

Familiar faces filled the screen, one after the other, the entire, unsmiling membership of the Mapleton Chapter. Meg appeared near the end, along with the other Trainees, and Laurie squeezed her leg in congratulations.

WE ARE LIVING REMINDERS.

Two male Watchers stood on a train platform, staring at a well-dressed businessman who was trying to pretend they weren't there.

WE WON'T LET THEM FORGET.

A pair of female Watchers accompanied a young mother down the street as she pushed her baby in a stroller.

WE WILL WAIT AND WATCH AND PROVE
OURSELVES WORTHY.

The same two pictures reappeared, with the Watchers obliterated, conspicuous by their absence.

THIS TIME WE WON'T BE FORGOTTEN.

A clock, the second hand ticking.

IT WON'T BE LONG NOW.

A worried-looking man gazed at them from the wall. He was middle-aged, a bit puffy, not particularly handsome.

THIS IS PHIL CROWTHER. PHIL IS A MARTYR.

Phil's face was replaced by that of a younger man, bearded, with the burning eyes of a fanatic.

JASON FALZONE IS A MARTYR, TOO.

Laurie shook her head. Poor boy. He was hardly older than her own son.

WE ARE ALL PREPARED TO BE MARTYRS.

Laurie wondered how Meg was taking this, but couldn't read her expression. They'd talked about Jason's murder and understood the danger they were in every time they left the compound. Nonetheless, there was something about the word *martyr* that gave her chills.

WE SMOKE TO PROCLAIM OUR FAITH.

An image of a cigarette appeared on the wall, a white and tan cylinder floating over a stark black background.

LET US SMOKE.

A woman in the front row opened a fresh pack and passed it around the room. One by one, the women of Blue House lit up and exhaled, reminding themselves that time was running out, and that they weren't afraid.

~~~~~

THE GIRLS slept late, leaving Kevin to fend for himself for a good part of the morning. He listened to the radio for a while, but the cheerful holiday music grated on him, a depressing reminder of busier and happier Christmases past. It was better to turn it off, to read his newspaper and drink his coffee in silence, to pretend that it was just an ordinary morning.

Evan Balzer, he thought, the name floating up, unbidden, from the swamp of his middle-aged memory. *That's how he did it.*

Balzer was an old college friend, a quiet, watchful guy who'd lived on Kevin's floor sophomore year. He mostly kept to himself, but spring semester he and Kevin had the same Econ lecture class; they got into the habit of studying together a couple of nights a week, and then heading out for a few beers and a plate of wings when they were finished.

Balzer was a fun guy to hang out with—he was smart, wryly funny, full of opinions—but hard to get to know on a personal level. He talked fluently about politics and movies and music, but clammed up like a P.O.W. if anyone asked about his family or his life before college. It took months before he trusted Kevin enough to share a little about his past.

Some people have interesting crappy childhoods, but Balzer's was just plain crappy—a father who walked out when he was two, a mother who was a hopeless drunk but pretty enough that there was usually a man or two hanging around, though rarely for very long. Out of necessity, Balzer learned to take care of himself at an early age—if he didn't cook or shop or do the laundry, then it probably wasn't going to get done. Somehow he also managed to excel in school, getting good enough grades to earn a full scholarship at Rutgers, though he still had to bus tables at Bennigan's to keep himself afloat.

Kevin marveled at his friend's resilience, his ability to thrive in the face of adversity. It made him realize how lucky he'd been by comparison, growing up in a stable, reasonably happy family that had more than enough love and money to go around. He'd gone through the first two decades of his life taking it for granted that everything would always be okay, that he could only fall so far before someone would catch him and set him back on his feet. Balzer had never assumed that for a minute; he knew for a fact that it was possible to fall and just keep falling, that people like him couldn't afford a moment's weakness, a single big mistake.

Though they remained close until graduation, Kevin never succeeded in convincing Balzer to come home with him for Thanksgiving or Christmas. It was a shame, because Balzer had broken off contact with his mother—he claimed to not even know where she was living—and never had any plans of his own for the holidays, except to spend them alone in the tiny off-campus apartment he'd rented at the beginning of junior year, hoping to save a little money by cooking his own meals.

"Don't worry about me," he always told Kevin. "I'll be fine."

"What are you gonna do?"

"Nothing much. Just read, I guess. Watch TV. The usual."

"The usual? But it's Christmas."

Balzer shrugged. "Not if I don't want it to be."

On some level, Kevin admired Balzer's stubbornness, his refusal to accept what he saw as charity, even from a good friend. But it didn't make him feel any better about his inability to help. He'd be home, sitting at the crowded table with his big extended family, everyone talking and laughing and chowing down, when, out of nowhere, he'd be struck by a sudden, bleak vision of Balzer alone in his cell-like apartment, eating ramen noodles with the shades pulled down.

Balzer headed off to law school right after they graduated, and he and Kevin eventually fell out of touch. Sitting in his kitchen on Christmas morning, Kevin thought it might be interesting to look him up on Facebook, find out what he'd been up to for the past twenty years. Maybe he'd be married by now, maybe a father, living the full, happy life he'd been denied in his youth, allowing himself to love and be loved in return. Maybe he'd appreciate the irony if Kevin confessed that he was now the one hiding from the holidays, employing the Balzer Method with pretty good results.

But then the girls came down and he forgot about his old friend, because all at once it really did feel like Christmas, and they had things to do—stockings to empty and presents to unwrap. Aimee thought it would be nice to have some music, so Kevin turned the radio back on. The carols seemed fine this time, corny and familiar and somehow reassuring, the way they were supposed to be.

There weren't all that many presents under the tree—at least not like there used to be back when the kids were little and it took most of the morning to open them all—but the girls didn't seem to mind. They took their time with each gift, studying the box and removing the paper with great deliberation, as if you got extra points for neatness. They tried on the clothing right there in the living room, modeling shirts and sweaters over their pajama tops—in Aimee's case, a precariously thin sleeveless T-shirt—telling each other how great they looked, even making a big deal over stuff like warm socks and fuzzy slippers, having such a good time that Kevin wished he'd gotten a few more gifts for both of them, just to prolong the fun.

"Cool!" Aimee said, tugging on the woolen hat Kevin had found at Mike's Sporting Goods, the kind with goofy-looking earflaps that snapped beneath the chin. She wore it low on her forehead, almost level with her eyebrows, but it looked good on her all the same, just like everything else. "I can use one of these."

She got up from the couch, her arms unfolding as she approached, and gave him a thank-you hug. She did this after every gift, to the point where it had become a kind of joke, a rhythmic punctuation to the proceedings. It was a little easier for him now that her skimpy morning ensemble had been augmented by a new sweater, a scarf, the hat, and a pair of mittens.

"You guys are so sweet to me," she said, and for a second, Kevin thought she might start to cry. "I can't remember the last time I had such a nice Christmas."

Kevin got a few things, too, though only after suffering through the usual round of complaints about how hard it was to buy presents for a man his age, as if adult males were completely self-sufficient beings, as if a penis and a five o'clock shadow were all they would ever need to get by. Jill gave him a biography about the early years of Teddy Roosevelt, and Aimee got him a pair of spring-loaded hand exercisers, because she knew he liked to work out. The girls also presented him with two identical packages, dense little objects wrapped in silver paper. Inside the one from Jill was a novelty mug that proclaimed him #1 DAD.

"Wow," he said. "Thanks. I knew I was in the top ten, but I didn't think I'd made it all the way to number one."

Aimee's mug was exactly the same, except that this one was labeled WORLD'S BEST MAYOR.

"We should celebrate Christmas more often," he said. "It's good for my self-esteem."

The girls started cleaning up after that, gathering the used wrapping paper and discarded packaging, jamming the debris into a plastic garbage bag. Kevin pointed at the solitary gift under the tree, a little box tied with ribbon that looked like it might contain jewelry.

"What about that one?"

Jill looked up. There was a red adhesive bow plastered to her scalp, making her look like a large, troubled baby.

"It's for Mom," she said, watching him closely. "In case she stops by."

Kevin nodded, as if this made perfect sense to him.

"That's really thoughtful," he told her.

~~~~~

THEY RANG Gary's doorbell but no one answered. Meg shrugged and took a seat on the cold concrete stoop, content to wait in plain sight for her ex-fiancé to return from wherever he happened to be on Christmas morning. Laurie sat down beside her, doing her best to ignore the dull sense of dread that had plagued her since they'd set out from Ginkgo Street. She didn't want to be here, and she didn't want to go to the next stop on their itinerary, either.

Unfortunately, their instructions were clear. It was their job to visit their loved ones, to do what they could to disrupt the cozy rhythms and rituals of the holiday. Laurie could see the point of this in the grand scheme of things: If the G.R. had one essential mission, it was to resist the so-called Return to Normalcy, the day-to-day process of forgetting the Rapture, or, at the very least, of consigning it to the past, treating it as a part of the ongoing fabric of human history, rather than the cataclysm that had brought history to an end.

It wasn't that the G.R. had anything special against Christmas—they disliked holidays across the board—nor were they enemies of Jesus Christ, as many people mistakenly assumed. The Jesus issue was a little confusing, Laurie had to admit that. She'd struggled with it herself before joining, puzzled by the way the G.R. seemed to embrace so many elements of Christian theology—the Rapture and Tribulation, of course, but also the inherent sinfulness of humanity, and the certainty of the Final Judgment—while completely ignoring the figure of Jesus himself. Generally speaking, they were much more focused on God the Father, the jealous Old Testament deity who demanded blind obedience and tested the loyalty of his followers in cruelly inventive ways.

It had taken Laurie a long time to figure this out, and she still wasn't sure if she'd gotten it right. The G.R. wasn't big on spelling out its creed; it had no priests or ministers, no scripture, and no formal system of instruction. It was a lifestyle, not a religion, an ongoing improvisation rooted in the conviction that the post-Rapture world demanded a new way of living, free from the old, discredited forms—no more marriage, no more families, no more consumerism, no more politics, no more conventional religion, no more mindless entertainment. Those days were done. All that remained for humanity was to hunker down and await the inevitable.

It was a sunny morning, much colder out than it looked, Magazine Street as still and silent as a photograph. Though he supposedly earned a good salary right out of business school, Gary was still living like a student, sharing the top floor of a shabby two-family house with two other guys, both of whom also had girlfriends. Weekends were crazy there, Meg had explained, so many people having sex in such a small space. And if you didn't do it, if you weren't in the mood or whatever, you almost felt like you were violating the terms of the lease.

They must have sat on the porch for a half hour before they saw another soul, a crabby old guy out walking his shivering chihuahua. The man glared at them and muttered something that Laurie couldn't quite hear, though she was pretty sure it wasn't *Merry Christmas*. Until she'd joined the G.R., she'd never really understood just how rude people could be, how free they felt to abuse and insult total strangers.

A few minutes after that a car turned onto Magazine from Grapevine, a sleek dark vehicle that looked like a shrunken SUV. Laurie could sense Meg's excitement as it approached, and her disappointment as it rumbled past. She was all keyed up about seeing Gary, despite Laurie's many warnings not to expect too much from the encounter. Meg was going to have to learn for herself what Laurie had figured out over the summer—that it was better to leave well enough alone, to avoid unnecessary encounters with the people you'd left behind, to not keep poking at that sore tooth with the tip of your tongue. Not because you didn't love them anymore, but because you did, and because that love was useless now, just another dull ache in your phantom limb.

~~~~~

NORA HAD been training herself not to think too much about her kids. Not because she wanted to forget them—not at all—but because she wanted to remember them more accurately. For the same reason, she tried not to look too often at old photographs or videos. What happened in both cases was that you only remembered what you already knew, the same trusty handful of occasions and impressions. *Erin was so stubborn. Jeremy had a clown at his party. She had such fine flyaway hair. He sure liked applesauce.* After a while, these scraps hardened into a kind of official narrative that crowded out thousands of equally valid memories, shunting the losers to some cluttered basement storage area in her brain.

What she'd discovered recently was that these leftover memories were much more likely to surface if she wasn't straining to retrieve them, if they were simply allowed to emerge of their own accord in the normal course of the day. Biking was an especially fruitful activity in this regard, the perfect retrieval engine, her conscious mind occupied by a multitude of simple tasks—scanning the road, checking the speedometer, monitoring her breathing and the direction of the wind—the unconscious part left free to wander. Sometimes it didn't go far: There were rides when she just kept singing the same scrap of an old song over and over—*Shareef don't like it! Rockin' the Casbah, Rock the Casbah!*—or wondering why her legs felt so dead and heavy. But then there were those magical days when something just clicked, and all kinds of amazing stuff started popping into her head, little lost treasures from the past—Jeremy coming downstairs one morning in yellow pajamas that had fit the night before, but now seemed a full size too small; tiny Erin looking panicked, then delighted, then panicked again as she nibbled on her first sour cream and onion potato chip. The way his eyebrows turned lighter in the summer. The way her thumb looked after she'd been sucking it all night, pink and wrinkled, decades older than the rest of her. It was all there, locked in a vault, an immense fortune from which Nora could make only small, all-too-infrequent withdrawals.

She was supposed to go to her sister's to open presents and eat a late breakfast of omelettes and bacon, but she called Karen and told her to go ahead without her. She said she was a bit under the weather, but thought she'd be okay with a little extra sleep.

"I'll just meet you at Mom's this afternoon."

"You sure?" She could hear the suspicion in Karen's voice, her almost uncanny ability to sense concealment or evasion. She must be a formidable parent. "Is there anything I can do? You want me to come over?"

"I'll be fine," Nora assured her. "Just enjoy the day. I'll see you later, okay?"

~~~~~~~

SOMETIMES, WHEN she waited too long in the cold, Laurie drifted into a kind of fugue state, losing track of where she was and what she was doing. It was a defense mechanism, a surprisingly effective way of blocking out physical discomfort and anxiety, though also a bit scary, since it seemed like the first step on the road to freezing to death.

She must have spaced out like that on Gary's front stoop—they'd been sitting there for quite a while—because she didn't register the fact that a car had pulled up in front of the house until the people inside it were climbing out, by which point Meg was already in motion, heading down the steps and striding across the dead brown lawn with an urgency that was almost alarming after such a protracted interlude of calm.

The driver circled around the hood of the car—it was a sporty little Lexus, freshly washed and gleaming in the wan winter sunlight—and took his place at the side of the woman who'd just vacated the passenger seat. He was tall and handsome in his camel-hair overcoat, and Laurie's brain had thawed out just enough to recognize him as Gary, whose confident, smiling face she'd seen numerous times in Meg's Memory Book. The woman seemed vaguely familiar as well. Both of them stared at Meg with expressions that combined varying degrees of pity and astonishment, but when Gary finally spoke, all Laurie heard in his voice was a note of weary annoyance.

"What the hell are you doing here?"

True to her training, Meg remained silent. It would have been better if she had a cigarette in her hand, but neither one of them had been smoking when the car pulled up. That was Laurie's fault, a lapse of supervision.

"Did you hear me?" Gary's voice was louder now, as if he thought Meg might have developed a hearing problem. "I asked you a question."

His companion gave him a puzzled look. "You know she can't talk, right?"

"Oh, she can talk," Gary said. "She used to talk my fucking ear off."

Looking vaguely mortified, the young woman turned back to Meg. She was short and curvy, a bit unsteady on her stiletto heels. Laurie couldn't help admiring her coat, a shimmery blue parka with fur-lined cuffs and hood. The fur was probably synthetic, but it looked really warm.

"I'm sorry," the young woman told Meg. "I know this must be weird for you. Seeing us together."

Laurie leaned to the left, trying to get a look at Meg's face, but the angle wasn't right.

"Don't apologize to *her*," Gary snapped. "She's the one who should apologize."

"It started two weeks ago," the young woman continued, as if Meg had requested an explanation. "A bunch of us went to Massimo's and drank a lot of red wine, and I was too drunk to drive home. So Gary offered me a lift." She raised her eyebrows, as if the story told itself.

"I'm not sure if it's serious or anything. We're just kinda hanging out together. For now."

"Gina." Gary's voice was sharp with warning. "Don't do this. It's none of her business."

Gina, Laurie thought. *Meg's cousin. One of the bridesmaids.*

"Of course it's her business," Gina said. "You guys were together all those years. You were gonna get married."

Gary studied Meg with a disgusted expression.

"Look at her. I don't even know who that is."

"She's still Meg." Gina spoke so softly that Laurie could barely hear the words. "Don't be mean to her."

"I'm not being mean." Gary's expression softened a little. "I just can't stand to see her like this. Not today."

He gave his ex-fiancée a wide berth as he headed toward the house, as if he thought she might try to attack him, or at least block his way. Gina hesitated just long enough to shrug an apology, then set off after him. Neither one of them paid the slightest attention to Laurie as they trudged up the front steps, not a word, not even a glance in her direction.

After Gary and Gina went inside, Laurie lit a cigarette and headed across the lawn to join Meg, who was still standing with her back to the house, staring at the Lexus as if she were thinking about buying it. Laurie held out the cigarette, and Meg took it, sniffling quietly as she brought it to her lips. Laurie wished she could say a few words—*Nice going,* or *Good job*—to let Meg know how proud she was. But all she did was pat her on the shoulder, just once, very gently. She hoped that was enough.

〰〰〰

NORA HADN'T planned on going for a long ride. She was supposed to arrive at her mother's between one and two in the afternoon, a time-table that only allowed for a fifteen- or twenty-mile spin, half her usual distance, but hopefully enough to clear her head and get her heart pumping, maybe even burn off a few calories before the big meal. Besides, it was freezing, only in the mid-twenties according to the thermometer outside her kitchen window, hardly ideal conditions for a strenuous workout.

But the cold turned out to be less of an impediment than she'd anticipated. The sun was out, the roads were clear—snow and ice were the real dealbreakers for winter riding—and the wind wasn't all that stiff. She had high-tech gloves, neoprene shoe covers, and a polypropylene hood beneath her helmet. Only her face was exposed to the elements, and she could live with that.

She figured she'd turn around at the eight-mile mark, halfway out on the bike path, but when she got there she just kept going. It felt too good to be on the move, the pedals rising and falling beneath her feet, white vapor steaming from her mouth. So what if she was a little late to her mother's? There would be a big crowd—all her siblings and their families, some aunts and uncles and cousins—and they wouldn't even miss her. If anything, they'd be relieved. Without Nora around, they could laugh and open presents and compliment everyone else's kids without wondering if they'd inadvertently said something to hurt her feelings, without giving her those sad, knowing glances or making those tragic little sighs.

That was what made the holidays so exhausting. Not the callousness of her relatives, their inability to acknowledge her suffering, but precisely the opposite—their inability to forget it for even a second. They were always tiptoeing around her, so careful and considerate, so painfully sympathetic, as if she were dying of cancer or afflicted with some disfiguring disease, like her mother's aunt May—a pitiful figure from Nora's own childhood—whose face had been paralyzed into a permanent crooked grimace by Bell's palsy.

Be nice to Aunt May, her mother used to tell her. *She's not a monster.*

The dicey stretch of path beyond Route 23 was nearly empty today, no creeps or stray dogs in sight, no animal sacrifices or criminal activity, just the occasional rider traveling in the opposite direction, tossing her a comradely wave as they passed. It would have been close to idyllic if she hadn't had to pee so badly. During the warmer months, the county maintained a Porta-John at the end of the path—it was gross, barely tolerable in a pinch—but they took it away for the winter. Nora wasn't a big fan of squatting in the woods, especially when there wasn't a lot of greenery around to block the view, but there were days when you had no choice, and today was one of them. At least she found a Kleenex in the pocket of her windbreaker.

Before getting back on her bike, she dialed Karen's cell phone and was relieved to be sent straight to voice mail. Like a kid playing hooky, she coughed once or twice, then spoke in an artificially congested voice. She said she was feeling a little worse than before and didn't think it would be a good idea to leave the house, especially since whatever she had might be catching.

"I'm gonna make some tea and get back into bed," she said. "Tell everybody Merry Christmas for me."

The roads beyond the bike path were semirural, winding past isolated houses and the occasional small farm, corn stubble poking up from the frozen fields like the hairs on a leg that needed shaving. Nora didn't know where she was going, but she didn't mind getting lost. Now that she was off the hook for Christmas dinner, she didn't care if the ride lasted all day.

She wanted to be thinking about her kids, but for some reason, her mind kept returning to poor Aunt May. She'd been dead a long time, but Nora could still picture her with strange clarity. She used to sit quietly at family gatherings, her mouth slanted at a weird angle, her eyes swimming with desperation behind thick glasses. Every now and then she tried to talk, but nobody could understand a word she said. Nora remembered being coaxed into hugging her, and then given a piece of candy as a reward.

Is that who I am? she wondered. *Am I the new Aunt May?*

She rode for sixty-seven miles in all. When she finally got home, there were five messages blinking on her answering machine, but she figured they could wait. She headed upstairs, stripped off her clammy clothes—she was suddenly shivery—and took a long hot bath. While she soaked, she kept contorting her mouth so that the left side hung lower than the right, and trying to imagine how it would feel to live like that, your face permanently frozen, your voice garbled, everyone trying to be extra nice so you wouldn't feel like a monster.

THERE WAS something pathetic about watching *It's a Wonderful Life* all by yourself, but Kevin couldn't think of anything else to do. The Carpe Diem was closed; Pete and Steve were busy with their families. He gave a fleeting thought to phoning Melissa Hulbert, but decided it was a bad idea. She probably wouldn't be too thrilled to receive a halfhearted booty call on Christmas Day, especially since he hadn't tried to get in touch with her since their last ill-fated encounter, the night she'd spit on the Watcher.

The girls had left about an hour ago. The abruptness of their departure had startled him—they got a text and they were gone—but he couldn't say he blamed them for wanting to spend some time with their friends. They'd hung out with him all morning and most of the afternoon, and it had been a lot of fun. After they finished with the presents, Aimee had made chocolate chip pancakes and then they'd gone for a long walk around the lake. When they got home, they played three games of Yahtzee. So, really, he had nothing to complain about.

Except here he was, with the rest of the afternoon and all of the evening stretched out ahead of him, a vast expanse of solitude. It was incomprehensible how his once-crowded life had dwindled down to this, his marriage over, his son lost to the world, both his parents gone, his siblings scattered—brother in California, sister in Canada. A few relatives remained in the immediate area—Uncle Jack and Aunt Marie, a handful of cousins—but everybody just did their own thing. The Garvey clan was like the old Soviet Union, a once mighty power that had dissolved into a bunch of weak and cranky units.

This must be Kyrgyzstan, he thought.

On top of everything, he wasn't loving the movie. Maybe he'd seen it too many times, but the story seemed so labored, all that effort just to remind a good man that he was good. Or maybe Kevin was just feeling a little too much like George Bailey himself, with no guardian angel in sight. He kept flipping channels, searching for something else to watch and ending up right back where he started, repeating the cycle over and over until the doorbell rang, three harsh buzzes so sudden and thrilling that he rose a little too quickly from the couch and almost fainted. Before he could greet his visitors, he had to stop and close his eyes, giving himself a moment to absorb the shock of being upright.

~~~~~~

FOR A minute or two, Laurie couldn't think of anything except how good it felt to be out of the cold. Slowly, though, as her body warmed, the strangeness of being back home began to settle in. This was her house! It was so big and lovingly furnished, nicer than she'd allowed herself to remember. This soft couch she was sitting on—she'd picked it out at Elegant Interiors, anguishing for days over the swatches, trying to decide whether the gray-green worked better with the rug than the brick red. And that wide-screen LCD HD-TV—*It's a Wonderful Life* was on, of all things—they'd bought that at Costco a couple of months before the Rapture, thrilled by the lifelike clarity of its picture. They'd watched reports of the catastrophe on that very screen, the anchors visibly freaked out by what they were saying, the footage of traffic accidents and bewildered eyewitnesses playing over and over in a mind-numbing loop. And this man standing in front of them, grinning nervously, that was her husband.

"Wow," he was saying. "This is quite a surprise."

Kevin had seemed a bit flustered to find them standing on the front porch, but he'd recovered quickly, ushering them into the house as if they were invited guests, hugging Laurie in the hallway—she tried to avoid it, but it was impossible in that narrow space—and shaking Meg's hand, telling her how pleased he was to make her acquaintance.

"You guys look chilly," he observed. "You're not really dressed for the weather."

That was an understatement, Laurie thought. It was hard to find really warm clothes that also happened to be white. Pants and shirts and sweaters weren't a problem, but outerwear was another story. She felt lucky to have a white scarf she could wrap around her head, and a heavyweight cotton hoodie with an unobtrusive Nike swoosh on the pocket. But she needed better gloves—the cotton ones she had were ridiculously thin, the kind you wore to make a surprise inspection— and a pair of boots, or at least real shoes, something a little more substantial than the beat-up sneakers on her feet.

"You want something to eat?" Kevin said. "I can make coffee or tea or whatever. There's wine and beer, too, if you want. Feel free to help yourself. You know where everything is."

Laurie didn't respond to this offer, nor did she dare look at Meg. Of course they wanted something to eat; they were starving. But they couldn't say so, and they certainly couldn't help themselves. If he put some food in front of them, they would be more than happy to eat, but it would have to be his call, not theirs.

"Better not look too hard," he added as an afterthought. "We're not eating as healthy as we used to. I don't think you'd approve."

Laurie almost laughed. She would have been happy to devour a couple of hot dogs straight from the package to let him know where she stood these days on the subject of healthy eating. But Kevin didn't give her the chance. Instead of heading into the kitchen like a good host, he just sat down in the brown leather recliner Laurie had bought at Triangle Furniture, the chair she loved to read in on lazy weekend mornings, no lamp necessary, just the sunlight streaming in from the south-facing windows.

"You look good," he said, examining her with alarming candor. "I like the gray hair. It actually makes you look younger. Go figure."

Laurie felt herself blushing. She wasn't sure if she was embarrassed on her own account, or because Meg was sitting right next to her. Still, though, it was nice to receive a compliment. Kevin hadn't been as tight-lipped as some of her friends' husbands, especially in the early days of their marriage, but the praise had definitely gotten sparser in recent years.

"I'm going a little gray myself," he said, tapping himself on the side of the head. "I guess it goes with the territory."

It was true, Laurie realized, though she hadn't noticed the change until he pointed it out. *Distinguished,* she would have told him if she could. Like a lot of men of his generation, Kevin had seemed boyish long after he'd had any right to, and the gray hair—what little of it there was—added a welcome touch of gravity to his appearance.

"You lost a lot of weight," he continued, casting a wistful glance in the vicinity of his own belt buckle. "I've been working out, but I can't seem to get below one ninety."

Laurie had to make a conscious effort not to think too hard about his body. It was a little overwhelming seeing him up close after all this time, being confronted with his actual physical self, experiencing the subtle pride of ownership that had been one of the sweeter undercurrents of their marriage: *My husband's a good-looking man.* Not handsome exactly, but appealing in a broad-shouldered, friendly sort of way. He was wearing a gray zippered sweater that she used to borrow on rainy days, very roomy and soft to the touch.

"What I gotta do is cut out the late-night snacks. Microwave burritos and blueberry pie, crap like that. That's what's killing me."

Meg let out a soft groan, and Laurie glanced pointedly in the direction of the kitchen, but Kevin didn't take the hint. He was too distracted by the TV, Jimmy Stewart getting all worked up about something, stuttering and flailing his arms. He snatched the remote off the coffee table and hit the off button.

"I can't stand that movie," he muttered. "Remind me never to watch it again."

Without the TV going, the house seemed ominously quiet, almost funereal. The clock on the cable box said it was only twenty after four, but already the evening darkness was moving in, pressing up against the windows.

"Jill's not here," Kevin announced, though it wasn't really necessary. "She went out about an hour ago, with her friend Aimee. You know about Aimee, right? She's been living with us since the end of the summer. She's a good kid, but a little wild." Kevin chewed his lip, as if pondering a difficult question. "Jill's okay, I guess. But she's been having a tough year. She really misses you."

Laurie kept her face resolutely blank, not wanting to betray the relief she felt at her daughter's absence. Kevin she could deal with. He was a grown man, and she could count on him to behave like one, to accept the fact that their relationship had undergone a necessary and irrevocable change. But Jill was just a kid, and Laurie was still her mother, and that was a whole different thing. Kevin rose abruptly from the recliner.

"I'm gonna give her a call. She'll be really upset if she misses you."

He went into the kitchen to get the phone. As soon as he left, Meg pulled out her pad and scribbled **Bathroom?** She nodded gratefully when Laurie pointed toward the far end of the hall, and lost no time heading in that direction.

"No luck," Kevin announced upon his return, still holding the phone. "I left a message, but she doesn't always check. I know she'd like to see you."

They stared at each other. For some reason, things were a little more awkward with Meg out of the room. Air escaped from Kevin's mouth in a slow leak.

"I haven't heard from Tom. Not since summer. I'm a little worried about him." He waited a moment before continuing. "I'm worried about you, too. Especially after what happened last month. I hope you're being careful."

Laurie shrugged, trying to let him know she was okay, but the gesture felt more ambivalent than she'd meant it to. Kevin put his hand on her arm, a few inches above the elbow. There was nothing especially tender in the gesture, but Laurie's skin started to hum beneath his touch. It had been a long time.

"Look," he said. "I don't know why you're here, but it's really good to see you."

Laurie nodded, trying to convey the sentiment that it was good to see him, too. His hand was moving now, making a tentative up-and-down motion on her arm, not quite purposeful enough to qualify as a caress. But Kevin was one of those men who didn't go in for a lot of casual contact. He rarely touched her unless he was thinking about sex.

"Why don't you stay here tonight?" he said. "It's Christmas. You should be with your family. Just for tonight. See how it feels."

Laurie cast a worried glance in the direction of the bathroom, wondering what was taking Meg so long.

"Your friend can stay, too," Kevin went on. "I can make up the bed in the guest room if she wants. She can go back in the morning."

Laurie wondered what that meant: *She can go back in the morning.* Did that mean she herself would remain? Was he asking her to move back home? She shook her head, sadly but firmly, trying to make it clear that she wasn't here for a conjugal visit.

"Sorry," he said, finally getting the hint and removing that distracting hand from her arm. "I'm just feeling kinda down tonight. It's nice to have some company."

Laurie nodded. She felt sorry for him, she really did. Kevin had always loved the holidays, all that mandatory family togetherness.

"This is a little frustrating," he told her. "I wish you would talk to me. I'm your husband. I'd like to hear your voice."

Laurie felt her resolve weakening. She was on the verge of opening her mouth, saying something like, *I know, it's ridiculous,* undoing eight months of hard work in a single moment of weakness, but before she could do it, the toilet flushed. A moment after that, the bathroom door swung open. And then, just as Meg came into view, smiling an apology, the phone buzzed in Kevin's hand. He flipped it open without checking the display.

"Hello?" he said.

~~~~~~

NORA WAS so startled by the sound of his voice that she couldn't bring herself to speak. She'd somehow convinced herself, with the help of two glasses of wine on a mostly empty stomach, that Kevin wouldn't be home, that she could just leave a brief message on his voice mail and make a clean getaway.

"Hello?" he said again, sounding more confused than irritated. "Who's there?"

She was tempted to hang up, or pretend that she'd dialed the wrong number, but then she got hold of herself. *I'm a grown woman,* she thought, *not a twelve-year-old making a prank call.*

"It's Nora," she said. "Nora Durst. We danced at the dance."

"I remember." His tone was a little flatter than she might have hoped, a bit guarded. "How are you?"

"I'm okay. How about you?"

"Fine," he said, but not like he meant it. "Just, uh, enjoying the holiday."

"Same here," she said, but not like she meant it, either. "So . . . ?"

His not-quite-question hung there for a few seconds, long enough for Nora to take a sip of wine and mentally review the speech she'd rehearsed in the bathtub: *You want to go out for coffee sometime? I'm free most afternoons.* She had it all figured out. Afternoons were low-pressure, and so was coffee. If you met for coffee in the afternoon, you could pretend it wasn't even a date.

"I was wondering," she said. "You want to go to Florida?"

"Florida?" He sounded just as surprised as she was.

"Yeah." The word had just tumbled out of her mouth, but it was the right one, the one she'd meant. She wanted Florida, not coffee. "I don't know about you, but I could use some sun. It gets so depressing up here."

"And you want me to . . . ?"

"If you want to," she told him. "If you're free."

"Wow." He didn't sound unhappy. "What kinda time frame are we talking about?"

"I don't know. Is tomorrow too soon?"

"The day after would be better." He paused, then said, "Listen, I can't really talk right now. Can I call you later?"

~~~~~

KEVIN TRIED to look nonchalant as he pocketed the phone, but it was hard with Laurie and her friend staring at him with such frank curiosity, as if he owed them an explanation.

"Just an acquaintance," he muttered. "No one you know."

Laurie clearly didn't believe him, but what was he supposed to say? *A woman I barely know asked me to go to Florida and I think I just said yes?* He didn't quite believe it himself. He'd only been off the phone for a few seconds and already it seemed like there must be some kind of mistake—an elaborate misunderstanding, or possibly even a practical joke. What he needed to do was call Nora back and get a few things clarified, but he couldn't do that until he was alone, and he had no idea how long he was going to have to wait for that. Laurie and her sidekick looked like they'd be happy to stand there and stare at him for the rest of the evening.

"So." He clapped his hands softly, trying to change the subject. "Is anybody hungry?"

~~~~~

LAURIE WALKED slowly toward Main Street, lagging a step or two behind Meg, enjoying the unfamiliar sluggishness that comes with a full belly. The meal hadn't been fancy—there were no leftovers from an afternoon feast, the way there should have been on Christmas night—but it was delicious nonetheless. They'd devoured everything Kevin put in front of them—baby carrots, bowls of Campbell's Chicken Noodle Soup sprinkled with oyster crackers, salami and American cheese sandwiches on white bread—and then topped it off with a bag of Hershey's Kisses and a cup of fresh hot coffee.

They were approaching the corner when she heard footsteps, and Kevin's voice calling her name. She turned to see him jogging down the middle of the street, no coat or hat, waving one arm in the air as if he were trying to flag down a taxi.

"You forgot this," he said when he caught up. There was a little box in his hand, the orphaned present she'd noticed under the tree. "I mean, I did. It's for you. From Jill."

Laurie knew that much just from looking at it. A gift from Kevin would have been sloppier, a lumpy, slapdash affair with as few frills as possible. But the box he was holding had been wrapped with care, the paper taut, the corners sharp, the ribbon curled between scissors and thumb.

"She would've killed me," he added, breathing harder than she would've expected after such a short run.

Laurie accepted the gift, but made no move to open it. She could see that he wanted to stay and watch, but she didn't think it was a good idea. They'd already had enough of a family Christmas, way more than was good for them.

"All right," he said, taking the hint. "I'm glad I caught you. And thanks again for coming."

He started for home, and they continued on to Main Street, stopping beneath a streetlight near Hickory Road to open the present. Meg stood close, watching with an eager expression as Laurie methodically undid her daughter's work, pulling off the ribbon, breaking the tape, stripping off the paper. She guessed that the box contained jewelry, but when she removed the top, what she found was a cheap plastic lighter resting on a bed of cotton. Nothing fancy, just a red Bic disposable with three words painted on the barrel in what must have been Wite-Out.

Don't Forget Me.

Meg took out her cigarettes and they each lit up, taking turns with the new lighter. It was a really sweet gift, and Laurie couldn't help crying a little, picturing her daughter at the kitchen table, inscribing that neat, heartfelt message with a tiny brush. It was an object to treasure, full of sentimental value, which is why she had no choice but to kneel down and drop it into the first storm drain they saw, poking it through the grate like a coin into a slot. It fell for what seemed like a long time, and hardly made a sound when it landed.

Part *Four*

BE MY VALENTINE

A BETTER-THAN-AVERAGE GIRLFRIEND

THE COUNCIL CHAMBERS WERE PACKED for the January town meeting. Kevin had been home from Florida for two weeks by then, so he was a little surprised by the number of comments he received about his tan.

"Looking good, Mr. Mayor!"

"Little fun in the sun, huh?"

"Were you near Boca? My uncle's got a place there."

"I could use a vacation!"

Was I that pale? he wondered, taking his seat at the center of the long table at the front of the room, between Councilman DiFazio and Councilwoman Herrera. Or were people responding to something deeper than the ruddy glow of his skin, an inner change that they couldn't otherwise account for?

In any case, Kevin was delighted by the healthy turnout, a vast improvement on December's dismal showing, which had consisted of no more than a dozen of the usual suspects, most of them tightwad senior citizens opposed to all government spending—federal, state, and local—except for the Social Security and Medicare they depended on to get by. The only attendee under forty had been the reporter for the *Messenger,* a pretty girl fresh out of college who kept nodding off over her laptop.

He gaveled the meeting to order at seven on the dot, not bothering with the customary five-minute delay to accommodate the stragglers. He wanted to stick to the schedule for once, keep things moving, and adjourn as close to nine as possible. He'd told Nora to expect him around then, and didn't want to keep her waiting.

"Welcome," he said. "It's good to see you all here, especially on such a cold winter night. As most of you know, I'm Mayor Garvey and these good-looking folks up here on either side of me are your town council."

There was a polite smattering of applause, and then Councilman DiFazio rose to lead them all in the Pledge of Allegiance, which they recited in a rushed, vaguely embarrassed mumble. Kevin asked everyone to remain standing for a moment of silence in honor of Ted Figueroa, the recently deceased brother-in-law of Councilwoman Carney and a prominent figure in the world of Mapleton youth sports.

"Many of us knew Ted as a legendary coach and guiding force behind the Saturday Morning Basketball Program, which he co-directed for two decades, long after his own kids had grown up. He was a dedicated, generous man, and I know I speak for all of us when I say he'll be sorely missed."

He hung his head and counted slowly to ten, which someone had once told him was the rule of thumb for a moment of silence. Personally, he hadn't been all that crazy about Ted Figueroa—the guy was an asshole, in fact, an ultra-competitive coach who cherry-picked the best players for his own teams and almost always won the championship—but this wasn't the time or place for honesty about the dead.

"All right," he said, after they'd taken their seats. "Our first order of business is approval of the minutes from the December meeting. Is there a motion to approve?"

Councilman Reynaud made the motion. Councilwoman Chen seconded.

"All in favor?" Kevin asked. The ayes were unanimous. "The motion carries."

~~~~~

IN HER younger days, during the all-too-brief window of freedom between her first kiss and her engagement to Doug, Nora had come to think of herself as a top-notch girlfriend. At her current remove—half a lifetime and another world away—she found it difficult to reconstruct the origins of this belief. It was possible that she'd read an article in *Glamour* on "Ten Essential Girlfriend Skills" and realized that she'd mastered eight of them. Or maybe she'd taken "The Ultimate Good Girlfriend Quiz" in *Elle* and scored in the top category: *You're a Keeper!* But it was just as likely that the habit of self-esteem was so deeply ingrained in her psyche that it simply hadn't occurred to her to think otherwise. After all, Nora was pretty, she was smart, her jeans fit well, her hair was straight and shiny. Of course she was a better girlfriend than most. She was a better everything than most.

This conviction was such an integral part of her self-image that she'd actually spoken it out loud during a mortifying breakup argument with her favorite college boyfriend. Brian was a charismatic philosophy major whose library pallor and pudgy waistline—he cultivated a European disdain for exercise—didn't detract in the least from his brainy appeal. He and Nora had been a serious couple for most of sophomore year—they referred to themselves as "best friends and soul mates"—until Brian decided, upon his return from Spring Break, that they should start seeing other people.

"I don't want to see anyone else," she told him.

"That's fine," he said. "But what if I do?"

"Then it's over between us. I'm not gonna share you."

"I'm sorry to hear that. Because I'm already seeing someone."

"What?" Nora was genuinely baffled. "Why would you do that?"

"What do you mean? Why does anyone see anyone?"

"I mean, why would you need to?"

"I don't understand the question."

"I'm a really good girlfriend," she told him. "You know that, don't you?"

He studied her for a few seconds, almost as if he were seeing her for the first time. There was something disconcertingly impersonal in his gaze, a kind of scientific detachment.

"You're okay," he conceded, a bit grudgingly. "Definitely above average."

After she graduated, this story became one of her favorite college anecdotes. She told it so much that it eventually became a running gag in her marriage. Whenever she did something thoughtful—picked up Doug's shirts at the cleaners, cooked him an elaborate dinner for no apparent reason, gave him a back rub when he came home from work—he would scrutinize her for a moment or two, stroking his chin like a philosophy major.

"It's true," he'd say, with an air of mild astonishment. "You really are a better-than-average girlfriend."

"Damn right," she'd reply. "I'm in the fifty-third percentile."

The joke seemed a little less funny these days, or maybe just funny in a different way, now that she was trying to be Kevin Garvey's girlfriend and doing such a crappy job of it. Not because she didn't like him—that wasn't the problem at all—but because she couldn't remember how to play a role that had once been second nature. What did a girlfriend say? What did she do? It felt a lot like her honeymoon in Paris, when she suddenly realized that she couldn't speak a word of French, even though she'd studied the language for all four years of high school.

It's so frustrating, she told Doug. *I used to know this stuff.*

She wanted to say the same thing to Kevin, to let him know that she was just a little rusty, that one of these days it would all come back to her.

Je m'appelle Nora. Comment vous appellez-vous?

I'm a really good girlfriend.

~~~~~~

COUNCIL MEETINGS were a bit like church, Kevin thought, a familiar sequence of rituals—Appointments, Resignations and Retirements, Announcements ("Congratulations to Brownie Troop 173, whose second annual gingerbread cookie fund-raiser netted over three hundred dollars for Fuzzy Amigos International, a charity that sends stuffed animals to impoverished indigenous children in Ecuador, Bolivia, and Peru . . ."), Proclamations ("February twenty-fifth is hereby proclaimed to be Dine Out in Mapleton Day!"), Permit Applications, Budgetary Resolutions, Committee Reports, and Pending Ordinances—that was both tedious and oddly comforting at the same time.

They moved through the agenda at a pretty good clip—the only speed bumps were the committee reports on Buildings and Grounds (too much detail on the paving contract selection process for municipal lot #3) and Public Safety (an evasive summary of the stalled investigation into the Falzone murder, followed by extensive discussion of the need for more nighttime police presence in and around Greenway Park)—and managed to conclude official business a little ahead of schedule.

"All right," Kevin told the audience. "It's your turn. The floor's open for Public Comment."

In theory, Kevin was eager to hear directly from his constituents. He said so all the time: "We're here to serve you. And we can't do that if we don't know what's on your mind. The most important job we can do is listen to your concerns and criticisms, and find innovative, cost-effective ways of addressing them." He liked to think of the Public Comment period as high school civics in action—self-government on a truly intimate scale, a face-to-face dialogue between the voters and the people they'd elected, democracy as the founders had intended it.

In practice, though, Public Comment was usually a bit of a freak show, a forum for cranks and monomaniacs to air their petty grievances and existential laments, most of which fell far outside the purview of municipal government. One of the regular speakers felt the need to provide her fellow citizens with monthly updates on a complicated billing dispute she was having with her health insurance provider. Another felt passionately about the abolition of Daylight Saving Time within the borders of Mapleton, an admittedly unorthodox move that he hoped would inspire other towns and states to follow suit. A frail elderly man frequently expressed his unhappiness with the poor delivery service provided by the *Daily Journal,* a newspaper that had ceased publication more than twenty years ago. For a while the council had tried to screen the speakers, barring those whose comments failed to address "relevant local issues," but this policy caused so many hurt feelings that it was quickly abandoned. Now they were back to the old system, informally known as "One Nut, One Speech."

The first person to address the January meeting was a young father from Rainier Road who complained about the speeding cars that used his street as a cut-through during evening rush hour, and wondered why the police were so lax in enforcing the traffic laws.

"What's it gonna take for you people to do something?" he asked. "Is some little kid gonna have to die?"

Councilwoman Carney, chair of the Public Safety Committee, assured the man that the police were planning a major traffic safety initiative for the summer driving season, a campaign that would include both a public information component and a robust enforcement component. In the meantime, she would personally ask Chief Rogers to keep an eye on Rainier Road and the surrounding streets at evening rush hour.

The next speaker was a friendly-looking middle-aged woman on crutches who wanted to know why so many sidewalks in Mapleton weren't properly shoveled after snowstorms. She herself had slipped on a patch of ice on Watley Terrace and had torn her ACL.

"Snow removal is mandatory in Stonewood Heights," she pointed out. "And it's a lot safer to walk there in wintertime. Why don't we do something like that here?"

Councilman DiFazio explained that hearings had been held on this very subject on three separate occasions that he could remember. Each time, large numbers of senior citizens had testified in opposition to any change in the law, for both health and financial reasons.

"We're kind of in a box here," he said. "It's a damned-if-you-do, damned-if-you-don't situation."

"I'll tell you what I'd like to see," Kevin interjected. "I'd like to compile some kind of registry of people who need help shoveling, and maybe share that with the high school volunteer office. That way, kids could get community service credit for doing something that actually needs to be done."

Several council members liked this idea, and Councilwoman Chen, chair of the Education Committee, agreed to follow up with the high school.

Things got a little more heated when the next speaker—an intense young man with deep-set eyes and a patchy beard—took the floor. He identified himself as the chef/owner of a recently opened vegan restaurant called Purity Café, and said he wanted to go on record protesting the unfair grade his establishment had received from the Health Inspector.

"It's ridiculous," he said. "Purity Café is spotless. We don't handle meat, eggs, or dairy, which are the main sources of food-borne illnesses. Everything we serve is fresh and lovingly prepared in a brand-new, state-of-the-art kitchen. But we get a B and Chicken Quick gets an A? *Chicken Quick?* Are you kidding me? You ever hear of salmonella? And Chumley's Steakhouse? *Really?* Have you ever seen the kitchen at Chumley's Steakhouse? Are you actually gonna look me in the eye and tell me it's cleaner than the Purity Café? That's a joke. Something doesn't smell right, and you can bet it's not the food in my restaurant."

Kevin wasn't crazy about the chef's condescending tone or his misguided decision to criticize his competitors—it definitely wasn't the way to win friends and influence people in a small town—but he had to admit that a grade of A for Chicken Quick seemed a bit improbable. Laurie had made him stop going there years ago, after she found a coin-sized battery in a container of garlic sauce. When she brought it back to show the owner, he laughed and said, *So that's where it went.*

Bruce Hardin, Mapleton's longtime health inspector, asked for permission to respond directly to the chef's "reckless allegations." Bruce was a hefty guy in his mid-fifties who had lost his wife in the Sudden Departure. He didn't seem especially vain, but it was hard to account for the disconcerting contrast between his dark brown hair and his silver-gray mustache without factoring in a certain amount of L'Oreal for Men. Speaking with the bland authority of a veteran bureaucrat, he pointed out that his reports were a matter of public record and that they usually contained photographs documenting each cited violation. Anyone who wished to examine his report on the Purity Café or any other food purveyor was welcome to do so. He was confident that his work could withstand the strictest scrutiny. Then he turned and stared at the bearded chef.

"I've served in this position for twenty-three years," he said, with an audible tremor in his voice. "And this is the first time my integrity has ever been questioned."

Backtracking a bit, the chef insisted that he hadn't questioned anyone's integrity. Bruce said that wasn't how it sounded to him, and that it was cowardly to try to deny it. Kevin intervened before things got out of hand, suggesting that it might be more constructive for the two of them to sit down in a calmer setting and have a forthright discussion about measures the Purity Café might take to improve its grade during the next inspection period. He added that he'd heard great things about the vegan restaurant and considered it a valuable addition to the town's eclectic roster of eateries.

"I'm not a vegetarian by any means," he said, "but I'm looking forward to eating there soon. Maybe lunch next Wednesday?" He glanced at the council members. "Who wants to join me?"

"You buying?" Councilman Reynaud quipped, drawing an appreciative chuckle from the crowd.

Kevin checked his watch before calling on the next speaker. It was already a quarter to nine, and there were at least ten people with their hands in the air, including Daylight Savings Guy and the gentleman who never got his newspaper.

"Wow," he told them. "Looks like we're just getting warmed up."

～～～

FOR SOME reason, she was always a little surprised to find Kevin on her doorstep, even when she was expecting him. There was just something a little too normal and reassuring about the whole situation, a big, friendly man pressing a brown paper bag into her hands, the neck of a wine bottle poking out.

"Sorry," he told her. "The council meeting ran late. Everybody had to put their two cents in."

Nora opened the wine and he told her all about it, in a lot more detail than she required. She did her best to look alert and interested, nodding at what seemed like the appropriate junctures, supplying the occasional comment or question to keep things moving along.

A good girlfriend is a good listener, she reminded herself.

But she was just pretending, and she knew it. In her former life, Doug used to sit across this very table and try her patience in a similar way, with long-winded soliloquies about whatever deal he happened to be working on at the moment, filling her in on the arcane legal and financial details of the transaction, thinking out loud about the various stumbling blocks that might arise, and what he might do to overcome them. But no matter how bored she was, she always understood that Doug's work *mattered* to her on a personal level, that it would have consequences for their family, and that she needed to pay attention. As much as she appreciated Kevin's company, she couldn't quite convince herself that she needed to care about the intricacies of the building code or a deadline extension for pet licenses.

"Is that just for dogs?" she wondered.

"Cats, too."

"So you're waiving the late fee?"

"Technically, we're extending the registration period."

"What's the difference?"

"We'd rather encourage compliance," he explained.

⁓⁓⁓

THEY SAT together in front of the flat-screen TV, Kevin's arm around Nora's shoulder, his fingers toying with her fine dark hair. She didn't object to being touched like that, but she gave no sign of enjoying it, either. Her attention was riveted to the screen, which she studied with an air of brooding intensity, as if *SpongeBob* were a Swedish art film from the 1960s.

He was happy enough to watch it with her, not because he enjoyed the show—he found it shrill and peculiar—but because it gave him an excuse to finally stop talking. He'd been babbling for too long about the council meeting—going on and on about overruns in the snow removal budget, the wisdom of replacing downtown parking meters with a ticket machine, etcetera, etcetera—just to spare them the awkwardness of sitting in prolonged silence like an old married couple with nothing left to say.

What made it so maddening was that they barely knew each other, even after all the time they'd spent together on vacation. There was still so much left to discover, so many questions he wanted to ask, if only she would let him. But she'd made it clear in Florida that the personal stuff was off-limits. She wouldn't talk about her husband or her kids, or even about her life before that. And he'd seen how she'd tensed up the few times he'd tried telling her about his own family, the way she'd winced and looked away, as if a cop were shining a flashlight in her eyes.

At least in Florida they'd been in an unfamiliar environment, spending most of their time outdoors, where it was easy to break the silence with a simple exchange about the temperature of the ocean, or the beauty of the sunset, or the fact that a pelican had just flown by. Back here in Mapleton, there was none of that. They were always inside, always at her house. Nora wouldn't go to the movies, to a restaurant, or even to the Carpe Diem for a nightcap. All they ever did was make labored small talk and watch *SpongeBob*.

She wouldn't even tell him about that. He understood that it was a rite of remembrance, and was touched that she let him be part of it, but he would've liked to know a little more about what the show meant to her, and what she wrote in her notebook when it was over. But apparently *SpongeBob* was none of his business, either.

~~~~~

NORA DIDN'T want to be like this, distant and shut down. She wanted to be the way she'd been in Florida, openhearted and alive, free with her body and spirit. Those five days had passed like a dream, both of them drunk on sunshine and adrenaline, perpetually amazed to find themselves together in the unfamiliar heat, liberated from the prison of their daily routines. They walked and they biked and they flirted and they swam in the ocean, and when they ran out of things to talk about, they had another drink, or sat in the Jacuzzi, or read a few pages of the thrillers they'd bought at the airport bookstore. In the late afternoons, they split up for a few hours, retiring to their separate rooms for a shower and a nap before reconvening for dinner.

She'd invited him back to her room the very first night. After a bottle of wine at dinner and a giddy makeout session on the beach, it seemed like the polite thing to do. She wasn't nervous taking her clothes off, didn't ask him to turn out the light. She just stood there naked, soaking up his approval. Her skin felt like it was glowing.

What do you think? she asked.

Nice collarbones, he said. *Pretty good posture, too.*

Is that all?

Come to bed and I'll tell you about the back of your knees.

She climbed in, snuggling against him. His torso was a pale slab, reassuringly solid. The first time she'd hugged him, it had felt like she was embracing a tree.

What about the back of my knees?

Honestly?

Yeah.

His hand wandered down the back of her thigh.

They're a little clammy.

She laughed and he kissed her and she kissed him back and that was it for the conversation. The only hitch came a few minutes later, when he tried to enter her and discovered she was too dry. She apologized, said she was out of practice, but he shushed her, licking his way down the center of her body, moistening her with his tongue. He took his time, letting her know it was all right to relax, coaxing her along an unfamiliar path until she stopped worrying about where it was leading and realized with a soft cry that she was already there, that something had loosened inside of her and something warm had come leaking out. When she caught her breath, she crawled down the bed and returned the favor, not thinking once about Doug or Kylie as she took him in her mouth, not thinking about anything at all until it was over, until he finally stopped whimpering and she was sure she'd swallowed every drop.

~~~~~

KEVIN FELT a brief flutter of suspense when the show was over and Nora closed her notebook.

"Excuse me." She covered her mouth, politely stifling a yawn. "I'm a little tired."

"Me, too," he admitted. "It's been a long day."

"It's so cold out." She gave a sympathetic shudder. "I'm sorry you have to go."

"I don't *have* to," he reminded her. "I'd love to stay here. I've been missing you."

Nora gave this some thought.

"Pretty soon," she told him. "I just need a little more time."

"We don't have to do anything. We could just keep each other company. Just talk until we fall asleep."

"I'm sorry, Kevin. I'm really not up for it."

Of course you are, he wanted to tell her. *Don't you remember what it was like? How could you not be up for that?* But he knew it was hopeless. The moment you started pleading your case, you'd already lost it.

She walked him to the door and kissed him good night, a chaste but lingering send-off that felt like an apology and a rain check at the same time.

"Can I call you tomorrow?" he asked.

"Sure," she said. "Call me tomorrow."

~~~~~

NORA LOCKED the door and carried the wineglasses to the sink. Then she went upstairs and got ready for bed.

I'm a terrible girlfriend, she thought as she brushed her teeth. *I don't know why I even bother.*

It was embarrassing, knowing that it was all her fault, that she'd volunteered for the position and misled Kevin into giving her the job. She was the one who'd invited him to Florida, after all, the one who'd managed to impersonate a functional, relatively cheerful human being for five days. By the end of the vacation, she'd almost started to believe that she actually *was* a functional, reasonably cheerful human being—the kind of person who might hold hands with another person under the table, or feed that other person little forkfuls of dessert—so she could hardly blame him for sharing in that misconception, or feeling confused and betrayed when she took it all back.

But she wasn't that person, not here in Mapleton anyway, not even close, and there was no use hiding from the truth. She had no love to give Kevin or anyone else, no joy or energy or insight. She was still broken, still missing some crucial parts. This knowledge had almost crushed her when she got back home, the unsupportable weight of her own existence, a lead-lined cape draped across her frail shoulders. *Welcome home, Nora.* It seemed so much heavier than she remembered, so much more oppressive, which was apparently the price you paid for sneaking out from under it for a few days. *Did you have a nice trip?*

THE OUTPOST

ON A WINDLESS MORNING IN late January, with light snow sifting down, Laurie and Meg walked from Ginkgo Street to their new quarters on Parker Road, a quiet residential enclave on the eastern edge of Greenway Park.

Outpost 17 was small, but nicer than Laurie had expected, a dark blue Cape Cod, dormered, with white trim around the windows. Instead of a concrete path, a walkway of clay-colored paving stones led to the main entrance. The only thing she didn't like was the front door itself, which looked a little too ornate for the rest of the house, gleaming brown wood with an elongated oval of smoked decorative glass cut into it, the kind of thing you'd expect to see on a McMansion in Stonewood Heights, not a modest Mapleton dwelling like this one.

"It's cute," Meg whispered.

"Could be a lot worse," Laurie agreed.

They liked it even better once they saw the inside. The downstairs was cozy without feeling cramped, enlivened by lots of nice little touches—a gas fireplace in the living room, area rugs with bold geometric designs, comfortable mix-and-match furniture. The high point was the renovated kitchen, a bright open space with stainless steel appliances, a restaurant-quality stove, and a window over the sink that looked out on a soothing vista of wooded parkland, the bare tree limbs frosted with a thin layer of white powder. Laurie could easily imagine her old self standing at the soapstone counter on a weekend afternoon, chopping vegetables while NPR murmured in the background.

The tour was guided by their new housemates, a pair of middle-aged men who'd answered the door with homemade name tags affixed to their shirts. "Julian" was tall and a bit stooped, with round, wire-framed glasses and a pointy nose that seemed to sniff inquisitively at the air. His face was clean-shaven, an anomaly in the G.R. "Gus" was a stocky, red-haired guy with a ruddy complexion; his beard was neatly trimmed, generously flecked with gray.

Welcome, he wrote on a communication pad. **We've been waiting for you.**

Laurie felt uneasy, but did her best to ignore it. She'd known the outposts could be coed, but hadn't anticipated anything quite so intimate, two men and two women sharing a small house on the edge of the woods. But if that was the assignment, then so be it. She understood what an honor it was to be selected for the Neighborhood Settlement Program—it was at the heart of the G.R.'s long-term expansion plans—and wanted to prove herself worthy of the trust that had been placed in her by the leadership, who were undoubtedly doing the best they could with the resources at their disposal.

Besides, she and Meg would have the whole second floor to themselves—two small bedrooms and a shared bathroom—so privacy shouldn't be a problem. Meg chose the pink room overlooking the street; Laurie took the yellow one with the park view, which had probably belonged to a teenager. The bed—it looked like it came from IKEA—was built low to the floor, a thin, futon-style mattress resting inside a frame of blond wood. The walls were bare, but you could see the empty spaces where some posters had recently hung, three rectangles slightly brighter than the space that surrounded them.

She'd only brought one suitcase—all her worldly belongings—and got unpacked in a matter of minutes. It felt anticlimactic somehow—more like checking into a hotel than settling into a new home—almost enough to make her nostalgic for the hectic moving days of her previous life: the weeks of preparation, the boxes and the tape and the markers, the big truck pulling up, the anxiety of watching your whole life disappear into its maw. And then the reverse peristalsis on the other end, all those boxes coming back out, the thud when they landed on the floor, the shriek when you ripped them open. The weird letdown of a new house, that nagging sense of dislocation that feels like it'll never go away. But at least you knew in your gut that something momentous had happened, that one chapter in your life had ended and another had begun.

A year, she used to say. *It takes a year to really feel at home. And sometimes longer than that.*

After she'd placed her clothes in the chest of drawers—also blond, also IKEA—she stayed on her knees for a long time, not praying, just thinking, trying to get her mind around the fact that she lived here now, that this place was home. It helped to know that Meg was nearby, just a few steps away. Not quite as close as in Blue House, where they'd shared a room, but close enough, closer than she could reasonably have hoped for.

. . .

AS A general rule, friendships were discouraged within the G.R. The organization was structured to prevent people from spending too much time together or relying too much on specific individuals for their social sustenance. In the Ginkgo Street Compound, members lived in large groups that were frequently reshuffled; jobs were rotated on a regular basis. Watchers were paired up by lottery and rarely worked with the same partner twice in a single month. The point was to strengthen the connection between the individual and the group as a whole, not between one individual and another.

This policy made sense to Laurie, at least in theory. People were extremely vulnerable when they joined the G.R. After expending so much energy tearing themselves away from their old lives, they were dazed and exhausted and deeply vulnerable. Without proper guidance, it was all too easy for them to lapse into familiar patterns, to unwittingly re-create the relationships and behavior patterns they'd left behind. But if they were allowed to do that, they'd miss out on the very thing they'd come for: a chance to start over, to strip away the false comforts of friendship and love, to await the final days without distractions or illusions.

The main exception to this policy was the highly charged relationship between Trainer and Trainee, which the organization tended to view as a necessary evil, a statistically effective but emotionally perilous strategy for easing new members into the fold. The problem wasn't so much the formation of an intense, exclusive bond between the two individuals involved—that was the whole point—as it was the trauma of dissolving this bond, of separating two people who had essentially become a unit.

It was the Trainer's job to prepare the Trainee for this eventuality. From the very beginning, Laurie had stuck to the protocol, reminding Meg on a daily basis that their partnership was temporary, that it would come to an end on January 15th—Graduation Day—at which point Meg would become a full-fledged member of the Mapleton Chapter of the Guilty Remnant. From then on, the two of them would be colleagues, not friends. They would treat each other with common courtesy—nothing more, nothing less—and strictly adhere to their vows of silence in each other's company.

She'd tried her best, but it hadn't done either of them much good. As the end of Meg's probation approached, they grew increasingly agitated and depressed. There were several nights that ended with one or both of them in tears, lamenting the unfairness of the situation, wondering why they couldn't just go on living as they had, sticking to an arrangement that was working fine for both of them. In a way, it was worse for Laurie, because she knew exactly what she was returning to—a crowded room in Gray House, or maybe Green, a sleeping bag on a cold floor, long nights without a friend nearby to help pass the time, nothing to keep her company but the frightened voice in her own head.

A WEEK EARLIER, on the morning of Meg's Graduation Day, they'd reported to the Main House with heavy hearts. Before setting off, they'd hugged each other for a long time and reminded themselves to be brave.

"I won't forget you," Meg promised, her voice soft, a bit hoarse.

"You'll be fine," Laurie whispered, not even convincing herself. "We both will."

Patti Levin, the first and only Director of the Mapleton Chapter, was waiting in her office, sitting like a high school principal behind an enormous beige desk. She was a petite woman with frizzy gray hair and a stern but surprisingly youthful face. She gestured with her cigarette, inviting them to sit down.

"It's the big day," she said.

Laurie and Meg remained silent. They were only allowed to speak in response to a direct question. The Director studied them, her face alert but expressionless.

"I see you've been crying."

There was no sense denying it. They'd barely slept and had spent a good part of the night in tears. Meg looked like a wreck—hair tangled, eyes raw and puffy—and Laurie had no reason to believe she looked any better.

"It's hard!" Meg blurted out like a heartbroken teenager. "It's just really hard!"

Laurie winced at the breach of decorum, but the Director let it pass. Pinching her cigarette between thumb and forefinger, she brought it to her mouth and sucked hard on the filter, as if it weren't drawing right, squinting with grim determination.

"I know," she said on the exhale. "It's the path we've chosen."

"Is it always this bad?" Meg sounded like she was about to start crying again.

"Sometimes." The Director shrugged. "It's different for different people."

Now that Meg had broken the ice, Laurie decided it was okay to speak up.

"It's my fault," she explained. "I didn't do my job. I got too attached to my Trainee and let things get out of hand. I really screwed up."

"That's not true!" Meg protested. "Laurie's a great mentor."

"It's our fault, too," the Director admitted. "We could see what was happening. We probably should have separated you two a month ago."

"I'm sorry." Laurie forced herself to meet the Director's eyes. "I'll try to do better next time."

Patti Levin shook her head. "I don't think there's going to be a next time."

Laurie didn't argue. She knew she didn't deserve a second chance. She wasn't even sure if she wanted one, not if she was going to feel like this when it was over.

"Please don't hold it against Meg," she said. "She's worked really hard these past couple of months and made a lot of progress, in spite of my mistakes. I really admire her strength and determination. I know she's going to be a great asset to the Chapter."

"Laurie taught me so much," Meg chimed in. "She's just a really good role model, you know?"

Mercifully, the Director let that pass. In the silence that followed, Laurie found herself staring at the poster on the wall behind the desk. It showed a classroom full of adults and children, all of them dressed in white, all of them with their hands in the air, like eager A students. Every raised hand held a cigarette.

WHO WANTS TO BE A MARTYR? the caption asked.

"I guess you've noticed that it's a little crowded around here," the Director told them. "We keep getting new recruits. In some of the houses we've got people sleeping in the hallways and the garages. It's just not a sustainable situation."

For a miserable moment or two, Laurie wondered if she was being kicked out of the G.R. to make room for someone more worthy than herself. But then the Director glanced at a sheet of paper on her desk.

"You're being transferred to Outpost 17," she said. "You move in next Tuesday."

Laurie and Meg exchanged wary glances.

"Both of us?" Meg asked.

The Director nodded. "That's your preference, right?"

They assured her that it was.

"Good." For the first time since they'd arrived, Patti Levin smiled. "Outpost 17 is a very special place."

~~~~

THE ONE thing life had taught Jill was that things change all the time—abruptly, unpredictably, and often for no good reason. But knowing that didn't do you that much good, apparently. You could still get blindsided by your own best friend, right in the middle of a macaroni and cheese dinner.

"Mr. Garvey," Aimee said. "I think it's time I started paying some rent."

"*Rent?*" Her father chuckled, as if he enjoyed having his leg pulled as much as the next guy. He'd been in a pretty good mood for the past few weeks, ever since he'd come back from Florida. "That's ridiculous."

"I mean it." Aimee looked completely serious. "You've been really generous to me. But I'm starting to feel like a freeloader, you know?"

"You're not a freeloader. You're a guest."

"I've been living here a looong time." She paused, daring him to disagree. "I'm sure you guys are really sick of me."

"Don't be silly. We enjoy your company."

Aimee frowned, as if his kindness just made things harder.

"I'm not just sleeping here, I'm eating your food, using your washer and dryer, watching your cable TV. I'm sure there's other stuff, too."

Internet, Jill thought. *Heat and AC, tampons, makeup, shampoo and conditioner and toothpaste, my underwear . . .*

"It's really okay." He glanced at Jill, wondering if she had a different opinion. "Right?"

"Absolutely," Jill said. "It's been fun."

And she meant it, too, despite her occasional complaints about Aimee's lengthy, open-ended crash at their house. Sure, there'd been some rocky times in the fall, but things had gotten better in the past month or two. Christmas had been really nice, and they'd thrown a great New Year's party while her father was on vacation. In the weeks since then, Jill had made a point of asserting her independence from Aimee, no longer going out every night, making a good-faith effort to keep up with her schoolwork and spend a little more time with her dad. It seemed like they'd finally come up with a balance everyone could live with.

"I've never paid rent before," Aimee said, "so I have no idea what the going rate would be, especially in a beautiful house like this. But I guess the landlord decides that, right?"

Her father winced at the word *landlord.*

"Don't be ridiculous," he said. "You're a high school student. How're you going to pay rent?"

"That's the other thing I wanted to tell you." Aimee seemed suddenly unsure of herself. "I think I'm done with school."

"What?"

Jill was startled to see that Aimee was blushing, because Aimee never blushed.

"I'm dropping out," she said.

"Why would you do that?" he asked. "You're gonna graduate in a few months."

"You didn't see my report card," Aimee told him. "I failed everything last semester, even gym. If I want to graduate I'm going to have to go back next year, and I'd rather shoot myself than be a fifth-year senior." She turned to Jill, requesting backup. "Go ahead, tell him what a fuckup I am."

"It's true," Jill said. "She can't even remember how to open her locker."

"Look who's talking," he said.

"I'm gonna do better this term," Jill promised, thinking how much easier it would be to buckle down with Aimee out of the picture. They wouldn't be walking to school every morning, getting stoned behind the supermarket, or sneaking out for two-hour lunches. *I can be myself again,* she thought. *Grow my hair back, start hanging out with my old friends . . .*

"Besides," Aimee added. "I got a job. You remember Derek from the yogurt store? He's managing the new Applebee's over at Stonewood Plaza. He hired me as a server. Full-time, starting next week. The uniforms are ugly, but the tips should be pretty good."

"Derek?" Jill didn't try to hide her disgust. "I thought you hated him."

Their old boss was a sleazeball, a married guy in his mid-thirties—his key chain was an LCD cube that flashed pictures of his baby son—who liked to buy alcohol for his underage female employees and ask lots of probing questions about their sex lives. *Ever use a vibrator?* he'd asked Jill one night, totally out of the blue. *I bet you'd like it.* He'd even offered to buy her one, just because she seemed like such a nice person.

"I don't *hate* him." Aimee took a sip of water, then heaved an exaggerated sigh of relief. "God, I can't wait to get out of that school. I get depressed every time I walk down the hall. All those *assholes* on parade."

"Guess what?" her father said. "They'll all come to Applebee's, and you'll have to be nice to them."

"So? At least I'll be getting paid for it. And you know what the best part is?" Aimee paused, smirking proudly. "I get to sleep in every day, as late as I want. No more waking up hungover at the crack of dawn. So I'd really appreciate it if you guys kept your voices down in the morning."

"Ha ha," Jill said, trying to fend off a sudden troubling vision of the house after she left for school, Aimee wandering through the kitchen in nothing but a T-shirt and panties, her father watching from the table as she guzzled OJ straight from the carton, every day a disaster waiting to happen. It made her really glad that he had a new girlfriend, a woman close to his own age, even if she was a little spooky.

"Listen." He seemed seriously concerned, as if Aimee were his own daughter. "I really think you should reconsider. You're too smart to quit school."

Aimee exhaled slowly, like she was beginning to lose her patience.

"Mr. Garvey," she said, "if you're really uncomfortable with this, I guess I can find somewhere else to live."

"This isn't about where you live. I just don't want you to sell yourself short."

"I get that. And I really appreciate it. But you're not gonna change my mind."

"All right." He closed his eyes and massaged his forehead with three fingertips, the way he did when he had a headache. "How about this? In a month or two, after you've been working for a while, we can sit down and figure out the rent situation. In the meantime, you're our guest, and everybody's happy, okay?"

"Sounds good." Aimee smiled, as if this were the exact outcome she'd been hoping for. "I like it when everybody's happy."

LAURIE COULDN'T sleep. It was her third night at the Outpost, and the transition wasn't going as smoothly as she'd hoped. Part of it was the strangeness, after twenty-three years of marriage and nine months of communal living, of once again having a room of her own. She just wasn't accustomed to solitude anymore, the way that lying alone on a comfortable mattress could feel like tumbling endlessly through outer space.

She missed Meg, too, missed their sleepy bedtime talks, the schoolgirl camaraderie of the Unburdening. Some nights they had stayed awake for hours, two soft voices bouncing back and forth, recounting their life stories in random installments. In the beginning, Laurie had made a good-faith effort to keep them focused on Meg's training, to discourage idle gossip and nostalgic chatter, but the conversation always seemed to have a mind of its own. And the truth was, she enjoyed its meandering trajectory just as much as Meg did. She excused her weakness by reminding herself that it was a temporary condition, that Graduation Day would come soon enough, and she would, by necessity, have to resume her regimen of silence and self-discipline.

And here she was, trying to do just that, but with Meg in the very next room, so close that not being able to talk to her seemed absurd and almost cruel. It was hard to be alone under any circumstances, but even harder when you knew you didn't have to be, when all you had to do was throw off the blankets and tiptoe down the hall. Because she had no doubt—none at all—that Meg was wide awake at that very moment, thinking the exact same thoughts she was, resisting the exact same temptation.

It had been simple to behave at the Compound, with so many people around, so many watchful eyes. At the Outpost there was no one to stop them from doing what they wanted, no one to even notice except Gus and Julian, and those guys were in no position to criticize. They were sharing the master suite on the ground floor—it had a king-size bed and a whirlpool tub in the adjoining bathroom—and Laurie sometimes thought she could hear their voices late at night, frail bubbles of speech drifting through the quiet house, popping just before they reached her ears.

What are they talking about? she wondered. *Are they talking about us?*

She wouldn't have blamed them if they were. If she and Meg had been together, they would certainly have been talking about Gus and Julian. Not to complain—there wasn't all that much to complain about—but just to swap impressions, the way you do when new people enter your life and you're not quite sure what to make of them.

They seemed like sweet guys, she thought, though maybe a bit self-involved and entitled. They could also be a little bossy, but Laurie suspected that this attitude was more a fluke of circumstance than a flaw in their characters. They'd been the sole occupants of Outpost 17 for almost a month before Laurie and Meg had arrived, and they'd naturally come to think of the place as their own and to assume that the newcomers would have to abide by the rules they'd established. As a matter of principle, Laurie didn't think this was fair—the G.R. was based on equality, not seniority—but she figured she'd wait a little while before making a fuss about the decision-making process.

Besides, it wasn't like the house rules were particularly onerous. The only one that caused Laurie any personal inconvenience was the indoor smoking ban—she liked starting the day with a cigarette in bed—but she had no intention of trying to change it. The policy had been put in place to protect Gus, who suffered from a severe case of asthma. His breathing was often labored, and just the day before, he'd suffered a full-on attack right in the middle of dinner, leaping up from the table with a panicky expression, gulping and wheezing like he'd just been rescued from the bottom of a swimming pool. Julian ran to their room to retrieve an inhaler and rubbed Gus's back for several minutes afterward until his respiration returned to something like normal. It had been terrifying to watch, and if Laurie had to smoke on the back patio to give him a little relief, that was a sacrifice she was more than willing to make.

As a matter of fact, she was grateful for the opportunity to practice any kind of self-denial, because the Outpost offered so few of them. Life here was so much easier than at the Compound. Food was plentiful, if not fancy—mostly pasta and beans and canned vegetables—and the thermostat was kept at a civilized sixty-two degrees. You could go to bed when you felt like it, and sleep in as long as you liked. As for work, you set your own hours and filled out your own reports.

It was almost disturbingly cushy, which was one of the reasons she was trying so hard to maintain her distance from Meg, to not fall back into the easy routine of friendship. It was bad enough being warm and well-fed and free to do as you pleased. If, on top of all that, you were happy, too, if you had a good friend to keep you company at night, then what was the point of even being in the G.R.? Why not just go back to the big house on Lovell Terrace, rejoin her husband and daughter, wear nice clothes again, renew her membership at the Mapleton Fitness Club, catch up on the TV she'd missed, redecorate the living room, cook interesting meals with seasonal produce, pretend that life was good and the world wasn't broken?

After all, it wasn't too late.

"YOU'VE BEEN with us for quite a while," Patti Levin had said at the end of their meeting last week. "I think it's about time we made it official, don't you?"

The envelope she pressed into Laurie's hand contained a single sheet of paper, a Joint Petition for Divorce. Laurie had filled in the blanks, checked the necessary boxes, and signed her name in the space reserved for Petitioner A. All that remained for her to do was to take the form to Kevin and get him to sign as Petitioner B. She had no reason to believe he'd object. How could he? Their marriage was over—it had suffered what the state called an "irretrievable breakdown"—and they both knew it. The petition was a legal formality, a bureaucratic statement of the obvious.

So what was the problem? Why was the envelope still resting on the dresser, weighing so heavily on her conscience that it might as well have been glowing in the dark?

Laurie wasn't naïve. She understood that the G.R. needed money to survive. You couldn't run an organization that large and ambitious without incurring serious expenses—all those people needing food and housing and medical care. There were new properties to be acquired, old ones to be maintained. Cigarettes. Vehicles. Computers, legal advice, public outreach. Soap, toilet paper, whatever. It added up.

Naturally, members were expected to contribute whatever they could afford. If all you had was a monthly Social Security check, that was what you gave. If the sum total of your worldly goods consisted of a rusty Oldsmobile with a bad muffler, the G.R. could use that, as well. And if you were lucky enough to be married to a successful business-man, why shouldn't you dissolve that union and donate your share of the proceeds to the cause?

Well, why not?

She wasn't really sure how much money was involved—the law-yers would have to figure that out. The house alone was worth around a million—they'd paid one point six for it, but that was five years ago, before the market tanked—and the various retirement and investment accounts had to be worth at least that much. Whatever the final tally, fifty percent of it would be a serious outlay, substantial enough that Kevin might have to think about selling the house to meet his obliga-tions.

Laurie wanted to do her part for the G.R., she really did. But the thought of walking over there, ringing the doorbell, and asking Kevin for half of everything she'd turned her back on filled her with shame. She had joined the G.R. because she had no choice, because it was the only path that made any sense to her. In the process, she'd lost her family and her friends and her place in the community, all the comfort and security money could buy. That was her decision, and she didn't regret it. But Kevin and Jill had paid a high price, too, and they hadn't gotten anything in return. It seemed greedy—unseemly—to suddenly show up at their door with her hand out, asking for even more.

SHE MUST have drifted off because she woke with a start, conscious of some sort of movement nearby.

"Laurie?" Meg whispered. Her nightgown emitted a ghostly radiance in the doorway. "Are you awake?"

"Is something wrong?"

"Can't you hear it?"

Laurie listened. She thought she caught a muffled sound, a soft rhythmic tapping.

"What is that?"

"It's louder in my room," Meg explained.

Laurie got out of bed, hugging her bare arms against the chill, and followed Meg down the short hallway into the other bedroom. It was brighter on that side of the house, the glow of a streetlight filtering in from Parker Road. Meg crouched in front of an old-fashioned radiator, a bulky silver thing with claw feet like a vintage bathtub, and beckoned Laurie to join her.

"I'm right on top of them," she said.

Laurie inclined her head, placing her ear close enough to the metal that she could feel the faint residual heat coming off it.

"It's been going on for a long time."

The sound was clearer now, like listening to a radio. The tapping was no longer faint or mysterious. It was a straightforward percussion, headboard against wall, with an undertone of protesting bedsprings. She could hear voices, too, one gruff and monotonous—it just kept saying the word *fuck* over and over—and the other higher-pitched, with a more varied vocabulary—*oh* and *God* and *Jesus* and *please*.

Laurie wasn't sure which one belonged to Julian and which to Gus, but she was glad to hear that neither one seemed to be suffering from shortness of breath.

"How am I supposed to sleep?" Meg demanded.

Laurie didn't trust herself to speak. She knew she was supposed to be scandalized, or at least upset, by what she was hearing—the G.R. didn't permit sex between members, gay or straight—but at that moment, she wasn't feeling anything except muddled surprise and a little more interest than she would have liked to admit.

"What are we gonna do?" Meg went on. "Do we have to report them?"

It took an effort of will for Laurie to move away from the radiator. She turned to Meg, their faces just inches away in the darkness.

"It's none of our business," she said.

"But—"

Laurie took Meg by the wrist and helped her to her feet.

"Grab your pillow," she said. "You can sleep in my room tonight."

BAREFOOT AND PREGNANT

TOM PUT ON THE SKI jacket he'd borrowed from Terrence Falk, taking care not to get his beard tangled in the zipper, which he pulled all the way up to his chin. He'd gotten snagged a couple of times, and it had hurt like hell getting it free.

"Where you going?" Christine asked from the couch.

"Harvard Square." He withdrew a cashmere watch cap from his coat pocket and smoothed it over his head. "Wanna come?"

She glanced down at her pajamas—polka-dot pants and a tight gray top that hugged the fertile swell of her belly—as if that were an answer in itself.

"You can get changed," he told her. "I'm in no hurry."

She pursed her lips, tempted by the offer. They'd been in Cambridge for a month, and she'd only been out of the house a handful of times—once to see a doctor, and twice to go shopping with Marcella Falk. She never complained about it, but Tom figured she must be going a little stir-crazy.

"I don't know." She glanced nervously toward the kitchen, where Marcella was baking cookies. "I probably shouldn't."

The Falks had never explicitly said that she wasn't allowed to leave the house on her own—they weren't bossy like that—but they discouraged her on a daily basis. It just wasn't worth the risk—she could slip on the ice, or catch a cold, or draw the attention of the police—especially now that she was in the third trimester of a pregnancy whose importance to the world could not be overstated. And this wasn't just their personal opinion—they were in direct contact with Mr. Gilchrest, through his attorney, and he wanted her to know how deeply concerned he was for her safety, and for the health and well-being of his unborn child.

He wants you to take it easy, they told her. *He wants you to eat good food and get lots of rest.*

"It's a ten-minute walk," Tom said. "You can bundle up."

Before Christine could reply, Marcella Falk hustled in from the kitchen, wearing a striped apron and balancing a plate of cookies on her upturned hand.

"Oatmeal raisin!" she sang out as she approached the couch. "Someone's favorite!"

"Yummy." Christine reached for a cookie and took a bite. "Mmm. Nice and warm."

Marcella set the plate down on the coffee table. As she straightened up, she glanced at Tom with an expression of bogus surprise, as if she hadn't known he was there, hadn't been eavesdropping the whole time.

"Oh—" She had short dark hair, watchful eyes, and the stringy physique of a fiftysomething yoga addict. "Are you going out?"

"Just for a walk. Christine might come along."

Marcella did her best to look interested rather than alarmed.

"Do you need something?" she asked Christine a little too sweetly. "I'm sure Tom will be happy to get it for you."

Christine shook her head. "I don't need anything."

"I thought she might like a little fresh air," Tom suggested.

Marcella looked puzzled, as if "fresh air" were an unfamiliar concept.

"I'm sure we could open a window," she said.

"That's okay." Christine made a show of yawning. "I'm kinda tired. I'll probably just take a nap."

"Perfect!" Marcella's face relaxed. "I'll wake you around two-thirty. The personal trainer's coming at three for your workout."

"I could use some exercise," Christine admitted. "I'm turning into a blimp."

"That's ridiculous," Marcella told her. "You look beautiful."

She was right about that, Tom thought. Now that she was indoors and eating properly, Christine was gaining weight and getting lovelier by the day. Her face was glowing, her body ripening gracefully. Her breasts still weren't that big, but they were rounder and fuller than before, and he sometimes got a little hypnotized by the sight of them. He also had to make a conscious effort not to reach out and rub her belly whenever she was nearby, not that she would've objected. She didn't mind if Tom touched her. Sometimes she even grabbed his hand and placed his palm right on top of the baby, so he could feel the movement inside of her, the little creature doing slow-motion somersaults, swimming blindly in its bubble. But it was a whole different thing to just fondle her without permission, to treat her body like it was public property. The Falks did that all the time, closing their eyes and cooing dreamily at the baby, as if they were the proud grandparents, and Tom thought it was rude.

He started toward the door, resisting the temptation to grab a cookie on the way out.

"You sure you don't want boots?" Marcella asked him. "I'm sure Terrencc has an extra pair."

"That's okay. I'm fine like this."

"Have fun," Christine called after him. "Tell the hippies I said hi."

IT WAS a damp gray afternoon, not especially cold for February. Tom headed east on Brattle, trying not to obsess about Terrence Falk's boots. If they were anything like his coat, or his super-lightweight, mysteriously toasty gloves, they'd probably been designed to withstand the rigors of an Antarctic expedition. An ordinary winter day would have been nothing for boots like that. You wouldn't even have to look where you were going.

But no, he taunted himself, hopscotching an archipelago of slushy puddles on Appleton Street. *I have to do it the hard way.*

At least he had his flip-flops. That was what the New England Barefoot People were allowed to wear when there was snow on the ground. Not boots, not shoes, not sneakers, not even Tevas—just plain rubber flip-flops, which were better than nothing, but not by much. He'd recently seen a couple of nerds wearing plastic bags over them— they were held in place by rubber bands around the ankles—but this modification was widely scorned around Harvard Square.

In California, it was frequently claimed that bare feet toughened up over time and became "as good as shoes," but no one believed this in Boston, at least not in the middle of winter. Your soles got leathery after a few months, that much was true, but your toes never got accustomed to the cold. And it didn't matter what else you wore—if your feet were frozen, the rest of you was miserable, too.

But there was no point in complaining, because all Tom's suffering in this regard was self-inflicted and totally unnecessary. He'd completed his mission, delivered Christine safe and sound to her comfortable new home, to the generous couple who'd promised to take care of her for however long it took for Mr. Gilchrest to resolve his legal difficulties. There was nothing to stop Tom from scrubbing off his bullseye, putting some shoes on his feet, and getting on with his life. But for some reason, he couldn't do it.

Christine hadn't hesitated. The night they'd arrived at the Falks', she'd disappeared into the bathroom right after dinner and taken a long, hot shower. When she emerged, her forehead was clean, her face pink and deeply relieved, as if the memory of the road were a bad dream she'd been happy to wash away. Ever since then, she'd been lounging around the house—a spectacularly renovated Victorian on Fayerweather Street—in organic cotton maternity clothes. In an attempt to repair the damage inflicted by months of exposure to the elements, the Falks had arranged for a house call from a Korean pedicurist, though they'd made Christine wear a face mask to protect herself and the baby from potentially harmful fumes. There had also been visits from a massage therapist, a dental hygienist, a nutritionist, and the nurse/midwife who would be assisting with what everyone hoped would be a home delivery.

All these professionals were devoted Holy Wayners, and they all treated Christine like royalty, like it was a rare privilege to buff her toenails or scrape the tartar from her teeth. Terrence and Marcella were the most obsequious of all; they'd actually knelt at Christine's feet when she entered their house, bowing until their foreheads touched the ground. Christine was delighted by all the attention, happy to resume her life as Wife Number Four, the Special One, Mr. Gilchrest's Chosen Vessel.

It was different for Tom. Being around all these true believers made it clearer than ever that he was no longer one of them, that there was no former self left for him to reclaim. The Holy Wayne part of his life was over, and the next phase hadn't begun, nor did he have the slightest clue what it would be. Maybe that was why he was so reluctant to shed his disguise: Being a fake Barefoot Person was the only real identity he had left.

But it was more than that. He'd been happy on the road, happier than he'd realized at the time. The journey had been long and occasionally harrowing—they'd gotten mugged at knifepoint in Chicago and nearly froze to death in a blizzard in western Pennsylvania—but now that it was over, he missed the excitement and the closeness he'd shared with Christine. They'd been a good team, best friends and secret agents, improvising their way across the continent, dealing creatively with whatever obstacles came their way.

The disguises they'd chosen had worked better than they could have imagined. Everywhere they went, they met local Barefoot People and were treated like family, given food and rides and, often, a place to sleep. Christine had gotten sick in Harrisburg, and they'd ended up spending three weeks in a run-down group house near the state capitol, eating rice and beans from a communal pot, sleeping together on the kitchen floor. They hadn't become lovers, but there'd been a couple of close calls, mornings when they'd awakened in each other's arms and needed a few seconds to remember why that was a bad thing.

On the road, they rarely talked about Mr. Gilchrest. As the weeks went by, he became an abstraction, an increasingly hazy figure from the past. There were days when Tom forgot all about him, when he couldn't help thinking of Christine as his own girlfriend, and the baby as his child. He let himself imagine that the three of them were a family, that they would soon settle down and build a life together.

It's up to me, he told himself. *I have to take care of them.*

At the Falks', though, this fantasy died of embarrassment. Mr. Gilchrest was everywhere, impossible to ignore, let alone forget. There were pictures of him in every room, including a gigantic photograph affixed to the ceiling of the master suite, right over Christine's bed, so his face would be the first thing she saw when she opened her eyes in the morning. Everywhere he went, Tom could feel the great man smiling at him, mocking him, reminding him who the real father was. The image he hated most was the framed poster in the basement, on the wall beside the foldout couch where he slept, an action shot of Holy Wayne on an outdoor stage, one fist raised in triumph, his face streaming with tears.

You motherfucker, Tom thought, last thing every night and first thing every morning. *You don't deserve her.*

He knew he needed to get out of that house and away from that face. But he couldn't bring himself to leave, to just walk out on Christine and abandon her to the Falks. Not when they'd come this far together, when her due date was only ten weeks away. The least he could do was stick it out until the baby came, make himself useful in any way he could.

THE MANDRAKE was a basement coffee shop on Mount Auburn Street that was one of the main gathering spots for Barefoot People in Harvard Square. Like Elmore's in the Haight, it was owned and operated by people in the movement, and seemed to do a brisk business, not just in herbal teas and whole-grain muffins, but in weed and mushrooms and acid as well, at least if you knew the right person to approach, and the correct way to place an order.

Tom got a chai latte from the blissed-out kid behind the counter—the staff wore shirts that read, NO SHOES? WE LOVE YOU!—and then scanned the crowded room for a place to sit. Most of the tables were occupied by Barefoot People, but there were a handful of average citizens and slumming academics scattered among them, outsiders who had either wandered in by mistake or enjoyed the nostalgic contact high that came from being in close proximity to Grateful Dead music, face paint, and unwashed bodies.

Eggy waved at Tom from his table in the back corner—his bald head was impossible to miss in that sea of hirsute humanity—where he was engaged in yet another marathon backgammon session with Kermit, the oldest Barefoot Dude Tom had ever met. An unfamiliar blond girl around Tom's age was the sole spectator.

"Yo, North Face!" Eggy called out. "Kill any caribou?"

Tom gave him the finger as he pulled up a chair. He took lots of ribbing at the Mandrake about the winter gear he'd borrowed from Terrence Falk, which was several cuts above the thrift-store crap most of the customers wore.

Kermit gazed at Tom with the bleary fascination of the permanently stoned. He had long, greasy yellowish gray hair that he liked to groom with his fingers when he was deep in thought. Rumor had it that he was a former English professor at B.U.

"You know what we should call you?" he said. "Jack London."

The bestowing of nicknames was serious business at the Mandrake. In the few weeks he'd been hanging out there, Tom had already been dubbed Frisco, Your Excellency, and, most recently, North Face. Sooner or later, he thought, something would have to stick.

"Jack London." Eggy murmured the name, testing it on his tongue. "I like that."

"I read a story by him," said the girl. She looked like a part-timer, round-faced and healthy, with the biggest bullseye on her forehead Tom had ever come across, a green-and-white swirl the size of a beer mat. "In high school English. This guy in the North Pole keeps trying to light a fire so he won't get hypothermia, but the fire keeps going out. And then his fingers freeze, and he's totally fucked."

"Man versus Nature." Eggy nodded sagely. "The eternal conflict."

"There are actually two versions of that story," Kermit pointed out. "In the first one, the guy survives."

"So why'd he write the second?" the girl asked.

"Why, indeed?" Kermit chuckled darkly. "Because the first version was bullshit, that's why. In his heart of hearts, Jack London knew that we can never build a fire. Not when we really need to."

"You know what's gross?" the girl asked cheerfully. "The guy wanted to kill his dog, cut it open, and warm his hands inside the guts. But by the time he tried to do it, he couldn't even hold the knife."

"Please." Eggy looked a bit queasy. "Could we not talk about this?"

"Why not?" the girl asked.

"He's a dog lover," Kermit explained. "Hasn't he told you about Quincy?"

"I just met her last night." Eggy sounded indignant. "What do you think, I meet someone and immediately start blabbing about my dog?"

Kermit directed an amused glance at Tom, who knew all too well how often Eggy talked about Quincy, a two-hundred-pound mastiff who'd wandered off after the Sudden Departure and hadn't been seen since. Instead of a wallet, Eggy carried a small album containing about a dozen photographs of the big dog, often in the company of a tall, unsmiling woman with scraped-back hair. This was Emily, Eggy's departed fiancée, a former graduate student at the Kennedy School of Government. Eggy didn't talk so much about her.

Kermit reached for the dice. "It's my turn, right?"

"Yup." Eggy pointed to a white blot on the middle bar. "I just took this guy prisoner."

"Again?" Kermit looked pissed. "You could show a little mercy, you know?"

"What are you talking about? Why should I show any mercy? That's like telling a football player not to tackle a player on the other team just because he has the ball."

"There's no law that says you have to tackle someone."

"No, but you'd be a shitty football player if you didn't."

"Point taken." Kermit shook the dice. "But let's not remove free will from the equation."

Tom rolled his eyes. The Barefoot People he'd known played different games in different cities—Monopoly in San Francisco, cribbage in Harrisburg, backgammon in Boston—but no matter what they played, the action always unfolded at a glacial pace, interrupted at every turn by pointless disputes and obscure philosophical digressions. More often than not, the games ended in midstream, called on account of boredom.

"I'm Lucy, by the way," the girl told Tom. "But these guys call me Ouch."

"*Ouch?*" Tom said. "Where's that come from?"

Eggy looked up from the board. He wore round wire-framed glasses that, along with his shaved head, gave him a monkish air.

"She was one of the original Harvard flagellants. You know about that?"

Tom nodded. He'd seen a video on the Internet a while back, a procession of college kids marching through Harvard Yard in their bathing suits, mortifying their flesh with homemade whips and cat-o'-nine-tails, some of which had nails and tacks affixed to the business end. Afterward, the kids would sit on the grass and rub ointment into one another's backs. They claimed to feel purified by their agony, temporarily cleansed of their guilt.

"Wow." Tom looked at Ouch a little more closely. She was wearing a pale blue cotton sweater that looked freshly laundered. Her complexion was clear, her hair fine and soft, like she still had access to showers and a meal plan. "That's pretty hard-core."

"You should see her scars," Eggy said with admiration. "Her back is like a topographic map."

"I saw you idiots once," Kermit told her. "I was sitting outside at Au Bon Pain, beautiful spring day, and the next thing I know, a dozen kids are lined up on the sidewalk like an a cappella group, yelling out their SAT scores and flogging the crap out of themselves. *Seven Twenty, Critical Reading! Whack! Seven Eighty, Math! Whack! Six Ninety, Writing! Whack!*"

Ouch was blushing. "We did it like that at the beginning. But then we started to personalize it. Somebody would scream, *Lead role in Godspell!* and the next one would say, *Congressional Page!* or *Lampoon Staff!* I had a really long one: *Two-Sport Varsity Scholar-Athlete!*" She laughed at the memory. "This one guy who came a couple of times, he used to scream about what a stud he was, and how proud he was about the size of his penis. *Eight Inches! I Measured It! I Even Posted Pictures on Craigslist!*"

"Fucking Harvard guys," said Eggy. "Always bragging about something."

"It's true," Ouch admitted. "The whole idea was that we were supposed to be atoning for the sins of excessive pride and selfishness, but we were even competitive about that. This one kid I knew, all he ever yelled was *I'm the Biggest Asshole Ever!*"

"There's a tall order," said Kermit. "Especially at Harvard."

"How long did you keep this up?" Tom asked.

"Couple months," she said. "But where can you go with something like that? It just doesn't *lead* anywhere, you know? After a while, you even get bored with the pain."

"So what happened? You just throw away your whip and go back to school?"

"They made me take a year off." She gave a vague shrug, like it wasn't worth talking about. "I did a lot of snowboarding."

"But now you're back?"

"Technically. But I'm not really going to class or anything." She touched her bullseye. "I'm more interested in this right now. It seems like a really good fit, you know? A lot more social and intellectual stimulation. I think I need that."

"More sex and drugs, too," Eggy added with a smirk.

"Definitely more of that." Ouch looked a bit troubled. "My parents aren't too happy about it. Especially the sex."

"They never are," Kermit told her. "But that's part of the deal. You gotta break free of those middle-class conventions. Find your own way."

"It's hard," she said. "We're a really close family."

"She's not kidding," Eggy informed them. "They phoned last night while we were fucking and she took the call."

"Hello?" asked Kermit. "Ever hear of voice mail?"

"That's our agreement," Ouch explained. "I can do whatever I want as long as I answer the phone. They just want to know I'm alive. I feel like I owe them that much."

"It goes way beyond that." Eggy sounded genuinely exasperated. "They talked for like a half hour, this big convoluted discussion about morality and responsibility and self-respect."

Kermit looked intrigued. "While you were fucking?"

"Yeah," Eggy grumbled. "It was a real turn-on."

"They made me so mad." Ouch was blushing again. "They wouldn't even concede that casual sex is healthier than hurting myself. They kept trying to draw a moral equivalence between the two, which is so ridiculous."

"Then—get this—she put me on the phone." Eggy pretended to shoot himself in the head. "She made me talk to her parents. I'm naked with a fucking hard-on. Unbelievable."

"They wanted to talk to you."

"Yeah, but I didn't want to talk to them. How do you think I felt, getting interrogated by these people I never met—what's my real name, how old am I, am I practicing safe sex with their little girl? Finally I just said, *Look, your little girl's a consenting adult,* and they're like, *We know that, but she's still our child, and she means more to us than anything in the world.* What the fuck am I supposed to say to that?"

"It's just because of my sister," Ouch told him. "They still haven't gotten over that. None of us have."

"Anyway," Eggy said wearily, "by the time she got off the phone, I didn't even feel like fucking anymore. And it takes a lot to make me not feel like fucking."

Ouch gave him a look. "You got over it pretty fast."

"You were very persuasive."

"Ah," said Kermit. "So there was a happy ending after all."

"Two, as a matter of fact." Eggy's expression was smug. "She's quite the scholar-athlete."

Tom wasn't surprised by this—Barefoot dudes bragged about their sexual exploits all the time—but he couldn't help feeling offended on Ouch's behalf. In a world that made any sense, she wouldn't even be talking to Eggy, let alone going to bed with him. She must have sensed his sympathy, because she turned to him with a curious expression.

"What about you?" she asked. "Are you in touch with your family?"

"Not really. Not for a while."

"Did you have a fight?"

"We just kinda drifted apart."

"Do your parents know you're alive and well?"

Tom wasn't sure how to answer that.

"I probably owe them an e-mail," he muttered.

"Whose turn is it?" Eggy asked Kermit.

Ouch took out her phone and slid it across the table.

"You should call," she said. "I bet they'd like to hear from you."

AT THE GRAPEFRUIT

NORA BOUGHT A NEW DRESS for Valentine's Day and immediately regretted it. Not because it didn't look good; that wasn't the problem at all. The dress was lovely—a blue-gray silk/rayon mix, sleeveless, with a V-neck and empire waist—and it fit her perfectly right off the rack. Even in the dispiriting light of the changing room, she could see how flattering it was, the way it emphasized the elegance of her shoulders and the length of her legs, the pale matte fabric calling attention to the darkness of her hair and eyes, her enviable cheekbones, her finely formed chin.

My mouth, she told herself. *I have a very pretty mouth.* (Her daughter had had the exact same mouth, but she preferred not to think about that.)

It was easy to imagine the looks she'd get in that dress, the heads that would turn when she walked into the restaurant, the pleasure in Kevin's eyes as he admired her across the table. *That* was the problem, the ease with which she'd allowed herself to get swept up in the excitement of the holiday. Because she already understood that it wasn't really working out, that she'd made a mistake getting involved with him, and that their days together were numbered—not because of anything he had or hadn't done, but because of her, because of who she was and everything she was no longer capable of. So what was the point of looking this good—better than she had any right to, really—of eating a nice meal in a fancy restaurant, drinking expensive wine and sharing some kind of decadent dessert, starting something that would probably lead to bed and then end in tears? Why put either of them through that?

The thing was, Kevin hadn't given her any advance warning. He'd just sprung it on her a few days ago as he was heading out the door.

Thursday at eight, he said, as if it were already set in stone. *Mark it on your calendar.*

Mark what?

Valentine's Day. I made reservations for two at Pamplemousse. I'll pick you up at seven-thirty.

It happened so quickly and felt so natural that it hadn't occurred to her to object. How could she? He was her boyfriend, at least for the moment, and it was the middle of February. Of course he was taking her out to dinner.

Wear something nice, he told her.

ALL HER life she'd been a sucker for Valentine's Day, even back in college, when a lot of people Nora respected treated it like a sexist joke at best, a Hallmark fairy tale from the bad old days, Ward bringing June a heart-shaped box of chocolates.

Let me get this straight, Brian used to tease her. *I give you flowers and you spread your legs?*

That's right, she told him. *That's exactly how it goes.*

And he'd gotten the message, too. Even Mr. Post-Structuralist had brought her a dozen roses and taken her out for a dinner he couldn't afford. And when they got home, she held up her end of the bargain, a little more enthusiastically and inventively than usual.

See? she told him. *That wasn't so bad, was it?*

It was okay, he conceded. *I guess once a year won't kill me.*

As she got older, she realized there wasn't anything to apologize for. It was just who she was. She liked being wined and dined, made to feel special, liked it when the deliveryman showed up at the office with a big bouquet and a sweet little note, and her female coworkers told her how lucky she was to have such a romantic boyfriend, such an attentive fiancé, such a thoughtful husband. That was one thing she'd always appreciated about Doug: He'd never failed her on Valentine's Day, never forgot the flowers, never acted like he was just going through the motions. He enjoyed keeping her off balance, surprising her with jewelry one year, a weekend at a luxury hotel the next. Champagne and strawberries in bed, a sonnet in her honor, a home-cooked gourmet meal. She understood now that it was all for show, that he was probably rolling out of bed after she fell asleep and writing steamy e-mails to Kylie or some other other woman, but she hadn't known that at the time. Back then every gift had seemed like one more nice gesture in a series that would go on forever, a tribute she deserved from the sweet man who loved her.

~~~~~

THERE WAS a candle between them and Nora's face looked younger than usual in its flickering glow, as if the tension lines had been erased from the corners of her eyes and mouth. He hoped the soft light was doing him the same favor, giving her a glimpse of the handsome fellow he used to be, the one she'd never had a chance to meet.

"This is a nice restaurant," he said. "Really down-to-earth."

She glanced around the dining room as if seeing it for the first time, taking in the rustic decor with an air of grudging approval—the high ceiling with exposed beams, the bell-shaped light fixtures suspended above rough-hewn tables, the plank floor and exposed brick walls.

"Why do they call it the grapefruit?" she asked.

"Grapefruit?"

"Pamplemousse. It's *grapefruit* in French."

"Really?"

She held up the menu, pointing to a big yellow orb on the cover.

He squinted at the image. "I thought that was the sun."

"It's a grapefruit."

"Whoops."

Her eyes strayed toward the bar, where a festive crowd of walk-ins was clustered, waiting for some tables to open up. Kevin couldn't understand why they all looked so cheerful. He hated that, killing time on an empty stomach, not knowing when the hostess would wander over and call your name.

"Must've been hard to get a reservation," she said. "Eight o'clock and everything."

"Just good timing." Kevin shrugged, as if it were no big deal. "Somebody canceled right before I called."

This wasn't precisely true—he'd had to call in a favor from the restaurant's wine supplier, who'd started out as a salesman for Patriot Liquors—but he decided to keep that information to himself. There were a lot of women who would've been impressed by his string-pulling abilities, but he was pretty sure Nora wasn't one of them.

"I guess you're just a lucky guy," she told him.

"That's right." He tilted his glass in her direction, suggesting a toast without insisting on it. "Happy Valentine's Day."

She mimicked his gesture. "Same to you."

"You look beautiful," he said, not for the first time that evening.

Nora smiled unconvincingly and opened her menu. He could see that it was costing her something just to be here, exposed like this, letting the whole town in on their little secret. But she'd done it—*she'd done it for him*—and that was the important thing.

HE HAD to hand it to Aimee. Without her encouragement, he never would've forced the issue, wouldn't have had the courage to nudge Nora out of her comfort zone.

"I don't want to push her," he'd said. "She's a pretty fragile person."

"She's a survivor," Aimee had reminded him. "I bet she's a lot tougher than you think."

Kevin knew it was an iffy proposition, taking relationship advice from a teenager—a high school dropout, no less—but he'd gotten to know Aimee a lot better in the past couple of weeks and had come to think of her more as a friend and a peer than as one of his daughter's classmates. For someone who'd made some pretty bad decisions in her own life, she actually had a lot of insight into other people and what made them tick.

It had been awkward at first, the two of them alone in the house after Jill left for school, but they'd gotten past that pretty quickly. It helped that Aimee was on her best behavior, coming downstairs wide-awake and fully dressed, no more sleepy Lolita in a tank top. She was polite and friendly and surprisingly easy to talk to. She told him about her new job—apparently, waitressing was a lot harder than she'd thought it would be—and asked a lot of questions about his. They discussed current events and music and sports—she was a pretty big NBA fan—and watched funny videos on YouTube. She was also curious about his personal life.

"How's your girlfriend?" she asked him almost every morning. "You guys getting serious?"

For a while, Kevin just said, *She's fine,* and moved on, trying to let her know that it was none of her business, but Aimee refused to take the hint. Then one morning last week, without making a conscious decision, he blurted out an honest answer.

"Something's wrong," he said. "I like her a lot, but I think we're running out of gas."

He told her the whole story, minus the meager sexual details—the parade, the dance, the impulsive trip to Florida, the rut they'd fallen into when they got back home, his sense that she was pushing him away, that he wasn't really welcome in her life.

"I try to get to know her, but she just clams up on me. It's frustrating."

"But you want to stay together?"

"Not if it's gonna be like this."

"Well, what do you want it to be?"

"A normal relationship, you know? As normal as she can handle right now. Just going out once in a while, to the movies or whatever. Maybe with friends, so it's not just the two of us. And I'd like to be able to have a real conversation, not to have to always worry that I'm saying the wrong thing."

"Does she know this?"

"I think so. I don't see how she couldn't."

Aimee studied him for a few seconds, her tongue pressing against the inside of her cheek.

"You're too polite," she said. "You have to tell her what you want."

"I try. But when I ask her to go out, she just says no, she'd rather stay at home."

"Don't give her a choice. Just say, 'Hey, I'm taking you out to dinner. I already made the reservations.'"

"Sounds kinda pushy."

"What's the alternative?"

Kevin shrugged, as if the answer were obvious.

"Give it a shot," she said. "What have you got to lose?"

〜〜〜

NICK AND Zoe were going at it pretty good. They were kneeling on the rug, close enough for Jill to touch, Zoe purring happily as Nick licked and nuzzled her neck in what looked like a vampire's idea of foreplay.

"It's heating up, folks." Jason spoke into an imaginary microphone, using a sports-announcer voice that wasn't as funny as he thought it was. "Lazarro's totally focused, working his way methodically downfield . . ."

If Aimee had been there, she would've made some clever, condescending remark to break Nick's concentration and remind him not to get carried away. But Aimee wasn't playing—she'd dropped out of the game a month ago when she started up at Applebee's—so if anyone was going to intervene, it would have to be Jill.

But Jill kept her mouth shut as the kissing couple toppled onto the floor, Nick on top, Zoe's fishnet leg wrapped around the back of his knees. She was surprised by the depth of her indifference to this spectacle. If it had been Aimee beneath Nick, she would've been sick with jealousy. But it was just Zoe, and Zoe didn't matter. If Nick wanted her, he was welcome to have her.

Knock yourself out, she thought.

It was almost embarrassing to remember how much time and emotional energy she'd squandered on Nick in the fall, pining for the one boy she couldn't have, the prize Aimee had claimed for herself. He was still beautiful, with that square jaw and those dreamy lashes, but so what? Back in the summer, when she'd first gotten to know him, he'd also been sweet and funny, so attentive and alive—she remembered laughing with him more than she remembered the sex they'd had—but these days he was like a zombie, all grim business, just another jerk with an erection. And it wasn't just his fault—Jill felt clumsy and tongue-tied in his presence, unable to think of anything to say that might disturb the blankness on his face, make him remember that they were friends, that she was something more than an obliging mouth, or a hand with some greasy lotion on it.

But the real problem wasn't Nick, and it wasn't Jill or Zoe or any of the other players. It was Aimee. Until she stopped coming to Dmitri's, Jill hadn't realized how important she was, not just to the game, but to the group as a whole. She was the one essential member, the sun in their little solar system, the magnetic force that held them all together.

She's our Wardell Brown, Jill thought.

Wardell Brown had been the center on her brother's high school basketball team, a six-foot-six superstar who had regularly scored more points than the rest of his teammates combined. It was almost comical to watch them play together, four average-sized, perfectly competent white guys hustling to keep up with a graceful black giant who played the game on a whole different level. During Tom's senior year, Wardell led the Pirates all the way to the final round of the state tournament, only to sit out the championship game with a sprained ankle. Deprived of his services, the team fell apart, losing in a humiliating blowout.

"Wardell's our glue," the coach said afterward. "He's not there and the wheels come off."

That was how Jill felt, playing Get a Room without Aimee nearby. Inept. Unglued. Adrift. Like a small planet wobbling through deep space, cut loose from its orbit.

~~~~~~

THE ENTRÉES were taking forever. Or maybe it just felt that way. Nora wasn't used to eating in restaurants anymore, at least not restaurants in Mapleton, where everyone did such a bad job of pretending not to stare at her, sneaking sideways glances and peering over the tops of their menus, directing sly beams of pity in her direction, though it was possible that this was just her imagination, too. Maybe she just wanted to think she was the center of attention so she'd have an excuse for how conspicuous she felt, as though she were up onstage with a white-hot spotlight shining in her face, trapped in one of those bad dreams where you had a starring role in the school play, but had somehow neglected to memorize your lines.

"What were you like as a kid?" he asked.

"I don't know. Like everyone else, I guess."

"Not everyone's the same."

"They're not as different as they think."

"Were you a girly girl?" he pressed on. "Did you wear pink dresses and stuff like that?"

She could sense some scrutiny coming from a table slightly behind her and a little to the right, where a woman she recognized, but whose name was escaping her, was sitting with her husband and another couple. The woman's daughter, Taylor, had been a student at Little Sprouts Academy during Nora's stint as an assistant teacher. The girl had a wispy, barely audible voice—Nora was always asking her to repeat herself—and she talked obsessively about her best friend, Neil, and all the fun they had together. Nora must have known Taylor for six months before she figured out that Neil was a Boston terrier and not a boy from the neighborhood.

"I wore dresses sometimes. But I wasn't a little princess or anything."

"Were you a happy kid?"

"Happy enough, I guess. I had a couple of bad years in middle school."

"Why?"

"You know. Braces, acne. The usual."

"Did you have friends?"

"Sure. I mean, I wasn't the most popular kid in the world, but I had friends."

"What were their names?"

God, Nora thought. *He's relentless.* He'd been grilling her like this ever since they'd sat down, as if he were a reporter writing an article for the local paper—"My Dinner with Nora: The Heartbreaking Saga of a Pathetic Woman." The questions were benign enough—*What did you do today? Did you ever play field hockey? Have you had any broken bones?*—but they annoyed her nonetheless. She could tell they were just warm-ups, stand-ins for the questions he really wanted to ask: *What happened that night? How did you go on living? What's it like to be you?*

"That was a long time ago, Kevin."

"Not that long."

She spotted the waiter moving in their direction, a short, olive-skinned man with the face of a silent movie idol and a plate in each hand. *Finally,* she thought, but he just floated by, on his way to another table.

"You really don't remember their names?"

"I remember their names," she said, speaking more sharply than she'd meant to. "I'm not brain damaged."

"Sorry," he said. "I was just trying to make conversation."

"I know." Nora felt like a jerk for snapping at him. "It's not your fault."

He glanced worriedly toward the kitchen. "I wonder what's taking so long."

"It's a busy night," she said. "Their names were Liz, Lizzie, and Alexa."

~~~~~~

MAX STARTED undressing as soon as Jill shut the door, as if she were a doctor who didn't like to be kept waiting. He was wearing a wool sweater over a T-shirt, but he removed both garments in a single hurried tug, the static electricity causing his wispy hair to crackle and float up into a boyish halo. His chest was narrow compared to Nick's, smooth and unmuscled, his belly taut and sunken, but not in a way that made you think of sexy underwear models.

"It's been a while," he said, unbuckling his pants, letting them slide down his skinny thighs and pool around his ankles.

"Not that long. Just a week or so."

"Way longer than that," he said, stepping out of his jeans and kicking them against the wall, on top of his shirt and sweater. "Twelve days."

"But who's counting, right?"

"Yeah." His voice was flat and bitter. "Who's counting."

He was still mad at her, offended by the eagerness with which she'd pounced on Nick the moment he became available. But that was the game. You had to make choices, express preferences, cause and suffer pain. Every now and then, if you were lucky the way Nick and Aimee had been lucky, your first choice chose you as well. But most of the time it was messier than that.

"Well, I'm here now," she told him.

"That's right." He sat down on the edge of the bed, pulling off his socks and tossing them onto the pile of discarded clothes. "You get the consolation prize."

It would have been easy enough to contradict him, to remind him of how willingly she'd just surrendered the alleged first prize—on Valentine's Day, no less, not that any of them cared about that—but for some reason she withheld the kindness. She knew it wasn't fair. In a more logical world, her disappointment with Nick would have made her more appreciative of Max rather than less, but it hadn't worked out that way. All the contrast had done was highlight the shortcomings of both guys, the fact that the sexy one wasn't nice, and the nice one wasn't sexy.

"What's the matter?" he asked.

"Nothing. Why?"

"You're just standing there. Why don't you come to bed?"

"I don't know." Jill tried to smile, but it didn't really work. "I'm just feeling a little shy tonight."

"Shy?" He couldn't help laughing. "It's a little late for shy."

She moved her arm in a vague arc, trying to encompass the game, the room, and their lives in the gesture.

"You ever get tired of this?"

"Sometimes," he said. "Not tonight."

She didn't move. After a few seconds, he stretched himself out on the bed, ankles crossed, fingers interlaced beneath his head. His briefs were unfamiliar, brown tighties with orange piping, unusually stylish.

"Nice undies," she told him.

"My mom got them at Costco. Eight-pack, all different colors."

"My mom used to buy me underwear," she said. "But I told her it was weird, so she stopped."

Max rolled onto his side, propping his chin on his hand, studying her with a thoughtful expression. Now he really did look like an underwear model, if there was a world where underwear models had hairy pipe-cleaner legs and bad muscle tone.

"I forgot to tell you," he said. "I saw your mother the other day. She followed me home from my guitar lesson. Her and this other woman."

"Really?" Jill tried to sound casual. It was embarrassing, the way her heart leaped every time someone mentioned her mother. "How's she doing?"

"Hard to tell. They just did that thing, you know, where they stand really close and stare at you."

"I hate that."

"It's creepy," he agreed. "But I didn't say anything mean. I just let them walk me home."

Jill felt almost sick with longing. She hadn't caught a glimpse of her mother for months and never bumped into her on the streets of Mapleton, though she was apparently a familiar figure around town. Other people saw her all the time.

"Was she smoking?"

"Yeah."

"Did you see her light a cigarette?"

"Probably. Why?"

"I gave her a lighter for Christmas. I just wondered if she was using it."

"Beats me." His face tightened with thought. "No, wait. They had matches."

"You sure?"

"Yeah." The doubt had left his voice. "This was like last Friday. Remember how cold it was with the windchill? Her hand was shaking and she was having a really hard time striking the match. I offered to do it for her, but she wouldn't let me. It took her like three or four tries to get the thing lit."

Bitch, Jill thought. *Serves her right.*

"Come on." Max patted the bed. "Relax. You don't have to take your clothes off if you don't want to."

Jill considered the offer. She used to like resting with Max in the dark, two warm bodies under the covers, talking about whatever came into their heads.

"I won't touch you," he promised. "I won't even jerk off."

"That's sweet of you," she said. "But I think I'm gonna go home."

<center>~~~~~</center>

THEY WERE both relieved when the food finally arrived, partly because they were hungry, but mainly because it gave them an excuse to suspend the conversation for a little while, take a breather, and maybe start over on a lighter note. Kevin knew he'd made a mistake, peppering her with so many questions, turning the small talk into an interrogation.

Be patient, he told himself. *This is supposed to be fun.*

After a few silent bites, Nora looked up from her mushroom ravioli.

"Delicious," she said. "The cream sauce."

"Mine, too." He held up a morsel of lamb for her perusal, showing her how perfectly grilled it was, brown at the edges, pink in the middle. "Melts in your mouth."

She smiled a bit queasily, and he remembered, too late, that she didn't eat meat. Did it disgust her, he wondered, being asked to admire a piece of cooked flesh skewered on a fork? He understood all too well how you could talk yourself into vegetarianism, teach yourself to think "dead animal" rather than "tender and succulent." He'd done it himself on numerous occasions, usually after reading articles about factory farms and slaughterhouses, but his qualms always vanished the moment he picked up a menu.

"So how was your day?" she asked. "Anything interesting happen?"

Kevin only hesitated for a second. He'd seen this moment coming and had been planning on playing it safe, saying something bland and innocuous—*Not really, just went to work and came home*—saving the truth for later, some unspecified time in the future when he knew her a little better and their relationship was a little stronger. But when would that be? How could you get to know someone a little better if you couldn't give an honest answer to a simple question, especially about something so important?

"My son called this afternoon," he told her. "I hadn't heard from him since the summer. I was really worried about him."

"Wow," she said after a brief silence that didn't quite thicken to the point of awkwardness. "Is he okay?"

"I think so." Kevin wanted to smile, but did his best to resist the impulse. "He sounded pretty good."

"Where is he?"

"He wouldn't say. The cell phone he used had a Vermont area code, but it wasn't his. I was just so relieved to hear the sound of his voice."

"Good for you," she said a bit stiffly, making an effort to sound pleased and sincere.

"Is this okay?" he asked. "We can talk about something else if you—"

"It's fine," she assured him. "I'm happy for you."

Kevin decided not to press his luck.

"What about you? Do anything fun this afternoon?"

"Not really," she said. "Got my eyebrows waxed."

"They look good. Nice and neat."

"Thanks." She touched her forehead, tracing her fingertip over the top of her right eyebrow, which did seem a little more sharply defined than usual. "Is your son still part of that cult? That Holy Wayne thing?"

"He says he's done with that." Kevin looked down at the fat candle in its stubby glass holder, the quivering flame floating on a puddle of melted wax. He felt an urge to plunge his finger into the hot liquid, letting it harden in the air like a second skin. "Says he's thinking about maybe coming home, going back to school."

"Really?"

"That's what he said. I hope it's true."

Nora picked up her knife and fork and cut into a ravioli. It was big and pillowy, crimped along the edges.

"Were you close?" she asked, still looking down, slicing the halves into quarters. "You and your son?"

"I thought we were." Kevin was surprised by the shakiness in his voice. "He was my little boy. I was always so proud of him."

Nora looked up with an odd expression on her face. Kevin could feel his mouth stretching, the pressure building inside his eyeballs.

"I'm sorry," he said, in the instant before he clapped his hand over his mouth, trying to muffle the sound of his blubbering. "Just give me a second."

~~~~~

IT WAS maybe fifteen degrees out, but the night air felt clean and invigorating. Jill stood on the sidewalk and took a good long look at Dmitri's house, her home away from home for the past six months. It was a shabby little place, a generic suburban box with a concrete stoop and a picture window to the left of the front door. In the day-time the exterior was a dirty shade of beige, but right now it was no color at all, just a dark shape against an even darker background. An odd sense of melancholy took hold of her—it was the same feeling she got walking past her old ballet school, or the soccer fields at

Greenway Park—as if the world were a museum of memories, a collection of places she'd outgrown.

Good times, she thought, but only as an experiment, just to see if she believed it. Then she turned and started for home, the street so quiet and the air so thin that her footsteps sounded like a drumbeat on the pavement, loud enough to wake the neighbors.

It wasn't that late, but Mapleton was a ghost town, not a pedestrian or a stray dog in sight. She turned onto Windsor Road, reminding herself to look alert and purposeful. She'd taken a self-defense course a couple of years ago, and the instructor had said that not looking like a victim was Rule Number One. *Keep your head up and your eyes open. Look like you know exactly where you're going, even when you don't.*

At the corner of North Avenue, she paused to consider her options. It was a fifteen-minute walk from here to Lovell Terrace, but only half that if she cut across the railroad tracks. If Aimee had been there she wouldn't have hesitated—they took the shortcut all the time—but Jill had never done it on her own. To get to the crossing, you had to walk down a desolate stretch of road, past auto repair shops, the Department of Public Works, and mysterious factories with names like Syn-Gen Systems and Standard Nipple Works, and then slip through a hole in the chain-link fence at the rear of the school bus parking lot. Once you crossed the tracks and circled around the back of Walgreens, you were in a much better area, a residential neighborhood with lots of streetlights and trees.

She didn't hear the car. It just whooshed up from behind, a sudden alarming presence at the edge of her vision. She let out a gasp, then whirled into an awkward karate stance as the passenger window slid down.

"Whoa." A familiar blissed-out face was peering at her, framed by reassuring blond dreadlocks. "You okay?"

"I was." Jill tried to sound exasperated as she lowered her hands. "Until you scared the shit outta me."

"Sorry about that." Scott Frost, the unpierced twin, was the passenger. "You know karate?"

"Yeah, Jackie Chan's my uncle."

He grinned his approval. "Good one."

"Where's Aimee?" Adam Frost called from the driver's seat. "We haven't seen her for a while."

"Working," Jill explained. "She got a job at Applebee's."

Scott squinted at her with puffy, soulful eyes. "Need a ride somewhere?"

"I'm good," she told him. "I live right across the tracks."

"You sure? It's fucking freezing out."

Jill gave a stoic shrug. "I don't mind walking."

"Hey." Adam leaned into view. "If you see Aimee, tell her I said hi."

"Maybe we could party sometime," Scott suggested. "All four of us."

"Sure," Jill said, and the Prius departed as quietly as it had arrived.

~~~~~~

IN THE men's room, Kevin splashed cold water on his face and wiped it off with a paper towel. He felt like a fool, breaking down in front of Nora like that. He could see how uncomfortable it made her, the way she froze up, like she'd never seen a grown man cry and didn't even know it was possible.

He'd caught himself by surprise, too. He'd been so worried about her reaction to what he was saying, he wasn't even thinking about his own. But something had snapped inside of him, a rubber band of tension that had been wound so tight for so long he'd forgotten it was even there. It was the phrase *little boy* that had done it, the sudden memory of an easy weight on his shoulders, Tom perched up there like a king on a throne, gazing down upon the world, one delicate hand resting on top of his father's head, the heels of his Velcro-fastened sneakers knocking softly against Kevin's chest as they walked.

Despite what had happened, he was glad he'd shared his good news with her, glad he'd resisted the temptation to spare her feelings. *For what?* So they could continue hiding from each other, eating their meal in uneasy silence, wondering why they had nothing to talk about? This way was harder, but it felt like a breakthrough, a necessary first step on a road that might actually lead somewhere worth going.

I don't know about you, he thought he would tell her when he got back, *but a nice dinner always makes me cry.*

That would be the way to handle it—no apology, just a little joke to smooth things over. He crumpled the towel and dropped it into the wastebasket, checking himself one last time in the mirror before heading out the door.

A small seed of alarm sprouted in his chest as he made his way across the dining room and saw that their table was empty. He told himself not to worry, that she must have taken advantage of his absence to make her own trip to the restroom. He poured himself a little more wine and ate a forkful of roasted beet salad, trying not to stare at the balled-up napkin resting beside her plate.

A couple of minutes went by. Kevin thought about knocking on the ladies' room door, maybe sticking his head inside to see if she was okay, but the handsome waiter stopped by the table before he had a chance. The man looked at Kevin with an expression that seemed to combine equal parts sadness and sympathetic amusement. His voice had a slight Spanish accent.

"Shall I clear the lady's plate, sir? Or would you just prefer the check?"

Kevin wanted to protest, to insist that the lady would be right back, but he knew it was futile.

"Did she—?"

"She asked me to convey her apologies."

"But I drove," Kevin said. "She doesn't have a car."

The waiter lowered his gaze, nodding toward the food on Kevin's plate.

"Shall I box that up for you?"

JILL CROSSED the street, keeping her chin up and her shoulders back as she hustled past Junior's Auto Body, a hospital for cars with shattered windshields and dimpled doors, dangling fenders and crumpled front ends. Some of the bad ones had deflated air bags drooping from the steering wheels, and it wasn't unusual for a bag to be spotted with blood. She knew from experience not to look too hard or think too much about the people who'd been inside.

She felt like an idiot for declining the twins' offer of a ride home. It was just injured pride that made her do it, anger at them for sneaking up on her like that, even if they hadn't meant to. There was also a certain amount of good-girl caution at work, the little voice in her head that reminded her not to get into cars with strangers. It was kind of self-defeating in this case, since the alternative seemed even dicier than the danger she was supposedly trying to avoid.

Besides, the twins weren't really strangers, nor was Jill the least bit scared of them. Aimee said they'd been total gentlemen the day she'd cut school and hung out at their house. All they'd wanted to do was get high and play Ping-Pong, hours and hours of Ping-Pong. Apparently they were really good at it, even when they were wasted. If they ever had a Pothead Olympics, Aimee figured that the Frost twins would probably win gold and silver medals in table tennis, dominating the competition like Venus and Serena.

In the course of that same conversation, Aimee floated her suspicion that Scott Frost had a little crush on Jill, a possibility Jill had refused to take seriously at the time. Why would Scott have a crush on *her*? He didn't even know her, and she wasn't the kind of girl that guys got crushes on from afar.

There's a first time for everything, Aimee had told her.

Except when there's not, Jill had replied.

But now she wondered, thinking about the way Scott had been looking at her, the disappointment in his eyes when she told him she felt like walking, and even the way he'd chortled at her stupid Jackie Chan joke, which meant that he was either very stoned or very well disposed toward her, or both.

Maybe we could party together, he'd said. *All four of us.*

Maybe we could, she thought.

JILL HEARD the whistle of an approaching train as she entered the Stellar Transport parking lot, home to a vast herd of yellow buses, more than enough to evacuate the entire town. They seemed otherworldly at night, row upon row of hulking beasts, their front ends staring straight ahead, a regiment of identical stupid faces. She hurried past them, eyes darting warily left and right, checking the dark alleys that separated one from the next.

The whistle sounded again, followed by the clanging of alarm bells and a sudden *whomp* of displaced air as a double-decker commuter train blew by on the eastbound track, a speeding wall of dull steel and luminous glass. For a few deafening seconds, there was nothing else in the world, and then it was gone, the earth trembling in its wake.

Continuing on her way, she rounded the bumper of the last bus and turned left. She didn't see the bearded man until they were right on top of each other, trapped between the bus on her left and the eight-foot-high chain-link fence on her right. She opened her mouth to scream, but by then she'd realized it wasn't necessary.

"You scared me," she said.

The bearded man stared at her. He was a Watcher, short and stocky, dressed in a white lab coat and painter's pants, and he seemed to be having a medical emergency.

"Are you okay?" she asked.

The man didn't respond. He was hunched over, hands on his thighs, gulping for air like a fish out of water, making a strangled sound every time he opened his mouth.

"Do you want me to call 911?"

The Watcher shook his head and straightened up. Reaching into his pants pocket, he pulled out an inhaler and brought it to his mouth, pressing the button and sucking hard. He waited a few seconds before exhaling, and then repeated the operation.

The medicine worked fast. By the time he put the inhaler back in his pocket, he was already breathing easier, still panting a bit, but no longer making that horrible noise. He dusted off his pants and took a small step forward. Jill backed up to give him room, flattening herself against the fence so he could squeeze past.

"Have a good night," she called after him, just to be nice, because so many people weren't.

~~~~~

KEVIN LEFT the restaurant in a funk, the bag of leftovers bouncing gently against his leg. He hadn't wanted to take it, but the waiter had insisted, telling him it would be a shame to waste so much good food.

Nora's house was at least a mile away, so there was no way she could have made it home by now. If he wanted to find her, he could just cruise down Washington Boulevard, keeping his eye out for a lone pedestrian. The hard part would come after that, when he pulled up beside her and lowered the passenger window.

Get in, he'd say. *Let me drive you home. It's the least I can do.*

Because why did she deserve that courtesy? She'd left of her own free will, without a word of explanation. If she wanted to walk home in the cold, that was her prerogative. And if she wanted to call him later and apologize—well, that ball was in her court, too.

But what if she didn't call? What if he waited for hours and the phone never rang? At what point would he lose his nerve and call her, or maybe even drive over to her house, ring the bell until she opened the door? Two A.M.? Four in the morning? Daybreak? The one thing he knew for sure was that he wouldn't be able to get to sleep until he'd at least talked to her, gotten some kind of explanation for what had just happened. So maybe the smartest thing was just to go after her right now, have it out as soon as possible, so he didn't have to spend the rest of the night wondering.

He was so caught up in this quandary that he barely noticed the two Watchers standing by his car, didn't even realize who they were until he'd already opened the locks with his remote key.

"Hey," he said, feeling a momentary sense of relief that Nora wasn't there, that they didn't have to go through that particular drama just now, the new girlfriend meeting the estranged wife. "You guys okay?"

They didn't answer, but they didn't have to, not when it was this cold out. The partner looked hypothermic—she was hugging herself and rocking from side to side, a cigarette stuck in one corner of her mouth like it had been glued in place—but Laurie was gazing at him with a tender, unwavering expression, the kind of look people give you in the funeral home when the deceased is a member of your family and they want to acknowledge your pain.

"What's the matter?" he asked.

There was a manila envelope in Laurie's hand. She held it out, jabbing it at his chest like it was something he needed to see.

"What is it?"

She gave him a look that said, *You know what it is.*

"Oh, Jesus," he muttered. "Are you kidding me?"

Her expression didn't change. She just held out the envelope until he took it.

"I'm sorry," she said, breaking her vow of silence. The sound of her voice was shocking to him, so strange and familiar at the same time, like the voice of a dead person in a dream. "I wish there was some other way."

〰〰〰

JILL SQUEEZED through the hole in the fence and trudged up the gravel embankment, pausing at the top to check for oncoming trains. It was an exhilarating place to be, all alone in that wide-open space, like she had the whole world to herself. The tracks flowed into the

distance on either side of her like a river, the rails catching the light of
the three-quarter moon, two parallel gleams fading into the darkness.

She balanced on one like a tightrope walker, tiptoeing with her
arms outstretched, trying to imagine what would have happened if
the Watcher she'd met back there had been her mother. Would they
have laughed and hugged each other, amazed to find themselves alone
in such an unlikely place? Or would her mother have been angry to
find her there, disappointed by the alcohol on her breath, her deplor-
able lack of judgment?

Well, whose fault is that? Jill thought, hopping off the rail. *Nobody's
looking out for me.*

She headed down the embankment on the other side, descending
toward the service road that ran behind Walgreens, her sneakers slipping on the loose gravel. Then she stopped.

A sound got trapped in her throat.

She knew that the Watchers always traveled in pairs, but the encounter with the bearded man had been so brief and awkward that
she hadn't stopped to wonder where his partner was.

Well, now she knew.

She took a few reluctant steps forward, moving closer to the white-
clad figure on the ground. He was lying facedown near a big Dumpster that said GALLUCCI BROS., his arms spread wide as if he were
trying to embrace the planet. There was a small pool of liquid near his
head, a luminous substance she badly wanted to believe was water.

Part *Five*

MIRACLE CHILD

ANY MINUTE NOW

IT WAS WAY TOO CHILLY to be sitting on the back deck with a cup of morning coffee, but Kevin couldn't help himself. After being cooped up all winter, he wanted to take advantage of every minute of sunshine and fresh air that the world allowed, even if he had to wear a sweater, a jacket, and a woolen cap to enjoy it.

Spring had come quickly in the past few weeks—snowdrops and hyacinths, flashes of yellow in the suddenly undead bushes, and then a riotous explosion of birdsong and dogwood blossoms, more new green every time you turned your head. The winter hadn't been harsh by historical standards, but it had felt long and stubborn, almost eternal. March was especially bleak—cold and damp, gray sky pressing down—the gloomy weather reflecting and intensifying the mood of foreboding that had afflicted Mapleton ever since the murder of the second Watcher on Valentine's Day. In the absence of any evidence to the contrary, people had convinced themselves that a serial killer was on the loose, some unhinged loner with a grudge against the G.R. and a plan to eliminate the organization, one member at a time.

It would have been bad enough if Kevin had simply been dealing with the crisis as an elected official, but he was involved as a father and a husband, too, worried about the psychological well-being of his daughter and the physical safety of his soon-to-be-ex-wife. He still hadn't signed the divorce papers Laurie had given him, but it wasn't because he thought their marriage could be saved. He was delaying for Jill's sake, not wanting to dump more bad news on her now, when she was still recovering from the shock of finding the body.

It had been an awful experience, but Kevin was proud of the way she'd responded, calling 911 on her cell phone, waiting alone in the dark with the dead man until the cops arrived. Since then, she'd done everything she could to assist the investigation, submitting to multiple interviews with detectives, helping an artist produce a sketch of the bearded Watcher she'd seen in the Stellar Transport parking lot, even visiting the Ginkgo Street compound to see if she could spot the man in a series of lineups that supposedly included every male resident over the age of thirty.

The lineups were a bust, but the sketch bore fruit: The bearded man was identified as Gus Jenkins, a forty-six-year-old former florist from Gifford Township who'd been living in a G.R. "outpost" on Parker Road—the same group home, Kevin was startled to learn, into which Laurie had recently moved. The victim, Julian Adams, lived in the same house and had been seen with Jenkins on the night of the murder.

After repeated denials, the G.R. leadership finally admitted that Jenkins was a member of the Mapleton Chapter, but insisted—

unconvincingly, according to investigators—that the organization had no idea as to his current whereabouts. This stonewalling infuriated the cops, who'd made it clear that they were seeking Jenkins as a witness, not a potential suspect. A couple of detectives even wondered out loud if the G.R. *wanted* the killer to remain at large, if they might be secretly pleased to have a homicidal maniac turning their members into martyrs.

Two months had passed without any breakthroughs in the case, but also without a third murder. People got a little bored with the story, started to wonder if maybe they'd overreacted. As the weather changed, Kevin sensed a shift in the collective mood, as if the whole town had suddenly decided to lighten up and stop obsessing about dead Watchers and serial killers. He'd seen this process before: It didn't matter what happened in the world—genocidal wars, natural disasters, unspeakable crimes, mass disappearances, whatever—eventually people got tired of brooding about it. Time moved on, seasons changed, individuals withdrew into their private lives, turned their faces toward the sun. On balance, he thought, it was probably a good thing.

"There you are."

Aimee stepped through the sliding door that connected the kitchen to the deck, then turned to shut the door with her elbow. She had a mug in one hand, the coffee carafe in the other.

"Want a refill?"

"You read my mind."

Aimee poured the coffee, then pulled up a cushionless metal chair, giving an exaggerated shudder as her butt touched the seat. She was wearing a Carhartt jacket over a nightgown she'd borrowed from Jill, but her feet were bare on the rough wood.

"It's quarter after nine," she said through a yawn. "I figured you left for work."

"Pretty soon," Kevin said. "There's no rush."

She nodded vaguely, not bothering to point out that he was *never* home after nine in the morning, or to suggest that he might have delayed his departure on her account, because he'd grown attached to their morning talks and didn't want to leave while she was still asleep. But he didn't have to say it; it was in the air, obvious to both of them.

"What time did you get in last night?"

"Late," she said. "A bunch of us went out to a bar."

"Derek, too?"

She made a guilty face. She knew he didn't approve of her relationship with her married boss, though she'd explained numerous times that it wasn't much of a relationship—just a bad habit, really, something to pass the time.

"Did he drive you home?"

"It's on the way."

Kevin swallowed his usual lecture. He wasn't her father; she was entitled to her mistakes, just like everyone else.

"I told you," he said. "You can use the Civic anytime you want. It's just sitting in the garage."

"I know. But even if I had a car last night, I was in no condition to drive."

He looked at her a little more closely as she sipped her coffee, both hands wrapped around the mug for warmth. She seemed alert and upbeat, not visibly hungover. At that age, he remembered, you just bounced right back.

"What?" she asked, uncomfortable with the scrutiny.

"Nothing."

She put down the mug, slipped her hands into her coat pockets.

"Gonna be a cold night for softball," she said.

Kevin shrugged. "The weather's part of the game, you know? You're out there under the sky. Cold in the spring, hot in the summer. That's why I never liked those domed stadiums. You lose all that."

"I could never get into softball." She turned her head, distracted by a bluejay flashing by. "I played one season when I was a kid, and I couldn't believe how boring it was. They used to stick me in the outfield, a million miles away from home plate. All I wanted to do was lie down in the grass, put my glove over my face, and take a nap." She smiled, amused by the memory. "I did it a couple of times. Nobody even missed me."

"Too bad," he said. "I guess I won't try to recruit you for next season."

"Recruit me for what?"

"My team. We're thinking about going coed. We need more players."

She bit her bottom lip, looking thoughtful.

"I might give it a try," she told him.

"But you just said—"

"I've matured. I have a much higher tolerance for boredom."

Kevin plucked a peach blossom from the surface of his coffee and flicked it over the railing. He caught the teasing lilt in Aimee's voice, but also the truth that lay beneath it. She *had* matured. Somehow, in the past couple of months, he'd stopped thinking of her as a high school girl, or his daughter's cute friend who stayed out too late. She was *his* friend now, his coffee buddy, the sympathetic listener who'd helped him through his breakup with Nora, a young woman who brightened his day every time he saw her.

"I promise I won't put you in the outfield," he said.

"Cool." She gathered her long hair with both hands as if making a ponytail, but then changed her mind, letting it spill back over her shoulders, soft and pretty against the rough twill of her jacket. "Maybe we could play catch sometime. When it's warmer out. See if I even remember how to throw."

Kevin looked away, suddenly embarrassed. In the far corner of the yard, two squirrels raced up a tree trunk, their little feet scrabbling frantically on the bark. He couldn't tell if they were having a good time or trying to kill each other.

"Oh, well," he said, playing the tabletop like a bongo. "Guess I better get to work."

〰〰

TOM WAS Christine's alarm clock. It was his job to wake her by nine in the morning. If she slept any later than that, it made her cranky and threw off her whole circadian rhythm. He hated to disturb her, though: She looked so blissful lying there on her back, her breathing slow and shallow, one hand behind her head, the other by her side. Her face was empty and serene, her belly huge beneath the thin blanket, a perfect human igloo. Her due date was just a week away.

"Hey, sleepyhead." He took her hand, tugging gently on her index finger, then her middle finger, moving methodically toward the pinkie. "Time to get up."

"Go 'way," she muttered. "I'm tired."

"I know. But you need to get up."

"Leave me alone."

This went on for another minute or two, Tom coaxing, Christine resisting, hampered by the fact that she could no longer roll onto her side without a massive amount of willpower and logistical calculation. Her preferred evasive maneuver—flopping onto her stomach and burying her face in the pillow—was totally out of the question.

"Come on, sweetie. Let's go downstairs and have breakfast."

She must have been hungry, because she finally deigned to open her eyes, blinking against the dim light, squinting at Tom as though he were a distant acquaintance whose name was on the tip of her tongue.

"What time is it?"

"Time to get up."

"Not yet." She patted the mattress, inviting him to join her. "Just a few more minutes."

This was part of the ritual, too, the best part, Tom's reward for performing an otherwise thankless task. He stretched out beside her on the bed, turning onto his side so he could look at her face, the one part of her body that hadn't changed dramatically over the past few months. It remained thin and girlish, as if it still hadn't gotten the news about the pregnancy.

"Ooh!" Wincing with surprise, she took his hand and placed it on her belly, right on top of her popped-out navel. "He's really busy in there."

Tom could feel a swirling movement beneath his palm, a hard object pressing against her abdominal wall—a hand or a foot, maybe an elbow. It wasn't easy to distinguish one fetal extremity from another.

"Somebody wants out," he said.

Unlike Christine and the Falks, Tom refused to refer to the fetus as "he." There hadn't been an ultrasound, so nobody knew for sure if it was a boy or a girl. The baby's supposed maleness was an article of faith, based on Mr. Gilchrest's certainty that the miracle child was a replacement for the son he'd lost. Tom hoped he was right, because it was sad to imagine the alternative, an infant girl being welcomed into the world with groans of shock and dismay.

"Are they home?" Christine asked.

"Yup. They're waiting for you."

"God," she sighed. "Can't they go away for the weekend or something?"

They'd been living with the Falks for three and a half months, and by now, even Christine was sick of them. She didn't dislike Terrence and Marcella the way Tom did, couldn't afford to resent their generosity, or laugh at their slavish devotion to Mr. Gilchrest. She just felt suffocated by their constant attention. All day long they hovered, trying to anticipate her needs, fulfill her smallest desire, as long as it didn't involve leaving the house. Tom knew that was the only reason he was still here—because Christine needed him, because she would've gone crazy, trapped for so long with just the Falks for company. If it had been up to their hosts, he would've been out on his ass a long time ago.

"You kidding?" he said. "They're not going anywhere, not this close to the big day. They wouldn't want to miss out on the fun."

"Yeah." She nodded with deadpan enthusiasm. "It's gonna be so great. I can't wait to go into labor."

"I hear it's a blast."

"That's what everybody tells me. Especially when it lasts really long and you don't have any pain medication. That part sounds awesome."

"I know," Tom agreed. "I'm totally jealous."

She patted her stomach. "I just hope the baby's really big. With one of those gigantic melon heads. That'll make it even better."

They joked like this all the time. It was Christine's way of calming her nerves, preparing herself for the ordeal of natural childbirth. That was how Mr. Gilchrest wanted it—no doctors, no hospital, no drugs. Just a midwife and some ice chips, a little Motown on the iPod, Terrence standing by with the video camera, ready to record the big event for posterity.

"I shouldn't complain," she said. "They've been really nice to me. I just need a break, you know?"

She'd been restless lately, tired of being pregnant and housebound, especially now that the weather was so nice. Just last week, she'd persuaded the Falks to take her for a drive in the country, but they'd been so nervous about having her in the car—unable to talk about anything except how horrible it would be if they got into an accident—that it hadn't been any fun for anybody.

"Don't worry." He reached for her hand, gave it a reassuring squeeze. "You're almost there. Just a few days to go."

"You think Wayne'll be out by then?"

"I don't know," he said. "I don't really understand the legal system."

For the past several weeks, the Falks had been claiming that Mr. Gilchrest's lawyers were making real progress on his case. From what they'd heard, a deal was in the works that would allow him to plead guilty to some minor charges and get off without any additional jail time. *Any minute now,* they kept saying. *We should hear some good news any minute.* Tom was skeptical, but the Falks seemed genuinely excited, and their optimism had rubbed off on Christine.

"You should come back to the Ranch with us," she told him. "You could live in one of the guesthouses."

Tom appreciated the offer. He'd grown attached to Christine and the baby—at least the *idea* of the baby—and would have liked to stay close to them. But not like that, not if it meant living in Mr. Gilchrest's shadow.

"You'd be welcome there," she promised. "I'll tell Wayne what a good friend you've been. He'll be really grateful." She waited for a response that didn't come. "It's not like you have anywhere else to go."

That wasn't exactly true. After the baby came, when Christine didn't need him anymore, Tom figured he'd head back home to Mapleton, spend a few days with his father and sister—he'd been thinking a lot about them in the past few months, though he hadn't called or e-mailed—maybe say hi to his mom if he could find her. After that, though, Christine was right—his life was a blank slate.

"Wayne's a good man," she said, gazing up at the poster on the ceiling, the one Tom didn't like to look at. "Pretty soon the whole world's gonna know it."

~~~~~

LAURIE AND Meg arrived early for their nine o'clock meeting, but they weren't invited into the Director's office until close to noon. Patti Levin seemed genuinely embarrassed about the delay.

"I didn't forget about you," she assured them. "It's just really hectic this morning. My assistant's out with the flu, and the whole operation just falls apart without her. I promise it'll never happen again."

Laurie was puzzled by the apology, which seemed to be based on the assumption that she and Meg were busy people who didn't like to be kept waiting. In her previous life, Laurie *had* been that sort of person, an overscheduled suburban mom juggling errands and kids, forever racing from one obligation to the next. Back then, when everybody thought the world would last forever, nobody had time for anything. No matter what she was doing—baking cookies, walking around the lake on a beautiful day, making love to her husband—she felt rushed and jittery, as if the last few grains of sand were at that very moment sliding through the narrow waist of an hourglass. Any unforeseen occurrence—road construction, an inexperienced cashier, a missing set of keys—could plunge her into a mood of frantic despair that could poison an entire day. But that was her old self. Her new self had nothing to do but smoke and wait, and she wasn't all that particular about where she did it. The hallway outside the Director's office was as good a place as any.

"So how's it going?" Patti Levin asked with a smile. "How are things at Outpost 17?"

Laurie and Meg traded glances, pleasantly surprised by the Director's friendly tone. The summons they'd received had been terse and a bit ominous—*Report to HQ, 9 A.M. tomorrow*—and they'd spent a good part of the previous evening trying to figure out if they might be in some kind of trouble. Laurie thought she might get scolded for her failure to return the divorce petition. Meg toyed with the idea that their house was bugged, that the leadership not only knew how regularly they violated their Vows of Silence, but exactly what they said as well. *You're being paranoid,* Laurie told her, but she couldn't help wondering if it might be true, racking her brain to see if she'd said anything over the past couple of months that might come back to haunt her.

"We like it there," Meg said. "It's a really nice place."

"It's got a great backyard," Laurie added.

"Doesn't it?" the Director agreed, touching a match flame to the tip of her cigarette. "I bet it's lovely this time of year."

Meg nodded. "It's so lush. And there's a little tree with the prettiest pink blossoms. I'm not sure if it's cherry or—"

"I'm told it's a redbud," the Director said. "Fairly unusual in these parts."

"The only problem is the birds," Laurie observed. "You wouldn't believe how loud they are in the morning. It's like they're right there in the bedroom. Hundreds of 'em, all chirping at one another."

"We think it might be nice to plant a vegetable garden," Meg said. "Green beans, zucchini, tomatoes, stuff like that. Totally organic."

"It would pay for itself," Laurie chimed in. "We just need a small investment to get started."

They were really excited about the garden plan—they had a lot of time on their hands and wanted to do something constructive with it—but the Director blew right past the subject as though she hadn't even heard them.

"Where do you sleep?" she asked. "Have you moved into the master bedroom?"

Laurie shook her head. "We're still upstairs."

"Separate rooms," Meg added quickly, which was technically true, but a bit misleading, since her own mattress had taken up permanent residence on the floor of Laurie's bedroom. They both felt better that way, close enough to whisper, especially now that they were alone at the outpost.

Patti Levin squinted in disapproval, exhaling a jet of smoke from the corner of her mouth.

"The master bedroom's much nicer. Isn't there a Jacuzzi down there?"

Meg blushed. It was a rare night at the outpost when she didn't avail herself of the Jacuzzi. Laurie liked it okay, but the novelty had worn off pretty quickly.

"The only reason I bring it up," the Director went on, "is because your new housemates will be arriving next week. If you want to make a move, this would be a good time to do it."

"Housemates?" Meg said without a whole lot of enthusiasm.

"Al and Josh," the Director said. "Really special guys. I think you'll like them."

This news wasn't unexpected—it was one of the first possibilities they'd discussed last night—but Laurie was surprised by the depth of her disappointment. She and Meg were happy on their own. They were like sisters or college roommates, totally relaxed and unself-conscious, familiar with each other's quirks and moods. She wasn't looking forward to the intrusion of newcomers, the awkwardness of once again sharing the house with strange men. The whole domestic chemistry would change, especially if one of them got a crush on Meg, or Meg got a crush on one of them. Laurie didn't even want to think about that, all the sexual tension and twentysomething drama, no peace for anyone.

"You've got a beautiful tradition at Outpost 17," the Director told them. "I hope you two can keep it going."

"We'll do our best," Laurie promised, though she wasn't quite sure what the tradition was, or how she and Meg might go about preserving it.

Patti Levin seemed to catch her uncertainty.

"Gus and Julian are heroes," she said in a firm and quiet voice. "We need to honor their sacrifice."

"Gus?" Meg said. "Did he get killed, too?"

"Gus is fine," the Director said. "He's a very brave man. We're taking very good care of him."

"What did he do?" Meg asked, giving voice to Laurie's own confusion. All they knew was that Gus hadn't come home the night Julian got killed, and that the police were still looking for him. "What was his sacrifice?"

"He loved Julian," the Director said. "Can you imagine the courage it took to do what he did?"

"What did he did do?" Meg asked again.

"He did what we asked him to."

Laurie felt suddenly light-headed, as if she might pass out. She remembered squatting by the radiator on those cold winter nights, listening to the shameless, almost desperate noise Gus and Julian were making in the master bedroom, as if they were beyond all caring.

Patti Levin sucked on her cigarette, staring at Meg for a long moment, and then shifting her gaze to Laurie, filling the space between them with a cloud of grayish smoke.

"The world went back to sleep," she said. "It's our duty to wake it up."

~~~~~

KEVIN KNEW it was overkill, reading the paper with the TV on and his laptop open while eating his pregame sandwich, but it wasn't as bad as it looked. He wasn't really using the laptop—he just liked to keep it handy in case he felt like checking his e-mail—nor was he reading the paper in any formal sense. He was just sort of scanning it, exercising his eyes, letting them roam over the headlines in the Business section without absorbing any information. As for the TV, that was just background noise, an illusion of company in the empty house. All he was thinking about was the sandwich itself, turkey and cheddar on wheat, a little mustard and some lettuce, nothing fancy, but perfectly adequate nonetheless.

He was almost finished when Jill came in through the back door, pausing in the mudroom to drop her heavy backpack on the floor. She must've been in the library, he thought. That was what she'd been doing lately, making sure she didn't get home from school until Aimee had left for work. They had it down to a science, at least on the weekdays, timing their arrivals and departures so that they never overlapped in the house unless one of them was sleeping, though they both insisted that they were getting along just fine.

He smiled sheepishly when she entered the kitchen, expecting her to tease him about his multimedia meal, but she didn't even notice. She was too busy squinting at her phone, looking surprised and impressed at the same time.

"Hey," she said. "You hear about Holy Wayne?"

"What's going on?"

"He pled guilty."

"Which charges?"

"Bunch of them," she said. "Looks like he's going away for a long time."

Kevin woke up his laptop and checked the news. The story was right there at the top. HOLY WAYNE FESSES UP: EXTRAORDINARY MEA CULPA FROM DISGRACED CULT LEADER. He clicked the link and started to read:

Surprise deal . . . prosecutors recommend twenty-year sentence . . . eligible for parole in twelve . . . "After my boy disappeared, I lost my bearings . . . All I wanted to do was help people who were in pain, but the power went to my head . . . I took advantage of so many vulnerable kids . . . betrayed my wife and the memory of my son, not to mention the trust of the young people who looked to me for healing and spiritual guidance . . . Especially the girls . . . They weren't my wives, they were my victims . . . I wanted to be a holy man, but I turned into a monster."

Kevin tried to concentrate on the words, but his eyes kept straying to the picture that accompanied the story, the all-too-familiar mug shot of a sullen, unshaven man in a pajama top. He was surprised to realize that he felt no satisfaction, no vengeful pleasure at the thought of Holy Wayne rotting in prison. All he felt was a dull throb of sympathy, an unwelcome sense of kinship with the man who'd broken his son's heart.

He loved you, Kevin thought, staring at the mug shot as if he expected it to reply. *And you failed him, too.*

SO MUCH TO LET GO OF

BEFORE SHE STARTED HUNTING IN earnest for a new name, Nora changed the color of her hair. That was the proper order, she thought, the only sequence that made any sense. Because how could you know who you were until you saw what you looked like? She'd never understood those parents who had their baby's name picked out months or even years before it was born, as if they were putting a label on an abstract idea rather than a flesh-and-blood person. It seemed so presumptuous, so dismissive of the actual child.

She would have preferred to do the dye job at home, in secret, but she could tell it would be too elaborate and risky an operation to handle on her own. Her hair was very dark brown, and every website she consulted warned her to think twice about trying to go blond without professional assistance. It was a complicated, time-consuming process that required harsh chemicals and often resulted in what the experts liked to call "unfortunate outcomes." The comments that followed the articles were full of second thoughts from rueful brunettes who wished they'd been a little more accepting of their natural coloration. *I used to have pretty brown hair,* one woman wrote. *But I bought into the propaganda and bleached it blond. The color came out fine, but now my hair's so dull and lifeless my boyfriend says it feels like plastic grass growing out of my scalp!*

Nora read these testimonies with some trepidation, but not enough to change her mind. She wasn't dyeing her hair for cosmetic purposes, or because she wanted to have more fun. What she wanted was a clean break with the past, a wholesale change of appearance, and the quickest, surest way to do that was to become an artificial blonde. If her pretty brown hair turned into plastic grass in the process, that was collateral damage she could live with.

In her whole life, she'd never once colored her hair, or added any highlights, or even touched up the smattering of gray that had appeared over the past few years, despite the repeated urging of her stylist, a stern and judgmental Bulgarian named Grigori. *Let me get rid of that,* he told her at every appointment, in his ominous Slavic accent. *Make you look like teenager again.* But Nora had no interest in looking like a teenager; if anything, she wished there was a little more gray up there, wished she was one of those still-youngish people whose hair had turned snow-white as a result of the shock they'd suffered on October 14th. It would've made her life easier, she thought, if strangers could take one look at her and understand that she was one of the stricken.

Grigori was a highly respected colorist with an upscale clientele, but Nora didn't want to involve him in her transformation, didn't want to listen to his objections or explain her reasons for doing something so drastic and ill-advised. What was she supposed to say? *I'm not Nora anymore. Nora's all finished.* That wasn't the kind of conversation she wanted to have in a hair salon with a man who talked like a movie vampire.

She made her appointment at Hair Traffic Control, a chain that catered to a younger, more budget-conscious consumer, and presumably handled lots of foolish requests without batting an eye. Even so, the punky, pink-haired stylist looked dubious when Nora told her what she wanted to do.

"Are you super sure about this?" she asked, brushing the back of her hand across Nora's cheek. "Because your skin tone doesn't really—"

"You know what I'm thinking?" Nora said, cutting her off in midsentence. "I'm thinking this'll go a lot faster if we skip the small talk."

~~~~~

JILL WASN'T making much headway with *The Scarlet Letter.* It was partly Tom's fault, she thought; back when he was in high school, he'd complained so bitterly about the book that it must have poisoned her mind. Actually, he hadn't just complained; she'd come home from school one afternoon and found him stabbing his paperback edition with a steak knife, the tip of the blade penetrating the cover and sinking far enough down into the early chapters that he sometimes had trouble pulling it out. When she asked what he was doing, he explained in a calm and serious voice that he was trying to kill the book before it killed him.

So maybe she wasn't approaching the text with the respect it deserved as a timeless classic of American literature. But she was at least making a good-faith effort. She'd sat down with the book on three separate occasions in the past week and still hadn't made it through Hawthorne's introduction, which Mr. Destry claimed was an important part of the novel that shouldn't be skipped. It was like she was allergic to the prose; it made her feel slow and stupid, not quite fluent in English: *These old gentlemen—seated, like Matthew, at the receipt of the custom, but very liable to be summoned thence, unlike him, for apostolic errands—were Custom-House officers.* The longer she stared at a sentence like that, the less sense it made, as if the words were dissolving on the page.

But the real problem wasn't the book, and it wasn't spring fever, or the fact that graduation was just around the corner. The problem was Ms. Maffey and the I.M. chat they'd started up a few days ago. It had gotten under Jill's skin and was pulling her in a direction she didn't want to go. And yet she couldn't seem to stop herself, couldn't find a good reason to disengage, to sever a connection that had renewed itself so unexpectedly, after so many years.

Ms. Maffey, *Holly*—Jill was still trying to get used to calling her by her first name—had been Jill's fourth-grade teacher at Bailey Elementary and her all-time favorite, though it hadn't started out that way. Holly had taken over the class in January, after Ms. Frederickson left to have a baby. All the kids resented her at first and treated her like the interloper she was. After a week or two, though, they began to realize that they'd lucked out: Ms. Maffey was young and vibrant, way more fun than stuffy old Ms. Frederickson (not that anyone had thought of Ms. Frederickson as stuffy or old until Holly showed up). Almost a decade later, Jill couldn't remember much about fourth grade, or what had made that spring so special. All she remembered was the goldfish tattoo above Ms. Maffey's ankle, and the feeling of being a little in love with her teacher, wishing every day that summer would never arrive.

Ms. Maffey only taught in Mapleton those few months. The following September, Ms. Frederickson returned from her maternity leave, and Holly took a job at a school in Stonewood Heights, where she'd remained until a year ago. She'd been married for a short time to a man named Jamie, who'd disappeared in what she naturally referred to as the Rapture. They hadn't had time to have kids, which was something Holly had mixed feelings about. She'd always wanted to be a mom and was sure that she and Jamie would have made beautiful babies, but she knew that this was no time to be reproducing, bringing new people into a world without a future.

I guess it's a blessing, she wrote to Jill in one of their first exchanges. *To not have to worry about little ones.*

They'd met a couple of months ago, at the height of the murder investigation. Jill had gone to Ginkgo Street with Detective Ferguson, who'd arranged for what he called a "beauty pageant," in the hope that she might be able to spot the asthmatic Watcher he was so keen on questioning. It had turned out to be a waste of time, of course, and a weird one at that—fifty grown men, all dressed in white, parading in front of her like contestants in a creepy religious version of *The Bachelorette*—but it had been redeemed at the very end by the reunion with her old teacher, whom she happened to pass on her way out of the main building. They recognized each other right away, Jill crying out with delight, Ms. Maffey spreading her arms, wrapping her former student in a long and heartfelt embrace. It wasn't until Jill got home and found the handwritten note that had been slipped into her coat pocket—*Please e-mail me if you want to talk about <u>anything</u>!*—that she realized it hadn't been a chance encounter at all.

Jill wasn't stupid; she understood that she was being recruited—probably with her mother's blessing—and resented the fact that someone so important to her had been given the job. Ms. Maffey had even decorated the note with a smiley-face emoticon, the same little flourish she used to scrawl at the top of fourth-grade homework assignments. Jill took the note and tucked it away in her jewelry box, promising herself that she wouldn't get in touch, wouldn't allow herself to be manipulated like that.

It would've been easier to keep this vow if she'd had a little more going on that spring, if she'd found some new friends to replace Aimee and the gang, but it hadn't worked out that way. Most nights she was stuck at home, no one to talk to but her dad, who seemed a little more distracted than usual, depressed about Nora, consoling himself with dreams of softball glory. Max had been texting her a lot, encouraging her to come back to Dmitri's, or maybe just hang out with him sometime, but she never replied. She was done with all that—the sex and the partying and all those people—and she wasn't going back.

After a while it started to feel inevitable, almost mathematical—Jill was looking to fill the vacuum in her life, and Holly was the only plausible candidate. It had been such a shock to see her that day, looking so washed out and dreamy in her white clothes, so unlike the vivacious woman Jill remembered. *Please e-mail me if you want to talk about anything!* Well, there was a lot Jill wanted to talk about, questions she wanted to ask about Ms. Maffey's spiritual journey and her life at the compound. She thought it might help her to understand her mother a little better, give her some insight into the G.R. that so far had eluded her. Because if a person like Holly could be happy there, maybe there was something Jill was missing, something she needed to find out about.

Do u like it there? she'd asked when she finally worked up the nerve to get in touch. *It doesn't seem like much fun.*

I'm content, Ms. Maffey had replied. *It's a simple life.*

But how can u live w.o. talking?

There's so much to let go of, Jill, so many habits and crutches and expectations. But you have to let go. It's the only way.

～～～～

THE DAY after she became a blonde, Nora sat down to write her goodbye letters. It turned out to be a daunting task, made even more difficult by the fact that she couldn't seem to sit still. She kept getting up from the kitchen table and wandering upstairs to admire herself in the full-length bedroom mirror, this blond stranger with the oddly familiar face.

The dye job was an unqualified success. It wasn't just that the unfortunate outcomes she'd been warned about had failed to materialize: There were no bald spots or greenish undertones, and her bleached hair felt as soft and sleek as ever, miraculously impervious to the noxious chemicals in which it had been steeped. The big surprise wasn't that nothing bad had happened, it was how good she looked as a blonde, far better than she had with her natural hair color.

The stylist had been right, of course: There was something jarring about the contrast between Nora's Mediterranean complexion and this pale Swedish hair, but it was a riveting mismatch, the kind of mistake that made you want to stare, to try to figure out why something that should have looked so tacky actually looked kind of cool. All her life she'd been pretty, but it was an unremarkable, vaguely reassuring sort of beauty, the kind of everyday good looks people barely even noticed. Now, for the first time, she struck herself as exotic, and even a bit alarming, and she liked the way it felt, as if her body and soul had come into closer alignment.

Some selfish part of her was tempted to call Kevin and invite him over for a farewell drink—she wanted him to see her in this new incarnation, tell her how great she looked, and beg her not to leave—but the more reasonable part of her understood that this was a terrible idea. It would just be cruel, getting his hopes up one last time before crushing them forever. He was a good man, and she'd already hurt him enough.

That was the main thing she was hoping to express in her letter— the guilt she felt for the way she'd behaved on Valentine's Day, walking out on him without a word, and then ignoring his calls and e-mails in the weeks that followed, sitting quietly in the darkness of her living room until he got tired of ringing the bell and slipped one of his plaintive notes under the door.

What did I do wrong? he wrote. *Just tell me what it was so I can apologize.*

You didn't do anything, she'd wanted to tell him, though she never had. *It was all my fault.*

The thing was, Kevin had been her last chance. From the very beginning—the night they'd talked and danced at the mixer—she'd had a feeling that he might be able to save her, to show her how to salvage something decent and functional from the ruins of her old life. And for a little while there, she'd thought it had actually started to happen, that a chronic injury was slowly beginning to heal.

But she was just kidding herself, mistaking a wish for a change. She'd suspected it for a while, but didn't see it clearly until that night at Pamplemousse, when he tried to talk to her about his son, and all she'd felt was bitterness and envy so strong it was indistinguishable from hatred, a burning, gnawing emptiness in the middle of her chest.

Fuck you, she kept thinking to herself. *Fuck you and your precious son.*

And the awful thing was, he didn't even notice. He just kept talking like she was a normal person with a functioning heart, someone who'd understand a father's happiness and share in a friend's joy. And she just had to sit there in agony, knowing that there was something wrong with her that could never be repaired.

Please, she'd wanted to tell him. *Stop wasting your breath.*

THEY WERE sleeping together now, in the same king-size bed that had previously been used by Gus and Julian. It was a little creepy at first, but they'd gotten past the awkwardness. The bed was huge and comfy—it had some kind of high-tech Scandinavian mattress that remembered the shape of your body—and the window on Laurie's side opened on to the backyard, which was teeming with spring vitality, the scent of lilacs wafting in on the morning breeze.

They hadn't become lovers—not the way the guys had been, anyway—but they weren't just friends anymore, either. A powerful sense of intimacy had grown between them in the past few weeks, a bond of complete trust that went beyond anything Laurie had shared with her husband. They were partners now, connected for all eternity.

For the moment, nothing was required of them. Their new

housemates would arrive soon, and their little idyll would be over, but for now it felt like a sweet vacation, cuddling in bed until late morning, drinking tea and talking in quiet voices. Sometimes they cried, but not as often as they laughed. On pleasant afternoons, they walked together in the park.

They didn't talk too much about what was coming. There wasn't much to say, really; they had a job to do, and they would do it, just like Gus and Julian had, and the pair before them. Talking about it didn't help; it only disturbed the peaceful bubble they were living in. Better to just concentrate on the present moment, the precious days and hours that remained, or let your mind drift backward, into the past. Meg spoke frequently about her wedding, the special day that had never happened.

"I wanted it to be traditional, you know? Classic. The gown and the veil and the train, the organ playing, my father walking me to the altar, Gary standing there with a tear rolling down his cheek. I just wanted that dream, those few minutes when everybody who mattered was looking at me and saying, *Isn't she beautiful? Isn't he the luckiest guy in the world?* Is that how it was for you?"

"My wedding was a long time ago," Laurie said. "All I remember is being really stressed out. You plan for so long, and the actual event never measures up to what you wanted it to be."

"Maybe it's better this way," Meg speculated. "Reality never messed up my wedding."

"That's a nice way to think about it."

"Gary and I fought about the bachelor party. His best man wanted to hire a stripper and I thought that was tacky."

Laurie nodded and did her best to look interested, though she'd already heard this story several times. Meg didn't seem to realize she was repeating herself, and Laurie didn't bother to point it out: This was the mental space in which her friend had chosen to dwell. Laurie herself was more focused on the years when her kids were little, when she had felt so necessary and purposeful, a battery all charged up with love. Every day she used it up, and every night it got miraculously replenished. Nothing had ever been as good as that.

"I just hated the idea," Meg went on. "A bunch of drunk guys cheering for this pathetic girl who's probably a drug addict from an abusive home. And then what? Does she actually . . . *service* them while the others watch?"

"I don't know," Laurie said. "I guess that happens sometimes. Depends on the guys, I guess."

"Can you imagine?" Meg squinted, as if straining to visualize the scene. "You're in church, on the biggest day of your life, and here comes your bride, walking down the aisle like a princess dressed in white, and your parents are right over there in the front row, maybe even your grandparents, and all you can think about is the skank who gave you a lap dance the night before. Why would you do that to yourself? Why would you ruin a beautiful moment?"

"People did all sorts of crazy things back then," Laurie said, as if referring to ancient history, a bygone era barely visible through the mists of time. "They had no idea."

~~~~~

Dear Kevin,

By the time you read this, Nora will no longer exist.

Sorry—I guess that sounds more ominous than I meant it to. I just mean that I'll be leaving Mapleton, heading somewhere else to start a new life as another person. You won't see me again.

I hope it's not rude to be telling you this in a letter, instead of face-to-face. But it's hard enough for me to even do it like this. What I'd really like to do is just dissolve into thin air like the rest of my family, but you deserve better than that (not that people always get what they deserve).

What I want to tell you is: Thanks. I know how hard you tried to make things work with me—how many allowances you made, and how little you got in return. It's not that I didn't want to hold up my end—I would have given a lot to have risen to that occasion. But I couldn't find the strength to make it happen, or maybe just the mechanism. Every minute we were together, I felt like I was wandering in the dark through a strange house, groping for a light switch. And then, whenever I found one and turned it on, the bulb was dead.

I know you wanted to know me, and that you had every right to try. That's why we get involved with other people, right? Not just for their bodies, but for everything else, too—their dreams and their scars and their stories. Every time we were together, I could feel you holding back, tiptoeing around my privacy, giving me room to guard my secrets. I guess I should thank you for that. For your discretion and compassion—for being a gentleman.

But the thing is, I knew what you wanted to know, and I resented you for it. How's that for a catch-22? I was mad at you for the questions you didn't ask, the ones you didn't ask because you thought that asking them would upset me. But you were biding your time, waiting and hoping, weren't you?

So let me at least try to give you an answer. I feel like I owe you that much.

We were having a family dinner.

It sounds so quaint when you put it that way, doesn't it? You imagine everyone together, talking and laughing and enjoying their meal. But it wasn't like that. Things were tense between me and Doug. I understand now why that was, but at the time it just felt to me like he was distracted by work, not fully present in our life. He was always checking that damn Blackberry, snatching it up every time it buzzed like it might contain a message from God. Of course it wasn't God, it was just his cute little girlfriend, but either way, it was more interesting to him than his own family. I still kind of hate him for that.

The kids weren't happy, either. They were rarely happy in the evening. Mornings could be fun in our house, and bedtimes were usually sweet, but dinners were often a trial. Jeremy was cranky because . . . why? I wish I could tell you. Maybe because it's hard to be six years old, or maybe because it was hard to be him. Little things made him cry, and his crying over little things irritated his father, who sometimes spoke sharply to him and made Jeremy even more upset. Erin was only four, but she had an instinct for getting under her brother's skin, pointing out in a matter-of-fact voice that Jeremy was crying again, acting like a little baby, which made him absolutely furious.

I loved them all, okay? My cheating husband, my fragile boy, my sneaky little girl. But I didn't love my life, not that night. I had worked really hard on the meal—it was this Moroccan chicken recipe I'd found in a magazine—and nobody cared. Doug thought the breasts were a little dry, Jeremy wasn't hungry, blah blah blah. It was just a crappy night, that's all.

And then Erin spilled her apple juice. No big deal, except that she'd made a big fuss about drinking from a cup without a top, even though I told her it was a bad idea. So what, right? It happens. I wasn't one of those parents who gets all upset about something like that. But that night I was. I said, "Damn it, Erin, what did I tell you!" And then she started to cry.

I looked at Doug, waiting for him to get up and get some paper towels, but he didn't move. He just smiled at me like none of this had anything to do with him, like he was floating above it all on some superior plane of existence. So of course I had to do it. I got up and went into the kitchen.

How long was I there? Thirty seconds, maybe? I gathered a handful of towels, winding them off the roll, wondering if I'd taken enough sheets, or had I possibly taken too many, because I didn't want to make a second trip but didn't want to be wasteful, either. I remember being conscious of the chaos I'd left behind, feeling relieved to be away from it, but also resentful and overburdened and unappreciated. I think maybe I closed my eyes, let my mind go *blank for a second or two. That was when it must have happened. I remember noticing that the crying had stopped, that the house felt suddenly peaceful.*

So what do you think I did when I got back to the dining room and found them gone? Do you think I screamed or cried or fainted? Or do you think I wiped up the spill, because the puddle was spreading across the table and would soon start dripping onto the floor?

You know what I did, Kevin.

I wiped up the fucking apple juice and then I went back into the kitchen, put the soggy paper towels in the garbage can, and rinsed my hands under the faucet. After I dried them, I went back to the dining room and took another look at the empty table, the plates and the glasses and the uneaten food. The vacant chairs. I really don't know what happened after that. It's like my memory just stops there and picks up a few weeks later.

Would it have helped if I told you this story in Florida? Or maybe on Valentine's Day? Would you have felt like you knew me better? You could have told me what I already think I know—that the crying and the spilled juice aren't really that important, that all parents get stressed out and angry and wish for a little peace and quiet. It's not the same as wishing for the people you love to be gone forever.

But what if it is, Kevin? Then what?

I wish you every happiness. You were good to me, but I was beyond repair. I really did like it when you danced with me.

Love,

N

~~~~~~

GRgrl405 (10:15:42 P.M.): how r u?

Jillpill123 (10:15:50 P.M.): just chillin. u?

GRgrl405 (10:15:57 P.M.): thinking bout u (:

Jillpill123 (10:16:04 P.M.): me 2 (:

GRgrl405 (10:16:11 P.M.): u shld come 4 a visit

Jillpill123 (10:16:23 P.M.): idk...

GRgrl405 (10:16:31 P.M.): ull like it here

Jillpill123 (10:16:47 P.M.): what wld we do?

GRgrl405 (10:16:56 P.M.): sleepover (:

Jillpill123 (10:17:07 P.M.): ???!

GRgrl405 (10:17:16 P.M.): just a night or 2—c what u think

Jillpill123 (10:17:29 P.M.): what wd i tell my dad?

GRgrl405 (10:17:36 P.M.): yr call

Jillpill123 (10:17:55 P.M.): ill think about it

GRgrl405 (10:18:08 P.M.): no pressure when ur ready

Jillpill123 (10:18:22 P.M.): im scared

GRgrl405 (10:18:29 P.M.): its ok 2 b scared

Jillpill123 (10:18:52 P.M.): maybe next week?

GRgrl405 (10:18:58 P.M.): that wd be perfect (:

I'M GLAD YOU'RE HERE

TOM WAS TELLING CHRISTINE ABOUT Mapleton as he drove, trying to sell her on the idea of an extended visit with his family, rather than an overnight stopover on the way to Ohio.

"It's a pretty big house," he said. "We could stay in my old room for as long as we want. I'm sure my father and sister would be happy to help with the baby."

This was a bit presumptuous, since his father and sister didn't even know he was on the way, let alone that he had company. He'd meant to give them a heads-up, but things had been pretty chaotic in the past few days; he figured it made more sense to play it by ear, keep his options open until they got within striking distance. The last thing he wanted to do was get his father's hopes up and then disappoint him, as he had so many times in the past.

"It's really nice there in the summer. There's a big park a couple blocks away, and a lake where you can go swimming. One of my friends has a hot tub in his yard. And there's a pretty good Indian restaurant downtown."

He was improvising now, not sure if she was even listening. This side trip to Mapleton was a Hail Mary on his part, a way to buy a little more time with Christine and the baby before they drifted out of his life.

"I just wish my mother was still there. She's the one who really—"

The baby let out a wail from her bucket in the backseat. She was a tiny thing, barely a week old, and didn't have a lot of lung power. All she could produce was a strained little mewling sound, but Tom was amazed by how viscerally it affected him, jangling his nerve endings, filling him with a sense of urgency just short of total panic. All he could do was glance at her scrunched, angry face in the rearview mirror and plead with her in a syrupy voice that was already starting to feel like a second language.

"It's okay, little one. Nothing to worry about. Just be patient, sweet pea. Everything's copacetic. You go back to sleep now, okay?"

He pressed on the gas pedal and was startled by the engine's eager response, the heroic leap of the speedometer needle. The car would've been happy to go even faster, but he eased off, knowing he couldn't afford to get pulled over in a BMW that was either borrowed or stolen, depending on how the Falks chose to look at it.

"I think it's about ten miles to the next rest area," he said. "Did you see the sign a while back?"

Christine didn't respond. She seemed almost catatonic in the passenger seat, sitting with her feet up and her knees tucked beneath her chin, staring straight ahead with a disconcertingly placid expression.

She'd been like this the whole way, acting as though the infant in the backseat were a hitchhiker Tom had picked up, an unwelcome guest with absolutely no claim on her attention.

"Don't cry, honey bun," he called over his shoulder. "I know you're hungry. We're gonna get you a baba, okay?"

Amazingly, the baby seemed to understand. She released a few more sobs—soft, hiccupy whimpers that sounded more like aftershocks than actual protests—and then fell back asleep. Tom glanced at Christine, hoping for a smile, or even just a nod of acknowledgment, but she seemed just as oblivious to the quiet as she'd been to the noise.

"A nice big baba," he murmured, more to himself than his passengers.

CHRISTINE'S INABILITY to connect with the baby had begun to frighten him. She still hadn't given the child a name, rarely spoke to her, never touched her, and avoided looking at her whenever possible. Before leaving the hospital, she'd gotten a shot that stopped her from lactating, and since then she had been more than happy to let Tom handle all the feeding, changing, and bathing duties.

He couldn't blame her for feeling a little shell-shocked; he was still a little shell-shocked himself. Everything had fallen apart so quickly after Mr. Gilchrest's guilty plea and humiliating confession, in which he publicly outed himself as a serial rapist of teenage girls and begged for forgiveness from his "real wife," who he claimed was the only woman he'd ever loved. Furious at his betrayal, Christine had gone into labor the very next day, shrieking in agony at the first contraction, demanding that she be taken to the hospital and given the strongest drugs available. The Falks were too demoralized to object; even they seemed to understand that they'd reached the end of the road, that the prophecies that had sustained them were nothing but pipe dreams.

Tom stayed with Christine throughout the nine-hour labor, holding her hand while she drifted in and out of a drug-induced delirium, cursing the father of her child so bitterly that even the delivery room nurses were impressed. He watched in amazement as the baby squirted into the world, fists clenched, puffy eyes glued shut, her jet-black hair plastered with blood and other murky fluids. The doctor let Tom cut the cord, then placed the child in his arms, as if she belonged to him.

"This is your daughter," he told Christine, offering the naked, squirmy bundle like a gift. "Say hi to your little girl."

"Go away," she told him, turning her head to keep from looking at the Miracle Child who no longer seemed like such a miracle. "Get it away from me."

They returned to the Falks' the following afternoon, only to find Terrence and Marcella gone. There was a note on the kitchen table—*Hope it went okay. We're out of town until Monday. Please be gone when we return!*—along with an envelope containing a thousand dollars in cash.

"What are we gonna do?" he asked.

Christine didn't have to think for long.

"I should go home," she said. "Back to Ohio."

"Really?"

"Where else can I go?"

"We'll figure something out."

"No," she said. "I need to go home."

They stayed at the Falks' for four more days, during which Christine did almost nothing but sleep. That whole time, while he was changing diapers and mixing formula and stumbling around the dark house in the middle of the night, Tom kept waiting for her to wake up and tell him what he already knew, which was that it was all okay, that everything had actually worked out for the best. They were a little family now, free to love one another and do as they pleased. They could go barefoot together, a band of happy nomads, drifting with the wind. But it hadn't happened yet, and there weren't that many miles between here and Ohio.

· · ·

TOM WAS aware of the fact that he wasn't thinking clearly. He was too exhausted for sober reflection, too focused on the baby's bottomless needs, and his fear of losing Christine. But he knew he needed to prepare himself for the ordeal of going back home, the questions that would arise when he pulled up in front of his father's house in a German luxury sedan he didn't own, with a bullseye on his forehead, accompanied by a severely depressed girl he'd never mentioned and a baby that wasn't his. There was going to be a lot of explaining to do.

"Listen," he said, slowing down as they approached the entrance to the rest area. "I hate to keep bugging you about this, but you really need to give the baby a name."

She nodded vaguely, not really agreeing, just letting him know she was listening. They headed up the access ramp to the main parking lot.

"It's weird, you know? She's almost a week old. What am I supposed to say to my dad? *This is my friend, Christine, and this is her nameless baby?*"

Traffic had been light on the highway, but the rest area was packed, as if the whole world had decided to pee at the same time. They got stuck in a slow parade, no one pulling in unless someone else pulled out.

"It's not that big a deal," he went on. "Just think of a flower or a bird or a month. Call her Rose or Robin or Iris or April or whatever. Anything is better than nothing."

He waited for a Camry to back out, then slipped into the space it had vacated. He put the car into park but didn't shut off the engine. Christine turned to look at him. There was a maroon-and-gold bullseye on her forehead—it matched his own and the baby's—that Tom had painted on in the morning, right before they left Cambridge. It was like a team insignia, he thought, a mark of tribal belonging. Christine's face was pale and blank below it, but it seemed to be emitting a painful radiance, reflecting back the love he was beaming in her direction, the love she refused to absorb.

"Why don't you choose," she told him. "It really doesn't matter to me."

~~~~~

KEVIN CHECKED his phone. It was 5:08; he needed to grab something to eat, change into his uniform, and get to the softball field by six. It was doable, but only if Aimee left for work in the next few minutes.

The sun was low and hot, blazing through the treetops. He was parked near the closed end of the cul-de-sac, four doors down from his own house, facing into the glare. Not ideal, but the best he could do under the circumstances, the only vantage point in Lovell Terrace that allowed him to keep tabs on his front door without being immediately visible to anyone entering or leaving the house.

He had no idea what was taking Aimee so long. She was usually gone by four, off to serve the early birds at Applebee's. He wondered if she was under the weather, or maybe had the night off and had neglected to mention it. If that was the case, then he'd have to rethink his options.

It was ridiculous that he didn't know, because he'd just talked to her on the phone a few minutes ago. He'd called for Jill, as he often did in the late afternoon, checking to see if they needed anything from the grocery store, but it was Aimee who picked up.

Hey, she said, sounding more serious than usual. *How was your day?*

Fine. He hesitated. *Kinda weird, actually.*

Tell me about it.

He ignored the invitation.

Is Jill there?

No, just me.

That was his opening to ask why she hadn't left for work, but he was too flustered for that, too distracted by the thought of Aimee alone in the house.

No problem, he said. *Just tell her I called, okay?*

He slumped down in the driver's seat, hoping to make himself a little less conspicuous to Eileen Carnahan, who was heading down the sidewalk in his direction, taking her geriatric cocker spaniel for his pre-dinner stroll. Eileen craned her head—she was wearing a floppy tan sun hat—and squinted at him with a puzzled expression, trying to figure out if something was wrong. Pressing his phone to his ear, Kevin fended her off with an apologetic smile and a *can't-talk-now* wave, doing his best to look like a busy man taking care of important business, and not a creep who was spying on his own house.

Kevin comforted himself with the knowledge that he hadn't crossed any irrevocable lines, at least not yet. But he'd been thinking about it all day, and no longer trusted himself to be alone with Aimee, not after what had happened that morning. Better to keep his distance for a while, reestablish the proper boundaries, the ones that seemed to have dissolved in the past few weeks. Like the fact that she no longer called him Mr. Garvey, or even Kevin.

Hey Kev, she'd said, wandering sleepy-eyed into the kitchen.

Morning, he'd replied, walking toward the cupboard with a stack of small plates balanced on his palm, still warm from the dishwasher.

He wasn't aware of anything flirtatious in her voice or manner. She was wearing yoga pants and a T-shirt, pretty tame by her standards. All he registered was his usual feeling of being happy to see her, grateful for the jolt of good energy she always provided. Instead of heading for the coffeemaker, she veered toward the refrigerator, opening the door and looking inside. She stood there for a while, as if lost in thought.

Need something? he asked.

She didn't reply. Turning away from the cupboard—just trying to help—he drifted up behind her, peering over her head into the familiar jumble of cartons and jars and Tupperware containers, the meats and vegetables in their transparent plastic drawers.

Yogurt, she said, turning and smiling up at him, her face so close that he caught a subtle whiff of her morning breath, which was a little stale but not unpleasant—not at all. *I'm going on a diet.*

He laughed, as if this were a ridiculous project—which it was—but she insisted she was serious. One of them must have moved—either he leaned forward or she leaned back, or maybe both those things happened at the same time—because suddenly she was right *there,* pressing up against him, the warmth of her body passing through two layers of fabric so that it felt to him like skin against skin. Without thinking, he placed a hand on her waist, just above the gentle flare of her hipbone. At almost the same moment, she tilted her head back, letting it rest against his chest. It felt completely natural to be standing like that, and also terrifying, as if they were perched on the edge of a cliff. He was intensely aware of the elastic waistband of her pants, an intriguing tautness beneath his palm.

On the door, he told her after a hesitation that was a lot longer than it needed to be.

Oh yeah, she said, abruptly breaking the connection as she turned. *Why didn't I know that?*

She grabbed the yogurt and headed for the table, flashing him a sidelong smile as she sat. He finished emptying the dishwasher, his mind buzzing, the memory of her body like a physical sensation, imprinted on his flesh as if he were made of very soft clay. A whole day had gone by and it was still there, right where she'd left it.

"Fuck," he said, closing his eyes and shaking his head, not quite sure if he was regretting the incident, or trying to remember it a little more clearly.

~~~~~

LAURIE COULDN'T blame the pizza guy for looking surprised, not when she was standing in the doorway in her white clothes, holding up a hand-lettered sign that read: HOW MUCH?

"Uh, twenty-two," he mumbled, doing his best to sound casual as he withdrew two boxes from an insulated pouch. He was just a kid, about the same age as her own son, broad-shouldered and appealingly scruffy in cargo shorts and flip-flops, as if he'd stopped off at Parker Road on his way to the beach.

They performed the awkward exchange, Laurie taking possession of the pizzas, the kid relieving her of two tens and a five, a huge expenditure of petty cash. She stepped back from the doorway, shaking her head to let him know that no change was necessary.

"Thanks." He pocketed the bills, tilting his head in an attempt to catch a glimpse of whatever was going on inside the house, losing interest when he realized there was nothing behind her but an empty hallway. "Have a nice night."

She carried the warm, flimsy boxes into the dining room and set them on the table, registering the anxious but clearly excited looks on the faces of the new guys, Al and Josh. After months of meager rations at the Ginkgo Street compound, takeout pizza from Tonnetti's must have seemed like an impossible, almost indecent luxury, as if they'd died and gone to a heaven of self-indulgence.

They'd moved in just three days ago and had quickly established themselves as ideal housemates—clean, quiet, and helpful. Al was around Laurie's age, a short, impish guy with a gray-flecked beard, a former environmental consultant for an architecture firm. Josh was in his early thirties, a good-looking former software salesman, lanky and morose, with a tendency to stare at everyday objects—forks and sponges and pencils—as if encountering them for the first time.

Not too long ago, Laurie thought, she and Meg would have been intrigued by the arrival of two reasonably attractive, age-appropriate men in their lives. They would have stayed up late, whispering in the dark about the newcomers, commenting on Al's cute smile, wondering if Josh was one of those emotionally stunted guys who would turn out not to be worth the work you'd have to put in to get him to come out of his shell. But it was too late for that sort of entertainment. They'd cut their ties; Al and Josh belonged to a world they'd already left behind.

Guessing correctly, Laurie opened the box that contained the mushroom and black olive pizza—there was also a sausage and onion for the carnivores—that Meg had specifically requested. The aroma that engulfed her was rich and complex, as full of memories as an old song on the car radio. Laurie was unprepared for the tenacity of the melted cheese as she lifted out the first slice, the improbable weight in her hand when it broke free. Moving slowly, trying to invest the act with the sense of ceremony it deserved, she set the slice on a plate and offered the plate to Meg.

I love you, she said, speaking only with her eyes. *You're so brave.*

I love you, too, Meg silently replied. *You're my sister.*

They ate in silence. Al and Josh tried not to look too greedy, but they couldn't restrain themselves, reaching for slice after slice, taking way more than their fair share. Laurie didn't mind. She wasn't very hungry, and Meg had only taken a single bite of the food she claimed to have been dreaming about for months. Laurie smiled sadly at the ravenous men across the table. They were innocents, just like she and Meg had been when they'd arrived at Outpost 17, blissfully unaware of the beautiful tradition they'd been chosen to uphold.

It's okay, she thought. *Enjoy it while you can.*

~~~~~

CHRISTINE HURRIED off to the restroom, leaving Tom to prepare the bottle in the front seat, heating the water with a handy device that connected to the cigarette lighter. When it was the right temperature, he added a single-serving packet of formula, shaking vigorously to make sure it was all mixed in. He performed these actions in a state of exquisite suspense, checking the mirror every few seconds to make sure the baby was still asleep. He knew from experience how hard it was to properly assemble a bottle when she was squealing with hunger. Something always went wrong: The plastic bag wouldn't open, or it would slip out of the holder, or it had a tiny pinhole in the bottom, or you didn't screw the top on right, or whatever. It was amazing how many ways there were to botch such a simple operation.

This time, though, the gods were on his side. He got the bottle all set, extricated the baby from her bucket without waking her, and carried her to the picnic area, where they found a shady bench. The baby didn't open her eyes until the nipple touched her lips. She snuffled around a bit and then pounced, latching on hard, sucking with a ferocity that made Tom laugh out loud, the bottle jerking rhythmically in his hand. It reminded him of fishing, the jolt when you got a bite, the shock of being connected to another life.

"You're a hungry little thing, aren't you?"

The baby gazed up at him as she gulped and snorted—not adoringly, Tom thought, or even gratefully, but at least tolerantly, like she was thinking, *I have no idea who you are, but I guess I'm okay with that.*

"I know I'm not your mother," he whispered. "But I'm doing the best I can."

Christine was gone for a long time, long enough for the baby to drain the bottle and Tom to start worrying. He hoisted the baby upright, patting her back until she released a cute little burp that seemed a lot less cute when he felt a familiar, disheartening dampness on his shoulder. He hated the sour smell of spit-up, the way it clung to your clothes and lingered in your nostrils, a far more insidious substance than baby poop.

The baby started fussing, so Tom took her for a walk around the grounds, which she seemed to appreciate. The rest area was a modest one—no restaurant or gas station, just a bland one-story building with bathrooms, vending machines, and shelves of informational brochures about the wonders of Connecticut—but it took up a surprising amount of space. There was a six-table picnic area, a dog walk, and a secondary parking lot for trucks and RVs.

Wandering past the big vehicles, Tom was hailed by a group of Barefoot People in a maroon Dodge Caravan with Michigan plates. There were five of them, three guys and two girls, all of them college-aged.

While the girls were cooing at the baby—they seemed especially charmed by the dime-sized bullseye on her forehead—a red-haired guy with a knotted bandana head rag asked Tom if he was heading to Mount Pocono for the monthlong solstice festival.

"It'll be raucous," he said, grimacing as he raised one arm and scratched diligently at his rib cage. "Way better than last year."

"I don't know," Tom said with a shrug. "Kinda hard with a baby."

One of the girls looked up. She had a hot body, a bad complexion, and one missing tooth.

"I'll babysit," she said. "I don't mind."

"Yeah, right," laughed one of her friends, a handsome dude with an unpleasant expression. "In between gang bangs."

"Fuck you," she told him. "I'm really good with kids."

"Except when she's tripping," the third guy chimed in. He was big and beefy, a football player going to seed. "And she's tripping all the time."

"You guys are assholes," the second girl observed.

CHRISTINE WAS waiting by the BMW, watching him with a pensive expression, her black hair gleaming in the afternoon sun.

"Where were you?" she asked. "I thought maybe you ditched me."

"Feeding the baby." He held up the empty bottle for her inspection. "She took the whole thing."

"Huh," she grunted, not even bothering to pretend that she cared.

"I ran into some Barefoot People. A whole van full. They said there's a big festival in the Poconos."

Christine said she'd talked to one of the girls in the bathroom. "She was all excited. Said it was the biggest party of the year."

"We could maybe check it out," Tom said cautiously. "If you want. I think it's on the way to Ohio."

"Whatever," she said. "You're the boss."

Her voice was dull, profoundly uninterested. Tom felt a sudden impulse to slap her across the face—not to hurt her, just to wake her up—and had to restrain himself until it passed.

"Look," he said. "I know you're upset. But you shouldn't take it out on me. I'm not the one who hurt you."

"I know," she assured him. "I'm not mad at you."

Tom glanced at the baby. "What about your daughter? Why are you so mad at her?"

Christine rubbed her stomach, a habit she'd developed during pregnancy. Her voice was barely audible.

"I was supposed to have a son."

"Yeah," he said. "But you didn't."

She squinted past Tom, watching a family of blond people emerge from an Explorer across the way—two tall parents, three little kids, and a yellow Lab.

"You think I'm stupid, don't you?"

"No," he said. "That's not the problem at all."

She laughed softly. It was a bitter, helpless sound.

"What do you want from me?"

"I want you to hold your daughter," he said, stepping forward and pressing the baby into her arms before she had time to resist. "Just for a couple minutes, while I go to the men's room. You think you can manage that?"

Christine didn't answer the question. She just glared at him, holding the baby as far away from her body as she could manage, as if it were the source of a troubling odor. He gave her an encouraging pat on the arm.

"And think about those names," he told her.

～～～～～

THE GAME calmed Kevin's nerves, as he knew it would. He loved the way time slowed down on the baseball diamond, the way your focus narrowed down to the facts at hand: two down, bottom of the third, runners on first and second, a count of two balls and one strike.

"All you, Gonzo!" he called from the outfield, not sure if his voice was loud enough to reach the ears of Bob Gonzalves, the Carpe Diem's ace pitcher, or if Gonzo was even listening. He was one of those guys who got into the zone when he pitched, disappeared deep into his own head. He probably wouldn't have noticed if the handful of women in the bleachers took off their shirts and started screaming out their phone numbers.

Call me, Gonzo! Don't make me beg!

That was another thing Kevin loved about softball: the fact that you could be a middle-aged, beer-bellied construction estimator like Gonzo—a guy who could barely jog to first base without risking a heart attack—and still be a star, a slow-pitch wizard whose deceptive underhand tosses seemed to float like cream puffs toward the batter, only to plummet over the strike zone like a shot duck.

"You da man!" Kevin chanted, pounding his mitt for emphasis. "Nothing to worry about!"

He was standing out in left center with huge expanses of grass on either side of him. Only eight Carpe Diem guys had shown up, and the team had decided to play with one less outfielder than usual, rather than leave a gaping hole in the infield. That meant a lot of extra ground for Kevin to cover, with the coppery, low-hanging sun shining directly into his eyes.

He didn't mind; he was just happy to be there, doing the best possible thing a man could be doing on a beautiful evening like this. He'd made it to the field with just a few minutes to spare, saved by Jill's timely appearance at twenty after five. With his daughter running interference, Kevin was able to pop inside and change into his uniform—white stretch pants and a pale blue T-shirt with *Carpe Diem* written in old-fashioned script above the image of a beer mug—then grab an apple and a bottle of water, all without even catching a glimpse of Aimee, let alone having to navigate any potentially awkward situations.

The next pitch was way outside, bringing the count to three and one on Rick Sansome, a mediocre hitter at best. The last thing Gonzo wanted to do was walk Sansome and have to face Larry Tallerico with the bases loaded. Tallerico was a beast, a scowling, sunburned bruiser who'd once hit a ball so far it had never been found.

"Easy does it!" Kevin shouted. "Make him swing!"

He wiped the back of his hand across his forehead, trying to ignore the lingering sense of shame that had dogged him all day. He knew just how close he and Aimee had come to making a terrible mistake, and he was determined not to let it happen again. He was a grown man, a supposedly responsible adult. It was up to him to take charge of the situation, to lay out the ground rules in an honest and forthright manner. All he had to do was sit down with her first thing in the morning, acknowledge what was going on between them, and tell her that it needed to stop.

You're a very attractive girl, he would say. *I'm sure you know that. And we've gotten pretty close in the past few weeks—a lot closer than we should have.*

And then he would explain, as bluntly as he needed to, that there could never be anything romantic or sexual between them. *It's not fair to you and it's not fair to Jill, and I'm not the kind of man who would put either of you in that position. I'm sorry if I gave you that impression.* It would be uncomfortable, there was no question about that, but not nearly as uncomfortable as doing nothing, allowing themselves to feign innocence as they continued down the dangerous path they were on. What would be next? A chance encounter in the hallway outside his bedroom? Aimee in nothing but a towel, mumbling an apology as she squeezed by, their shoulders brushing as she passed?

Sansome fouled off the next pitch and the one after that, hanging on for dear life. Gonzo's next pitch sailed so high over his head that Steve Wiscziewski had to leap out of his crouch to grab it.

"Ball four!" bellowed the umpire. "Take your base!"

The runners advanced as Sansome trotted to first. Hoping to calm Gonzo's nerves, Steve called time-out and walked out to the mound for a conference. Pete Thorne wandered in from shortstop to put his two cents in. While they chatted, Kevin retreated deeper into the outfield, showing his respect for Tallerico's power. With Carpe Diem up by three, they could afford to give up a run or two. What he wanted to avoid was a scenario in which the ball sailed over his head, and he had to chase it down and nail a long throw to the relay man to prevent a grand slam.

"Let's play ball!"

Pete and Steve returned to their positions. Tallerico lumbered up to the plate, tapping the surface with the fat end of his bat, doing an amused double-take when he saw how far away Kevin was standing, maybe ten yards from the edge of the woods. Kevin took off his blue hat and waved it in the air, hailing the big man, inviting him to bring it on.

Gonzo wound up and pitched, dropping a fat one right over the plate. Tallerico just stood there and watched it fall, not the least bit fazed when the ump called strike one. Kevin tried to imagine the conversation he would have to have with Aimee at the breakfast table, wondering how she'd take it, and how he'd feel when it was over. He'd lost so much in the past few years—everyone had—and had worked so hard to stay strong and keep a positive attitude, not only for himself, but also for Jill, and for his friends and neighbors, and for everybody else in town. For Nora, too—especially for Nora, though that hadn't worked out so well. And right now he was feeling the weight of all those losses, and the weight of the years that were behind him, and the weight of the ones that were still ahead, however many there might be—three or four, twenty or thirty, maybe more. He was attracted to Aimee, sure—he was willing to admit that much—but he didn't want to sleep with her, not really, not in the real world. What he was going to miss was her smile in the morning, and the hopeful feeling she gave him, the conviction that fun was still possible, that you were more than the sum of what had been taken from you. It was hard to think about giving that up, especially when there was nothing waiting to replace it.

The *chink* of the aluminum bat snapped him out of his reverie. He saw the flash of the ball as it rose, then lost it in the sun. Raising his bare hand to shield his eyes, he stumbled backward, then a little bit to the right, instinctively calibrating the trajectory of an object he couldn't see. It must have been a towering shot, because it seemed for a second or two that the ball had left the earth's atmosphere and wouldn't be coming down. And then he saw it, a bright speck streaking across the sky, arcing downward. He lifted his arm and opened his glove. The ball dropped into the pocket with a resounding smack, as if it had been heading there the whole time and was happy to reach its destination.

~~~~~

JILL ASKED if she should wear white to the sleepover, but Ms. Maffey told her it wasn't necessary.

Just bring yourself and a sleeping bag, she wrote. *Things are pretty casual at the Guest House. And don't worry about the Vow of Silence. We can talk in whispers. It'll be fun!*

As a gesture of when-in-Rome goodwill, Jill picked out a stretchy white T-shirt to wear with her jeans, and then packed an overnight bag with pajamas, a change of underwear, and a few toiletries. At the last second, she added an envelope containing a dozen family photographs—a sort of rough draft of a Memory Book—just in case her visit lasted longer than a single night.

Aimee wasn't usually home in the evenings, but Jill had heard her moving around in the guest room, so she wasn't all that surprised to go downstairs and find her sitting on the living room couch. What did surprise her were the suitcases flanking Aimee's feet, matching blue canvas wheelbags that Jill's parents had bought when Tom was still in high school, when the whole family went to Tuscany for spring vacation.

"Going somewhere?" she asked, conscious of the rolled-up sleeping bag dangling from her own hand. They could have been taking a trip together, waiting for a ride to the airport.

"I'm leaving," Aimee explained. "It's about time I got out of your hair."

"Oh." Jill nodded for longer than necessary, waiting for the meaning of Aimee's words to sink in. "My dad didn't tell me."

"He doesn't know." Aimee's smile lacked its usual confidence. "It was kind of a spur-of-the-moment thing."

"You're not going home, are you? Back to your stepfather's?"

"God, no." Aimee sounded horrified by the thought. "I'm never going back there."

"So where . . . ?"

"There's a girl I met at work. Mimi. She's pretty cool. She lives with her parents, but it's like a separate basement apartment. She says it's okay if I crash there for a while."

"Wow." Jill felt a twinge of jealousy. She remembered how amazing it had been when Aimee first moved in, the two of them as close as sisters, their lives all tangled together. "Good for you."

Aimee shrugged; it was hard to tell if she was proud of herself or embarrassed. "That's what I do, right? I make friends with people at work and then I move into their houses. Then I stay for way longer than I should."

"It was fun," Jill murmured. "We were happy to have you."

"What about you?" Aimee wondered. "Where you off to?"

"Just—to a friend's," Jill said after a brief hesitation. "No one you know."

Aimee nodded indifferently, no longer curious about the details of Jill's social life. Her eyes took a nostalgic tour of the living room—the wide-screen TV, the comfy sectional, the painting of a humble shack illuminated by a streetlight.

"I really liked it here," she said. "This was the best place I ever lived."

"You don't have to go, you know."

"It's time," Aimee told her. "I probably should've left a few months ago."

"My dad's gonna miss you. You really cheered him up."

"I'm gonna write him a letter," Aimee promised, speaking to Jill's feet instead of her face. "Just tell him I said thanks for everything, okay?"

"Sure."

It felt to Jill like there was something else that needed to be said, but she couldn't think of what it was, and Aimee wasn't helping. They were both relieved when a horn sounded outside.

"That's my ride."

Aimee stood up and looked at Jill. She seemed to be trying to smile.

"I guess this is it."

"I guess so."

Aimee stepped forward, reaching out for a farewell hug. Jill responded as best she could with her one free hand. The horn sounded again.

"Last summer?" Aimee said. "You kinda saved my life."

"It was the other way around," Jill assured her.

Aimee laughed softly and hefted up her luggage.

"I'm just borrowing these. I'll bring them back in a few days."

"Whenever," Jill replied. "There's no rush."

She stood in the doorway and watched her former best friend in the world roll the suitcases out to a blue Mazda waiting by the curb. Aimee opened the back hatch, stowed the bags, and then turned to wave goodbye. Jill felt an emptiness open inside of her as she lifted her arm, a sense that something vital was being subtracted from her life. It was always like that when somebody you cared about went away, even when you knew it was inevitable, and it probably wasn't your fault.

~~~~~

UNBELIEVABLE, TOM thought as he drove down Washington Boulevard for the first time in more than two years. *It looks exactly the same.*

He wasn't sure why this bothered him. Maybe just because he'd changed so much since the last time he'd been home, he figured that Mapleton should have changed, too. But everything was right where it was supposed to be—the Safeway, Big Mike's Discount Shoes, Taco Bell, Walgreens, that ugly green tower looming over the Burger King, bristling with cell phone antennae and satellite dishes. And then that other landscape, when he turned off the main drag onto the quiet streets where people actually lived, the suburban dreamworld of perfect lawns and groomed shrubbery, tipped-over tricycles and little insecticide flags, their yellow banners hanging limp in the evening doldrums.

"We're almost there," he told the baby.

It was just the two of them now, and she'd been sleeping the whole way. They'd waited around the rest area for a half hour, in case Christine decided to turn up, but that was just a formality. He knew she was gone, had known it the moment he returned from the bathroom and found the baby girl alone in the car, buckled into her little seat, gazing up at him with glassy, reproachful eyes. And, even worse, Tom knew it was his own fault: He'd spooked Christine, shoving the child into her arms like that, when she clearly wasn't ready.

He searched the car, but there was no note, no apology, not a word of thanks or explanation, not even a simple goodbye to the loyal friend who'd supported and protected her when no one else would, her cross-country traveling companion and almost-boyfriend, surrogate father to her child. He scoured the parking lot, too, but found no trace of her, or of the van full of Barefoot People headed for the Poconos.

Once the initial shock subsided, he tried to convince himself that it was all for the best, that his life would be easier without her. She was just dead weight in the car, one more burden he had to carry from place to place, every bit as selfish and demanding as the infant she'd abandoned, and a lot harder to satisfy. He'd been kidding himself, thinking she was going to wake up one morning and suddenly realize that she was better off with him than she would've been with Mr. Gilchrest.

You missed out, he thought. *I was the one who loved you.*

But that was the problem, the one his mind kept returning to as he steered the BMW toward the place that used to be home: He loved her and she was gone. It hurt to think of her rolling down the highway in that van full of Barefoot kids, all of them talking about the big party, all the crazy fun they would have. Christine probably wasn't even listening, just sitting there thinking how good it was to be free, away from the baby and from Tom, too, the two people who couldn't help reminding her of everything that had gone wrong, and what a fool she'd been.

It hurt him even more to think of her emerging from the fog a week or maybe a month down the road, discovering that the worst was over, that she could laugh and dance again, maybe even hook up with some lucky stoned idiot. And where would Tom be? Back home in Mapleton with his father and sister, raising a child who wasn't even his, still pining for a girl who'd left him at a rest stop in Connecticut? Was that where his long journey was going to deposit him? Right back where he started, just with a bullseye on his forehead and a dirty diaper in his hand?

The sun had set by the time he turned onto Lovell Terrace, but the sky was still a deep blue above his family's big white house.

"Little baby," he said. "What am I gonna do with you?"

〜〜〜

DON'T HESITATE. That was guideline number one. *The martyr's exit should be swift and painless.*

"Come on," Meg pleaded. She was leaning against a brick wall beneath an outdoor staircase at Bailey Elementary, her chest rising and falling with each ragged breath. The barrel of the gun was only an inch or so from her temple.

"Just a second," Laurie said. "My hand's shaking."

"It's all right," Meg reminded her. "You're doing me a favor."

Laurie took a deep calming breath. *You can do this.* She was prepared. She'd learned how to shoot the gun and had faithfully performed the visualization exercises included in the instructional memo.

Squeeze the trigger. Imagine a flash of golden light transporting the martyr directly to heaven.

"I don't know why I'm so nervous," she said. "I took a double dose of the Ativan."

"Don't think about it," Meg reminded her. "Just do it and walk away."

That was Laurie's mantra for the evening, her task in a nutshell: *Do it and walk away.* A car would be waiting at the corner of Elm and Lakewood. She didn't know where they were taking her, only that it would be far from Mapleton and very peaceful there.

"I'm gonna count down from ten," Meg told her. "Don't let me get to one."

The pistol was small and silver, with a black plastic grip. It wasn't that heavy, but it took all of Laurie's strength to hold it steady.

"Ten . . . nine . . ."

She glanced over her shoulder, making sure the schoolyard was empty. When they'd arrived a couple of adolescent girls were gossiping on the swings, but Laurie and Meg had stared at them until they left.

"Eight . . . seven . . ."

Meg's eyes were closed, her face tense with anticipation.

"Six . . ."

Laurie told her finger to move, but her finger wouldn't obey.

"Five . . ."

She'd gone to all that trouble to tear herself away from her family and friends, to withdraw from the world, to move beyond earthly comfort and human attachments. She'd left her husband, abandoned her daughter, shut her mouth, surrendered herself to God and the G.R.

"Four . . ."

It was hard, but she'd done it. It was as if she'd reached up with her own hand and plucked out one of her eyes, no anesthetic, no regret.

"Three . . ."

She'd made herself into a different person, tougher and more submissive at the same time. A servant without desire, with nothing to lose, ready to obey God's will, to come when called.

"Two . . ."

But then Meg had shown up, and they'd spent all that time together, and now she was right back where she'd started—weak and sentimental, full of doubt and longing.

"One . . ."

Meg clenched her teeth, preparing for the inevitable. After a few seconds went by, she opened her eyes. Laurie saw a flicker of relief in her face, and then a flood of annoyance.

"Goddammit," she snapped.

"I'm sorry." Laurie lowered the gun. "I can't do it."

"You have to. You promised."

"But you're my friend."

"I know." Meg's voice was softer now. "That's why I need you to help me. So I won't have to do it myself."

"You don't have to do it at all."

"Laurie," Meg groaned. "Why are you making this so hard?"

"Because I'm weak," Laurie admitted. "I don't want to lose you."

Meg held out her hand.

"Give me the gun."

She spoke with such calm authority, such utter faith in the mission, that Laurie felt a kind of awe, and even a certain amount of pride. It was hard to believe that this was the frightened young woman who'd cried herself to sleep her first night in Blue House, the Trainee who couldn't breathe in the supermarket.

"I love you," Laurie whispered as she handed over the pistol.

"I love you, too," Meg said, but there was an odd flatness in her voice, as if her soul had already left her body, as if it hadn't bothered to wait for the deafening explosion a moment later, and that imaginary flash of golden light.

〰〰

NORA KNEW it was ridiculous, walking all the way across town to deliver a letter she could just as easily have dropped into a mailbox, but it was a beautiful evening, and she didn't have anything else to do. At least this way she'd know for sure that the letter hadn't gotten lost or delayed by the Post Office. She could just cross it off her list and move on to the next task. That was the real point of this exercise—to do *something,* to stop procrastinating and take a small concrete step in the right direction.

Leaving town and starting a new life was turning out to be a bigger challenge than she'd expected. She'd had that manic burst of energy last week—that exhilarating vision of her blond pseudonymous future—but it had faded quickly, replaced by an all-too-familiar inertia. She couldn't think of a new name for her new self, couldn't decide where she wanted to go, hadn't called the lawyer or the real estate broker to arrange for the sale of her house. All she'd done was ride her bike until her legs ached and her fingers went numb, and her mind was too tired to put up a fight.

It was the prospect of selling the house that had tripped her up. She needed to get rid of it, she understood that, not just for the money, but for the psychological freedom that would come with leaving it behind, the bright line between before and after. But how could she do that when it was the only home her kids had ever known, the first place they'd go if they ever came back. She knew they weren't coming back, of course—at least she thought she knew that—but this knowledge didn't stop her from tormenting herself, letting herself imagine the disappointment and bewilderment they'd feel—the sense of abandonment—when a stranger answered the door instead of their own mother.

I can't do that to them, she thought.

Just this afternoon, though, she'd hit on a solution. Instead of selling the house, she could rent it through an agency, make sure someone knew how to get in touch with her in the event of a miracle. It wasn't the clean break she'd been fantasizing about—she'd probably have to keep using her own name, for one thing, at least for the rental agreement—but it was a compromise she could live with. Tomorrow morning she'd head down to Century 21 and work out the details.

She picked up the pace as she neared Lovell Terrace. The sky was dimming, the night settling in on its lazy warm weather schedule. Kevin's softball game would be over soon—she'd made sure to check the online schedule—and she wanted to be far away from this neighborhood by the time he got back. She had no desire to see him or talk to him, didn't want to be reminded of what a nice guy he was, or how much she enjoyed his company. There was nothing to be gained from that, not anymore.

She hesitated for a moment in front of his house. She'd never been there before—she'd made a point of staying away—and was startled by the size of it, a three-story colonial set way back from the street, with a gently sloping lawn big enough for a game of touch football. There was a small arched roof over the front entrance, a bronze mailbox mounted beside the door.

Come on, she told herself. *You can do this.*

She was nervous as she made her way up the driveway and across the stone path that led to the steps. It was one thing to have a fantasy of disappearing, of leaving your friends and family behind, and another thing to go ahead and make it real. Saying goodbye to Kevin was a real thing, the kind of action you couldn't take back.

You won't see me again, she'd written in the letter.

There was a lantern hanging in the archway, but it wasn't lit, and the area below it seemed darker than the rest of the world. Nora was so focused on the mailbox that she didn't notice the bulky object resting on the stoop until she almost tripped right over it. She let out a gasp when she realized what it was, then knelt down for a closer look.

"I'm sorry," she said. "I didn't see you there."

The baby was fast asleep in its car seat, a tiny newborn with squirrelly cheeks, vaguely Asian features, and a fine fuzz of black hair. A familiar smell rose from its body, the unmistakable sweet-and-sour fragrance of new life. There was a diaper bag next to the car seat, with a scrawled note tucked into an outside pocket. Nora had to squint to read what it said: *This little girl has no name. Please take good care of her.*

She turned back to the baby. Her heart was suddenly beating way too fast.

"Where's your mommy?" she asked. "Where'd she go?"

The baby opened her eyes. There was no fear in her gaze.

"Don't you have a mommy or daddy?"

The baby blew a spit bubble.

"Does anybody know you're here?"

Nora glanced around. The street was empty, as silent as a dream.

"No," she said, answering her own question. "They wouldn't just leave you here all by yourself."

The car seat doubled as an infant carrier. Out of curiosity, Nora raised the handle and lifted it off the ground. It wasn't that heavy, no more unwieldy than a bag of groceries.

Portable, she thought, and the word made her smile.

～～～

THE SLEEPOVER had seemed like a cool idea in the abstract. But now that she was actually walking toward Ginkgo Street, Jill could feel some resistance building up inside of her. What were she and Ms. Maffey going to do all night? The idea of talking in whispers had seemed exciting at first, even vaguely illicit, like campers staying up past curfew. On reflection, though, it struck her as dishonest, like serving people ice cream on their first night at the fat farm.

Hey, have some more hot fudge! You're gonna love it here at Camp Lose-a-Lot!

She wasn't as happy about Aimee moving out as she might have expected, either. Not for her own sake—they'd been over each other for a while now—but for her father's. He'd gotten pretty attached to Aimee in the past few months and would be sad to see her go. Jill had been jealous of their friendship, and even a bit worried about it, but she was also aware of how much pressure it took off her, and how much more her father would be needing from her in the coming days and weeks.

Not a great time to be leaving him alone, she thought, switching the sleeping bag from her left hand to her right as she made her way down Elm Street.

She stopped short, startled by what sounded like a gunshot coming from the direction of Bailey Elementary. *A firecracker,* she told herself, but a cold shudder ran through her body, accompanied by a harrowing vision of the dead man she'd found by the Dumpster on Valentine's Day—the liquid halo encircling his head, his wide eyes staring in amazement, the endless minutes they'd spent together waiting for the police to arrive. She remembered talking to him in a soothing voice, as if he were still alive and just needed a little encouragement.

Only a firecracker . . .

She wasn't sure how long she'd been turned away from the street, listening for a second explosion that never came. All she knew was that a car was veering toward her when she turned around, moving quietly and way too fast, as if it meant to run her down. It straightened out at the very last second, swooping in parallel to the curb, stopping neatly beside her, a white Prius facing in the wrong direction.

"Yo, Jill!" Scott Frost called from the driver's seat as the tinted window descended. A Bob Marley song was playing on the car stereo, the one about the three little birds, and Scott was grinning his usual blissed-out grin. "Where you been hiding?"

"Nowhere," she said, hoping she didn't look as rattled as she felt.

His eyes narrowed as he studied the sleeping bag in her hand, the overnight bag slung across her chest. Adam Frost was leaning in from the passenger seat, his identical handsome face stacked a little above and behind his brother's.

"You runnin' away?" Scott asked.

"Yeah," she told him. "I think I'm gonna join the circus."

Scott considered this for a few seconds, then chuckled approvingly.

"Awesome," he said. "You need a ride?"

~~~~~

THE GETAWAY car was right where it was supposed to be. There were two men up front, so Laurie opened the back door and climbed inside. Her ears were still ringing from the blast; it felt as though she were encased in the hum, as though a solid barrier of sound had intervened between her and the rest of the world.

It was better that way.

She was conscious of the men staring at her, and wondered if something was wrong. After a moment, the one in the passenger seat—he was a tanned, outdoorsy guy—opened the glove compartment and removed a Ziploc freezer bag. He peeled it open and held it out.

Right, she thought. *The gun. They want their gun back.*

She lifted it with two fingers, like a TV detective, and dropped it in, trying not to think about the difficulty she'd had removing it from Meg's hand. The man gave a businesslike nod and sealed the bag.

Evidence, Laurie thought. *Hide the evidence.*

The driver seemed upset about something. He was a moonfaced youngish guy, slightly bug-eyed, and he kept tapping himself in the forehead, like he was reminding a stupid person to think. Laurie didn't understand the meaning of the gesture until the guy in the passenger seat handed her a Kleenex.

Poor Meg, she thought, as she brought the tissue to her forehead. She felt something wet and sticky through the paper. *Poor, brave Meg.*

The guy in the passenger seat kept handing her tissues, and the driver kept touching various parts of his face to indicate where she needed to wipe. It would have been easier if she'd just looked in the mirror, but all three of them understood that that was a bad idea.

Finally, the driver turned around and started the car, heading down Lakewood toward Washington Boulevard. Laurie settled into her seat and closed her eyes.

Brave, brave Meg.

After a while she glanced out the window. They were leaving Mapleton now, crossing into Gifford, probably headed for the Parkway. Beyond that, she knew nothing about her destination and didn't really care. Wherever it was, she would go there, and she would wait for the end, her own and everyone else's.

She didn't think it would be long now.

~~~~

THE BMW had built-in satellite radio, which was pretty cool. Tom had tried listening a few times on the way down from Cambridge, but he had to keep the volume low so as not to disturb the baby or irritate Christine. Now he could just crank it up, switching from old-school hip-hop to Alternative Nation to Eighties nostalgia to Hair Metal whenever he felt the urge. He stayed away from the Jam Band channel, figuring there'd be more than enough of that when he got to the Poconos.

He was feeling a little less shaky now that he was on the highway. Escaping Mapleton had been the hard part. He kept heading out of town, then losing his nerve and circling back at the last minute to check on the baby. He did this three times before finally working up the courage to make the break, promising himself she'd be okay. He'd given her a bottle and changed her right before he left, so he figured she'd probably just sleep for a couple of hours, by which point somebody would get home to take care of her, or one of the neighbors would hear her crying. Maybe he could call his father from the next rest stop to say hi, pretend it was a coincidence, just to make sure everything was okay. If nobody answered, he could always call the cops from a pay phone, make an anonymous tip about a baby abandoned on Lovell Terrace. But he hoped it wouldn't come to that.

In his heart, he was pretty sure he'd made the right decision. He couldn't stay in Mapleton, couldn't go back to that house, that kind of life, at least not without Christine. But he couldn't take the baby with him, either. He wasn't her father, and he had no job, no money, no place to stay. She'd be better off with his dad and Jill, if they decided to keep her, or with a loving adoptive family that would give her the kind of secure, stable life Tom could never provide, at least not if he didn't want to be completely miserable.

Maybe someday he and Christine could go back to Mapleton and reclaim her baby, re-create the family that Tom had dreamed about. It was a long shot, he knew that, and there was no point in getting ahead of himself. What he needed to do right now was find that solstice festival, join those Barefoot kids dancing under the stars. They were his people now, and that was where he belonged. Maybe Christine would be there, and maybe she wouldn't. Either way, it sounded like a pretty good party.

~~~~~

JILL SAT on a raspberry-colored sling chair in the finished basement, watching the ball fly back and forth across the Ping-Pong table. For a pair of stoners, the Frost twins played with surprising skill and intensity, their bodies loose and fluid, their faces taut with concentration and controlled aggression. Neither one made a sound except for the occasional grunt, and a matter-of-fact announcement of the score before each serve. Otherwise it was just the hypnotic chatter of ball-against-table-against-paddle-against-table, over and over and over again, until one of the brothers seized his advantage, rearing back for a monster smash, which the other one more often than not managed to return.

There was a beautiful symmetry to their game, as if a single person were occupying both sides of the table, hitting the ball to himself in a kind of self-sustaining loop. Except that one of the players—Scott, the one on the right—kept searching out Jill's eyes in the lull between volleys, carrying on a silent conversation, letting her know that she hadn't been forgotten.

I'm glad you're here.

I'm glad, too.

The score was tied eight to eight. Scott took a deep breath and hit a wicked spinning serve, slashing his paddle down on a sharp diagonal. Adam was caught off guard, leaning to the right before realizing his mistake, lurching all the way across the table to make an awkward backhand stab, hitting a feeble lob that barely cleared the net. And just like that they were back into the rhythm, a steady, patient *pock-pocketa-pock,* the white blur bouncing from one orange-padded paddle right back to the other.

Maybe another person would have found it tedious, but Jill had no complaints. The chair was comfortable, and there was nowhere else she'd rather be. She felt a little guilty, picturing Ms. Maffey standing by the entrance gate of the Ginkgo Street compound, wondering what had happened to her new recruit, but not guilty enough to do anything about it. She could apologize tomorrow, she thought, or maybe the day after.

I ran into some friends, she could write.

Or: *There's this cute boy, and I think he likes me.*

Or even: *I forgot what it feels like to be happy.*

~~~~~~

THE HOUSE was dark when Kevin pulled into the driveway. He turned off the engine and sat for a few seconds, wondering what he was even doing here when he could have been back at the Carpe Diem with his teammates, celebrating their hard-won victory. He'd left after a single beer, his festive mood dampened by the text he'd received from Jill: *I'm at a friend's. In case ur wondering, Aimee moved out. She said to tell u gdbye and thnx for everything.*

In a way he was relieved—it was easier not to play the heavy, not to have to ask her to leave—but the news saddened him nonetheless. He was sorry it had happened like this, that he and Aimee hadn't had the chance for one last morning talk out on the deck. He wanted to tell her how much he'd enjoyed her company, and to remind her not to sell herself short, not to settle for a guy who didn't deserve her, or get stuck in a job that didn't give her any room to grow. But he'd told her those things on numerous occasions, and just had to hope that she'd been listening, that his words would have sunk in by the time she really needed them.

For now, though, he'd just have to add her name to the list of people he cared about who'd moved on. It was getting to be a long list, and it contained some pretty important names. In time, he thought, Aimee would probably seem like a footnote, but just now her absence felt bigger than that, like maybe she deserved a whole page to herself.

He got out of the car and headed across the driveway to the bluestone path that had been Laurie's first big project when they moved into this house. She'd spent weeks on it—choosing the stones, plotting the winding course, digging and leveling and fine-tuning—and the results had made her proud and excited.

Kevin paused at the edge of the lawn to admire the fireflies that were rising like sparks from the lush grass, lighting up the night in a series of random exclamations, turning the familiar landscape of Lovell Terrace into an exotic spectacle.

"Beautiful," he said, realizing even as he spoke that he wasn't alone.

A woman was standing at the bottom of the front steps, facing in his direction. She seemed to be holding something in her arms.

"Excuse me?" he said. "Who's there?"

The woman began walking toward him at a slow, almost stately pace. She was blond and slender, and reminded him of someone he knew.

"Are you okay?" he asked. "Can I help you?"

The woman didn't reply, but by now she was close enough for him to recognize her as Nora. The baby in her arms was a complete stranger, the way they always are when we meet them for the first time, before we give them their names and welcome them into our lives.

"Look what I found," she told him.